SEXUAL NUTRITION

HOW TO NUTRITIONALLY IMPROVE, ENHANCE, AND STIMULATE YOUR SEXUAL APPETITE

DR. MORTON WALKER

A DR. MORTON WALKER HEALTH BOOK

Avery Publishing Group
Garden City Park, New York

This book has been written and published strictly for informational purposes, and in no way should it be used as a substitute for recommendations from your own medical doctor or healthcare professional. All the facts in this book came from medical files, clinical journals, scientific publications, personal interviews, published trade books, self-published materials by experts, magazine articles, and the personal-practice experiences of the authorities quoted or sources cited. You should not consider educational material herein to be the practice of medicine or to replace consultation with a physician or other medical practitioner. The author and publisher are providing you with the information in this work so that you can have the knowledge and can choose, at your own risk, to act on that knowledge.

The author and publisher also urge all readers to be aware of their health status, as well as that of their partners, and to always practice safe sex.

Cover artist: Jürek, Provincetown, MA
In-house editor: Elaine Will Sparber
Typesetter: Bonnie Freid
Printer: Paragon Press, Honesdale, PA

The excerpt on pages 225–227 is from *Dr. Mandell's 5-Day Allergy Relief System* by Marshall Mandell, M.D., and Lynne Waller Scanlon. Copyright © 1979 by Marshall Mandell, M.D., and Lynne Waller Scanlon. Reprinted by permission of HarperCollins Publishers, Inc.

Publisher's Cataloging-in-Publication Data

Walker, Morton.
   Sexual nutrition : how to nutritionally improve, enhance, and
stimulate your sexual appetite / Morton Walker.
      p. cm.
   Includes index.
   ISBN 0-89529-565-2

   1. Sex (Biology)—Nutritional aspects. 2. Sex. I. Title.

QP251.W26   1994   613.9'5
                                               QBI93-22227

CONTENTS

To the woman of my dreams,
Joan Walker.

PREFACE

Sex can be supreme, but it requires work. Having a wonderfully fulfilling sex life does not just happen. To be able to successfully accomplish lovemaking—the act of giving and receiving emotional and erotic pleasure—you must nurture the involved body systems. You must give these body systems the nutrients they need.

Neither sexual responsiveness nor sexuality is merely instinctive; they both require a healthy internal signaling system of nerves, brain, gonads, endocrine glands, blood vessels, and other parts. In addition, the entire sexual apparatus must function effectively in the presence of erotic stimuli. Sexual decline is not an inevitable result of growing older or of losing interest in a relationship. Rather, it results mostly from the body's loss of ability to receive and metabolize nutrients efficiently and in sufficient amounts. The nutritional substances that may be lacking could include those responsible for generating sexual interest, allowing sexual response, or maintaining sexual performance.

In the beginning of a marriage or other relationship of deep physical and emotional affinity, the intensity of love and sexual attraction may be so strong that lovers feel sure their passion for each other will never diminish. As time passes, however, they may experience a decline in sexual enthusiasm or ability that may leave them feeling unloved or unfulfilled. Research indicates that such a loss of libido or sexual capacity does not have to occur.

The fact is that sexual desire, along with the ability to fulfill sexual desire, is greatly affected by physical health. The problem of a lackluster sex life—or even of just a good as opposed to fantastic sex life—frequently comes from nutritional shortcomings or dietary indiscretions. This became quite apparent to me from the letters my wife and I received in response to a series of articles on sexual nutrition that we wrote for *Soma, Forum,* and *Swank* magazines. Over 3,000 letters arrived within a two-year period! Some of the letters were funny, others were sad, a number were kooky, many were serious, plenty were effusive, a few were disgusting, several were frightening—but all were from people seeking good nutritional advice about sexual difficulties. My wife and I were repeatedly amazed that the letter writers provided us with the most intimate and revealing details of their sexuality, organ functions, fantasies, infidelities, compulsions, physical disabilities, and diseases.

In *Sexual Nutrition*, I use composites of these letters to present a typical letter from a man and a typical letter from a woman at the beginning of each chapter. The names of the letter writers are pseudonyms, and the hometowns show the diversity of the areas from which the real letter writers came. I am not disguising the identities of the health professionals I quote, though; in many instances, I personally interviewed them.

Sexual Nutrition provides you with a complete program of diet, supplements, and techniques for a lifetime of optimal sexual health. My premise is that a healthy body enjoys greater sexuality than does an unhealthy body. Now, instead of missing out on the enjoyment and satisfaction your sex instinct urges, you will have the correct information to improve your health and increase your sexual pleasure, desirability, and consummation. Yet, remember that nothing I suggest in this book should be taken as a substitute for the individualized recommendations of a licensed medical professional skilled in nutritional, sexual, or health counseling. A professional's education, licensing, and experience make him or her the proper authority for appropriate remedial treatment of sexual dysfunction. I cannot provide you with foolproof cures, correctives, prophylactics, or any other type of therapeutic aid.

Sexual Nutrition, in keeping with the current changes in attitude toward sexual attractiveness, sexual responsiveness, and sexuality, is an answer to the needs and wishes of modern, sexually enlightened men and women who also have a renewed interest in becoming and staying healthy and are searching for knowledge about nutrition. "Sexy" has in many ways come to mean "healthy," with health brought about in large measure by the quality of what is consumed.

Today, being sexy means, for both men and women, being well-nourished, fit, and trim; being active and vital. My intent in this book is to furnish you with a compendium of nutritional information that has a direct bearing on sexual vigor and enjoyment. I believe that *Sexual Nutrition* will be referred to continually in public and private by those who want to feel sexually healthy, look attractive, react well to erotic stimuli, and perform superbly in satisfying their bedmates. I hope you will agree that I have accomplished my intention.

Chapter 1

THE TOTALLY
BALANCED LOVER

After four years of marriage, Marvin and I enjoy sex very much. I am an attractive twenty-six, and he's a handsome, athletic thirty. He agrees that our sex is great. We have tremendously strong orgasms, sometimes together and sometimes separately. He's gentle, kind, generous, inventive, and very sexy. Marvin tells me that I am, too. However, we have a problem. It may be no problem at all, only that we want even more from our sexual relations.

Our lovemaking is easy, slow, and smooth, and it involves a lot of foreplay. Kissing and touching stimulate me. Marvin brings me to an earth-shattering orgasm with his tongue. I do the same for him. We love the taste of each other. During the time we are recovering from the sensations of climaxing, we often fall asleep in each other's arms. Not infrequently, we actually forget or feel no need to have sexual intercourse in the usual way. Our love and excitement so overwhelm us when we first reach orgasm, we don't often go on to do what is considered "normal" among other couples. Is this a sexual problem, or isn't it? Should we try reaching orgasm from intercourse first, eliminating oral stimulation? In other words, should we vary the way in which we go about making love when we are quite satisfied with what is occurring in bed now? We do want to be healthy and normal. Are we?

Betty M.
Boston, Massachusetts

The lady next door calls me Superstud. We have been lovers for three years, ever since I began doing odd jobs for her when I was sixteen years old. My mother thinks I'm still doing neighborly chores, but actually, Marge and I spend most of our time together in the sack.

Marge is divorced. She says I'm a better lover than either of her former husbands. She's forty-two, well-built, really good looking for an older woman, and quite experienced, and she has taught me a lot about making love. I never seem to get enough. My penis is in a constant state of erection, except just after having had sex.

My question to you involves sexual frequency. Marge and I usually have sex twice a day—every day—and I also masturbate twice a day on the average. I fantasize

all the time about having sex. Before learning from this woman, I never felt an urge
to make love so much. What I want to know is how much sex is "too much" sex?
Am I oversexed? Is Marge? Could there be something wrong with the way my body
produces hormones? Or am I doing what comes naturally for a nineteen-year-old
who has access to a willing, available, and sexy older woman?

Richard S.
Phoenix, Arizona

No norm has been defined concerning how much or what type of sexual activity should be engaged in. Body chemistry is unique. Every person is biochemically matchless and cannot compare his or her desires or behavior to anyone else's. Between consenting adults enjoying each other in private and doing no harm to themselves or to others, anything goes. Lovemaking in whatever form it takes—as long as it is mentally, emotionally, morally, physically, and spiritually uplifting for the participants—may be indulged in for its homeostatic benefits.

No matter how the conditions around you change, if your internal systems regulating temperature, blood pressure, acid–base balance, and the like stay normal and maintain equilibrium, you are in *homeostasis*. The homeostatic person feels high-level wellness.

Having high-level wellness does not mean simply that you are not sick or that you are living in a way that does not induce illness. Instead, it means that you are trim, eat properly, enjoy sexual relations regularly, exercise often, sleep soundly, do not smoke, and do not drink to excess. You have learned to relax deeply and completely, and you know how to counterbalance stress. You think positively about yourself and feel confident about your social interactions. Having high-level wellness also means that you express your emotions effectively, are creatively involved with those around you, are concerned about your physical and psychological environment, and are aware of other levels of consciousness.

When you have high-level wellness, you are able to interpret illness as a message from within. You also accept your mortality and see the dying process as another aspect of human reality. Neither illness nor the acceptance of eventual death should inhibit your acceptance of life or your treasuring of the optimal health that enables the achievement of fullest potential. At high-level wellness, you function at your greatest potential. Ideally, you remain at high-level wellness all the time, so that your body can cope with the ecology that continually is being altered by industry and modern technology.

Two people who are drawn together by a strong physical attraction may experience a flood of passion, anticipation, and excitement. These feelings could be fleeting or everlasting, depending upon the two people's commitment to each other. When together the two people satisfy their erotic and affectional needs, they are lovers.

To be a homeostatic lover, you need to focus on achieving and maintaining good health, along with giving and receiving sexual fulfillment. Enjoying sensual intimacy with another person while at the same time feeling your own sexuality enables excellent health to permeate your whole being. Each of your sixty trillion body cells functions at its best in this homeostatic state. When you maintain your mental and physical health from within, you are able to recognize and act, in a wholesome way, upon the stresses that are encountered in the ordinary course of daily living. High-level wellness holds the mental, emotional, and physical upsets to a minimum in all difficult situations.

When you are a homeostatic lover, you consider sexual dysfunction in any form as an important feedback message, to be dealt with consciously as part of the whole life process. You do not regard yourself as a victim of nature or of today's hostile technology; rather, you realize that your body will know how to heal itself after you remove any stressors or misunderstandings. You endeavor to restore the internal environment that is best for your body and mind.

In addition, the homeostatic lover offers his or her sexual partner the pleasure of choosing the course of action—the learning pattern—that provides the ultimate joy in closeness, shared intimacy, orgasm, and love. Sexual fulfillment of the other is a restorative for each partner. It is nourishing. During the course of lovemaking, you allow yourself to build and release tension, breathe quickly and deeply, and enjoy the supportive contact of your lover's body. The sex act brings with it a system of mutual healing and awakening of the spirit.

Havelock Ellis, the renowned sex therapist who was fashionable in the 1960s, called sex "the chief and central function of life . . . ever wonderful, ever lovely." He also said that coitus under normal circumstances was "entirely beneficial." For Ellis, abstinence was unhealthy; the world needed not greater restraint but more passion.

I agree with Havelock Ellis, although I am by no means encouraging total lack of restraint. Instead, I am suggesting sexual gratification through careful management of erotic resources; the most ecstatic sexual experiences will be inaccessible to you if you expend your resources indiscriminately. Without a certain amount of selectivity, your sex life may quickly degenerate into a series of trivial orgasms that have no meaning. You will just be using other peoples' bodies as instruments of masturbation.

Being a homeostatic lover requires that sexual relations merge with personal relations; that physical actions extend into the emotional realm. Let sexual lust evolve into sexual love for your bedfellow, even if only during the time you are in bed together.

ACTS OF SEX AND LOVE BEFORE INTERCOURSE

Lovemaking does not necessarily begin when the man inserts his penis into the woman's vagina. This action is just one stage—coitus. The activity leading up to coitus is as important (or more important) to many men and women, especially to impotent males and preorgasmic females (see Chapter 10). The acts before intercourse can provide each partner with feelings of closeness and affection, which all human beings need.

Kissing can be a prelude to intercourse. Begin by kissing your lover around the face—the cheeks, the neck, the eyelids, the mouth—in a gentle and light manner. You can become more fervent as your kisses are returned. You might progress to probing with your tongue deep in your partner's mouth, or vice versa. Nibble on your lover's tongue, lips, or earlobes.

Fondling and light touching are another natural prelude in the act of lovemaking. You can stroke a shoulder, feel a biceps, inhale the fragrance of hair, stroke a breast, grasp a bulging penis, squeeze a buttock, or remove clothing that is impeding your hands' exploration of your lover's warm, bare flesh.

A woman can unbutton her partner's shirt from the neck down. When you reach his belt, let your hand stray down to his crotch. Remove his shirt; unbuckle his belt. Untie his shoes and have him step out of them. Unzip his fly, then work his pants down his legs and have him step out of them. Fondle the bulge in his underpants. Embrace him and, while standing close, slide his shorts down his legs so that he can step out of them. Remove his socks.

A man can kiss his partner, holding her against his naked body. Begin to undress her, working slowly. Undo her dress without hurrying or tearing the zipper, buttons, or snaps. Gently lift the garment over her head. Unhook her bra. Kiss her neck, eyes, ears, and lips, and tenderly slip off the bra. Again kiss her neck and then work your lips along her shoulders down to her breasts. Kiss the nipples; tease them with your tongue. Suck them.

Move your hands to her hips, preparing to slide off her pantyhose. Have her step out of her shoes. Lower the waistband of her undergarment, then pull off her pantyhose, along with her panties. Embrace her with ardor. Kiss and touch her all over.

A man can give pleasure and sexually excite his partner by touching her genitals. Caress the labia of her vagina; separate the labia to expose the clitoris, then lightly stroke this female erectile tissue. The clitoris is an elongated bump or slight bulge in front of the vaginal opening. It is anywhere from a quarter of an inch to almost one inch long. Tipped with a glans similar to the glans penis, it is, in fact, covered with a hood just like the male foreskin. Running a finger along the face of the clitoris will cause heightened sexual arousal and enjoyment for your lover. You will also be preparing her for intercourse, as arousal stimulates the secretion of lubricating fluids into the vagina.

Press and rub your penis and testicles against her body—around her breasts, along her abdomen, about her groin. Do not penetrate her vagina yet; use your mouth as an instrument of pleasure. (*Cunnilingus* is the oral stimulation of a woman's clitoris. *Fellatio* is the oral stimulation of a man's penis. Both are accepted techniques of lovemaking, practiced by well-educated people who know that clean genitals have lower microorganism counts than the average person's mouth.) You can do this through kissing, sucking, licking, or simulating intercourse with your mouth. For a woman, sensitivity is intense from the edge of the clitoris to near the anus, and oral stimulation given over a prolonged period will almost always bring forth an ecstatic response. The tongue, teeth, and lips work better than fingers do.

Make sure your fingernails are well-clipped because next you should use your hands. Gently slip one, two, or more fingers in and out of her vagina like a penis during intercourse; be careful not to be harsh or haphazard in your movements. Coitus will be easier if you take the time to do this, since you will be spreading additional moisture throughout the vaginal vault.

In the excitement of this lovemaking, your partner's body will respond to the desire for coitus and will prepare the vagina. The vagina is a flexible tube about four inches long. When relaxed, its folded walls touch, so almost no opening exists. But when the vagina is stimulated—that is, when the outer one-third is responding to gonadal commands—it spontaneously becomes ready to accept a penis. The muscles controlling the vaginal entrance automatically relax, and the tube becomes longer and wider. The vaginal walls become smoother, more sensitive, and more flexible, the better to expand and to grasp the penis when it is finally inserted.

A woman can bring a man acute pleasure by using her mouth like a vagina. Shape your mouth and throat into a hollow tube and take his penis in. Use your lips and tongue like a vagina's muscular walls to suck, pull, and siphon his erect organ. Move your head in a pumping action, while he pushes forward. Stop when he tells you his semen is going to be released, or continue pushing all the way to ejaculation. If you choose the latter, you can either swallow the ejaculate or hold it in your mouth until you have a chance to spit it out. Freshly ejaculated semen is nothing more than a bodily fluid of pure protein; it is not harmful to swallow unless you have a protein allergy. Ejaculate can even be considered a source of nourishment.

The only hazard in giving pleasure by fellatio is the teeth. Pain can make a penis flaccid. Protect his penis from your teeth by covering your front teeth with your lips and by keeping the penis away from your back teeth by taking it down the hollow tube you have shaped with your tongue and throat.

In 1948, Alfred Kinsey wrote in *Sexual Behavior in the Human Male* that 30 percent of all men have experienced fellatio. Sex researchers and writers say that the numbers today are probably triple Kinsey's figures, since our society is more enlightened and more tolerant when it comes to sex. Oral sex is reported by sexologists to be practiced by 85 percent of all people under age twenty-five and by an even higher percentage of older, married couples looking for sexual variety.

GONADAL RESPONSE TO SEXUAL STIMULATION

In anticipation of, during, or resulting from these various acts of sex and love, your gonads will probably respond if you are indeed a homeostatic lover. William Masters and Virginia Johnson Masters, describing the gonadal reaction in their landmark book *Human Sexual Response*, said that the physiology of a man and a woman engaged in lovemaking can be divided into four phases—excitement, plateau, orgasm, and resolution.

The duration of the *excitement phase* varies with the quality and quantity of stimulation and any effects of anticipation. General muscular tension is one of the sexual processes that anticipation can affect; it begins for the man in the form of a penile erection and for the woman with clitoral erection. Nerves in these organs cause valves in the erectile tissue to close, trapping blood, producing swelling, and heightening sensitivity.

Both men and women experience an increase in heart and breathing rates and an elevation of blood pressure. Also, early in the excitement phase, the nipples of both stand out, swell, and become more sensitive.

In women, the labia majora open and spread flat, while the labia minora swell and extend outward. The clitoris steadily increases in length and diameter. The vagina becomes wet with a lubricant that leaches through its walls. More lubricating fluid is secreted by the Bartholin's glands. The uterus and cervix pull back and away from the vagina, leaving more room for the deposit of semen. The entire length of the vagina expands somewhat, but the inner two-thirds opens more to create a channel that is ready to receive the penis. Parts of the female body flush darker in color, especially the labia.

In men, the penis begins to engorge with blood, which makes its spongy tissue expand. It grows longer and thicker, and becomes stiff and upright. The nerves in the penis receive further stimulation from the gonads. Another automatic reflex increases the blood flow even more. The spongy mass around the urethra swells and presses against its sheath of skin, stretching the sheath to its maximum. The penis will by now have increased in circumference by at least two and a half times. The penis continues to jut slightly upward until ejaculation is accomplished.

Meantime, the testes are pulled in ever closer to the body by contractions of the attaching tendons and muscles. The scrotal sac shrinks to maintain this condition for a long period, although the condition may be lost and regained repeatedly without orgasm.

Masters and Johnson said that most penises are equal in action, no matter how large or small they are. Like the law, the vagina is impartial and recognizes few distinctions of penis length or breadth. No man should think himself the sexual superior of his fellow man merely because he is greater endowed.

In the *plateau phase*, the testes draw still closer to the body. Masters and Johnson described what happens:

> As excitement-phase levels of tension develop, there is a specific elevation of both testes toward the perineum. . . . Actually, only partial elevation of the testes is accomplished during the excitement phase, unless there is to be a fulminating completion of the sexual response cycle. . . . As male sexual tensions rise through plateau phase toward orgasmic-phase release, the specific reaction of testicular elevation progresses until the final pre-ejaculatory positioning in tight apposition to the male perineum is attained.[1]

What Masters and Johnson described is something between a two-stage process and a continuous progression—the buildup to a crescendo of sensation. The plateau phase is a continuation of the effects of stimulation, with the reactions becoming stronger and more constant. Breathing quickens. The penis increases slightly in diameter near its tip. The opening into the urethra from which the semen will ejaculate becomes more slitlike. The tip and the head of the penis change color to a deeper reddish purple. Finally, the erection is intensified to the point of completion, and involuntary nervous tension is so strong that the organ goes into tiny muscular spasms.

The penis provides its own lubrication by releasing small amounts of semen containing sperm. Even without physical manipulation, the lubricating ejaculate may drip from the penis. If the penis is in a woman's vagina at this moment, even if neither partner experiences any sensation close to orgasm, the sperm deposited—no matter how few—can cause pregnancy.

For females, the inner two-thirds of the vagina balloons, while the outer third narrows to about half its excitement-phase diameter. This helps the vaginal muscles both to grasp the penis more effectively and to produce a slight vacuum to suction out the seminal fluid. The vagina, after all, has been fashioned by nature to act as a repository of the stuff for survival of the species. In the plateau phase, the vaginal vault resembles a funnel, with the penis inserted in the narrow end and the sperm cradled in the wide end. This narrowing indicates the woman is nearly at the pinnacle of arousal; coitus will be most pleasurable now, as the outer portion of the vaginal tunnel is at its most sensitive.

The inner lips of the woman's labia minora now become a brighter red, as they become congested with blood. More fluid "sweats" through the vaginal walls for lubrication. Wetness is felt between the legs. Inside, the uterus, which had begun to elevate during the excitement phase, now elevates fully; the muscles contract in the abdomen, around the groin, and through the buttock region. Both the pulse and breathing are fast, and a "sex flush" appears on certain parts of the body.

The man, too, is nearing the end of the plateau phase, better described as the preejaculatory phase. Masters and Johnson explained:

> The penis that apparently has achieved full erection during the

excitement phase undergoes a minor involuntary vasocongestive increase in diameter as the orgasmic (ejaculatory) phase approaches. This additional plateau-phase tumescence is confined primarily to the corona glandis area of the glans penis. A color change also may develop in the glans penis in the plateau phase of the sexual cycle.[2]

In the *orgasm phase*, both the man's and woman's heart rates elevate to anywhere from 140 to 180 beats per minute (the normal is about 70 beats per minute). The genital muscles of both partners go through a patterned series of contractions. In fact, all the muscles of their bodies react much like the genitals by contracting involuntarily. Arms and legs grip, faces contort, buttocks tighten, sphincters close, eyes shut, and skin tingles.

The belief that all women have multiple orgasms is a myth. While females are physically capable of multiple orgasms, they are not likely to experience them often, and many may not even want them. Another myth is that intercourse that is "right" results in simultaneous orgasm. If the partners do experience simultaneous orgasm, it is just a happy coincidence and not a result of the "right" technique. A woman may not climax at all—despite this, many women feel satisfying sexual pleasure from having a man's penis inside them and from watching how the man gets lost in the orgasmic experience.

An orgasm for a man occurs when the muscles around the urethra go through a number of rapid, involuntary contractions. These contractions begin at the back of the penis and in the genital area and move forward along the line of the urethra. Near the end of the plateau phase, semen that has gathered within the head of the penis is pumped to the top of the urethra. In the orgasmic phase, a great pressure builds at the head of the penis to force the semen out through the penile opening. Ejaculation is accomplished in three or four strong bursts, each lasting about eight-tenths second, with each burst separated by that same amount of time. On the average, about three and a half milliliters (less than one teaspoon) of semen is ejaculated, the quantity diminishing with each repeated ejaculation. Men can enjoy another orgasm in about a half-hour. With the next orgasm, the muscular contractions feel pleasurable but are weaker and more irregular.

For the female, rhythmic contractions build at the outside of the vagina and move in waves down its length. The uterus contracts as well. The intensely pleasurable contractions of the vagina are repeated many times, depending on the amount of stimulation. Just before orgasm, there is a feeling of tension lasting approximately three seconds as the small muscles in the pelvis surrounding the vagina and uterus contract. This is followed by a series of rhythmic muscular contractions every eight-tenths second. The series lasts for ten to fifteen seconds. The feeling spreads from the outer third of the vagina backward and upward to the uterus. The average orgasm contains eight contractions, but there may be more or fewer depending on the quality of the foreplay and the current clitoral massage. A second orgasm can be experienced if excitement can be held at the plateau level. Some women can experience three or more orgasms in a half-hour.

In the *resolution phase*, climax has come and gone, and a gradual muscular and physiological relaxation sets in for both partners. It takes about a half-hour for the various muscles to relax completely, with the different swellings subsiding, skin discolorations or rashes disappearing, and organs returning to their normal sizes and positions in the body.

In men, first there is a rapid reduction in penis size. The organ shrinks to approximately 50 percent of its erect size during the resolution phase. With the elapse of additional time, it slowly reduces to its normal length and breadth.

If ejaculation did not occur, the great amount of blood in the pelvic region will take more time to dissipate. In this case, the blood will dribble out of the congested blood vessels and slowly return to the general circulation. A sensation of pressure in the testes, scrotum, perineum, and penis will be annoying for a time; this is the discomfort known euphemistically as blue balls. If allowed to happen repeatedly, blue balls will jeopardize the health of the prostate. Ejaculation affords an immediate release of the tension and blood-vessel engorgement in the pelvic region. Ejaculation is also healthy. (If a man's sexual system is in homeostasis, plenty of semen is constantly being produced and stored.)

In a woman, the nipples return to normal in the resolution phase. The excess blood drains from the vaginal lips, with the color of the genitals returning to normal. The muscle spasms and nervous tension subside, and a great peacefulness is felt. Even so, women can easily go from the resolution to the plateau level again with some additional stimulation. Another orgasm can be reached without the waiting period necessary for males.

As with men, however, if a woman did not achieve orgasm, it will take her quite a while longer during resolution to attain the physiological state of relaxation that she was in before stimulation. Orgasm allows the sudden release of blood from the pelvic blood vessels and of nerves from their heightened functioning; without this release, the return to normal takes longer.

THE GRAFENBERG SPOT FOR VAGINAL ORGASM

Unfortunately, according to Shere Hite in *The Hite Report*, 70 percent of all women do not regularly achieve orgasm through sexual intercourse. The type of orgasm that I have been describing results specifically from stimulation of the clitoris. In 1966, Masters and Johnson tersely dismissed the possibility of orgasm from stimulation of the vagina. They argued that only clitoral stimulation, whether direct or indirect, is involved in orgasm and that the vagina has no important nerve endings to cause a sensation sufficient for the feeling. Yet, in 1950, the originator of human intrauterine devices, a German gynecologist named Dr. Ernst Grafenberg, had written about an especially sensitive spot inside the vagina that when stroked can evoke an intense orgasmic response. Gynecologists today call this the Grafenberg spot, or G-spot.

About the size of a nickel, the Grafenberg spot is located in the upper wall of the vagina about one inch beneath the vaginal surface, halfway between the back of the pubic bone and the front edge of the cervix, near the urethra and just under the bladder. A woman can locate her Grafenberg spot with her lover's help. First, she should lie on her back, knees apart and slightly elevated. Her partner should place his index finger, pad up, in her vagina and look for her pubic bone, directly behind the clitoris. By firmly yet gently sliding his finger back into the vagina toward the cervix, he will come upon the Grafenberg spot, on the upper wall of the vagina. The woman will know he has found the spot when he touches it. The first sensation she will feel will be an urgency to urinate, but this will be quickly replaced by sensations of pleasure, especially if he gently strokes the spot for a few seconds, causing it to swell and become more definable. Then the woman will feel a vaginal orgasm that is deeper than a clitoral orgasm and that can be repeated with direct stimulation. In coitus, the face-to-face position is best for achieving vaginal orgasm because it allows the penis to rub the Grafenberg spot.

Stimulation of the Grafenberg spot, which can also be done with a long, narrow vibrator inserted into the vagina, leads to contractions of the deeper muscles of the pelvis and of the uterus itself. Some sex experts think of the Grafenberg-spot orgasm as a uterine orgasm rather than a vaginal one. Even women who have never experienced a clitoral orgasm can have a vaginal one by finding the Grafenberg spot and stimulating it.

John D. Perry, Ph.D., and Beverly Whipple, R.N., M.Ed., dispelled another myth—about women not ejaculating. In their article "Can Women Ejaculate? Yes!" in *Forum: The International Journal of Human Relations*, these two sexologists declared that women are not only able to have a vaginal orgasm but can also ejaculate.

Perry and Whipple reported that one in ten women experiencing orgasm from stimulation of the Grafenberg spot has an ejaculation of fluid from the Skene's glands, which are mucous glands in the wall of the urethra. The wetness that escapes from the vagina directly after orgasm is not urine, as some women believe, but rather a secretion from these so-called female prostate glands. The chemical composition of this female ejaculate, according to Edwin Belzer, M.D., of Halifax, Canada, quoted in the article, is prostatic acid, phosphatase, glucose, urea, and creatinine, the same ingredients of male ejaculate.[3]

THE ANATOMICAL AND PHYSIOLOGICAL BASIS
FOR INTERCOURSE

People use a plethora of scientific, medical, cultural, euphemistic, and street-corner terms in referring to the act of sex and love. We speak of *coitus, copulation, intercourse, intromission, making love, sleeping with, having sex with, going to bed with, fornicating, laying, mating with,* and *coupling with.* In animal husbandry, dogs and cats *mate,* sheeps *tup,* bulls *bull,* and stallions *cover.* What do two consenting heterosexual human adults do? What do two consenting homosexual adults do? What is the anatomical and physiological basis for what they do?

No human male is wholly male; no human female is wholly female. Both possess hormones that, given the opportunity, can cause them to develop either form of sexual system. The news media advises us that sex reversal is not only possible but also not uncommon. A narrow sexual fence separates the two sexes physically, spiritually, mentally, and emotionally. Doctors at the Gender Identity Clinic of Baltimore believe, "If the mind cannot be changed to fit the body, we should consider changing the body to fit the mind."

There are three types of distinctions separating men and women—primary, secondary, and tertiary. Tertiary characteristics are suicide patterns, ways of thinking, amount of red blood cells, brain weight, and life span—among other things. The secondary characteristics distinguishing males from females include body size and shape, distribution of fat tissue, bone structure, voice, and hair growth. The primary characteristics are, of course, the internal and external sexual organs.

The systems of sexual reproduction of both men and women are wondrous combinations of many parts. The penis, for example, increases in length and rigidity strictly for the purpose of intercourse. There is no other reason for penis enlargement. Suitable nervous stimulation, whether directly physical or merely mental, starts the erection process.

The penis works just like a water hose, with water flowing freely out of one end. Seal that end and the accumulating water pressure will distend and stiffen the hose. Similar hydraulics cause the blood vessel running along the upper surface of the penis to become compressed when sexual excitement begins. The blood's outlet gets plugged. The muscular coatings on the small arteries branching off the blood vessel begin to stretch from the surge of blood being shunted into the arteries. The penis becomes distended because of the blood. The spongy tissue that forms the bulk of the penis quickly absorbs this added fluid, swelling just like a saturated sponge.

While the blood already present in the penis is being trapped, the heart sends down more blood; this additional blood comes at a faster rate than normal because of the heart's elevated beat. The dorsal vein of the penis becomes compressed, and the pressure makes the penis become even more rigid. The base of the penis swells to about one and a half inches on average.

The head alone of the penis makes up about one-quarter of the total erect-organ length. A survey conducted in the United States by Kinsey and his colleagues indicated that 90 percent of American men can get erections at the age of fifty, over 80 percent at the age of sixty, 70 percent at the age of seventy, and 25 percent at eighty. In fact, in Chapter 12, I describe Ecuadorian men over one hundred years old whose healthy lifestyle keeps them sexually young and still enjoying sexual intercourse. These long-lived men may or may not achieve orgasm, but their bodies continue to form sperm up to the time they die. Fifty-year-old American men report averaging two orgasms a week; seventy-year-old American men report an average of one a week.

All future generations of the human species depend on the testicles, which hang precariously low and in front of the body, where they are exposed to injury. Their owners sit on them, and many men strangle them by wearing tight pants. The testicles lie in the scrotum, anatomical sacs just behind the penis, in a rather defenseless position. This exterior position provides sperm with a place to be born that is slightly cooler than internal body temperature.

Each testis is about two inches long, about one inch wide, and less than one inch thick. Sperm production is continuous, with forty-six days required to form a complete spermatozoon. Sperm become mature and motile in the epididymis, the main sperm storehouse—a small lump of tissue attached to each testicle. They remain vital for several weeks, degenerating, liquifying, and being reabsorbed by the body if not ejaculated.

Ejaculation takes sperm on a journey up a thin tube called the vas deferens. During the twelve-inch trip, the sperm are bathed in a yellow fluid that forms much of the semen. The fluid comes from the seminal vesicles, small glands near the prostate gland, which adds its own secretion. Prostate fluid is thin and gives ejaculate its characteristic smell. Small bulbourethral glands furnish another secretion. The resultant assortment of fluids and sperm is 90.3 percent water, with a total ejaculation comprised of two to seven milliliters of liquids.

About 200,000,000 spermatozoa are released into the vagina during an average ejaculation. Only one will make a baby if it reaches the woman's egg. The trip is long, and the sperm travel at just half an inch per minute.

Since the urethra is used for both urine and semen, a sphincter closes to prevent sperm from being shot into the bladder and to keep urine, which is spermicidal, from mixing with the semen. Sperm live no longer than forty-eight hours in a woman's uterus or cervix; if they remain in the vagina, they stop moving after one hour. Contractions of the vagina during orgasm tend to cause the semen to be sucked up toward the fallopian tubes, where fertilization will take place if an egg is in the vicinity.

While the male's sole reproductive function is to manufacture sperm and then transfer the sperm to a female, the female's function is to produce eggs, receive sperm, provide protection and nourishment for a developing fetus, and then expel the fetus from her body. Yet a woman's reproductive system is not a great deal more complex than a man's.

The woman's two ovaries are equivalent to the man's two testes. The ovaries contain all of the woman's eggs, which total at her birth between 200,000 and 400,000. By puberty, the egg supply has shrunk to approximately 10,000. But to experience 10,000 menstrual periods, the woman would have to live about eight hundred years, assuming she reached puberty at age thirteen. Actually, only about 400 ova are shed from the ovaries in a lifetime, so that the childbearing ability of an average woman lasts about thirty-three years, to age forty-six.

The ovaries are slightly smaller than the testes and sit within the body, roughly three inches to either side of the point that is midway between the vagina and navel. Leading from the ovaries are thin tunnels called fallopian tubes, which can be described as forming the two arms of the letter Y. The fallopian tubes join at the center of the Y, in the uterus, or womb.

Roughly pear-shaped and pear-sized, the uterus is a muscular organ that swells enormously when housing and nourishing a fetus. The "stalk" side of the organ points downward, ending in the cervix, or neck of the uterus. The vagina forms the bottom leg of the Y, leading down from the cervix.

The symmetrical arrangement of a woman's reproductive system is simple enough. However, the functioning of the system is slightly more complicated. Not only does menopause, over a period of years, alter the system's functioning drastically, but ovulation and menstruation cause systemic changes on a monthly basis. I will describe menstruation and menopause in Chapters 4 and 7, respectively, when I discuss nutritional methods for easing them. Here I will concentrate on ovulation.

Ovulation is the production or release of an ovum, or egg. It occurs once a month as part of the menstrual cycle. Each month, an egg in one of the ovaries awakens. A swelling bundle of cells known as the graafian follicle surrounds it. The bundle then enlarges within the ovary to almost a half inch in diameter. If by some whim of nature two eggs form follicles at the same time, it is possible for both eggs to drop and become fertilized, resulting in twins.

Once ready, or ripe, the egg moves to the edge of the ovary and bursts through. This is the moment of ovulation, which usually occurs thirteen to seventeen days after the start of the last menstrual period. Ovulation may bring on a bit of lower abdominal pain, known as *mittelschmerz* ("middle pain"), which some women can feel. Women who usually do not feel this minor pain can determine the precise time of ovulation through body temperature. Ovulation is usually accompanied by a slight reduction in temperature. First, the woman needs to determine her normal temperature, either orally, rectally, or under the arm. Then, she must take her temperature first thing every morning, before getting out of bed for *anything*. Ovulation will be signaled by a temperature that is a bit below what she has found to be her norm.

Although the released egg may have awaited the opportunity to do its job for thirty years, since before the woman's birth, it has only a little more than thirty hours to live unless it is fertilized. It slowly travels through the few inches of fallopian tube waiting to be fertilized, heading for the small cavity within the uterus. If it is not fertilized, the egg becomes infertile and begins to deteriorate.

After ovulation, the follicle that produced the egg continues to care for its solitary charge. The follicle secretes the hormones estrogen and progesterone. Estrogen, which comes from the ovary itself, causes the woman to desire coitus and prepares the vagina to receive a penis. Progesterone supports the changes that occur in the uterus in preparation for the embedding of a fertilized egg. If pregnancy does not occur, the follicle grows in size (it is then called the corpus luteum) and pours out its hormones. When the corpus luteum stops supplying hormones, menstruation begins about twelve to fourteen days after ovulation and the follicle degenerates. If pregnancy does occur, the follicle continues to produce hormones and grows into a large yellow tissue locked into the uterine wall. Halfway through the pregnancy, when the placenta has grown and is itself producing hormones, including progesterone, the old follicle degenerates.

EXAMINATION OF THE GENITALS

One of the primary ways in which you can maintain yourself as a totally homeostatic lover is to make sure your reproductive system remains in good health. To do this, you should self-examine your genitals—at least the external parts you can reach and see. Following are a number of clinical examinations that you and your mate can perform either on yourselves or on each other.

Mirror Examination for Inguinal Hernia

An inguinal hernia is a rupture in the lower abdomen. In an inguinal hernia, the tissue or muscle at the lower end of the abdominal cavity is either congenitally weak or has become weak from lifting, coughing, or straining with bowel movements. A sac of peritoneum (the membrane that lines the abdominal cavity) containing fat or part of the bowel protrudes through the weak part of the abdominal wall. This protrusion is the hernia.

One method a man can use to examine himself for an inguinal hernia is to stand before a mirror with his genitals in view. Cough hard and strain. Watch the area just above the scrotum and note any bulge that appears. A bulge may be a hernia.

A lump of any size under the pubic hair can indicate an inguinal hernia. It is possible for the lump to disappear when you lie down, as the loop of intestine may fall back into the abdominal cavity. Exertion may bring on lower abdominal pain, which might radiate to the testes. Bring anything unusual to the attention of a doctor.

Examination for Scrotal Hernia

An inguinal hernia so large that it passes into the scrotum is called a scrotal hernia. This type of hernia can be detected by examining the scrotum with a bright beam of light.

Unwrinkle the scrotum by stretching it, then shine a flashlight beam against and through the sac. A hernia will be opaque rather than translucent to the beam. Grasp the root of the sac between your thumb and forefinger to see if there is any unusual thickness or bulging. Insert your index finger into the subcutaneous inguinal ring by gently pushing upward through the scrotum; feel for a cough impulse from any possible hernia. If you feel or see something suspicious, consult a physician.

Examination for Undescended Testicles

A hernia is found in 90 percent of men with undescended testicles, a condition in which one or sometimes both testicles fail to come down into the scrotum at birth. An undescended testicle is usually found somewhere between the scrotum and abdomen. The medical reason for the condition remains unknown. However, the effects are not unknown—if both testicles are undescended, sterility will result, since sperm cannot be produced at normal body temperature and need the cooler environment of the scrotum.

To look for an undescended testicle, compare both testes by gently grasping one with each hand, using the thumb and forefinger. The testicles should be spongy-firm and egg-shaped. Any lump or difference in shape should be brought to the attention of a urologist.

Examination for Testicular Tumors

Cancer of the testes accounts for only 1 percent of all cancers in men. It is most common between the ages of twenty and thirty-four, with 75 percent of the cases seen in men between the ages of twenty and forty-nine. White men in the Western hemisphere show rates four times higher than those of black men.

It is important to examine the testes regularly to check for tumors. Some testicular tumors are associated with undescended testes, but it is not clear if one causes the other or if both are the result of hormonal imbalances. Although injury is a possible initiating factor, it also may just call attention to a tumor that was already present.

While testicular tumors cannot be prevented, they can be detected early through prompt attention to symptoms and close examination for undescended testicles. Testicular tumors often develop slowly and silently. An early symptom may be simply a sensation of discomfort resulting from the weight of the tumor. A mass, either soft or hard, may be felt in the scrotum. A dull scrotal ache or pain may be present. Occasionally, there is a backache. Tumors producing changes in hormone levels may bring about early sexual development in children or feminization in adult men. Check out suspicious symptoms or signs with a doctor.

Examination of the Epididymes

Locate each epididymis by feeling the smooth testis through the scrotum until you find a vertical ridge of soft nodules. The ridge of nodules should begin at the upper pole and extend to the lower pole. Feel for any lumps. If there are any, consult a physician immediately.

Examination of the Spermatic Cords

Compare the spermatic cords simultaneously by gently taking hold of each one with a different hand at the neck of the scrotum. With the thumbs in front and the forefingers behind, lightly compress the cords. Feel the distinct hard whipcord of the normal vas deferens and trace the cords down to the testes. There should be no unusual thickening, which would be due to inflammation of the vas deferens or the collection of fluid in a sac surrounding the testicle (hydrocele of the cord). Seek a doctor's advice if you find something abnormal.

Examination of the Vulva

For a woman, self-examination of the genitals is slightly more complicated than it is for a man. A woman either has to be something of a contortionist or must use a mirror. It can be accomplished, though, and it is worth the effort.

Put a mirror on the floor and squat over it, looking down into the mirror to inspect the external organs of the vulva. Look for any swelling, ulcers, or changes in color. Separate the labia with your thumb and forefinger to see the clitoris and vestibule, the part surrounded by the labia minora. Check the urethral opening for any discharge, lumps, or abscesses. Do the same thing with the vaginal opening. Look for vulvitis, a condition in which the skin around these external genitalia is hot, swollen, and red. An inflammation with discharge may be the result of vaginitis. Diseases such as gonorrhea and trichomoniasis are also characterized by an irritating discharge. Consult a physician immediately if you see suspicious signs.

A vulval tumor may result from a venereal disease. Swelling of one or both of the labia majora could be connected to failure of the peritoneal pouch to disappear after childbirth. (The peritoneum, the membrane lining the abdominal walls and surrounding the contained organs, stretches into a pouch during pregnancy.) The condition is similar to a scrotal hernia in a man. Injury to the existing pouch could cause a large, painful, bluish swelling. Additionally, a tumor might arise from a vulvovaginal gland abscess.

Urethritis, an inflammation of the urethra, may cause redness and swelling of the vulva, along with a profuse discharge of pus from the urethra and vulva. Nonspecific urethritis often occurs after menopause.

Medical attention is recommended for any of these problems.

Examination of the Vagina

From its opening, the vagina extends back into the pelvis, inclining at an angle of about forty-five degrees. Normally, the vagina is a collapsed tube nine centimeters (about three and a half inches) long that ends at the cervix, or neck of the uterus. It becomes an engorged and distended tube when sexually stimulated, and it changes into a remarkably elastic birth canal when receiving a baby.

An educated layperson can perform a vaginal examination using just fingers. To begin, empty your bladder, disrobe from the waist down, lie on your back on a table or bed, and bend your knees. If you want a smear taken for a Pap test, have it done now. Otherwise, or afterward, the examiner should don a rubber glove, apply lubricating jelly to the two examining fingers, and shine a bright light onto the perineum, which is the tissue between the anus and vagina.

Keeping the index and middle fingers straight and close together, the thumb spread out, and the fourth and fifth fingers folded into the palm, the examiner should insert the two extended fingers into the vaginal cavity with the finger pads facing upward, toward the front of your body. He should feel for tenderness and inflammation; thickening from scars, lumps, strictures, or narrowing of the vaginal walls; and adhesions from abnormal fibers binding organs together. With the two fingers inside the vagina, and the thumb opposite and outside on the rear portion of the labia majora, the examiner should rotate his hand to move the fingers around the vaginal walls, checking for abscesses and tenderness. Tenderness of the vaginal walls and a foul-smelling discharge are signs of vaginitis.

With the fingers still inserted in the vagina, the examiner should press the fingers of the other hand deep into the abdomen above your mons pubis and push the top of the uterus downward and forward, so that it can be felt by the two fingers within. Again, the examiner should look for such abnormalities as tenderness, blockage, lumps, and inflammation. Additional disorders could include pelvic relaxation from childbirth, indicated by the accommodation of three fingers instead of two; a floppy-walled vagina; and abnormalities such as infection from trichomonads or monilial yeasts. Seek medical attention for any abnormalities.

Pap Test

The pap smear must be taken before the vaginal finger examination because lubricating jelly on a cellular specimen interferes with the stain that is used for the test. Dr. George Papanicolaou developed the unique tissue-staining technique that detects and identifies both normal and abnormal cells, especially cancer cells, in vaginal tissue. The technique requires that the interior of the vagina is swabbed with a *sterile* cotton-tipped applicator to gather epithelial cells that have sloughed off the walls. The cells are smeared onto a clean glass slide and immediately rushed to a laboratory for fixing. Or, the examiner can fix the specimen by immersing the slide in a solution of equal parts ether and 95-percent ethyl alcohol. The slide is removed and dried, and sent to a cytotechnologist or pathologist for staining and analysis.

The sloughing of cells from tissue is a natural event, and by studying them, an expert can diagnose a malignant condition before it has advanced to the stage at which overt symptoms are noticed by the patient. A biopsy should follow any positive (Grade III or higher) report concerning a Papanicolaou smear.

The Pap test is reported according to a five-point scale:

Grade I.   Absence of atypical cells. The patient's condition
                is excellent.
Grade II.   Atypical cytology but no evidence of malignancy.
                The patient's condition is normal.
Grade III.   Cytology suggestive of, but not conclusive for,
                malignancy. The patient should be retested monthly
                until the results obtained are normal.
Grade IV.   Strongly suggestive of malignancy. The patient should
                seek medical attention.
Grade V.   Conclusive for malignancy. The patient should consult
                her gynecologist immediately.

Warning: Gynecologists report that even family practitioners often do not probe the swab stick for a Pap smear deeply enough—right up against the neck of the uterus. The result is that cervical cancer cells are not identified and a false Grade I or Grade II report is issued. Although you now have the instructions for performing a Pap test at home, it is still best to have this examination done by a medical specialist. In fact, none of these home examinations of the male or female genitalia is an alternate to the knowledgeable clinical inspection of a physician. What self-examination can do is to put you in close touch with your genitals and give you the opportunity to become aware of a health problem long before it reaches serious proportions. The best medicine against any type of health problem is to nip it in the bud.

Chapter 2

THE DIET FOR HEALTHY LOVEMAKING

I am an extremely orgasmic woman and have been sexually inclined since I was about six years old. I've masturbated for as long as I can remember and have been obsessed with sex since the first time I stimulated myself. Now, at age twenty-seven, I've finally found the man who makes me happiest, and our wedding is arranged for next month. He makes me feel fantastic in bed.

When Robert rubs his penis over my clitoris in just the right way, he builds me up to an incredible excitement. Then I erupt in orgasm for almost a full minute. The impact is so tremendous that I shoot my legs straight out from the tension, go into a semiconvulsion, and finally relax, while pleasure seeps throughout my being. A few minutes later, I'm ready to do it all over again.

I think I owe this healthy response to my parents, who raised me on a farm and fed me only freshly killed meat and poultry, fish from nearby streams and lakes, raw whole milk, vegetables grown in our own gardens, whole grains from our fields, and fruits off our own trees. My life has consisted of good nutrition and plenty of exercise. Even now I do everything I can to keep myself strong and healthy. I love my body. I view it wholistically and want to retain sexual health to the end of my years.

Because of this, I'm open to any new knowledge concerning sexual nutrition. There's no objection on my part to having better sex and even more pleasurable orgasms! What do you have to offer?

Sally W.
St. Paul, Minnesota

I recently retired from a Fortune 500 company and am having a rousing good time with the widows and divorcées in the retirement community in which I have settled. I'm a widower, formerly married to a loving and giving woman for thirty-seven years. My wife and I had an extremely satisfying sex life, which produced three strong sons and two daughters. For me, lovemaking was always a life force that gave me incentive to do bigger and better things in business. Now, in retirement, when I'm able to relax and am not under daily pressure to reach a specific goal, I find myself more sexually fulfilled than ever.

The women in this neighborhood compete for me. Age is no factor at all. I am attractive to, and feel an attraction for, women from fifty-five to seventy-five—and there are lots of them in this community. They can't do enough for me. I'm having a ball!

I have never regarded a spontaneous, firm erection as a birthright, and I have experienced my share of failures, usually because I was tired, troubled, or intoxicated. But this never happens to me now, maybe because I'm eating well, sleeping nine hours, golfing daily, laboring under no emotional stress, and seeking nothing more than to fulfill my wants and needs.

Do I have a problem? Not really, unless it's in selecting from a range of preferences in arousal and lovemaking. What I am looking for, however, is a way of satisfying more than one woman in a twenty-four-hour period. Would you have suggestions for edibles that might let me "rise to the occasion" more frequently?

Harry B.
Ft. Lauderdale, Florida

Adult macho adventure novels invariably feature heroes with penises that are twelve inches long, stiff as steel, and functional all night. These fictional male organs usually come in three sizes—large, gigantic, and so big that their muscular owners can barely carry them around. The heroines of adult women's romance fantasies often flow vaginally like fountains, explode in orgasm, and do it again and again and again. These imaginary women groan in ecstasy and make themselves available at every opportunity. Ardent, detailed lovemaking scenes are the highlights of these writings, which would be all right if the sessions described were accurate.

In real life, however, one or both lovers too often experience some sexual difficulty. The greatest obstacle to effective sexual functioning is the feeling that particular goals must be achieved. These goals may include attaining an erection and sustaining it until orgasm, always having an orgasm, being naturally lubricated enough for easy penetration, or having simultaneous orgasms. Performance has become blindly revered. Underlying this performance anxiety, or fear of sexual failure, is the belief that you are not a "real" man or woman if your performance is not first-rate. People put very irrational demands on themselves when it comes to their sexuality.

Sex is a psychological as well as a physical need. You require sexual relations as much for the state of your mind as for the state of your body. Sexual intercourse is a physiological fulfillment—the confirming act of your sexuality. And sexuality is your psychosocial attitude toward, interest in, feelings about, belief in, and comfort with sex and all its ramifications in your relations with the environment and the people around you. Your concept of your personal sexuality laps over into all the spheres of your life.

Sex is a natural gift, inherited by almost everyone. How you use sex affects your self-image and conditions your sexuality. You may be anatomically, physically, mentally, and emotionally talented in sexual gratification of yourself or a partner, but when your gratification is suppressed, frustrated, or perverted, the wholeness of your life is temporarily shattered. If allowed to continue, temporary damage to sexuality can stabilize into a more permanent sexual problem.

Dr. Mary S. Calderone, a sexologist and former medical director of the Planned Parenthood Federation of America, and Eric W. Johnson, a sex educator, defined "sexual" and "sexuality" as concerning your *whole* self, not just your physical body but also your male or female role in life. Sexuality encompasses the relationships you have with people of the opposite sex and of your own sex, and at any age. Therefore, when I discuss ways in which you can improve your diet to enhance your physical and emotional sexual pleasure, I simultaneously am delineating wholistic actions you can take to raise your entire personhood to a higher degree. What is good for your neurogenital response is also beneficial for your whole being.

Sex—the physical aspect of an intimate relationship—is a wholistic activity. Wholism of self exists when the body, emotions, mind, spirit, and sexuality all are functioning in harmony. Healing involves the growth, strengthening, repair, and striving of the total human organism. You are a psychosomatic organism endeavoring to maintain complete health and to promote the full soundness of your being. Your personal responsibility is to become an active participant in your psychosomatic enhancement, and one of the main tools you can use is lovemaking. Making love is best done with a partner who lives your same wholistic lifestyle.

Years ago, women accepted sex as the man's domain and saw themselves as passive and submissive partners; most repressed their sexual desires. Fortunately, these attitudes have changed. Today's women—as well as men—recognize that there are choices for both sexes. Equality in lovemaking has become the new reality.

Gerald G. Griffin, Ph.D., said in *The Silent Misery: Why Marriages Fail* that there are six types of relationships possible between two loving people:

1. A flexible, responsible relationship that is continuously growing and free of manipulation, self-centeredness, jealousy, and possessiveness.

2. A cooperative, liking relationship based on tolerance and trust, and nourished by undistorted, realistic expectations.

3. A friendship of respect and gratitude.

4. A loyal intimacy continuously nurtured by genuine care, affection, concern, acceptance, encouragement, support, and open communication.

5. A relationship that is individualistic, private, and honest but also molded by social vogue, pressures, indoctrination, expectations, pretense, and façade.

6. A relationship based on a passionate time in bed.[1]

SEXUAL TROUBLES IN INDUSTRIALIZED WESTERN SOCIETIES

Good, regular sex both encourages good health and is a sign that good health is prevailing. This being true, it is apparent that all is not healthy for the people living in the industrialized Western nations. As many of us become more open about sex, and as the pressure builds for us to perform well in bed, surprising statistics about sexual health are surfacing.

One out of ten young men in the West is totally impotent. Over 50 percent are struggling with potency problems more than just occasionally. Of Western women, more than half have never had an orgasm or are the victims of exceedingly low sex drives.

A man in his mid-twenties, Raymond M. of Newtown, Connecticut, told me he is being divorced following only two years of marriage because any sexual desire he felt for his wife disappeared directly after their honeymoon.

Another man, Morris R. of New York City, age thirty-six, reports that he has been sexually repulsed by his wife since the birth of their last child— three years ago.

A forty-four-year-old woman, Cynthia H. of Indianapolis, Indiana, told her physician that she wants to revive her sexual interest in her husband— an interest that dissipated five years earlier, when she took up golf and became a fanatic of the game.

Babette O. of Alexandria, Virginia, says that she has never experienced much desire for her spouse in the thirty-two years of their marriage but now feels that she has been missing out on something.

These troubled people are manifesting physical, mental, and emotional changes in their sexuality. They are typical of the husbands and wives being seen in sex therapy clinics throughout the Western world and suffering from what psychiatrists label inhibited sexual desire. This inhibition is defined as one of many sexual dysfunctions in *The Diagnostic and Statistical Manual of Mental Disorders* of the American Psychiatric Association.

Inhibited sexual desire is not an unusual problem among American men and women, and you, recognizing some latent tendency, might ask: "Am I a highly enthusiastic lover with boundless energy and a seemingly insatiable sexual appetite? Or do I look on lovemaking as a chore that never really gets me terribly turned on?"

Your ability to satisfy and be satisfied, your views on what healthy sex comprises, your sexual responsiveness, your desirability, all infiltrate the deepest fabrics of life.

While there are scores of reasons for chronic sexual dysfunctions—including pressures at work, mental illness, everyday stress, effects of medication, poisoning from pollution, and anxiety and depression—the leading underlying pathology is probably poor diet. Inadequate nutrition keeps your body from being able to cope adequately with all the many sources of dysfunction. Yet diet is the one sexual-distress factor that is most within your control. While people may try to improve their sex lives through the use of vibrators, pornographic films, waterbeds, mood music, drugs, and the Kama Sutra, it is becoming evident that what is kept in the kitchen has a greater effect on sexual responsiveness than the gimmicks used in the bedroom.

To maintain the highest possible energy levels, to follow through fully on inclinations to engage in sexual activity, to reach the heights of sexual bliss, and to enjoy repeated and ageless sex, you must get your body's cellular structures and fluids into perfect harmony. This can be achieved with a full program of sexual nutrition.

You do not need to be obviously sick to have a sex life that is less than ideal; many people today are living on the borderline between sickness and minimal good health. Wholistic health practitioners call this border-line condition *low-level worseness*. Being minimally healthy in this way is a far cry from the *high-level wellness* that would have you feeling very energetic and sexually receptive.

AN EXAMPLE OF LOW-LEVEL WORSENESS

Maryanne F., age twenty-three, a homemaker living in Seattle, Washington, was feeling acute anxiety, tension, depression, and dissatisfaction with her marriage, mainly due to concerns related to her infrequent sexual intercourse with her husband of two years. The couple had an eight-month-old baby girl whom they adored, but this did not stop them from fighting often. Their relationship was deteriorating drastically.

Both Maryanne and her husband desired different things from the marriage. Maryanne wanted activity and excitement. After being confined to the house and caring for the baby all day, she was full of energy and anxious for adult stimulation, especially the sexual kind. In contrast, her mate came home tired, dragging, and hoarse from his day's activities selling low-cost life insurance door to door in a vast housing project. Peter F., who was twenty-five, found himself too fatigued to perform as a social companion after dinner or as a lover in bed. The fault for the marital conflicts, of course, belonged to both Peter and Maryanne. Maryanne was suffering from the *tired homemaker syndrome*, and Peter was a victim of the *tired businessperson syndrome*.

After discussing the problem with her mother, the young woman took her complaint to her family doctor. On his advice, she traveled to see a psychiatrist, Abram Hoffer, M.D., Ph.D., of Victoria, British Columbia, Canada.

Maryanne had no mental disease, yet her visit to the psychiatrist was a major event in her marriage. The relationship was saved not by counseling but by a change in nutrition.

"The woman told me that she and her husband simply could not get along," said Dr. Hoffer, as quoted in my book *Total Health.* "They were fighting all the time and considering divorce even though they acknowledged their love for each other."

Maryanne described her tension to Dr. Hoffer and said she believed that her husband had an emotional problem, too. According to Dr. Hoffer:

> In a marriage counseling situation, I explore all the reasons for a marriage's deterioration. I interviewed the wife very carefully to see if she had evidence of any psychiatric disorder. She did not. Then I interviewed Peter. He did not have any mental problem, either. The main difficulty for both of them was incorrect eating. For instance, let me describe Maryanne's reaction.
>
> At first she refused to accept my diagnosis of acute anxiety caused from malnourishment, but she did admit to often feeling fatigued and tense, being irritable and short-tempered, feeling easily frustrated and sometimes coming close to hysteria because of a seeming inability to breathe. In fact, Maryanne had the classic form of malnutrition common to this decade of eating processed foods almost exclusively—the "tired homemaker syndrome."

Dr. Hoffer explained that the tired homemaker syndrome is a complex of symptoms that arises from poor eating habits.

Dr. Hoffer continued:

> Typically, a newly married person such as Maryanne, who feels quite tired in the morning—even after a night's sleep—exhibits the syndrome from consuming the wrong diet. She goes back to bed after giving her baby an early morning feeding, and upon arising takes coffee and something sweet to eat—a really poor breakfast. Her lunch may be better, with soup and a sandwich. She'll begin to feel slightly less tired in the afternoon from eating lunch. In the evening she'll have her first proper meal that is more filled with nutrients. She begins to wake up. The rest of the evening she will be cheerful and energetic.
>
> But consider this young woman's husband. Peter is forced to rise early and go to work. He eats a poor breakfast, may eat a substantial lunch for more energy needed in selling, and arrives home for dinner feeling rather tired from walking for miles and interacting with people all day. In the evening he prefers to write up his sales accounts and then sit back and relax, maybe doze in front of the television set, and isn't much interested in exchanging ideas. His wife hungers for activity and conversation after being home all day with their child and now feels lively from an intake of proper nourishment. The result is likely to be a major personality clash

because of their different needs and energy levels. Their nutritional patterns are similar. Their blood sugars have been kept at mostly hypoglycemic level.

In *hypoglycemia*, the body's blood-sugar level is lower than normal, due to either too much insulin being present in the body or inadequate food having been consumed. Maryanne, as do many other homemakers, put off every morning fulfilling her body's need for nourishment to break the long fast during sleep. Her diet was lacking in fiber and heavy in refined starches. Maryanne was courting a carbohydrate intolerance by having either no breakfast or just coffee and toast with jam. Caffeine and starchy foods were causing her blood sugar to surge temporarily and then drop sharply. Such serum-glucose fluctuation can cause depression, anxiety, irritability, and other forms of emotional discomfort. Hypoglycemia is one of the main conditions that cause distress in sexual relationships.

Wholistic physicians who treat hypoglycemia with nutrition usually employ the methods of orthomolecular medicine. Orthomolecular medicine is a nontraditional therapeutic approach in which the optimal molecular concentration of substances normally present in the body is determined and is then provided both to preserve health and to treat illness. The word "orthomolecular" was coined in 1968 by Linus Pauling, Ph.D., American chemist and two-time Nobel laureate. "Ortho" means "right," so "orthomolecular" refers to the supplying of the body with "the right molecules in the right amounts." This concept was developed over thirty years ago by Dr. Hoffer and Humphrey Osmond, M.R.C.P., M.D., who worked together in a psychiatric hospital in Saskatoon, Saskatchewan, Canada. These two orthomolecular psychiatrists first began using vitamins, minerals, amino acids, and other natural physiological substances to balance the body chemistry and restore the health of mentally ill patients. They tried to avoid substances alien to the body, such as synthetic drugs. Drs. Hoffer and Osmond had incredibly successful results, and through publication of their research, orthomolecular nutrition—including sexual nutrition—came to be further tested and then established as a legitimate medical therapy. Now orthomolecular medicine is available to anyone experiencing difficulty with his or her sexuality. The possible antidotes for sexual dysfunction that I discuss in this book evolved from the clinical practices of orthomolecular physicians and other professionals who correct health problems using no-junk nutrition.

An excellent diet based on natural foods is a mainstay of the orthomolecular nutrition program. Said Dr. Hoffer:

My treatment of the tired homemaker syndrome was to persuade Maryanne to start each morning with a substantial breakfast. I advised her to eat hot cereal, two eggs, maybe some tuna fish, and whole wheat toast. Frequently such a patient will be horrified, as was this woman. "I never eat breakfast," she said. "Well, you must!" I answered. "You have no choice. In a week you'll enjoy it." That kind of breakfast releases energy steadily and raises the blood-sugar level sufficiently for it to stay elevated throughout the day.

The homemaker must eat a larger lunch, too. It doesn't necessarily have to be higher in protein. I'm just a sugar-free advocate. Eating sugar-free furnishes an evenminded afternoon. A small dinner is in order, and giving up her cocktail will help. Such an eating program will have this formerly tired homemaker feeling good all day and no longer prone to anxiety or fluctuating in her personality.

An improvement in eating habits will often solve marital problems involving sexuality, as it did for Peter and Maryanne. In my opinion, physiological disturbances caused by improper nutrition and resultant anxiety are a serious cause of marital conflict.

Physiological disturbance was definitely the cause of Peter's inadequate performance in bed, as a full physical evaluation revealed. Peter suffered from an illness that is, for the most part, neglected by orthodox psychiatry and traditional psychology. This "sickness" does not produce obvious life-threatening symptoms. It cannot be described in a clear manner. Years pass before it kills, and no postmortem indicates that it had ever been present. This disease of our modern society, sometimes labeled the tired businessperson syndrome, is ubiquitous throughout the complex of industrialized nations.

The tired businessperson suffers from symptoms that are subjective and constantly present. The major one is fatigue. Also, the bowels are lax, appetite is gone, sleep is fleeting, desire to work is diminished, memory is unreliable, libido is practically absent, sexual function is far from satisfactory, anxiety is always near, and joy is missing from life.

From youths in their twenties to seniors past sixty, the number of people who look, behave, and feel older than they are is increasing every day. Some start to show signs of premature aging at as early as eighteen, and among those over forty, the people who do not are the exceptions. A good proportion of businesspeople over sixty, in view of their physical condition, should act and appear far younger than they do.

Of the many factors contributing to the tired businessperson syndrome, poor nutrition may be the most important. Incorrect eating habits can help wear out physical resistance. Poor resistance makes an individual easy prey to degenerative forces such as stress, air and water pollution, food additives, overwork, smoking, and insufficient rest. Modern society is filled with "half-invalids" whose inability to give or receive sexual joy has them and their mates exceedingly unhappy.

THE LOVER'S DIET AND DAILY WHOLE FOOD GUIDE

What can be done about the tired businessperson syndrome and the tired homemaker syndrome? Although the proponents of twentieth-century technology and the giant food industry would imply differently, the basic "treatment" is an alteration in eating habits and a more judicious food selection. The results of a national survey conducted by the U.S. Department of Agriculture indicated that out of 7,500 average American families, only half had diets that met the Recommended Dietary Allowances for calories, protein, iron, calcium, magnesium, vitamin A, thiamine (vitamin B1), riboflavin (vitamin B2), and vitamin C. The diets of the other half failed to meet the allowances for one or more of these essential nutrients. And vital trace elements such as zinc, chromium, and manganese were not even among the nutrients listed on the questionnaire.[2]

Industrialized peoples consume too many refined, processed, canned, frozen, precooked, or ready-to-serve items in place of fresh, whole foods prepared at home from scratch. They drink an overabundance of soft drinks, alcoholic beverages, coffee, tea, and water polluted with toxic heavy metals. They try to nourish themselves with doughnuts for breakfast, fast-food hamburgers for lunch, and heavy, sauce-laden entrées for dinner. In other words, they subsist on sugar, salt, white flour, fats, and unnecessary, potentially harmful chemical additives.

The price that is paid for such faulty food habits is low-level health. An early symptom of this modern scourge is an unpleasant alteration in sexual physiology. Although health authorities do not agree on the precise role diet plays in sexual dysfunction, they generally do agree that it is a major factor in many serious degenerative diseases. In the United States alone, the incidence of degenerative disease has reached more than one-half of the adult population—a staggering 125 million people. Treatment of these diseases has made the medical field the fourth-largest industry in the United States today. Americans are desperately trying to suppress the discomfort and anguish of the many resulting ills they are battling, particularly sex-related ills.

Sexual dysfunction is a degeneration of body parts. It can encompass a number of different organs or systems, including the mind, nerves, genitals, endocrine glands, or blood vessels. Diet-related problems with sexuality that commence in the twenties or thirties and steadily increase in the forties, fifties, and later ages are often tied to overeating, improper selection of foods, and lack of exercise.

To help protect yourself against or control ailments involving the sex organs, authorities recommend a diet that is low in fats (especially saturated fats), cholesterol, salt, sugar, and other refined or concentrated foods, and high in fresh fruits, fresh vegetables, and protein from plant sources. The Lover's Diet is such a regimen. The Daily Whole Food Guide, on page 28, is the basis for the Lover's Diet, which is presented beginning on page 31.

Daily Whole Food Guide

You can make many creative meals for yourself as you experiment with different combinations of the wholesome foods listed here. This list is designed to help you plan nutritious, low-cost meals to supply the vital nutrients that work together to build, repair, and reinforce your sexuality. This is easily accomplished by eating a variety of fresh, whole, natural foods from each of the following groups. The number of servings may vary according to your age, size, activity, and general health. A suggested daily menu is presented on page 33.

Whole Grains, Legumes, Nuts, and Seeds (Plant Protein Foods)

WHOLE GRAINS

- Wheat, rice, millet, oats, barley, rye, buckwheat, and triticale.
- Bulgur and cornmeal.

LEGUMES

- Lentils, peanuts, dried peas, dried beans, soybeans, mung beans, black kidney beans, red kidney beans, chick peas (garbanzos), pinto beans, lima beans, adzuki beans, great northern beans, black-eyed peas, navy beans, white beans, etc.
- Tofu.

NUTS AND SEEDS

- Almonds, cashews, Brazil nuts, walnuts, pecans, filberts, and pine nuts.
- Sunflower seeds, pumpkin seeds, sesame seeds, and squash seeds.
- Butters made from the above nuts or seeds.

SUBSTITUTES

- Brewer's (nutritional) yeast—three tablespoons per day for protein and the B vitamins.
- Eggs—one per day (up to three per week because of the high cholesterol content) if low-fat dairy products are used that day and no meat is eaten.
- Fish, poultry, and lean meat.

GUIDELINES AND SUGGESTIONS

- Serving suggestions—grain or bean loaves and patties, casseroles, spreads, soups, salads, pasta, cakes, muffins, pancakes, breads, sandwiches, pita, tortillas, flat breads, and cookies.
- Combining grains with dairy products, seeds, or legumes yields a high-quality protein. (See page 38.)

- Method of enrichment—for every two tablespoons of flour called for in a recipe, substitute one tablespoon of soy flour and one tablespoon of wheat germ or brewer's yeast.
- Use unsalted, unroasted nuts and seeds. Avoid rancid nuts and seeds.

Milk and Milk Products

MILK

- Low-fat milk, skim milk, and powdered milk.
- Buttermilk, yogurt, and kefir.

CHEESE

- Unprocessed natural hard cheeses, such as sapsago and mozzarella.
- Natural soft cheeses, such as Brie, Camembert, cottage cheese, ricotta, and farmer cheese.

SUBSTITUTES

- Goat's milk or soymilk products.

GUIDELINES AND SUGGESTIONS

- Serving suggestions—puddings, pies, toppings, blender drinks, patties, custards, salads, and dips.
- Method of enrichment—in bread, pancake, muffin, and cookie recipes, add one-quarter cup powdered milk for extra protein.
- Try making your own yogurt at home.
- Use low-fat milk products to reduce your intake of saturated fats and cholesterol.

Fruits and Vegetables

VITAMIN A FRUITS AND VEGETABLES

- Cantaloupes, papayas, persimmons, apricots, peaches, nectarines, prunes, and mangos.
- Carrots, winter squashes, sweet potatoes, sweet peppers, chives, broccoli, pumpkins, cabbage, yams, and dark leafy greens (spinach, Swiss chard, mustard greens, dandelion greens, beet greens, turnip greens, collard greens, kale, watercress, parsley, endive, etc.).

VITAMIN C FRUITS AND VEGETABLES

- Black currants, guavas, persimmons, strawberries, papayas, kumquats, mangos, cantaloupes, all berries, and citrus fruits (grapefruits, oranges, lemons, limes, and tangerines).

- Sweet peppers, cauliflower, asparagus, kohlrabi, Brussels sprouts, all cabbages, all sprouts, and all leafy greens (spinach, parsley, kale, collard greens, etc.).
- Potato skin.

OTHER FRUITS AND VEGETABLES

- Apples, bananas, plums, pineapples, cherries, pears, raisins, grapes, avocados, pomegranates, quinces, melons, figs, and dates.
- Beets, radishes, onions, garlic, cucumbers, celery, artichokes, green beans, peas, asparagus, okra, mushrooms, parsnips, corn, eggplant, etc.

GUIDELINES AND SUGGESTIONS

- Serving suggestions—juices, crudites, salads, cereal toppers, pies, cakes, muffins, pancakes, casseroles, soups, and stews.
- Some fruits and most vegetables can be lightly steamed, baked, or broiled, but all are most nutritious when eaten raw.
- Every day, serve at least one vitamin A fruit or vegetable and at least a few vitamin C fruits or vegetables.
- Try to enjoy at least one large, leafy salad each day.
- Try to choose fruits in season.

Other Items

FATS AND OILS

Use cold-pressed, unrefined, polyunsaturated vegetable oils in place of animal or hydrogenated fats to help reduce your consumption of saturated fats and cholesterol. These oils are available in health food stores and some supermarkets. Safflower, sunflower, soy, corn, and sesame oils are good choices. You can also substitute nut or seed butters or soft margarine for butter and hydrogenated fats.

SWEETENERS

Since refined white sugar adds calories but no nutrients to your diet, restriction of intake is recommended. Reduce your use of sugar by avoiding refined, processed, fabricated foods and by eliminating white sugar and products made with white sugar or glucose. Also bypass honey, syrups, dextrose, and other sweeteners.

SALT

Try to avoid adding salt to food. Salt occurs naturally in many foods and is found in almost all processed foods. Reduce your salt intake by eating fresh, whole, unsalted foods. If you must add salt, substitute tamari (soy sauce), sea salt, or miso. (One tablespoon of tamari equals one teaspoon of salt.)

Kelp or dulse, rich in iodine, iron, and other trace minerals, can also be used. Herbs, spices, and lemon juice substitute natural flavors for the salt flavor.

The Lover's Diet

The Lover's Diet not only is based on the Daily Whole Food Guide but also takes into account the need of sexually active people for a normally elevated blood-sugar level. The nerves, brain, and gonads depend on blood sugar in the form of glucose (the product of carbohydrate metabolism) in order to function efficiently. When the glucose-serum level drops too low, the organs and systems utilized for sex are weakened, potentially causing dysfunctioning. To avoid a drop in blood sugar, you need to guard against:

1. Sluggish adrenal-gland reaction, which slows the release of stored sugar from the liver.
2. A weak liver, which allows excess sugar to be dumped into the bloodstream.
3. Disrupted insulin response by the pancreas, which can cause excess secretion of insulin by the body and rapid removal of sugar from the blood.
4. Poor diet, especially the consumption of foods containing too many refined carbohydrates, which are high in simple sugars.

The sexual-response system is affected when the diet contains an overabundance of simple sugars. While it is true that a flood of refined carbohydrates into the digestive system will temporarily heighten energy and emotions, you will lose these sexual attributes approximately fifteen minutes later because of an overproduction of insulin. Eating simple sugars subjects you to an emotional and physical seesaw. After the initial energy rush, you will drop into depression and lose your energy.

The Lover's Diet takes into consideration the fact that Americans, Europeans, and the people of other high-technology societies are subjected to thousands of toxic pollutants, which put stress on the liver. In addition, large amounts of protein place increased burdens on the liver, which is the detoxifying organ of the body. A high-protein diet would be unsuitable for you if your sexual sluggishness is due partly to a malfunctioning or overworked liver.

Some high-protein, low-carbohydrate diets cause a double burden by failing to differentiate between simple and complex carbohydrates. White sugar, as a simple carbohydrate, is absorbed into the bloodstream too rapidly. Avoid using any concentrated, refined sugar. Whole grains, legumes, seeds, nuts, and other complex carbohydrates, being complicated sugar links, are broken down more gradually and absorbed into the bloodstream

The Lover's Fast

Sam Addanki, Ph.D., advised overweight men and women to "lose those extra pounds and develop good nutritional habits" in his article "Doctor Reveals How Being Overweight Causes Sexual Problems," published in the magazine "Body Forum." Addanki said, "Eat less fat and sugar and add more dietary fiber. Obesity is not beautiful in either sex, and it is not healthy.

"Literally thousands of obese couples are experiencing the trauma of sexual incompatibility," added Addanki. "I feel that there is a direct relationship between obesity and divorce."

According to Addanki, "A high level of estrogen present in an obese man is often the cause of impotence. A man's basic male hormone is testosterone, which is responsible for his sex drive," Addanki explained. "The liver makes the globulin that binds this sex hormone, but in the obese man, estrogens interfere with this function, causing the male hormone to be excreted instead of retained. This lowers the concentration of testosterone in the blood, and with less of this hormone, the man's sex drive diminishes and often disappears. The role of estrogen in altered sexual awareness of obese men went undetected for so long because, oddly enough, it does not cause any external signs of feminization."[3]

The solution for nonresponsiveness to sexual stimulation and reduced desire for sexual intercourse, felt Addanki, is to lose weight. And one way to lose weight is to go on a fast for perhaps five days. A fast has three phases. In the first phase, some hunger pangs are experienced. The second phase features withdrawal and detoxification from the substances commonly eaten to which you might be allergic. (A paradox is that people tend to be addicted to the foods to which they are allergic.) In the third phase, a tremendous sense of well-being and increased energy are felt, as both chronic sensitivity reactions and symptoms of withdrawal and detoxification have disappeared. In general, the first phase lasts one day and the second, two days. The third phase begins around the fourth day. It is on the fourth day that increased sexuality is felt. Many men and women report that fasting is an excellent aphrodisiac.

In any fast, water must be taken on a regular basis. In the book "Food, Mind and Mood," coauthor Dr. Michael Schachter, an orthomolecular psychiatrist who treated brain sensitivities using fasting as one of his several techniques, suggested: "When the hunger pangs strike, try taking several mouthfuls of water; this may effectively deal with the uncomfortable sensations. Besides, you should be drinking at least two quarts of water a day throughout the entire fast."[4]

A fast helps the body lose fluid and solid flab slowly but steadily. Better still, because it does not have to digest food and process accumulating waste products, the body also gets rid of toxic materials it has been storing that have been draining its energy. While symptoms of toxicity may be apparent during the first two or three days of a fast because of leaching of the body's wastes into the bloodstream, feelings of health take over once the waste materials have been released through the skin, kidneys, lungs, intestines, and liver. A feeling of sexual vigor then descends and grows into an appetite not for food but for sex.

During the fast, exercise—not vigorous, but moderate, regular muscular activity—done in fresh air is beneficial. It helps the body eliminate the toxins. Also, vitamins can be consumed, although a true therapeutic fast disallows the ingestion of anything except purified water. (Avoid drinking tap water because of its possible toxicity.) Vegetable juice or fruit juice squeezed fresh during the detoxification days can also be consumed.

over a longer period of time—up to six hours. This longer transit time allows the release of glucose into the circulatory system at a lower and more consistent rate. Eating complex-carbohydrate foods with an additional protein source, accompanied by a small amount of fats or oils, further slows absorption and keeps blood-sugar uptake even more gradual.

Other ways to keep your blood-sugar level even and normally elevated include supplying yourself with the nutrients required for the metabolism of carbohydrates. These carbohydrate metabolizers include the B-complex vitamins and the mineral chromium. Eat smaller portions of food more frequently. Chew your food thoroughly—this is the first step in proper digestion and also brings out the full flavor of whole, unrefined natural foods. Stay away from stressful situations. Use meditation or other relaxation techniques. Perform deep-breathing exercises. Get plenty of exercise. These collective actions will smoothen the metabolism of what you eat to keep your blood sugar normally elevated in accordance with your sexual requirements.

Even taking all of the aforementioned into account, the Lover's Diet is a satisfying, delicious way to eat. A daily menu might consist of the following:

Pre-Breakfast Snack (upon arising)

Fresh fruit.

Breakfast

Whole-grain cereal (cooked or cold) with skim milk and fresh fruit.
Whole-grain bread with a boiled egg or cottage cheese, tofu, or beans.
Beverage such as herb tea, water-processed decaffeinated coffee (such as
    Rombotz), or coffee substitute (such as Caffix, Pioneer, Duram, or Bambu).

Mid-Morning Snack

Tomato juice, plain yogurt with fresh vegetables, or hot homemade bouillon.

Lunch

Whole-grain bread.
Fresh vegetable or lentil soup.
Fresh raw salad.
Cottage cheese, hard cheese, or lean meat, fish, or poultry.
Beverage.

Mid-Afternoon Snack

Fresh fruit with nuts or seeds.

Dinner

Large raw salad of vegetables in season.
Lean meat, fish, or poultry.
Baked potato, fresh corn on the cob, or brown rice or another grain.
Fresh fruit.
Beverage.

Evening Snack

Fresh fruit and skim milk.

Other guidelines for following the Lover's Diet are:

- Limit beef, lamb, or pork meals to three per week.
- Choose fish or poultry over beef, lamb, and pork.
- Limit your use of salad dressings and other fats. The less you use, the better.
- Steam, bake, or broil foods; do not fry them.
- Eat plenty of raw foods.
- Limit your intake of eggs and hard cheese.
- Limit or exclude caffeine, which is present in tea, coffee, cocoa, and cola and other soft drinks.
- Limit your intake of alcohol.
- Limit your use of salt and sugar.
- Eat as many different foods as you can within each category of the Daily Whole Food Guide.
- Eat six to eight small meals per day, instead of three large meals. Do not overeat at any one meal. Consuming smaller portions of a variety of foods helps keep caloric consumption down. If weight reduction is necessary, adjust your food intake as required.

- Avoid drinking liquids with your larger meals. Instead, drink the beverage a half hour before or after the meals.
- Always eat a good breakfast, which should include tofu, beans, wholegrain pancakes, or other foods that are plentiful in protein and provide a slow release of energy into the day.
- Avoid candied or dried fruits. Whole fruits are preferable to fruit juices because of the fiber content of whole fruits. However, three to four ounces of diluted unsweetened fresh natural fruit or vegetable juice is preferable to a coffee substitute or herbal tea.
- Cultured dairy products such as yogurt, kefir, koumiss, acidophilus milk, cottage cheese, and buttermilk make excellent nutritional snacks, especially if you mix in seeds, wheat germ, brewer's yeast, lecithin, or another supplement.
- Use substitutes for salt whenever possible. Kelp, dulse, and miso are especially recommended, since they are also rich in nutrients.
- When baking, replace sugar or artificial sweeteners with herbs or spices, fruits, sprouted grains, nut butters, seed butters, pure vanilla extract, or anise.
- Avoid refined or processed foods containing white sugar or white flour. Limit canned or packed foods, soft drinks, roasted or salted nuts, candy, chocolate, rich desserts, chewing gum containing sugar, ice cream, jams, jellies, preserves, and pastries, doughnuts, and other sweetened baked goods.
- Eliminate cigarette smoking totally.

FEWER BUT BETTER PROTEIN FOODS FOR SEXUAL HEALTH

Protein is second only to water in the body, comprising 22 percent of the body's weight. It is part of every living cell; it supplies fuel for energy (one gram supplies four calories) and acts as a body regulator, enzyme producer, immune-system enhancer, and endocrine-gland stimulator. The National Research Council recommends fifty-six grams of dietary protein daily for an average man and forty-six grams daily for an average woman. But the average daily American consumption of protein is in the range of ninety to one hundred grams per person. This is far in excess of physiological requirements.

The animal-protein industry in North America has been greatly overemphasizing the need for protein by humans. Eating too much protein is a major cause of aggravated liver disturbances in Americans and Canadians. Liver disease is the seventh most frequent cause of death among Americans. Malfunctioning of the liver allows excesses of sugar to be dumped into the bloodstream. This gives rise to hyperinsulinism (too much insulin in the blood) followed by hypoglycemia (a marked drop in blood sugar), a combination that is one of the four physiological reasons for the tired home-maker syndrome and the tired businessperson syndrome—causes of sexual dysfunction.

Protein is composed of large complex molecules created from amino acids, which are made of carbon, hydrogen, oxygen, nitrogen, and sulfur molecules. The twenty-two building blocks of protein—amino acids—are manufactured by plants through the process of photosynthesis. The human body is able to synthesize all but eight amino acids, which are therefore termed "essential" because they must be supplied "ready-made" by our food. The essential amino acids are methionine, threonine, tryptophan, isoleucine, leucine, lysine, valine, and phenylalanine. (Infants also require histidine.) About 20 percent of an adult's daily protein intake should be in the form of these essential amino acids.[5] It is important to know which foods contain high-quality protein. Eating fewer but better protein foods is an important component of improving your sexual nutrition.

There is some protein in most foods. Table 2.1 lists some common food sources of animal and vegetable proteins and will help you calculate the approximate amount of protein you consume in your daily diet.

Animal protein comes from foods such as beef, pork, fish, poultry, eggs, and dairy products. Many spokespersons in the field of nutrition, especially those who favor vegetarianism, believe that humans eat too much protein from animal sources and should eat more from vegetable sources. The original source of all protein, indeed, is plants. Herbivorous animals, which humans eat, get their protein from plants. Some human cultures eat carnivorous animals, but carnivores get their protein from herbivorous animals.

The health hazards from eating large quantities of animal protein include increased consumption of saturated fats and cholesterol, which are associated with heart disease. Saturated fats and cholesterol are also dangerous to your sexual health. Many meats—especially luncheon meats, canned ham, bacon, and sausage—contain sodium nitrites, which in the body form nitrosamines, substances that are suspected of causing cancer of the prostate, testes, cervix, ovaries, uterus, and other organs. Furthermore, the food animal's own toxic cellular wastes are passed on to the consumer in concentrated form, along with environmental contaminants, bacteria from spoilage, and other chemical additives.

While I do not believe that vegetarianism is the way to total sexual health, I do believe that substituting plant foods for meats—in particular, pork, beef, and lamb—will help tremendously in ensuring long-lived sexuality.

Plant proteins can be combined with each other or with a small amount of animal protein such as milk, eggs, or cheese to achieve better sexual nutrition. The Chinese have created many naturally complementary dishes using mainly rice or millet and soybean products with a touch of sesame seeds or slivered meat. Using certain protein items makes it easier to prepare low-cost complete-protein meals. These foods include powdered

Table 2.1. **Common Food Sources of Animal and Vegetable Proteins**

Food	Amount	Grams of Protein
Whole milk	8 ounces	8.5
Cheddar cheese	1 ounce	7.1
Hamburger, cooked	2 ounces	20.0
Chicken or turkey, cooked	1 drumstick	12.0
Most meats, cooked	2 ounces	15.0–20.0
Most fishes, cooked	2 ounces	15.0–20.0
Whole wheat bread	1 slice	3.0
Most pancakes	2 medium	6.0–8.0
Most muffins	2 medium	6.0–8.0
Potato, baked	1 medium	3.0
Corn, cooked	1 ear	3.0
Orange	1 medium	1.8
Brewer's yeast	3 tablespoons	12.0
Avocado	½ medium	2.0
Kale, cooked	1 cup	5.0
Tofu	3 ounces	9.0
Dried beans, cooked	½ cup	10.0–15.0
Yogurt	1 cup	8.0
Egg, raw	1 medium	6.0
Cottage cheese	½ cup	15.0
Peanut butter	2 tablespoons	8.0
Split peas, cooked	½ cup	8.0
Most leafy greens, cooked	1 cup	2.0
Most nuts	½ cup	10.0–20.0
Most seeds	½ cup	10.0–20.0
Oatmeal, cooked	1 cup	5.0
Brussels sprouts, raw	1 cup	5.5
Carrot, raw	1 medium	2.0
Mushrooms, raw	1 cup	2.0

milk, cottage cheese, soy flour, powdered soymilk, soy grits, eggs, wheat germ, seeds (sunflower, sesame, squash), grated cheese, brewer's yeast, nuts (almonds, Brazil nuts, cashews, walnuts, pine nuts), and seed or nut butters.

Protein balance is essential because the human body cannot store the surplus of amino acids provided by the Western diet. The body excretes excess amino acids through the kidneys in the form of urea, accompanied by gout, arthritis, kidney stones, and urogenital-system troubles such as prostatitis, cystitis, and bladder inflammation.

Fine combinations of protein foods from plant sources include the following:

Legumes with seeds
- Peas with pumpkin seeds
- Tofu and tahini spread
- Lentil soup with sunflower seeds
- Chick pea salad with sesame-seed dressing
- Beans with nuts
- Bean and nut casserole
- Soymilk custard with chopped nuts
- Bean spread with nuts

Grains with seeds
- Rice with sesame seeds
- Bread with tahini
- Rice pudding with sunflower seeds

Grains with dairy products
- Whole wheat bread with milk
- Whole wheat pizza with cheese
- Millet pudding
- Yogurt with granola
- Wheat and cheese casserole

Grains with legumes
- Rice with beans
- Millet with peas
- Wheat-soy bread
- Baked beans with rye bread
- Bulgur and bean salad

In addition, combining grains, nuts, legumes, or seeds with even a small amount of animal protein (dairy, poultry, meat, or fish) will increase sexual nutrition.

Among the finest of plant-protein foods is the sesame seed. The sesame seed can be used to make a variety of superior items such as tahini, hummus, sesame butter, granola, sesame meal, breads, cookies, and natural candy. Sesame has a rare, rich amino-acid profile. While it is not totally complete as a food, since it is slightly deficient in the amino acid lysine, it achieves a very high protein efficiency ratio when it is mixed with soy. In fact, combining almost any vegetable or grain with sesame seeds will create a complete protein.

More than this, sesame has a surplus of methionine and tryptophan. Other vegetable proteins are fashioned the other way around, with an abundance of lysine and a deficiency of methionine and tryptophan. Thus, again, sesame and other plant proteins together provide a complete, or balanced, protein. Aside from honeybee pollen, sesame comes the closest of any plant food to supplying a protein balance that seems tailor-made for the human body.

To make a delicious sesame-milk drink, combine one-half cup of sesame seeds, one-third cup of powdered milk, and six ounces of cold water in a kitchen blender, then add a little honey or vanilla. Sesame seeds also make an excellent addition to soups, fish, salads, cereals, and drinks, and their slight crunchiness makes them a great topping for yogurt. A little sesame oil sprinkled on game fish such as trout eliminates the gamy odor.

To make a sesame mayonnaise, mix sesame meal with some water in a blender. Put the mixture through cheesecloth and mix the resulting milk with vegetable oil. Add some mustard, sea salt, and vinegar to taste, and you have created a wonderful sesame mayonnaise.

The protein in sesame seeds can be an important nutritional resource if the seeds are hulled pure and without chemicals, such as the product manufactured by International Protein Industries, Inc. (20 Oser Avenue, Hauppauge, New York 11788; 516–231–7940). When chemicals like caustics, acids, and bleaches are used to remove the sesame hull, which contains toxic calcium oxalate, a rather unpalatable product results. Some of the caustic substances penetrate the seed. Additional processing gets out the caustics, but the chemical methods of refining leave seeds whose nutritional value has been reduced by oxidation, sterilization, and bleaching. International Protein Industries uses a process that not only avoids these chemical methods but also leaves the seeds more crunchy, tasty, and palatable through reduction of the 8-percent moisture content to 4 percent.

REDUCED SATURATED FATS FOR SEXUAL HEALTH

The fats in the foods you eat help your body store fat-soluble vitamins A, D, E, and K, which are necessary for sexual functioning. With nine calories per gram, fats are the most concentrated source of bodily energy. During digestion, fats break down first into glycerol and fatty acids and then into glucose, the ultimate source of energy for body cells.

Most fats supply linoleic acid, which is not manufactured by the body and must be obtained from food, making it an "essential" fatty acid. Good sources of this essential fatty acid are unhydrogenated vegetable oils such as safflower, sunflower, corn, wheat germ, sesame seed, walnut, and soybean. Other sources are peanuts, olives, nuts, chicken, and fish.

All animal fats, including those in whole milk, butter, cheese, lard, and shellfish, are saturated. Saturated vegetable fat sources include coconut and palm oils. Saturated fats are imbued with hydrogen atoms, which make the fats solid at room temperature. Many wholistic and traditional doctors believe saturated fats are potentially unhealthy because they raise blood-cholesterol levels.

Unsaturated fats are healthier to eat. They are present in nuts, seeds, corn, peanuts, olives, and fish. Fish is the only animal food that contains large amounts of unsaturated fats.

Polyunsaturated fats have less hydrogen than do unsaturated fats and remain liquid at room temperature. Polyunsaturated fats can be found in unrefined vegetable oils such as safflower, sunflower, soybean, and corn. When eaten, they tend to lower blood-cholesterol levels.

Hydrogenated fats, artificially hardened with hydrogen, may increase blood cholesterol. The hydrogenation also decreases the amount of essential fatty acids. Margarines, shortening, most supermarket peanut butters, fast foods, and the majority of processed convenience foods contain hydrogenated fats.

The majority of medical authorities, as well as the members of the former U.S. Senate nutrition committee, believe that Americans would benefit from reducing their total consumption of fats, particularly animal fats. If ingesting fats is mandatory for you, substitute moderate amounts of polyunsaturated vegetable fats for some of the saturated fats in your diet. In Third World countries, where diets are adequately supplied with fruits, vegetables, nuts, seeds, and grains, problems with sexuality and reproduction are almost unknown. This is true of the Vilcabambans, people high in the Andes mountains of Ecuador (see Chapter 12 for a full discussion), where it is common for a couple to produce and raise a dozen children. The long-lived people of Vilcabamba have active sex lives even at one hundred years of age and beyond, partly because they eat little saturated fat.

Sexual difficulties, obesity, and other degenerative disorders have been linked to dietary factors including excessive intake of fats. Fried foods, especially deep-fat fried, are really troublesome to the gonads. The high heat used in cooking changes the chemical structure of the fat, creating indigestible toxins that interfere with sex-hormone formation.

In order to decrease the amount of fats in your diet, do not eat fried foods. Avoid deep-fat fried foods altogether, and do not eat grilled, pan-fried, or charcoal-broiled meats. Broil your foods, with the heat source above. Limit your intake of hot dogs, avocados, doughnuts, rich baked goods, and potato chips because of their high saturated-fat content. Use skim or low-fat dairy products such as farmer cheese, low-fat yogurt, and cottage cheese, rather than processed American cheese, Brie, bleu cheese, cream cheese, or cheddar or other hard cheeses. Buy only fresh, nonrancid seeds, nuts, oils, wheat germ, and whole-grain flours, and store them in a cool, dry, dark place.

Most Americans get up to 40 percent of their daily calories from fats, a practice that is the likely cause of the increased occurrence of sexual disorders in the United States. Do not let this be your practice. Most orthomolecular nutritionists believe just two tablespoons of added fat is the minimal daily requirement to supply all that you need.

COMPLEX CARBOHYDRATES FOR SEXUAL HEALTH

Carbohydrates supply four calories per gram and are a source of body fuel for carrying out daily activities. In the process of digestion, carbohydrates are changed into glucose, which is the form of sugar that the body can use. The glucose, or blood sugar, travels to the brain, the sex organs, and all the other body cells for utilization. Any surplus carbohydrate that is eaten is converted into glycogen and stored as reserve fuel or as fatty tissue.

There are two kinds of carbohydrates—good ones and bad ones. The bad carbohydrates are the refined ones, contained in soft drinks, alcohol, jams, cakes, cookies, candy, and ice cream. These foods are low in quality and high in calories, depleted of the essential nutrients necessary for their own proper metabolism. The good carbohydrates are the unrefined, complex carbohydrates, found in vegetables, legumes, nuts, seeds, and whole grains. Complex carbohydrates are converted to simple sugars that are released very gradually, requiring four to six hours for complete digestion. Fruits are high-quality carbohydrate foods, but they also contain the simple, quickly digested, natural sugar fructose.

Complex-carbohydrate foods incorporate vitamins, minerals, fiber, and other nutrients. Fiber, including cellulose and pectin, is not digestible, but it supplies the bulk, or roughage, necessary for the proper elimination of solid waste from the body. Sex research by physician members of the Academy of Orthomolecular Psychiatry indicated that certain types of dietary fiber—such as wheat bran, whole apples, the white pulp of citrus fruits, and the red skin covering peanut seeds—help maintain the integrity of the body organs involved with sexuality, such as the liver, adrenals, and pancreas. Fiber foods prevent constipation, aid in weight reduction, act as detoxifiers, reduce hypercholesterolemia (high blood cholesterol), counteract diseases of the large intestine, and help release simple sugars slowly to provide energy over a long period of time. The overall effect of slow energy release is a relatively stable blood-sugar level.

Since refined sugar and refined white-flour products do not offer the vitamins and minerals needed for their own digestion, these nutrients must be "borrowed" from the body's stores. Therefore, the need for these extra nutrients is increased when refined carbohydrates are consumed. Supplemental B vitamins are especially needed.

Following are some dietary tips to help you and your family counteract the refined-carbohydrate temptations put in your way by magazine advertisements, television commercials, and restaurant dessert menus:

- Decrease your sugar intake.
- Use unsweetened applesauce to flavor puddings and desserts. Avoid candy eggs for Easter; hide only real ones. For Halloween, give out wholesome homemade cookies, nuts, or fruit.
- Instead of frosting, top a cake with crushed fruits, nuts, or coconut.
- Snack on fresh fruit, vegetable sticks, or homemade candy made from healthy ingredients like nut butters, powdered milk, carob, and raisins.
- Make homemade fruit-juice ices, ice pops, ice cubes, or frozen yogurt for dessert.
- Replace the cookie jar with a fruit bowl, and fill the candy dish with nuts, raisins, and sunflower seeds.

- Serve hot mixed-grain cereal with sesame seeds, banana slices, and brewer's yeast, instead of ready-to-eat sugared cereals. Enjoy your own homemade granola.
- Replace the jam on your toast with old-fashioned unhydrogenated peanut butter, cashew butter, almond butter, sesame seed butter, cottage cheese, or bean spread (mashed leftover beans with seasonings).
- For bad breath, eat parsley instead of a breath mint.
- Use sprouted grains instead of sugar to effectively sweeten breads, breakfast cereals, and cookies.
- Replace soda water and carbonated beverages with fresh orange juice, apple cider, and blender drinks made with milk, fruit, carob, and molasses. Use a variety of fresh fruits, lemon juice, and mineral water. Iced herb teas are fine drinks, too.
- Mixed drinks usually have more sugar and calories than do unmixed drinks. Tomato, pineapple, cranberry, grape, and orange juices work well straight.
- Some commercial mayonnaises, baby foods, canned soups, prepared mixes, and fruited yogurts contain refined sugar; do not purchase them. Make your own products of this type using the spices and pure extracts in your kitchen cabinet.

Once you have cut down on refined carbohydrates, your craving for sweets will disappear and your improved sexual nutrition will give your sex life a boost.

Chapter 3

NUTRIENTS FOR THE LIBIDO

I am thirty-four years old and have been married once and divorced. A couple of years ago, I met a woman with whom I was very compatible sexually. Both of us liked oral sex a lot. But after about eight months of going together, I suddenly lost my sexual urge. For some unknown reason, I just didn't want sex anymore—with any woman. My girlfriend and I broke up. I lost not only a girlfriend but also a good drinking buddy. Each evening, we would knock off a quart of gin together and then bring each other to orgasm using our mouths.

Imbibing less may be better for me, since after my marriage dissolved, I drank excessively. My drinking eventually led to a touch of cirrhosis of the liver, damage to the pancreas and spleen, and the onset of diabetes. I must now inject myself with insulin every day.

I wonder if masturbating starting at age ten caused the early squandering of my semen supply. Is my semen all used up now? I masturbated a lot, even when I was married. Today I seem to have nothing left. Is this the reason I don't feel the urge for sex?

Please check out my situation and let me know what you think I should take for my lack of sexual desire. Are there some pills to pop? I will be grateful if you can help me feel better about myself.

Wilbur P.
Bowling Green, Kentucky

I am forty-three. About four years ago, I had my uterus and ovaries removed. Now I'm on Valium and Elavil because of the severe depression and nervousness that have followed the operation. Also, I had two nervous breakdowns from which I have never seemed to recover. But my biggest problem at present is that I feel no desire to make love.

My husband, who is forty-seven years old, can't warm me up no matter how hard he tries. I just have no feeling inside. I'm empty of sexual emotion, which makes me think my lack of desire is not from his lovemaking.

After my husband uses my body for his satisfaction, I cry. I feel cold, washed out, and less than a woman. In fact, if he just hints at having any sex, I get terribly nervous and irritable.

I even try warming myself up with a vibrator when I sense that he's going to want to fool around. I make myself so sore from two hours of masturbation to prepare that when he inserts his penis, it feels like a rod of metal.

The way I am right now, if Leroy never mentions sex again, it would be okay with me. I can't stand his quarreling and calling me bad names all the time because of my lack of response. I don't want to go on crying, being nervous, and letting this man use my body when I don't get anything out of it except a burning bottom. I need help! Are there some foods that would stimulate my sexual feelings—anything at all to make me feel sexy?

Mrs. Leroy R.
Parkersburg, West Virginia

Hundreds of factors directly or indirectly affect the ability to react sexually and the degree to which sexual feelings, stamina, energy, and drive are experienced. Perhaps the most influential and controllable factors are diet and lifestyle. What you eat is intimately involved with the way you feel about engaging in sex and with how you respond to your lover. Nutrition is a more potent element contributing to sexual capabilities than is breeding, environment, or education.

If you have a healthy body and a lucid mind, you should be able to enjoy a good sex life. Incitement to sexual action and overall sexual endurance are direct reflections of general good health. Think about it! A sexual encounter is probably one of the last things on your mind when you do not feel well. This is true for the millions of Americans who eat poorly because they know little about which foods they should be taking into their digestive systems. The bodies of many individuals who are not overtly "sick" are often in such a minimal state of good repair that the first activity to suffer from malnutrition is the energy-demanding act of sex.

The human body has been slowly and continually changing over the millennia in an effort to adapt itself to the Earth's environment, which is constantly changing. During this last century, however, the lifestyle and diet of the industrialized Western societies have shifted so radically and in such a short period of time that the body has not been able to adapt quickly enough. In this unnatural environment, you therefore are existing in a constant stamina-draining state of stress.

The term "homeostasis," as described in Chapter 1, refers to the condition in which the body should ideally be—with all hormones, body fluids, and enzymes functioning in perfect harmony. It is during homeostasis that you have the most energy and are at your sexual prime. You respond easily and naturally to a sexual stimulus, and can satisfy your partner and be satisfied yourself.

If some environmental abnormality acts upon your body and throws it out of homeostasis, you will suffer physiological distress. Anything that causes such stress is called a stressor. A literally countless number of stressors can affect bodily function, including air pollution, anxiety, liquor, drugs, illness, injury, surgery, junk food, obesity, extreme heat or cold, and toxic food additives. These common stressors can throw the body out of homeostasis. And there goes your sex life.

If you do nothing to rid yourself of a stressor or to overcome it with optimal nutrition, you will probably feel less inclined to enjoy the act of love. In the extreme, you may even become a victim of the same fate that has befallen the writers of the two letters at the start of this chapter.

So predominant among average people is this state of subclinical illness or minimal health that because of it, every tenth postpubescent American male is totally impotent. No matter how much he wants to, this chronically impaired man cannot become aroused. Even discounting the very old and the very sick, the number of sexually nonfunctioning men in the United States is outrageously and frighteningly high. Additionally, fully 50 percent of "normally functioning" men encounter potency problems more than just occasionally.

There are also thousands of women who are completely incapable of responding sexually. They derive little or no pleasure from the love act and often find sexual intercourse a painful rather than pleasurable experience.

In a society whose men and women pride themselves on their sexuality and are constantly seeking sexual contentment, the common problem of emotional indifference from a sexual partner is mortifying. Nevertheless, the problem often can be alleviated by some simple and basic dietary changes. Many of the troubles in an intimate relationship are brought about by the consumption of foods that are more harmful than helpful to physical and mental well-being.

In this chapter, I will identify which foods contain the nutrients that are necessary for a fabulous sex life. Foods that stimulate sexual feelings are frequently missing from the diets eaten in industrialized Western countries. Can certain foods greatly heighten sexual desire? Can they restore it if it is absent? To a certain extent, yes!

However, at this point, I would also like to caution you about taking too much of a supplemental nutrient, especially a mineral. Before taking supplements, have a hair mineral analysis made to determine your body's lack or overabundance of minerals. (For more information on hair mineral analyses, see page 214.) Let the hair test tell you what minerals you need, then use dosages that fall within the limits recommended by orthomolecular physicians, which are also presented in this book.

PHOSPHORUS MAKES YOU FEEL SEXY

A variety of foods can improve your sex drive and responsiveness. At the top of the list are those containing the essential metabolite phosphorus.

Phosphorus is among the most abundant minerals in the human body and was the first to be recognized as directly involved with libido (sexual desire).

Phosphorus functions in conjunction with calcium and is maintained by the metabolism in a specific calcium–phosphorus ratio. Besides joining with other minerals, such as calcium and magnesium, to make up the skeletal system, phosphorus plays a part in most metabolic reactions, including the formation of nucleoproteins, which are responsible for cell division and reproduction.

Phosphorus is included as a therapeutic substance in some of the more popular European medical genital tonics. It is also used by the Chinese in erotic cookery—for example, to make the celebrated Bird's Nest Soup, an avowed aphrodisiac. The nest of the sea swallow (*salangane*) is used for the soup. This nest consists of an edible seaweed that has been stuck together using the spawn of fish, which are extremely rich in phosphorus. The soup is said to have a powerful action in increasing libido and the ability to achieve and sustain an erection.

Phosphorus can also be found in curries, chutneys, and hot sauces, foods that irritate the sex organs. The sex organs become excited, which can lead to sexual stimulation.

The underground fungi known as truffles contain phosphorus. The two usual species in the marketplace are the *Tuber aestivum* and the *Tuber melanosporum*, the latter of which is used to make pâté de foie gras. Anthelme Brillat-Savarin, the French jurist, writer, and gastronome who wrote *Gastronomy as a Fine Art* and *The Physiology of Taste* (both fine literary analyses of the art of eating and drinking, interspersed with wise comments and humorous anecdotes), described truffles: "The tubercle is not only delicious to the taste, but it excites a power, the exercise of which is accompanied by the most delicious pleasures. . . . The truffle is a positive aphrodisiac. . . . It makes women more amiable, and men more amorous."

A diet that includes eggs and seafood greatly improves sexual functioning because these foods also contain especially high quantities of iodine. Dr. Arnold Lorand wrote in *Health and Longevity Through Rational Diet* of a specially adapted diet that helps increase sexual activity:

> Since the most remote periods of the existence of man, the eating of fish has been accredited with the property of increasing sexual activity. It was for this reason that the old Egyptians forbade the eating of fish by the priests. There must be some truth in this since the idea has persisted up to the present time. . . .
>
> Other articles of diet, particularly eggs and caviar, are also supposed to exert a stimulating action upon sexual activity . . . even medical science—which has undoubtedly frequently profited by such statements—should not pass them by without notice. . . .

It seems to me quite certain that a plentiful diet containing, in particular, much protein would have an exciting influence upon the sexual function.[1]

Dr. Lorand named lobster, crab, and truffles as excellent sources of phosphorus. He also said, "Foods containing iron and phosphorus appear to have a very favorable effect upon sexual activity."

Phosphorus combines with nitrogen, fatty acids, and glycerol to form phospholipid, a substance present in every body cell. The most widely distributed phospholipid is lecithin, which helps to promote the secretion of glandular hormones, including sex hormones. Lecithin also does many other good things in the body, such as aiding the passage of substances through cell walls, promoting healthy nerves and efficient mental activity, transporting fats and fatty acids, and preventing the accumulation of too much acid or too much alkali in the blood.

Raymond Bernard, Ph.D., said in *The Secret of Rejuvenation* that some European physicians are using lecithin to correct sexual weakness, glandular exhaustion, and nerve disorders. He noted that male reproductive fluid is high in lecithin; therefore, if a man is deficient in lecithin, his virility is simultaneously diminished.

The Dr. Rinse Formula is one recommended way of adding lecithin to your diet. Physical chemist Jacobus Rinse, Ph.D., of East Dorset, Vermont, recommended eating the "lecithin breakfast," a formula of certain food supplements. You can either buy the ingredients for the Dr. Rinse Formula at a health food store and mix them together in your kitchen, or you can use the prepackaged product.

Sunflower seeds, a main ingredient in the Dr. Rinse Formula, also provide necessary potassium and zinc. Additional zinc was also recommended by Dr. Rinse, as were calcium and magnesium. Take these minerals daily in the form of one multinutrient capsule or tablet, or separately as three individual-ingredient capsules or tablets, supplying 1,000 milligrams of calcium, 500 milligrams of magnesium, and 60 milligrams of zinc. Dr. Rinse also recommended taking vitamin B_6 because lecithin can be manufactured by the body only in the presence of the B vitamins, particularly B_6.

Lecithin is found in liver, egg yolks, and raw vegetables. It is also available at health food stores as tablets, granules, liquid, or powder. Use two tablespoons of lecithin granules every day if your diet does not supply enough phosphorus for your body to manufacture lecithin naturally. Most people, however, do get enough phosphorus in the foods they eat daily.

Foods High in Phosphorus

The following list names foods that are high in phosphorus. Also given for each food is the number of milligrams of phosphorus per 100 grams (3.5

ounces) of edible portion of food. For example, brewer's yeast has 1,753
milligrams of phosphorus in every 100 grams of edible food.

1,753	Brewer's yeast	79	Prunes, dried
1,276	Wheat bran	78	Broccoli
1,144	Pumpkin seeds	77	Figs, dried
1,144	Squash seeds	69	Yams
1,118	Wheat germ	67	Soybean sprouts
837	Sunflower seeds	64	Mung bean sprouts
693	Brazil nuts	63	Dates
592	Sesame seeds, hulled	63	Parsley
554	Soybeans, dried	62	Asparagus
504	Almonds	59	Bamboo shoots
478	Cheddar cheese	56	Cauliflower
457	Pinto beans, dried	53	Potatoes, with skin
409	Peanuts	51	Okra
400	Wheat	51	Spinach
380	English walnuts	44	Green beans
376	Rye grain	44	Pumpkins
373	Cashews	42	Avocados
352	Beef liver	40	Beet greens
338	Scallops	39	Swiss chard
311	Millet	38	Winter squashes
290	Barley, pearled	36	Carrots
289	Pecans	36	Onions
267	Dulse	35	Red cabbage
240	Kelp	33	Beets
239	Chicken	31	Radishes
221	Brown rice	29	Summer squashes
205	Eggs	28	Celery
202	Garlic	27	Cucumbers
175	Crab	27	Tomatoes
152	Cottage cheese	26	Bananas
150	Beef	26	Persimmons
150	Lamb	26	Eggplants
119	Lentils, cooked	26	Lettuce
116	Mushrooms	24	Nectarines
116	Green peas, fresh	22	Raspberries
111	Sweet corn	20	Grapes
101	Raisins	20	Oranges
93	Cow's milk, whole	17	Olives
88	Globe artichokes	16	Cantaloupes
87	Yogurt	10	Apples
80	Brussels sprouts	8	Pineapples

CALCIUM AND MAGNESIUM FOODS FOR WOMEN

In the last section, I mentioned that phosphorus works in conjunction with calcium and magnesium. In fact, during her mature years, a woman should try to maintain her calcium–phosphorus balance to prevent the annoying symptoms of menopause. The period in a woman's life marked by the glandular changes that denote the end of the menstrual cycle and reproductive years is also made easier by the upkeep of magnesium intake.

A specific phosphorus–calcium–magnesium ratio is necessary for the body to function optimally. The ideal proportion is two and a half times more calcium than phosphorus and twice as much calcium as magnesium. For every 1,000 milligrams of calcium, therefore, you need 500 milligrams of magnesium and 400 milligrams of phosphorus. But better than popping supplemental pills is getting your necessary mineral supply from foods.

Foods High in Calcium

The following list names foods that are high in calcium. Also given for each food is the number of milligrams of calcium per 100 grams (3.5 ounces) of edible portion of food. For example, kelp has 1,093 milligrams of calcium in every 100 grams of edible food.

1,093	Kelp	119	Wheat bran
925	Swiss cheese	118	Cow's milk, whole
750	Cheddar cheese	114	Buckwheat, raw
352	Carob flour	110	Sesame seeds, hulled
296	Dulse	106	Olives, ripe
250	Collard greens	103	Broccoli
246	Turnip greens	99	English walnuts
245	Barbados molasses	94	Cottage cheese
234	Almonds	93	Spinach
210	Brewer's yeast	73	Soybeans, cooked
203	Parsley	73	Pecans
200	Corn tortillas (lime added)	72	Wheat germ
187	Dandelion greens	69	Peanuts
186	Brazil nuts	68	Miso
151	Watercress	68	Romaine lettuce
129	Goat's milk	67	Apricots, dried
128	Tofu	66	Rutabagas
126	Figs, dried	62	Raisins
121	Buttermilk	60	Black currants
120	Sunflower seeds	59	Dates
120	Yogurt	56	Green snap beans
119	Beet greens	51	Globe artichokes

51	Prunes, dried	25	Cauliflower
51	Pumpkin seeds	25	Lentils, cooked
51	Squash seeds	22	Sweet cherries
50	Dried beans, cooked	22	Asparagus
49	Cabbage	22	Winter squashes
48	Soybean sprouts	21	Millet
46	Hard winter wheat	19	Mung bean sprouts
41	Oranges	17	Pineapples
39	Celery	16	Grapes
38	Cashews	16	Beets
38	Rye grain	14	Cantaloupes
37	Carrots	14	Jerusalem artichokes
34	Barley	13	Tomatoes
32	Sweet potatoes	12	Chicken
32	Brown rice	11	Orange juice
29	Garlic	10	Avocados
28	Summer squashes	10	Beef
27	Onions	8	Bananas
26	Lemons	7	Apples
26	Green peas, fresh	3	Sweet corn

Foods High in Magnesium

The following list names foods that are high in magnesium. Also given for each food is the number of milligrams of magnesium per 100 grams (3.5 ounces) of edible portion of food. For example, kelp has 760 milligrams of magnesium in every 100 grams of edible food.

760	Kelp	115	Rye grain
490	Wheat bran	111	Tofu
336	Wheat germ	106	Beet greens
270	Almonds	90	Coconut meat, dried
267	Cashews	88	Soybeans, cooked
258	Blackstrap molasses	88	Spinach
231	Brewer's yeast	88	Brown rice
229	Buckwheat	71	Figs, dried
225	Brazil nuts	65	Swiss chard
220	Dulse	62	Apricots, dried
184	Filberts	58	Dates
175	Peanuts	57	Collard greens
162	Millet	51	Shrimp
160	Wheat grain	48	Sweet corn
142	Pecans	45	Avocados
131	English walnuts	45	Cheddar cheese

41	Parsley	21	Beef
40	Prunes, dried	20	Asparagus
38	Sunflower seeds	19	Chicken
37	Common beans, cooked	18	Sweet peppers, green
37	Barley	17	Winter squashes
36	Dandelion greens	16	Cantaloupes
36	Garlic	16	Eggplants
35	Raisins	14	Tomatoes
35	Green peas, fresh	13	Cabbage
34	Potatoes, with skin	13	Grapes
34	Crab	13	Cow's milk, whole
33	Bananas	13	Pineapples
31	Sweet potatoes	13	Mushrooms
30	Blackberries	12	Onions
25	Beets	11	Oranges
24	Broccoli	11	Iceberg lettuce
24	Cauliflower	9	Plums
23	Carrots	8	Apples
22	Celery		

THE POTENCY OF ZINC

Zinc, another essential mineral, is needed for the synthesis of dihydroxytestosterone (DHT), the active enzyme of the male hormone, testosterone. The body of an average-weight twenty-year-old male at all times normally contains 2.2 grams of zinc, most of which accumulates in the testes. With less than this amount of the mineral, it is unlikely that the young man will feel much of a sexual urge, be able to sustain an erection, or produce any quantity of semen. A normal level of zinc in the body is necessary to perform sexually. Note, however, that the belief that masturbating a great deal as a youth could cause depletion of a man's semen supply later in life is erroneous. The male body continues to form semen, even as merely secretions from the prostate and other glands without spermatozoa, throughout life.

With age, the body does become less capable of absorbing zinc from foods. Such stressors as smoking, alcohol, coffee, infection, and medications also deplete any zinc reserves that may have accumulated over time. Without sufficient zinc, a man's body cannot produce DHT, resulting in a low testosterone level—often too low to allow for sexual arousal.

According to Dr. Carl Pfeiffer, former medical director of the Brain Bio Center in Princeton, New Jersey, a zinc deficiency can lead to several difficulties for men. These include impotence, a greatly reduced sperm count, and prostatitis (inflammation of the prostate gland), an affliction common among older men. Left unchecked, prostatitis can lead to cancer of the prostate. When zinc is deficient in prepubescent males, inadequate development of the penis or testes can result.

Medical scientists have found that men undergoing kidney dialysis (which filters out zinc, as well as other nutrients, from the blood) complain consistently of impotency. Zinc supplements can quickly rectify this condition.

Zinc is also needed by women to help sustain proper lubrication in the vaginal canal, thus making vigorous intercourse pleasurable instead of painful.

Dr. Pfeiffer discovered large amounts of zinc in the pineal and hippocampus glands, which are located in the brain, as well as in the retinas of the eyes. The pineal gland is linked directly to libido, while the hippocampus controls emotions. This discovery led Dr. Pfeiffer to suggest that adequate zinc levels are needed for a healthy sex drive by both men and women.

The typical Westerner eats a diet supplying 10 to 15 milligrams of zinc a day. However, the body can absorb only less than a third of this. Since the National Research Council recommends 15 milligrams of zinc daily for the average American adult, at least this dosage should be taken in tablet form as an addition to the diet.

If you use refined white sugar, refined cereal grains, frozen vegetables, alcoholic beverages, or vegetables grown in the soil of one of the thirty-two states deficient in zinc, you are likely to have insufficient zinc in your body. Dietary zinc is supplied by high-protein foods such as meat (steak and lamb chops), fish (haddock, sardines, and anchovies), and nuts; certain vegetables (split peas, lima beans, mushrooms, and onions); wheat germ; and grape juice. The most abundant source is the oyster—which may be why we attribute great sexual powers to eating this lowly marine bivalve. Oats, rye, whole wheat, raw eggs, peas, lentils, and liver are also good sources of zinc. Dr. Pfeiffer recommends supplementing your diet with 60 milligrams of zinc gluconate per day, divided into doses of 20 milligrams each at breakfast, lunch, and dinner. Zinc tablets are available from most health food stores and drug stores.

Remember, if what you normally eat is lacking in zinc, you should change your diet.

Foods High in Zinc

The following list names foods that are high in zinc. Also given for each food is the number of milligrams of zinc per 100 grams (3.5 ounces) of edible portion of food. For example, fresh oysters have 148.7 milligrams of zinc in every 100 grams of edible food.

148.7	Oysters, fresh	5.3	Lamb chops
6.8	Ginger root	4.5	Pecans
5.6	Ground round steak	4.2	Split peas, dried

4.2	Brazil nuts	0.9	Parsley
3.9	Beef liver	0.9	Potatoes
3.5	Egg yolks	0.6	Garlic
3.2	Whole wheat	0.5	Carrots
3.2	Rye grain	0.5	Whole wheat bread
3.2	Oats	0.4	Black beans
3.2	Peanuts	0.4	Cow's milk, whole, raw
3.1	Lima beans	0.4	Pork chops
3.1	Soy lecithin	0.4	Corn
3.1	Almonds	0.3	Grape juice
3.0	Walnuts	0.3	Olive oil
2.9	Sardines	0.3	Cauliflower
2.6	Chicken	0.2	Spinach
2.5	Buckwheat	0.2	Cabbage
2.4	Hazelnuts	0.2	Lentils
1.9	Clams	0.2	Butter
1.7	Anchovies	0.2	Lettuce
1.7	Tuna	0.1	Cucumbers
1.7	Haddock	0.1	Yams
1.6	Green peas, fresh	0.1	Tangerines
1.5	Shrimp	0.1	String beans
1.2	Turnips		

Black pepper, paprika, mustard, chili powder, thyme, and cinnamon are also high in zinc.

VITAMIN E FOR MENOPAUSE

Vitamin E, sometimes referred to as the sex vitamin, plays a vital role as an antioxidant. Antioxidants prevent the combination of body substances with oxygen, a union that results in the body substances' destruction.

During sexual intercourse, both the clitoris and the penis need additional oxygen and are flooded with blood, which carries oxygen. Vitamin E (alpha tocopherol) helps the blood transport the oxygen efficiently and quickly, and without oxidation resulting.

In postmenopausal women, vitamin E helps the body compensate for estrogen loss more effectively and safely than does estrogen replacement therapy (ERT). Vitamin E is well-known among doctors who use nutrition therapeutically to help women maintain a very exciting and satisfying sex life through the later years. Women who have had menopause induced prematurely through surgery (hysterectomy or ovariectomy) have found vitamin E extremely effective in reducing the otherwise severe problems caused by sudden estrogen loss.

As reported in *The Journal of the American Medical Association*, a physician

administered vitamin E to a woman who had undergone a complete removal of her uterus and ovaries due to the discovery of cancer in the ovaries.
Following the operation, the patient suffered from hot flashes. On being
given the small dosage of 75 International Units (IU) of alpha tocopherol
daily as part of her treatment, the woman reported the total disappearance
of her discomfort. Her hot flashes just stopped completely!

Complete absence of vitamin E from a man's diet may bring on irre-
versible degeneration of the epithelial or germinal cells of the testicles. Lack
of the vitamin in a pregnant woman's diet may cause death of the embryo
followed by internal absorption or spontaneous abortion. Vitamin E deficiency does not promote degeneration of the ovaries or prevent conception.
However, experiments on rats showed that when a group was fed a diet
adequate in proteins, minerals, and all the vitamins except E, the first
generation of rats became partially sterile, while the second generation
became completely sterile.

Vitamin E has a particular effect on the anterior lobe of the pituitary
gland, which has a profound control over the sexual organs, sexual characteristics, and sexual functions. Overactivity of this gland from insufficient
vitamin E in a man, for instance, results in unusually large genitalia.

In connection with the thyroid, vitamin E also has some effect on sexual
desire. The basophil cells of the thyroid's anterior lobe control the gonado-
tropic sex hormones. In men, these hormones catalyze the formation of
semen and testosterone, and in women, they control ovulation and stimulate the formation of progesterone, which promotes the implantation of ova.

The tocopherols play a major role in alleviating vaginitis (inflammation
of the vagina) and in preventing prostatitis.

How can you tell if you have enough vitamin E in your body for optimal
sexual health? It is not difficult. Have your blood tested for the tocopherols—alpha, beta, delta, epsilon, eta, gamma, and zeta. The normal adult
tocopherol blood level is 0.5 milligrams per 100 milliliters of blood plasma.
If you have less than this level, your sexuality will not be up to par. Your
ability to accept sexual stimuli will probably be very diminished. This may
already have manifested itself in apathy toward sex.

Vitamin E is found mostly in unrefined-flour products, such as whole
wheat bread, as well as in bran, unprocessed cereals, nuts, soybeans, and
wheat germ. Most wholistic physicians prescribe supplemental vitamin E.
The standard recommendation is for 600 IU of natural mixed tocopherols
(rather than synthetic d-alpha tocopherol) per day in capsules or tablets,
divided into two or three doses. Increase the dosage by 200 to 400 IU if you
are experiencing diminished sexual desire.

Foods High in Vitamin E

The following list names foods that are high in vitamin E. Also given for each food is the number of International Units of vitamin E per 100 grams (3.5 ounces) of edible portion of food. For example, wheat germ oil has 216.00 IU of vitamin E in every 100 grams of edible food.

216.00	Wheat germ oil	2.90	Asparagus
90.00	Sunflower seeds	2.50	Salmon
88.00	Sunflower seed oil	2.50	Brown rice
72.00	Safflower oil	2.30	Rye grain
48.00	Almonds	2.20	Rye bread, dark
45.00	Sesame oil	1.90	Pecans
34.00	Peanut oil	1.90	Wheat germ
29.00	Corn oil	1.90	Rye crackers
22.00	Wheat germ	1.90	Wheat crackers
18.00	Peanuts	1.40	Whole wheat bread
18.00	Olive oil	1.00	Carrots
14.00	Soybean oil	0.99	Split peas, dried
13.00	Peanuts, roasted	0.92	Walnuts
11.00	Peanut butter	0.88	Bananas
3.60	Butter	0.83	Eggs
3.20	Spinach	0.72	Tomatoes
3.00	Oatmeal	0.29	Lamb
3.00	Wheat bran		

VITAMIN C IN THE REPRODUCTIVE PROCESS

Birth control pills have been shown to deplete the body tissue of vitamin C (ascorbic acid).[2]

Medical Times reported that nineteen women who were "habitual aborters" and six women whose conditions threatened abortion were given ascorbic acid to prevent the problem. Of the total twenty-five women in the clinical study, eighteen experienced the normal delivery of a healthy, full-term infant, two had some unusual bleeding, and two delivered stillborn infants before term. Three of the women voluntarily ended their pregnancies before birth. All of the women had received 300 milligrams of vitamin C plus 100 milligrams of citrus bioflavonoid complex three times a day for up to eight months. In view of their histories, all of these women probably would have aborted without these daily supplements.

Vitamin C helps make pregnancy and labor more comfortable. Pregnant women taking large doses have fewer leg cramps, greater skin elasticity and fewer stretch marks, shorter labor time, less severe labor, and diminished tendency to postpartum hemorrhaging. However, I do not recommend the arbitrary use of any nutrient supplement, including vitamin C, by pregnant women. A pregnant woman should only take nutritional supplements if her doctor approves of them or actually prescribes them. The reason? Megadosing on a nutrient is tantamount to turning that nutrient into a drug. Just as a mother-to-be would not drug herself during pregnancy, she should not take too much nutritional supplementation for the sake of the fetus. An infant born to a mother who megadosed on vitamin C may suffer from scurvy soon after birth unless given supplemental vitamin C daily under a pediatrician's supervision.

Of possibly greater interest to most people than vitamin C's effects on pregnancy are the nutrient's effects on sexual pleasure. Men and women taking high doses of the vitamin to ward off colds advise that they sense a greater urgency for sexual intimacy, enjoy it more when they engage in it, and have more intense orgasms.

One of vitamin C's primary roles is as an aid in the formation of collagen, the gelatinous substance found in connective tissue, cartilage, and bone. The vitamin is also needed for the repair of wounds. Inasmuch as the requirement for collagen regeneration steadily increases over the years, the need for vitamin C also becomes greater.

Also as part of aging, a heightened need for vitamin C is developed by the sex glands. If the vitamin is not obtained from the diet, the sex glands will draw it out of other tissues, leaving these tissues vulnerable to disease. If these other tissues have no C to spare, sex-gland functioning will diminish or stop altogether and libido will drop or completely disappear.

For years, many physicians have been using vitamin C to treat sexual impairments, among other conditions, administering it either intravenously or orally at a dosage of 20 to 40 grams per day. This dosage is about six hundred times the Reference Daily Intake (RDI) of 45 milligrams of vitamin C.

To determine your need for vitamin C, you can test your urine for vitamin C content in the privacy of your own home. Buy aqueous silver nitrate, an inexpensive solution available at pharmacies. Then collect a urine specimen. Put ten drops of the aqueous silver nitrate solution in a cup, add ten drops of the urine, and wait two minutes. The solution should turn white to gray to charcoal in color. The darker it turns, the more vitamin C you are spilling, meaning you have an excess supply in your body and do not need any ascorbic acid supplementation or change in food intake. If the solution tends toward a whiter shade, you are excreting little or no vitamin C, meaning your body systems are using all they can get and you should provide them with more.

Another effective test for vitamin C is the lingual ascorbic acid test. It does not require either urine or blood. The lingual-C dispensing system is an accurate, fast-working, and completely painless tool for measuring the amount of vitamin C present in your body. The testing solution—a blue dye—is available from Advanced Medical Nutrition, Inc. (2247 National Avenue, P.O. Box 5012, Hayward, California 94540; telephone 800–437–8888 or 510–783–6969).

To conduct the test, rinse your mouth thoroughly with tap water. Sit in a well-lighted area and stick out your tongue. Have a friend or family member gently grasp the tongue with one gauze pad and dry it with another gauze pad. Have the friend stroke the tongue's papillae so that they stand erect and then, on a papillated area to the left or right of the tongue midline, deposit a single drop of dye. Finally, beginning as soon as the dye drop touches the tongue, the friend should use a stopwatch and time how long it takes the blue color to completely disappear.

If the blue color disappears within twenty seconds, you have a normal amount of vitamin C in your body. Longer than twenty seconds indicates that extra vitamin C supplements are needed.

If you do not eat plenty of citrus fruits and dark-green leafy vegetables, you probably consume less ascorbic acid than you should. According to members of the Academy of Orthomolecular Psychiatry, you will need to supplement your diet with vitamin C tablets, powder, or capsules at a dosage of up to 1,000 milligrams per day merely for maintenance of the sex glands and other body organs. It is possible to obtain 200 milligrams of ascorbic acid daily just from a well-balanced diet.

Foods High in Vitamin C

The following list names foods that are high in vitamin C. Also given for each food is the number of milligrams of C per 100 grams (3.5 ounces) of edible portion of food. For example, acerola fruit (which is also available in supplement form) has 1,300 milligrams of vitamin C in every 100 grams of edible food.

1,300	Acerola fruit	50	Oranges
360	Chili peppers, red	50	Orange juice
242	Guavas	47	Cabbage
204	Sweet peppers, red	46	Lemon juice
186	Kale	38	Grapefruits
172	Parsley	38	Grapefruit juice
152	Collard greens	36	Elderberries
139	Turnip greens	36	Calf liver
128	Sweet peppers, green	36	Turnips
113	Broccoli	35	Mangos
102	Brussels sprouts	33	Asparagus
97	Mustard greens	33	Cantaloupes
79	Watercress	32	Swiss chard
78	Cauliflower	32	Green onions
66	Persimmons	31	Beef liver
61	Red cabbage	31	Okra
59	Strawberries	31	Tangerines
56	Papayas	30	New Zealand spinach
51	Spinach	30	Oysters

29	Lima beans, young	25	Chinese cabbage
29	Black-eyed peas	25	Yellow summer squashes
29	Soybeans	24	Loganberries
27	Green peas, fresh	23	Honeydew melons
26	Radishes	23	Tomatoes
25	Raspberries	23	Pork liver

THE BIOFLAVONOIDS WORK WITH VITAMIN C

The same scientist who won the Nobel Prize in Medicine in 1937 for discovering vitamin C, Albert Szent-Györgyi, M.D., Ph.D., also isolated and identified bioflavonoids. These quasi vitamins, which often are present with vitamin C in food, are brightly colored nutrients. Nutritional therapists use them to prevent habitual and threatened abortion, excessive postpartum bleeding, heavy menstrual bleeding, and other difficulties with fragile or permeable capillaries.

Bioflavonoids collectively have been labeled vitamin P. They relieve menstrual cramping and irregular menstruation when taken separately as supplements or in foods. The bioflavonoid components consist of citrin, hesperidin, rutin, quercetin, and eriodictyol. They are present in citrus fruits mainly in the white pulp lying just under the skin but are absent from the juice.

Foods High in Bioflavonoids

The following list names foods that are high in bioflavonoids. However, the listing does not give the exact amount of bioflavonoids in each type of food because the concentration always varies.

Apricots	Lemons
Blackberries	Oranges
Black currants	Papayas
Broccoli	Parsley
Cabbage	Plums
Cantaloupes	Prunes, dried
Cherries	Rose hips
Grapefruits	Sweet peppers
Grapes	Tomatoes

VITAMIN A FOR HEALTHY SEX GLANDS

While most authorities recommend limiting the dietary intake of eggs to three per week because of their high cholesterol content, Dr. William J. Robinson, former chief of the Department of Genitourinary Diseases and Dermatology at Bronx Hospital, New York City, recommended eggs as a food to make you feel sexy. He did this because eggs are high in vitamin A. Dr. Robinson used vitamin A for his patients who suffered with impotence or frigidity. He wrote:

> The patient should eat plenty of eggs, oysters, raw and fried, meat and fish. I often make my patients eat two to six raw eggs a day, two or three the first thing in the morning, before breakfast, the rest during the day. It is best to drink the egg directly from the shell. Make a hole in the top, put in a pinch of salt and sip it. Caviar is also reputed to be beneficial. Spices and condiments are not only permissible, but desirable.[3]

The way Dr. Robinson suggested the eggs be eaten—raw and plain—is not a danger to the heart or blood vessels, since raw eggs contain lecithin, an antidote to dietary cholesterol. However, salmonella poisoning could be a serious problem.

Vitamin A maintains healthy testicular tissue. Eating foods with a high vitamin A content helps protect against cancer of the testes. "Further, vitamin A and some closely related substances can actually *reverse* precancerous changes in cells of the prostate gland," said Dr. Michael Lesser of San Francisco, former president of the Orthomolecular Medical Society.[4]

Vitamin A promotes the formation of a higher number of sperm in ejaculate. It is a required ingredient in the production of all sex hormones in both men and women. For this reason, a daily dose of cod-liver oil or beta-carotene tablets, both of which are high in vitamin A, is considered by sexologists to be sound advice for nutritionally improving sexual function.

Veterinarian J.L. Madsen reported in the *Journal of Animal Science* that bulls deficient in vitamin A suffered degeneration of their seminiferous tubules. The animals reportedly regained full potency after receiving strong doses of the vitamin. Scientists theorize that the same effect could be observed in human beings from variations in vitamin A nutrition.

Vitamin A insufficiency is one of the major nutritional problems experienced around the world—along with protein deficiency. It may surprise you to learn that this insufficiency is present more in industrialized Western countries than in Third World countries. Third World populations eat more natural diets, which contain higher amounts of vitamin A, while Western societies eat diets heavy in overprocessed foods, which have had their vitamin A contents refined away. But since refined diets are lacking in many nutrients, vitamin A deficiency is rarely isolated. Sexual malfunction as a result of a lack of vitamin A in the diet is rather subtle.

Vitamin A is soluble in fat and usually insoluble in water (although modern technology has perfected a water-soluble vitamin A). The vitamin is stored in the liver, where up to 600,000 International Units can accumulate before the liver begins to enlarge in size—a sign of potential toxicity. The usual dose of supplemental vitamin A in pill or capsule form suggested by orthomolecular nutritionists for daily maintenance is 25,000 IU.

Vitamin A is available in both animal-source and vegetable-source foods. In animal-source foods, it occurs mostly as active, preformed vitamin A, known as retinol; while in vegetable-source foods, it occurs as provitamin A, a carotenoid known as beta-carotene, which must be converted to active vitamin A by the body to be utilized. The efficiency of conversion varies among individuals, so some people are more likely to suffer from vitamin A deficiency than are others. Beta-carotene is converted more efficiently than are the other carotenoids. Green and deep-yellow vegetables as well as deep-yellow fruits are highest in beta-carotene.

Foods High in Vitamin A

The following list names foods that are high in vitamin A. Also given for each food is the number of International Units of vitamin A per 100 grams (3.5 ounces) of edible portion of food. For example, lamb liver has 50,500 IU of vitamin A in every 100 grams of edible food.

50,500	Lamb liver	3,300	Endive
43,900	Beef liver	2,700	Apricots
22,500	Calf liver	2,500	Broccoli
21,600	Chili peppers, red	2,260	Whitefish
14,000	Dandelion greens	2,000	Green onions
12,100	Chicken liver	1,900	Romaine lettuce
11,000	Carrots	1,750	Papayas
10,900	Apricots, dried	1,650	Nectarines
9,300	Collard greens	1,600	Prunes, dried
8,900	Kale	1,600	Pumpkins
8,800	Sweet potatoes	1,580	Swordfish
8,500	Parsley	1,540	Cream, whipping
8,100	Spinach	1,330	Peaches
7,600	Turnip greens	1,200	Acorn squashes
7,000	Mustard greens	1,180	Eggs
6,500	Swiss chard	1,080	Chicken
6,100	Beet greens	1,000	Cherries, sour red
5,800	Chives	970	Butterhead lettuce
5,700	Butternut squashes	900	Asparagus
4,900	Watercress	900	Tomatoes, ripe
4,800	Mangos	770	Chili peppers, green
4,450	Sweet peppers, red	690	Kidney, all kinds
4,300	Hubbard squashes	640	Green peas, fresh
3,400	Cantaloupes	600	Green beans
3,300	Butter, yellow	600	Elderberries

590	Watermelons	520	Okra
580	Rutabagas	510	Yellow cornmeal
550	Brussels sprouts	460	Yellow squashes

THE LIBIDINOUS POWERS OF SOME B VITAMINS

The B complex of vitamins exerts a definite influence on the production of testosterone, the male sex hormone. Dr. I. Fraser MacKenzie, a sex therapist in London, said:

It has been demonstrated that, in the case of the formation by the testes of another substance—testosterone—there is a reduction in output when nutrition is defective, and especially when there is a deficiency of the vitamin-B complex.[5]

The B-vitamin dosages I give in this section are recommended by physicians I interviewed who routinely use nutritional therapy as part of their patients' programs.

Thiamine, or vitamin B_1, given in 150-milligram daily doses, is crucially needed to help an underactive thyroid gland. Hypothyroidism not uncommonly is the source of a lack of desire or capacity for sex.

In the case of adrenal weakness or exhaustion, in which there is little or no libidinous response during sexual encounters, a daily combination of 100 milligrams of vitamin B_2 (riboflavin), 200 milligrams of vitamin B_3 (niacin), and 500 milligrams of pantothenic acid will be prescribed. If the niacin produces a hot skin sensation and flush that are intolerable, you can substitute 200 milligrams of niacinamide.

Another B vitamin, folic acid, works synergistically (as a team) with testosterone to develop mature sperm. A male adolescent requires a suitable concentration of folic acid in his diet to develop the normal sex characteristics, such as deepening of the voice, growth of a beard, and enlarging of the prostate gland for production of secretions for semen. In women, deficiency of folic acid eliminates the normal response of the reproductive organs to estrogen, resulting in abnormalities in pregnancy.

In *The Lancet*, a physician in the Department of Pathology of the Royal Berkshire Hospital in Reading, England, reported success with using vitamin B_{12} for the treatment of male sterility. Dr. Alan A. Watson aided the maturation of sperm cells by giving the men megadose injections of the vitamin. Vitamin B_{12} therapy is also useful for overcoming female infertility due to pernicious anemia, according to doctors at the Royal Infirmary in Glasgow, Scotland. Blood specialists sometimes suggest that when sterility or infertility exists, physicians should test the level of vitamin B_{12} in the patient's blood to see if it is inordinately low, prescribing supplements if it is.

Para-aminobenzoic acid (PABA) is used for relieving Peyronie's disease, a sexual problem of middle-aged men in which the tissue of the penis becomes abnormally fibrous. Victims of the condition find that an erection causes the penis to curve too much, which causes a lot of pain. They dread being stimulated. PABA apparently increases the oxygen supply to the fibrotic tissue, helping it to become more flexible and lessening the penile curvature. An average therapeutic megadose of 12 grams of PABA, given as four 500-milligram tablets six times a day, was taken by sixteen men with Peyronie's disease for up to two years; all the men got rid of their problem permanently. *Note:* A dose of PABA as high as 12 grams per day definitely requires a doctor's supervision. Do not take this large amount on your own.

The B vitamins are especially important for energy and nervous functions; therefore, their lack plays havoc with the workings of the sexual apparatus. Indeed, among the nutrients, the B vitamins are the most vital of the water-solubles. They combine with specific proteins to facilitate the breakdown of food for use by the body in individual cells. The B-complex vitamins are so interrelated that an insufficient supply of any single one can impair the usefulness of the others.

At the present time, twenty-five B vitamins have been discovered, although some of the discoveries duplicated others and thus have been discounted. The functions of the various vitamins in the B complex are closely related, but the individual vitamins do not act as substitutes for one another. Each B vitamin has its own set functions in maintaining the human body at peak performance.

A discussion of the actions of the separate B vitamins would require a book by itself, as would the lists of foods that contain the vitamins. Because of this, the lists that follow indicate only foods that have high concentrations of the vitamins. Eating a wide variety of these foods should provide you with sufficient amounts of the B vitamins for optimal functioning of your sex organs and libido. If you cannot tolerate certain of these foods or have no access to them, nutritional supplements can be substituted at the following dosages, recommended by the Academy of Orthomolecular Psychiatry:

- Vitamin B_1 (thiamine)—100 milligrams daily.
- Vitamin B_2 (riboflavin)—100 milligrams daily.
- Vitamin B_3 (niacin)— 200 milligrams daily.
- Vitamin B_4 (pantothenic acid)—100 milligrams daily.
- Vitamin B_6 (pyridoxine)—150 milligrams daily.
- Folic acid (folacin, folate)—400 micrograms daily.
- Vitamin B_{12} (cobalamin)—100 micrograms daily.
- Biotin—100 micrograms daily.
- Choline—300 micrograms daily.
- Inositol—100 milligrams daily.
- Para-aminobenzoic acid (PABA)—60 milligrams daily.

Foods High in Vitamin B₁ (Thiamine)

The following list names foods that are high in vitamin B₁. Also given for each food is the number of milligrams of B₁ per 100 grams (3.5 ounces) of edible portion of food. For example, brewer's yeast has 15.61 milligrams of vitamin B₁ in every 100 grams of edible food.

15.61	Brewer's yeast	0.46	Hazelnuts
14.01	Torula yeast	0.45	Lamb heart
2.01	Wheat germ	0.45	Wild rice
1.96	Sunflower seeds	0.43	Cashews
1.84	Rice polishings	0.43	Rye grain
1.28	Pine nuts	0.41	Lamb liver
1.14	Peanuts, with skins	0.41	Lobster
1.10	Soybeans, dried	0.38	Mung beans
1.05	Cowpeas, dried	0.38	Cornmeal
0.98	Peanuts, without skins	0.37	Lentils
0.96	Brazil nuts	0.36	Beef kidney
0.93	Pork, lean	0.35	Green peas, fresh
0.86	Pecans	0.34	Macadamia nuts
0.85	Soybeans, fresh	0.34	Brown rice
0.84	Pinto beans	0.33	Walnuts
0.84	Red beans	0.31	Chick peas
0.74	Split peas, dried	0.30	Pork liver
0.73	Millet	0.25	Garlic
0.72	Wheat bran	0.25	Beef liver
0.67	Pistachio nuts	0.24	Almonds
0.65	Navy beans	0.24	Lima beans, fresh
0.63	Veal heart	0.24	Pumpkin seeds
0.60	Buckwheat	0.24	Squash seeds
0.60	Oatmeal	0.23	Brain, all kinds
0.55	Whole wheat flour	0.23	Chestnuts, fresh
0.55	Whole wheat	0.23	Soybean sprouts
0.51	Lamb kidney	0.22	Chili peppers, red
0.48	Lima beans, dried	0.18	Sesame seeds, hulled

Foods High in Vitamin B₂ (Riboflavin)

The following list names foods that are high in vitamin B₂. Also given for each food is the number of milligrams of B₂ per 100 grams (3.5 ounces) of edible portion of food. For example, torula yeast has 5.06 milligrams of vitamin B₂ in every 100 grams of edible food.

5.06	Torula yeast	4.28	Brewer's yeast

3.28	Lamb liver	0.26	Brain, all kinds
3.26	Beef liver	0.26	Kale
3.03	Pork liver	0.26	Parsley
2.72	Calf liver	0.25	Cashews
2.55	Beef kidney	0.25	Rice bran
2.49	Chicken liver	0.25	Veal
2.42	Lamb kidney	0.24	Lamb, lean
1.36	Chicken giblets	0.23	Broccoli
1.05	Veal heart	0.23	Chicken, meat and skin
0.92	Almonds	0.23	Pine nuts
0.88	Beef heart	0.23	Salmon
0.74	Lamb heart	0.23	Sunflower seeds
0.68	Wheat germ	0.22	Navy beans
0.63	Wild rice	0.22	Beet greens
0.46	Mushrooms	0.22	Mustard greens
0.44	Egg yolks	0.22	Lentils
0.38	Millet	0.22	Pork, lean
0.36	Chili peppers, red	0.22	Prunes, dried
0.35	Soybean flour	0.22	Rye grain
0.35	Wheat bran	0.21	Mung beans
0.33	Mackerel	0.21	Pinto beans
0.31	Collard greens	0.21	Red beans
0.31	Soybeans, dried	0.21	Black-eyed peas
0.30	Eggs	0.21	Okra
0.29	Split peas, dried	0.13	Sesame seeds, hulled
0.29	Beef tongue		

Foods High in Vitamin B3 (Niacin)

The following list names foods that are high in vitamin B3. Also given for each food is the number of milligrams of B3 per 100 grams (3.5 ounces) of edible portion of food. For example, torula yeast has 44.4 milligrams of vitamin B3 in every 100 grams of edible food.

44.4	Torula yeast	11.4	Calf liver
37.9	Brewer's yeast	11.3	Turkey, light meat only
29.8	Rice bran	10.8	Chicken liver
28.2	Rice polishings	10.7	Chicken, light meat only
21.0	Wheat bran	8.4	Trout
17.2	Peanuts, with skins	8.3	Halibut
16.9	Lamb liver	8.2	Mackerel
16.4	Pork liver	8.1	Veal heart
15.8	Peanuts, without skins	8.0	Chicken, dark meat only
13.6	Beef liver	8.0	Swordfish

8.0	Turkey, dark meat only	4.7	Brown rice
7.7	Goose, meat only	4.5	Pine nuts
7.5	Beef heart	4.4	Buckwheat
7.2	Salmon	4.4	Chili peppers, red
6.4	Veal	4.4	Whole wheat
6.4	Beef kidney	4.3	Whole wheat flour
6.2	Wild rice	4.2	Mushrooms
6.1	Chicken giblets	4.2	Wheat germ
5.7	Lamb, lean	3.7	Barley
5.6	Chicken, meat and skin	3.6	Herring
5.4	Sesame seeds, hulled	3.5	Almonds
5.4	Sunflower seeds	3.2	Shrimp
5.1	Beef, lean	3.0	Haddock
5.0	Pork, lean	3.0	Split peas, dried

Foods High in Vitamin B_4 (Pantothenic Acid)

The following list names foods that are high in vitamin B_4. Also given for each food is the number of milligrams of B_4 per 100 grams (3.5 ounces) of edible portion of food. For example, brewer's yeast has 12.0 milligrams of vitamin B_4 in every 100 grams of edible food.

12.0	Brewer's yeast	1.4	Lentils
11.0	Torula yeast	1.3	Rye flour
8.0	Calf liver	1.3	Cashews
6.0	Chicken liver	1.3	Salmon, meat only
3.0	Beef kidney	1.2	Camembert cheese
2.8	Peanuts	1.2	Chick peas, dried
2.6	Brain, all kinds	1.2	Wheat germ, toasted
2.6	Heart, all kinds	1.2	Broccoli
2.2	Mushrooms	1.1	Hazelnuts
2.0	Soybean flour	1.1	Turkey, dark meat only
2.0	Split peas, dried	1.1	Brown rice
2.0	Beef tongue	1.1	Whole wheat flour
1.9	Perch	1.1	Sardines
1.8	Bleu cheese	1.1	Chili peppers, red
1.7	Pecans	1.1	Avocados
1.7	Soybeans	1.1	Veal, lean
1.6	Eggs	1.0	Black-eyed peas, dried
1.5	Lobster	1.0	Wild rice
1.5	Oatmeal, uncooked	1.0	Cauliflower
1.4	Buckwheat flour	1.0	Chicken, dark meat only
1.4	Sunflower seeds	1.0	Kale

Foods High in Vitamin B₆ (Pyridoxine)

The following list names foods that are high in vitamin B₆. Also given for each food is the number of milligrams of B₆ per 100 grams (3.5 ounces) of edible portion of food. For example, torula yeast has 3.00 milligrams of vitamin B₆ in every 100 grams of edible food.

3.00	Torula yeast	0.43	Beef kidney
2.50	Brewer's yeast	0.42	Avocados
1.25	Sunflower seeds	0.41	Veal kidney
1.15	Wheat germ, toasted	0.34	Whole wheat flour
0.90	Tuna, meat only	0.33	Chestnuts, fresh
0.84	Beef liver	0.30	Egg yolks
0.81	Soybeans, dried	0.30	Kale
0.75	Chicken liver	0.30	Rye flour
0.73	Walnuts	0.28	Spinach
0.70	Salmon, meat only	0.26	Turnip greens
0.69	Trout, meat only	0.26	Sweet peppers
0.67	Calf liver	0.25	Beef heart
0.66	Mackerel, meat only	0.25	Potatoes
0.65	Pork liver	0.24	Prunes, dried
0.63	Soybean flour	0.24	Raisins
0.60	Lentils, dried	0.24	Sardines
0.58	Lima beans, dried	0.23	Brussels sprouts
0.58	Buckwheat flour	0.23	Elderberries
0.56	Black-eyed peas, dried	0.23	Perch, meat only
0.56	Navy beans, dried	0.22	Cod, meat only
0.55	Brown rice	0.22	Barley
0.54	Hazelnuts	0.22	Camembert cheese
0.54	Chick peas, dried	0.22	Sweet potatoes
0.53	Pinto beans, dried	0.21	Cauliflower
0.51	Bananas	0.20	Popcorn, popped
0.45	Pork, lean	0.20	Red cabbage
0.44	Albacore, meat only	0.20	Leeks
0.43	Beef, lean	0.20	Molasses
0.43	Halibut, meat only		

Foods High in Folic Acid (Folacin, Folate)

The following list names foods that are high in folic acid. Also given for each food is the number of micrograms of folic acid per 100 grams (3.5 ounces) of edible portion of food. For example, brewer's yeast has 2,022 micrograms of folic acid in every 100 grams of edible food.

2,022	Brewer's yeast	57	Textured vegetable protein
440	Black-eyed peas	56	Peanuts, roasted
430	Rice germ	56	Peanut butter
425	Soybean flour	53	Broccoli
305	Wheat germ	50	Barley
295	Beef liver	50	Split peas, dried
275	Lamb liver	49	Whole wheat cereal
225	Soybeans	49	Brussels sprouts
220	Pork liver	45	Almonds
195	Wheat bran	38	Whole wheat flour
180	Kidney beans	33	Oatmeal
145	Mung beans	32	Cabbage
130	Lima beans	32	Figs, dried
125	Navy beans	30	Avocados
125	Chick peas	28	Green beans
110	Asparagus	28	Corn
105	Lentils	28	Coconut meat, fresh
77	Walnuts	27	Pecans
75	Spinach, fresh	25	Mushrooms
70	Kale	25	Dates
65	Filberts	14	Blackberries
60	Beet greens	7	Ground beef
60	Mustard greens	5	Oranges

Foods High in Vitamin B_{12} (Cobalamin)

The following list names foods that are high in vitamin B_{12}. Also given for each food is the number of micrograms of B_{12} per 100 grams (3.5 ounces) of edible portion of food. For example, lamb liver has 104.0 micrograms of vitamin B_{12} in every 100 grams of edible food.

104.0	Lamb liver	4.0	Brain, all kinds
98.0	Clams	4.0	Salmon, meat only
80.0	Beef liver	3.0	Tuna, meat only
63.0	Lamb kidney	2.1	Lamb
60.0	Calf liver	2.1	Sweetbreads (thymus)
31.0	Beef kidney	2.0	Eggs
25.0	Chicken liver	2.0	Whey, dried
18.0	Oysters	1.8	Beef, lean
17.0	Sardines	1.8	Edam cheese
11.0	Beef heart	1.8	Swiss cheese
6.0	Egg yolks	1.6	Brie cheese
5.2	Lamb heart	1.6	Gruyére cheese
5.0	Trout	1.4	Bleu cheese

1.3	Haddock, meat only	1.0	Mozzarella cheese
1.2	Flounder, meat only	1.0	Halibut
1.2	Scallops	1.0	Perch, meat only
1.0	Cheddar cheese	1.0	Swordfish, meat only
1.0	Cottage cheese		

Foods High in Biotin

The following list names foods that are high in biotin. Also given for each food is the number of micrograms of biotin per 100 grams (3.5 ounces) of edible portion of food. For example, brewer's yeast has 200 micrograms of biotin in every 100 grams of edible food.

200	Brewer's yeast	24	Oatmeal
127	Lamb liver	24	Sardines, canned
100	Pork liver	22	Eggs
96	Beef liver	21	Black-eyed peas
70	Soybean flour	18	Split peas, dried
61	Soybeans	18	Almonds
60	Rice bran	17	Cauliflower
58	Rice germ	16	Mushrooms
57	Rice polishings	16	Whole wheat cereal
52	Egg yolks	15	Salmon, canned
39	Peanut butter	15	Textured vegetable protein
37	Walnuts	14	Wheat bran
34	Peanuts, roasted	13	Lentils
31	Barley	12	Brown rice
27	Pecans	10	Chicken

Foods High in Choline

The following list names foods that are high in choline. Also given for each food is the number of micrograms of choline per 100 grams (3.5 ounces) of edible portion of food. For example, lecithin has 2,200 micrograms of choline in every 100 grams of edible food.

2,200	Lecithin	245	Chick peas
1,490	Egg yolks	240	Brewer's yeast
550	Beef liver	223	Lentils
504	Eggs	201	Split peas, dried
406	Wheat germ	170	Rice bran
340	Soybeans	162	Peanuts, roasted
300	Rice germ	156	Oatmeal
257	Black-eyed peas	145	Peanut butter

143	Wheat bran	66	Sweet potatoes
139	Barley	48	Cheddar cheese
122	Ham	42	Green beans
112	Brown rice	29	Potatoes
104	Veal	23	Cabbage
102	Rice polishings	22	Spinach
94	Whole wheat cereal	21	Textured vegetable protein
86	Molasses	15	Cow's milk, whole
77	Pork	12	Orange juice
75	Beef	5	Butter
75	Green peas, fresh		

Foods High in Inositol

The following list names foods that are high in inositol. Also given for each food is the number of milligrams of inositol per 100 grams (3.5 ounces) of edible portion of food. For example, lecithin has 2,200 milligrams of inositol in every 100 grams of edible food.

2,200	Lecithin	150	Grapefruits
770	Wheat germ	130	Lentils
500	Navy beans	120	Raisins
460	Rice bran	120	Cantaloupes
454	Rice polishings	119	Brown rice
390	Barley, cooked	117	Orange juice
370	Rice germ	110	Whole wheat flour
370	Whole wheat	96	Peaches
270	Brewer's yeast	95	Cabbage
270	Oatmeal	95	Cauliflower
240	Black-eyed peas	88	Onions
240	Chick peas	67	Whole wheat bread
210	Oranges	66	Sweet potatoes
205	Soybean flour	64	Watermelons
200	Soybeans	60	Strawberries
180	Peanuts, roasted	55	Lettuce
180	Peanut butter	51	Beef liver
170	Lima beans	46	Tomatoes
162	Green peas, fresh	33	Eggs
150	Molasses	13	Cow's milk, whole
150	Split peas, dried	11	Beef, round

Foods High in Para-Aminobenzoic Acid

The following list names foods that are high in para-aminobenzoic acid.

However, the listing does not give the exact amount of para-aminobenzoic acid in each type of food because the concentration always varies.

Beef liver	Oats
Cabbage	Spinach
Cow's milk, whole	Sunflower seeds
Eggs	Wheat bran
Mushrooms	Wheat germ

Most of the foods listed in this chapter are commonly available. However, if you find that you have little or no access to these edibles, or if you cannot eat them for some reason, you can substitute nutritional supplements in equivalent or higher dosages. Supplements can be purchased from health food stores, a few pharmacies, some supermarkets, and mail-order houses specializing in health products.

Chapter 4

SEXUAL HEALTH
WITH HERBS

For the last fifteen years—ever since I was fifty-seven—I've been running to the toilet to urinate six times a night. I don't know anymore what a full night's sleep is because of my prostate. First I had prostatitis, which hospitalized me. Then I developed chronic enlargement of the prostate gland. I've been to the urologist countless times for all kinds of treatments. He keeps recommending an operation that I don't want. I'm afraid that cutting into my prostate will make me impotent, and my wife and I still enjoy each other too much to let that happen.

I figure I can defeat the need for surgery by adopting better nutritional habits. As it is, I eat pumpkin seeds for their magnesium and zinc contents, and I take lecithin because I have read that it helps reduce enlarged glands. I take hot sitz baths, too, soaking half an hour for the soothing effect. I still run to the toilet, although I admit there was a time before I started eating healthy foods that I was running as many as ten times a night. I have no doubt I could improve my condition even more if I only knew what to do for a swollen prostate in particular. Have you any recommendations?

Lyle V.
Sidney, Australia

I am an unmarried twenty-one-year-old secretary in a real estate firm, and I suffer terribly from premenstrual tension and menstrual pain. About three days before my period starts, a headache hits; I feel miserable and weighed down, as if everything is too much or the world is against me. I become defensive, irritable, and unable to concentrate, and my boss complains about the mistakes I make.

When my period starts, I feel no better. I double over with cramps on all four days of menstruation. At times, the cramps radiate along the insides of my thighs and throughout my lower back. Awful cramps come even as I sit at my desk typing. I take aspirin, extra doses of birth control pills, painkillers, diuretics, and muscle relaxants, all of which my gynecologist has prescribed. I apply heat to my stomach region. I've even smoked marijuana as a treatment. Nothing helps! The symptoms all recur at the same time every month with maddening regularity.

Yet I do have three good weeks each month when I cannot understand how I could have felt so low. I can describe the bad feelings right now, though, since I am in the middle of my period.

Because I work, I can't just pull up short one week out of every month. I've therefore learned to repress the discomfort—to grin and bear it without sympathy from my fellow workers. But it's too much, and I hate it! Why must I be considered to be overreacting or lying during my bad days, as if I'm trying to avoid work? I'm not neurotic, although the realty brokers in my office treat me as if I am.

My doctor doesn't seem to have any additional suggestions except a dilatation and curettage. I don't want a D and C, but I don't know where to turn anymore. What can I do to help myself?

Constance F.
St. Louis, Missouri

Some women would suggest that the female reproductive mechanism could be improved upon as a system. The monthly blood flow, usually beginning around age thirteen and ending in the fifties, affects women in different ways.

Over 72 percent of all women menstruate approximately every twenty-eight days. The average bleeding period is four days, and the amount of blood discharged varies from one to five ounces.

The remaining 29 percent of women who menstruate experience considerable variations from the averages. Menstrual irregularities prevail. These include profuse and prolonged periods, a condition called *menorrhagia*; bleeding between periods, known as *metrorrhagia*; absence of bleeding, called *amenorrhea*; and painful cramps during the menstrual period, called *dysmenorrhea*. A woman whose periods are regular, predictable, and comfortable can consider herself lucky.

Until recently, premenstrual syndrome (PMS), or premenstrual tension (PMT)—the irritability, nausea, constipation, acne, backache, headache, breast enlargement and soreness, weight gain, abdominal bloating, fatigue, lack of concentration, tearfulness, food cravings, clumsiness, lethargy, and depression that occur during the three or four days just prior to blood flow—was not considered a true clinical entity. Doctors classified the problem as psychological and a characteristic of hypochondriacal women. It was a "woman's neurosis" and had to be tolerated. But as many victims have noted, if PMS had been a man's problem, it would have been diagnosed and treated years ago.

Gynecologists estimate that PMS affects about 60 percent of all women who menstruate. It is currently believed to be due mainly to the retention of water in the system, caused by disordered secretions of progesterone and adrenocortical hormone. The generally accepted treatment, according to the American College of Obstetricians and Gynecologists, is therefore a dehydration regimen beginning twelve to fourteen days before the expected menstrual date. Dehydration is achieved by limiting the amount of fluid consumed to one quart daily, eating a low-salt diet, and taking diuretics in the form of pills or injections. But for many women suffering mental or physical distress just before the onset of menstruation, this dehydration regimen is quite inadequate.

The majority of dysmenorrhea victims find no relief using the orthodox treatment. It is not unusual to feel a slight amount of discomfort during menstruation, but genuine pain and severe cramps are definitely abnormal, affirms the American Society for Psychoprophylaxis in Obstetrics, Inc. Painful menstruation is of two types—*primary* and *secondary*. *Primary dysmenorrhea* is more common among young women, such as our letter writer, Constance F. This type of menstrual cramping is associated with an endocrine imbalance and presents symptoms that usually diminish or disappear after childbirth. But what if you do not become a mother? Must you then accept discomfort indefinitely? Later in this chapter, I will examine some easy home remedies for relieving or preventing menstrual cramps that are now being recommended by physicians prescribing herbal medicines.

Secondary dysmenorrhea is a result of a serious pathological condition, such as inflammation of the pelvis, malpositioning of the uterus, or presence of fibroid tumors in the uterus. It is likely to occur somewhat later in life, perhaps as a result of chronic constipation or longstanding faulty posture. Emotional stress frequently intensifies the discomfort of both types of painful menstruation.

The treatment for primary menstrual pain is generally injections with hormones, especially estrogen. Mild analgesics are also usually prescribed, along with regulated exercises and the use of a heating pad to relieve the symptoms. When a physician decides that his young patient is totally incapacitated by the recurring pain, he may recommend psychotherapy.

An adolescent who has just begun to menstruate may complain of severe cramps with the onset of each cycle. Telling her that the cramps will disappear at some future time will not minimize the discomfort and is a bad practice. It is better to act to relieve the pain, either by standard medical treatment or by employing a few of the herbal methods suggested by wholistic doctors.

For some cases of secondary dysmenorrhea, surgery may be prescribed to reposition the uterus or remove the fibroid tumors. Dilatation and curettage (D and C) of the cervix is another technique that may remove the organic disorder causing the symptoms. A D and C operation is a standard procedure. Dysmenorrhea associated with infection is treated medically by other orthodox methods.

MORE NATURAL TREATMENT TECHNIQUES FOR PMS

The release of emotional tension through orgasm has been found by many women to offer temporary relief from PMS. Masters and Johnson have shown that an orgasm is a powerful valve opener when too much pressure has built up in the psyche. You should take your relief where you find it—by having sex with your mate just prior to menstruating or by masturbating.

Another natural treatment technique is exercise, particularly the exercise movements suggested for pregnant women. A good workout does wonders to dispel congestion and its accompanying bloated feeling. Swimming is good for relaxing the muscles of the uterus and for loosening tight limbs. Do movements that stretch out achy muscles and tendons without causing pain. Backache during PMS responds well to pressing the small of the back flat against the floor. Above all, keep fit where and when you are able.

Massage is excellent therapy for aching neck, shoulder, and back muscles. Also massage the abdomen, where congestion may actually have distended the stomach region. Try rubbing the abdomen with a deep-heating oil, cream, or lotion. Massaging with such a rubefacient, or with just the hands, stimulates blood circulation and promotes heat. You could help the heat do a better job by gently raising the temperature of the congested area with a heating pad or hot water bottle. Try hot baths as well, making sure that the temperature does not go above a comfortable range. Hot baths help some women but worsen the pain for others.

The best natural relief-giving technique for premenstrual syndrome is sexual nutrition using herbs. Herbology, the science of using herbs in the treatment of illness, has a remedy for most female reproductive-system problems. The following herbs are especially recommended to relieve PMS:

- Garlic (*Allium sativum*). Originally from India and central Asia, garlic is now cultivated everywhere. The whole plant contains an antibiotic essential oil consisting of allium, diallyl sulphide, and various enzymes. The oil also provides vitamin A, thiamine, riboflavin, and niacin. Garlic oil is so popular in Russian medicine that it is referred to as Russian penicillin, the way chicken soup is popularly known as Jewish penicillin. Russian hospitals and clinics use the volatile garlic extract almost exclusively in the forms of a vapor and an inhalant. It works exceedingly well for premenstrual trouble because of emmenagogic properties (an emmenagogue is a medicine that brings on the menstrual flow).

    It is not necessary to eat cloves of fresh garlic for PMS. The allium in garlic has been investigated by the Japanese and found in some instances to be a harmful substance. Allium is also what gives garlic its strong characteristic odor. The Japanese have created a special garlic preparation that is allium-modified to change the substance into a harmless and odorless one. Known as Kyolic, this product is exported all over the world.

    Allium-modified, odorless garlic is available in health food stores as capsules or tablets, or as a liquid to be put into your own gelatin capsules. Most of the symptoms of premenstrual tension, according to some physicians, are relieved by daily intake of 810 to 1,620 milligrams of this deodorized garlic, divided into three daily doses.

- Black cohosh (*Cimicifuga racemosa*). Native to Canada and the United States, black cohosh is often called squaw root because it was used by North American Indians to relieve menstrual difficulties. Five grains (about one-sixth teaspoon) of the powdered rhizome (a plant stem that sends roots from its lower surface) constitutes one dose. Indian women nibbled on the black cohosh rhizome or the blue cohosh (*Caulophyllum thalictroides*) root to bring on the menses, as well as to hasten childbirth.
- Wild yam root (*Dioscorea villosa*). Found in moist places down the east coast of the United States and across into Texas, the wild yam is not the common yam found in urban produce markets. Rather, it is a twining perennial vine, the smallish root of which, when dried, powdered, and made into a decoction, aids in easing PMS. Wild yam is often recommended by herbalists to combat the nausea of pregnant women as well.
- Camomile, or chamomile (*Anthemis nobilis*). Originally from Europe, camomile is now grown in home herb gardens all over the world for its soothing, sedative, and completely harmless tranquilizing effect. Camomile is drunk as a tea. It relieves the uterine congestion of PMS and stimulates the menstrual flow when taken cold.
- Tansy, or bitter buttons (*Tanacetum vulgare*). Widespread along roadsides, banks, and ditches in Europe, tansy is a robust perennial producing an essential oil that is a valuable agent for various female complaints. It is one of the finest remedies for PMS and other menstrual problems in medicine's herbal repertoire. Tansy should be taken in small doses on a regular basis as a decoction, powder, tincture, fluid extract, infusion, or solid extract *before* premenstrual syndrome strikes.

EXPLAINING HERBAL MEDICINE

Decoction? Infusion? Tincture? What do these terms mean? In every society that kept records, herbal medicine played an integral part. This includes the current Western civilization, which calls allopathic treatment the orthodox method. Herbology is not at all primitive, for new herbal discoveries are being made regularly and incorporated into the armamentarium of modern physicians. For example, most people know digitalis as a heart stimulant, part of the drug therapy of today's Western cardiovascular specialists. Digitalis is processed from an herb, foxglove, a discovery of old-time herbology. The effective anticlotting drug coumarin comes from the herb sweet clover. One of the most popular allopathic tranquilizer drugs, reserpine, is refined from the herb snakeroot. Quinine, used for the treatment of malaria and other high fevers, is made from Peruvian (cinchona) bark.

When a whole herb is utilized for relieving ills, there are usually no side effects. But when one component is extracted from a plant, as is done in modern drug manufacturing, the medicinal portion of the herb is altered from its whole natural state and many side effects may be produced. For instance, you can drink all the Peruvian-bark tea you want without any side effects, but take too much quinine extracted from that same bark and you will lose your hearing and maybe die.

In 1965, more than 130 million of the prescription drugs ordered by American physicians came from herbs. Today, about 50 percent of all pharmaceuticals are made from plants, and 75 percent of the hormones used for their medicinal effects are derived completely from herbs. Herbs are prepared by individuals for use at home by methods that are not unlike the manufacturing processes that produce prescription drugs. You can make your own remedies by following the directions in a good book on herbology. Many fine volumes are available at health food stores, bookstores, and libraries.

Traditional physicians in the United States and other countries are gradually recognizing the value of herbal medicine. They are now making use of herbs under the banner of "wholistic medicine"—the well-rounded, "whole" approach to health care. Today's herbalist-nutritionist is finding a new status within orthodoxy.

The herb leaf, flower, seed, root, or bark is turned into an herbal medicine using the method that will work best for the individual herb. The following are the types of preparations made from herbs:

- *Infusion.* Boil water, then pour it over the bruised roots, bark, seeds, or stems at a ratio of one pint of water to one ounce of herb. The usual infusion dose is approximately two tablespoonfuls.
- *Decoction.* Add cold water to the plant parts, then boil the mixture for about thirty minutes; cool and strain the liquid. Since some water always boils away, herbalists suggest using twenty-four ounces of water to one ounce of herb. A dose of decoction is approximately one tablespoonful.
- *Liquid extract.* Boil the herb parts in water, then strain the liquid and let it evaporate to the desired consistency. This process liberates the more active principals of an herb from the useless insoluble pulpy matter. Other fluids besides water can also be used. Brewing tea produces a typical liquid extract. A liquid extract dose is measured in teaspoons, with one dose equal to one teaspoonful.
- *Solid extract.* Dissolve the herb parts in a suitable solvent or plant juice to a point where the potency of one part of the extract equals five times the medicinal value of one part of the crude herb. You will recognize when this point has been reached by how thick and dark the solution has become, and through experience and judgment.) Then cook down the solvent to the consistency of honey or thicker. A dose of solid extract is about two teaspoonfuls.
- *Tincture.* Boil the herb parts the same way as when making a liquid extract

but use alcohol instead of water. This method should be used when the herb substance is gummy or resinous, which is why the alcohol is used. Tincture doses vary considerably.

Herb forms or vehicles also include powders, pills, capsules, suppositories, syrups, and teas. When an herbal therapy calls for an herbal tea, a decoction, or an infusion, many people unpracticed in herbal preparations ask, "How much herb, how much water?"

Herbal expert Dian Dincin Buchman, author of *Herbal Medicine*, explained how to best make an herbal tea. Use one level teaspoon of powdered herb or one rounded teaspoon of cut and sifted herb per cup of purified water; this is the standard concentration. The water should be brought to a boil, then removed from the heat source before the herbal material is added. (Herb parts other than bark or roots should be simmered. When bark or roots are boiled, the result is called a decoction.)

To make tea from encapsulated herbs, simply pull the capsules apart and add the contents to hot water. One regular-size (size 0) capsule holds about 7 grains, or roughly 453 milligrams, of herb. Three to four capsules contain approximately one teaspoon of herb.

Most herbal teas should be made by steeping the herb for fifteen to twenty minutes in a tightly covered glass or stainless steel vessel. Steep bark or roots for thirty minutes. Using only a stainless steel strainer or natural fiber cloth, strain the tea after steeping. Tea made from a powdered herb sometimes does not need straining; it may be cloudy, but it will be more beneficial to the drinker.

It is usually better to take a powdered herb in a capsule rather than as a tea. Many of the most important ingredients in herbs are not water soluble, and you could be throwing away essential ingredients by brewing tea and merely drinking the colored water.

HERBS FOR DYSMENORRHEA

During a conference at the College of New Rochelle in New Rochelle, New York, members of the Society for Menstrual Cycle Research described the hormonal changes involved in a woman's menstrual cycle. At the start of the usual monthly cycle, the hypothalamus, a part of the higher brain center, sends a signal to the nearby pituitary gland that the body's estrogen level is too low. The pituitary releases a hormone to stimulate the ovary to develop some follicles from its supply of eggs. The growing follicles cause more estrogen to be released into the bloodstream. Of the twenty or so follicles, only one survives to burst into a mature egg about midway during the menstrual cycle; this is called ovulation. Where the egg leaves the ovary, a scar, known as the corpus luteum, remains. This corpus luteum becomes a tiny gland that secretes the hormone progesterone. The progesterone thickens the uterus to provide a nutritive bed in which the egg, if fertilized, can develop into an embryo. If no egg implantation occurs in the uterus, all female hormone production stops. Twenty-four hours later, the thickened uterine lining is shed as part of the periodic hemorrhage called menstruation.

Investigative efforts by doctors at Cornell University Medical College have indicated that excessive prostaglandins are the source of the pain in women with dysmenorrhea. Prostaglandins are hormonelike substances that cause contraction of the uterus; for this reason, they have been used therapeutically to aid labor and induce abortion. The Cornell researchers have found up to three times the normal level of prostaglandins in women suffering from painful menstrual cramps. When the cramps are the worst, usually on the first day of menses, the amount of prostaglandins in the bloodstream is known to be the highest. The higher the level of prostaglandins is, the greater is the rate of uterine contraction.[1]

A treatment for dysmenorrhea approved by the Food and Drug Administration (FDA) is a drug formerly developed as an anti-arthritic that is 3,000 percent as potent as aspirin.

Additionally, a "circulating factor" in the bloodstream, discovered by Dr. John Irwin, Dr. Edward Morse, and Dr. Daniel Riddick of the University of Connecticut School of Medicine, is believed to bring on the full complement of dysmenorrheic symptoms. When women without dysmenorrhea (even those who have had hysterectomies) are injected with this unknown blood factor, taken from women suffering with menstrual cramps, the nonsymptomatic women feel typical menstrual discomfort within twelve hours.

When asked in an interview, "If a woman came to you with menstrual cramps, what herb would you recommend she take?" herbalist John R. Christopher, N.D. (Doctor of Naturopathy), replied:

> Without a doubt, I'd recommend an herb called cramp bark. It's an old-time remedy for cramps which the American Indians used. It's very effective—I've seen it relieve tense cramps in a matter of five to ten minutes.
>
> This is one herb all women should have close by. It not only relieves painful cramps once they start, but it prevents further cramps from developing. That's why it's a good idea if women take this herb about a week before their menstrual periods. . . . You simply take it as a hot tea. Mix one teaspoon of the ground-up bark in a cup of boiling distilled water, and let it steep for five minutes. The tea should start to relieve the cramped feeling. . . . If you are suffering from just mild cramps, three to four cups a day should be sufficient. However, if you are experiencing intensely painful cramps, you should take the tea every half hour until the cramps go away. If you don't want to go through all the trouble of prepar-

ing the tea, then just take one capsule of cramp bark powder instead of the cup of tea. But if you really want quick results, the tea is best.[2]

Cramp bark, or *Viburnum opulus*, is sometimes used as a substitute for the common cranberry, which it resembles. The dried stem bark of the cramp bark herb is highly regarded as an antispasmodic, tonic, relaxant, diuretic, expectorant, astringent, sedative, and reliever of menstrual cramps. Cramp bark is considered by herbalists to be one of the best female regulators and relaxants of the ovaries and uterus. It is highly effective in preventing miscarriages due to nervous causes. It soothes the pain of uterine and abdominal cramps.

Other herbs that work well for dysmenorrhea are the following:

- Red raspberry (*Rubus idaeus*). Raspberry tea is a valuable agent for menstrual problems of all types because of its soothing and toning effects. From many decades of experience with it, herbalists know that this tea decreases the menstrual flow without stopping it abruptly, reduces uterine cramps, helps labor pains, and eases prolapsed uterus. It generally acts as an astringent and contractive agent for the reproductive area before and during labor, and assists contractions and checks hemorrhage during labor. The herb is known for relieving childbirth afterpains and for strengthening, cleansing, and enriching mother's milk after delivery.

  Dr. Christopher said, "If I had just one herb to pick which all women should have in their cupboards, it would be red raspberry leaves. Red raspberry is an all-purpose woman's herb which can relieve all sorts of female problems. Whether it's irregular periods, irritability, swollen breasts, nausea, or mild cramps, red raspberry will do the trick." The dose is two tablespoonfuls four times a day.

  Red raspberry also makes a good douche for leukorrhea (a whitish discharge from the vagina, often caused by a fungus infection) and inflamed mucous membranes within the vagina.
- Snakeweed (*Polygonum bistorta*). As a decoction, fluid extract, infusion, or powder tincture, snakeweed helps to decrease or regulate the menstrual flow. But the decoction in a dose of one teaspoonful to one tablespoonful in a little water works the best. Used as a douche, the decoction reduces leukorrhea.
- Water lily (*Nymphaea odorata*). The root of the white pond lily made into a decoction acts therapeutically as an astringent, antiseptic, or tonic. One or two tablespoonfuls help relieve excoriations (abrasions) of the vulva. Water lily also makes a fine douche for leukorrhea. (*Note:* For men, water lily works exceedingly well as an antidote for prostate irritation and for excoriations of the penis foreskin.)
- Squaw vine (*Mitchella repens*). The herb or vine of the squaw vine makes a fine diuretic, astringent, tonic, or emmenagogue when taken as a

decoction (one wineglassful twice a day) or infusion (one teacupful twice a day). To relieve painful menstruation, squaw vine combines well with red raspberry leaves. The infusion or decoction is also a good vaginal douche for leukorrhea.

- Garden rue (*Ruta graveolens*). The leaves and oil of garden rue have a stimulating, emmenagogic, antispasmodic effect and are a wonderful aid for functional inactivity of the uterus or ovaries. Drink five drops of a decoction mixed with a glass of water to encourage ovulation. For menstrual problems in general, drink one wineglass of infusion every couple of hours in combination with any herb that has an antispasmodic action, such as caraway seed, anise seed, marjoram herb, cinnamon bark, fennel seed, or wintergreen herb.

- Motherwort (*Leonurus cardiaca*). For failure to menstruate and painful menstruation, two tablespoons of a tonic liquid made from motherwort sipped three times a day is therapeutic. Used as an infusion or decoction in a vaginal douche, motherwort also reduces senile vaginitis (vaginal inflammation in older women) and trichomoniasis (leukorrhea caused by the microorganism *Trichomonas vaginalis*).

- Life root (*Senecio aureus*). For a steady regulator of the female organs, life root infusion, taken at a dose of one teacupful three times daily, does a fine job. It is a stimulant for amenorrhea and reliever of leukorrhea, especially when combined with white pond lily and sipped as a beverage.

- Southernwood (*Artemisia abrotanum*). Southernwood has proven valuable for such menstrual problems as amenorrhea, dysmenorrhea, and menorrhagia when one wineglass of infusion is taken three or four times a day. An excellent formula for menstrual obstruction is one part each of southernwood herb, pennyroyal herb, and mugwort leaves. Put one ounce of the combined herbs in one pint of boiling water, cover the container, and steep for ten minutes. Strain the tea, sweeten it to taste, and allow it to cool. Drink one wineglassful.

- European pennyroyal (*Mentha pulegium*). As a reliable and effective emmenagogue, pennyroyal is especially useful for retarded or obstructed menstruation due to a sudden chill or cold. It is wonderful for treating amenorrhea, menorrhagia, and other menstrual problems. Take a teacup of infusion as a tea every two hours.

- Blessed thistle (*Carbenia benedicta*). Taken cold, an infusion of blessed thistle is a tonic for menstrual cramps. It also benefits nursing mothers by stimulating the mammary glands to give more milk. To purify her breast milk, a mother should drink blessed thistle as a cold infusion in a dose of half a teacupful three times daily.

- True unicorn root (*Liliaceae*). As a healing tonic for the female regenerative organs, true unicorn root has been proven to be especially effective for cases of habitual miscarriage due to chronic weakness. It may be safely used during the entire pregnancy. Because of its powerful uterine stimulative properties, true unicorn root is used for female sterility and male impotence. It increases the possibility of conception. It is also used for dysmenorrhea, menorrhagia, chronic uterine weakness, general debility, female sterility, and male impotency. The dose is a half cup of decoction three to six times a day.

In his book *School of Natural Healing*, Dr. Christopher focused attention on the many emmenagogue herbs. He wrote:

> There are some 150 botanical herbs that are presently classed as promoting menstrual normalcy. . . . Emmenagogues are herbal agents that are female correctives, and which provoke, stimulate, and promote the menstrual flow and discharge. Properly used, emmenagogues will readjust the entire genital areas, so that the menstrual flow and discharge will be at the normal minimum, instead of excessive or lacking.

Many herbs, including several just discussed, also make wonderful all-purpose tonics. To make a superb female tonic, combine one-quarter ounce each of true unicorn root, cramp bark, and wild yam root with one ounce of squaw vine herb. Place the mixture in one quart of water and simmer for twenty minutes. Strain the liquid, sweeten it to taste, and let it cool. Drink this tonic every day at a dose of three tablespoonfuls three times a day.

PROSTATE TROUBLE

The chief disorder that affects the prostate gland is the condition known as benign prostatic hypertrophy (BPH), which is a nonmalignant enlargement of the prostate. It was described in the letter from Lyle V. at the beginning of this chapter and is the same for approximately half the Western world's male population over the age of fifty.

The prostate gland is an accessory organ of the male reproductive system. It surrounds the urethra at the base of the bladder. The alkaline fluid that the prostate gland constantly secretes is thought to nourish and lubricate the sperm cells.

Because of the prostate's anatomical location, swelling of the gland can interfere with bladder function. A middle-aged man's earliest symptoms of BPH are increasing difficulty in beginning to urinate and a feeling that the bladder is never fully emptied. The need to urinate is felt more frequently, and a burning sensation may accompany the passing of urine, due in part to the onset of infection.

The most common prostate problem in young men is prostatitis, or inflammation of the gland, which may be a result of gonorrhea. Prostatitis symptoms include discomfort in the perineal region, itching around the end of the penis, and burning upon urination. On rectal examination, the prostate may be found to be enlarged and tender. Pressure may cause it to exude pus into the urethra. A smear of the discharge identifies the responsible germ, and a suitable antibiotic is administered.

BPH is not dangerous in 80 percent of cases, but it is malignant in 20 percent. The older a man is, the greater are his chances of developing prostate cancer. Of all male cancer deaths, 10 percent are from cancer of the prostate. Each year, 60,000 new cases are diagnosed in the United States, and at least 20,000 men each year die from the disease. Prostate cancer is suggested by occasional drops of blood in the urine; the urologist can feel hard lumps on the prostate during rectal examination. The symptoms resemble those of BPH.

The specific causes of benign prostatic hypertrophy and prostate cancer are unknown. The hormonal changes that accompany aging are thought to be a possibility. Of all the body's living tissues, the prostate gland and sperm have by far the highest concentrations of zinc. Not unsurprisingly, nutritionists and wholistic physicians firmly agree that zinc deficiency is associated with sperm abnormalities, sexual problems in general, and prostate enlargement (including cancer) in particular. Taking zinc supplements and eating foods high in zinc are recommended (see pages 51–53 for the recommended dosage and a list of foods high in zinc).

Dr. John Eichenlaub, in his book *A Minnesota Doctor's Home Remedies for Common and Uncommon Ailments*, described an easy home test to determine if a urination problem is due to prostatitis or urethritis (inflammation of the urinary tract in the penis). Using three glass containers, pass a few drops of urine into one container, almost all of what remains in the bladder into the second, and the last teaspoonful or so into the third. Examine the urine samples. Cloudiness in only the first sample points to urethritis, but cloudiness in both the first and third samples means prostatitis.

HERBS FOR PROSTATE TROUBLE

Certain herbs have healing and maintenance properties for ailing prostate glands. For example, a well-known prostate formula for reducing swelling of the gland includes a mixture of one part each of cayenne, ginger, golden seal root, gravel root, juniper berries, marshmallow root, parsley root, and uva ursi leaves. The herbs should be ground into a powder and put into size 00 capsules. The recommended dose is two or three capsules taken with a cup of parsley tea twice a day, in the morning and evening.

In his book *Own Your Own Body*, Stan Malstrom, N.D., recommended his own prostate formula, SP. The formula, he said,

consists of black cohosh, cayenne, ginger, goldenseal, gotu-kola, kelp, licorice, and lobelia; works beautifully for men who suffer from prostate problems. These tend to activate and stimulate the prostate to eliminate much mucus; and frequently men, after utilizing this formula for a period of several weeks, will suddenly begin to hemorrhage for a day or so: blood, old cellular material, and all types of debris from the urinary tract. After this, they heal and then they have very few further problems with urination at night; in fact, the formula tends to eliminate the old symptoms and problems, provided a reasonable diet is followed. This formula is also used by some women who are low in hormone balance, especially progesterone.

Ginseng (*Panax quinquefolia* or *Panax schinseng*) is especially good for prostate trouble. Also known as tartar root, five-finger, and red berry, among other names, ginseng is native to Canada, Korea, China, and the United States (the Appalachian and Ozark regions, and the Pacific Northwest). Ginseng has been used successfully for prostate trouble and, in fact, is prized as a near panacea for most sexual problems, including loss of libido in both sexes and especially impotence. It has been used to excite the fading virility of Chinese men for thousands of years. The wild Manchurian variety found in China has a particularly stimulating effect on the endocrine glands, increasing testosterone production and encouraging a rejuvenation that testosterone injections alone do not.

Ginseng has also been shown to have estrogenlike effects on female reproductive tissues. It prevents vaginal atrophy. The *Medical Tribune* reported that researchers at Finland's Turku University Central Hospital found ginseng can preserve the health of female organs in cases where natural estrogen is absent, such as following hysterectomy.

The first suspicions concerning the estrogenlike effects of ginseng cropped up when Dr. R. Punnonen examined a sixty-two-year-old woman who had undergone a complete hysterectomy fourteen years earlier but had never taken synthetic estrogens. The woman, who regularly used Rumanian ginseng in pill form, suffered no signs of atrophy of the vaginal tissues.

To confirm his suspicions that ginseng works like estrogen in preserving the vitality of the vagina, Dr. Punnonen used gas chromatography to analyze the ginseng tablets the woman had been swallowing. As he suspected, no trace of estrogen was apparent in the ginseng tablets. Dr. Punnonen then asked the woman to stop taking her ginseng tablets for three weeks.

At the end of the three-week period, an examination of the woman's vaginal tissues revealed an estrogen-deficient pattern. The condition was corrected when the patient resumed taking the ginseng.

While they remain unsure of exactly how ginseng works, Dr. Punnonen and his colleagues at Turku University Central Hospital are certain that it has an estrogenlike effect. They have been conducting further studies to determine its potential use in the treatment of a number of other female disorders.

Ginseng has been exhaustively examined by researchers in Japan, Germany, the United States, Russia, and former Eastern European countries. Numerous tests with animals have also been made. Mice and rats, for example, copulated more frequently when injected with a ginseng extract. Their organs, especially the gonads, showed increased growth due to the herb.

Researchers in the Department of Biologically Active Substances, Academy of Sciences, Russia, claimed in a paper entitled "New Substances of Plant Origin" that Korean ginseng root stimulates the central nervous system and serves the body as a "satisfying tonic." Ginseng contains steroidal saponins, which have a function very similar to that of cortisone. These saponins cause the body to be more responsive to the adrenaline it produces. In effect, then, ginseng is like the caffeine in coffee and the nicotine in tobacco—all three increase the sensitivity to adrenaline and increase the amount of adrenaline that the body produces.

Ginseng can help sexual performance—or perhaps it just provides an illusion of improved performance. It also may produce the same side effects as do other stimulants, such as insomnia, irritability, diarrhea, nervousness, hypertension, decreased appetite, and depression. Of course, ginseng advocates and herbalists do not agree and probably would be offended by this warning.

Chinese healers do not consider ginseng to be a sexual stimulant of the same ilk as an aphrodisiac. An aphrodisiac is anything that can elevate sexual desire. Ginseng works more subtly. It restores normally healthy sexual functioning that has become fatigued or worn out. Dr. I.I. Brekhman, a Russian physician who has studied ginseng root extensively, says that the herb "acts only by improving physiological processes. No bad effects are observed after taking it." And the good effects do not develop instantaneously; they build up as the healthy sexual functioning is gradually restored over time.

Ginseng is taken internally in various ways. You can drink it as a tea, chew portions of the root, swallow it in powder form, or pop it down in gelatin capsules. You can add the powder to soups, broths, juices, blended drinks, coffee, sodas, or other beverages. You can use it in the form of an elixir or tincture by adding the dose to a small glass of water.

Ferris H. of Oklahoma City, Oklahoma, became a widower at age sixty. After two years, he met a woman of thirty-nine with whom he fell in love. She returned his emotion with a passion, and they often visited overnight in her apartment. The only thing wrong was that Ferris could not perform well in bed. He had difficulty maintaining an erection, and he was repeatedly distracted during lovemaking by a frequent urgent need to urinate. The man suffered with benign prostatic hypertrophy.

"Then I began drinking tea made from the super type of compounded ginseng roots, consisting of sixteen roots imported from China," Ferris said. He explained:

> I brewed tea with the nugget type of root that makes an instant beverage when you slip a nugget in the cup and add boiling water. I stirred until the ginseng nugget melted and drank two or three cups at a time, sometimes three times a day. I also avoided eating citrus fruits or drinking any citrus fruit juices for three hours after drinking ginseng tea. This was the advice of the herbalist who supplied my ginseng.
>
> I can't say that any change took place in my impotence or frequency of urination for about a month. I still had prostate trouble. My lady friend had long since given up on having sexual intercourse, and I satisfied her in other ways. But then I noticed that I didn't go to the bathroom through the night so much. In a couple of weeks my trips reduced from five a night to only three. In another few weeks I began awakening in the morning with a good firm erection. It was then I began prodding my lady friend with my penis. And she was delighted. We enjoyed ourselves whenever the firmness was available no matter what time of the night or morning. We cooperated with my penis and, in turn, it got hard and stayed that way again and again.
>
> For the first time since my wife died, I felt macho again, like a young man. Suffice it to say I keep drinking my ginseng tea and wouldn't be without it. I've been able to cut down on the amount and drink only one steaming cup daily usually at dinner. My prostate trouble seems to be gone, too.

Other herbs that are good for prostate problems are:

- Burdock root (*Arctium lappa*). The leaves, seeds, stalk, and first-year growth of roots from the burdock root work well as a tonic for reducing the size of an enlarged prostate gland. The recommended dose is one wineglassful three or four times daily, until the symptoms of the urinary dysfunction disappear.
- Coneflower (*Echinacea angustifolia*). The aborigines of Australia and the American Indians are known to have used coneflower herb for helping frequent urination (probably due to prostate trouble). Eric Powell, N.D., Ph.D., of London, England, considered coneflower to be one of the finest *alternatives*. (In herbology, an *alternative* is a substance that changes a condition by producing a gradual alteration toward the restoration of health.) Quoted in *Health From Herbs* magazine, Dr. Powell said, "We have only recently discovered that echinacea (coneflower) has a marked

affinity for the prostate gland, and may be used for enlargement and weakness of this organ." He went on to describe the case of an elderly patient with an enlarged prostate and great difficulty in passing urine. "Five drops of the combined tinctures of echinacea and saw palmetto berries (*Serenoa serrulata*) normalized the gland in three months."

Peach tree leaves are said by herbalists to be useful for treating mild cases of prostatitis. Cornsilk, buchu, and blue flag herb have a special action when made into teas. Herb teas are more effective when consumed as part of a wholesome meal.

HERBS FOR THE SEX ORGANS

There are as many as 800,000 species of plants on the Earth and only a fraction of them have been investigated for medicinal effects.[3] About 40,000 have been studied for nutritional value during the last decade; probably 20 percent of these are useful for enhancement of health. I have presented only a limited number of herbs and herb combinations in this chapter because I have centered my attention strictly on sex-related benefits. Following are more extensive lists of herbs that provide advantages for the sex organs. Lack of space prevents a fuller discussion of each herb; more information about individual herbs can be found in books on herbology.

Herbs to Correct Impotence and Strengthen Sexual Power

Arrach	False unicorn	Quaker button
Betal	Garden sage	Saw palmetto berries
Black cohosh	Ginseng	Summer savory
Burr gockeroo	Guarana	Sundew
Camphor	Jamaica ginger	True unicorn
Carline thistle	Matico	Vanilla pods
Coca	Murira-puama	Virginia snakeroot
Damiana	Night-blooming cereus	Yohimbe
Echinacea	Nux vomica	

Herbs to Bring About Normal Menstrual Function

Acacia	Arrach	Beneset
Aloe	Asafetida	Beth root
American angelica	Balm	Birthwort
American centaury	Bamboo juice	Bistort
American pennyroyal	Barnet	Bitter root
Ammeniacum	Bayberry	Bittersweet
Arbor vitae	Beet	Black cohosh

Black haw
Black hellebore
Black horehound
Black mustard
Blessed thistle
Bloodroot herb
Blue cohosh
Brooklime
Buchu
Buckbean
Button snakeroot
Cajuput oil
Calamint
Camomile
Carrot
Catnip
Cedar berries
Celandine
Columbine
Comfrey
Contrayerba
Cornflower
Cotton root
Cramp bark
Crawley root
Cubeb
Culver's root
Dandelion
Devil's bit
Double tansy
Dyer's madder
Elecampane
European angelica
European ground pine
European pennyroyal
Evening primrose
False unicorn
Fennel
Fenugreek
Feverfew
Fever root
Figwort
Fringe tree
Galbanum

Garden sage
Garlic
Gelsemium
Gentian
German camomile
Ginger
Goldenrod
Golden seal
Gravel root
Ground pine
Guaiac
Guarana
Hemlock spruce
Horehound
Horsemint
Jacob's ladder
Jamaica dogwood
Jamaica ginger
Jerubeba
Jerusalem oak
Juniper berry
Lavender cotton
Lemon
Lemon thyme
Life root
Linden
Lobelia
Lovage
Lungwort
Magnolia
Mandrake
Manganita
Marigold
Masterwort
Mayweed
Meadow lily
Mistletoe
Motherwort
Mugwort
Myrrh
Oregon grape
Parsley seeds
Peach
Peppermint

Peruvian (cinchona) bark
Peruvian rhatany
Pilewort
Pitcher plant
Plantain
Pleurisy root
Prickly ash
Pulsatilla
Ragwort
Red cedar berries
Red raspberry
Red sage
Rosemary
Rue
Safflower
Saffron
St. John's wort
Sanicle
Santonica
Sassafras
Savin
Scabiosa
Senega
Shepherd's purse
Slippery elm
Smartweed
Sneezewort
Solomon's seal
Sorrel
Southernwood
Spruce
Squaw vine
Stinging nettle
Storax
Stramonium
Sumac berries
Sumbul
Summer savory
Sweet cicely
Sweet gale
Sweet marjoram
Sweet-scented golden-rod

Tamarack
Tanacetum balsamita
Tansy
Thyme
True unicorn
Turkey corn
Uva ursi
Valerian
Vervain
Virginia snakeroot

Wake robin
Watercress
White ash
White bryony
White pond lily
White poplar
Wild carrot
Wild columbine
Wild indigo
Wild marjoram

Wild mint
Wild yam
Wintergreen
Witch hazel
Wood betony
Wood sage
Wormwood
Yarrow
Yellow flag

Herbs to Counteract the Tendency to Miscarriage

Cramp bark
Lobelia

Red raspberry
Witch hazel

Herbs to Lessen Sexual Functions and Desires

American black willow
Black willow
Camphor
Celery

Cocoa
Garden sage
Hops
Life everlasting

Oregon grape
Skullcap
White pond lily

Herbs to Stimulate Uterine Contractions and Hasten Childbirth

American angelica
Beth root
Birthwort
Black cohosh
Blue cohosh
Cedar berries
Cinnamon bark
Cinnamon oil

Cotton
Cotton root
Cramp bark
Crawley root
Honeysuckle
Horehound
Lobelia
Red raspberry

Rue
St. John's wort
Shepherd's purse
Spikenard
Squaw vine
Sweet gale
Uva ursi

Herbs to Relieve the Symptoms of Venereal Diseases

American senna
Barberry
Bayberry
Bitter root
Bittersweet
Black catechu
Black walnut
Black willow

Bladderwrack
Bloodroot
Blue flag
Blue violet
Boldo
Boxwood
Burdock
Burr gockeroo

Button snake root
Caroba
Chaparral
Cleavers
Condurango
Copaiba
Corn silk
Cranesbill

Cubeb
Culver's root
Devil's bit
Echinacea
Elder bark (leaves and
  berries)
European birch
Fringe tree
Frostwort
Galla
Golden seal
Guaiac
Hardhack
Hydrangea
Hyssop
Indian sarsaparilla
Ivy
Juniper berry
Kava kava
Krameria root
Life everlasting
Lily of the valley
Manaca
Mandrake

Manganita
Marshmallow
Marsh rosemary
Matico
Mesereon
Mountain laurel
Mullein oil
Oregon grape
Pansy
Pareira
Parsley
Peruvian balsam
Peruvian rhatany
Pipsissewa
Plantain
Poke root
Prickly ash
Quince
Red clover
Red raspberry
Red root
Rock rose
Sandalwood
Sanicle

Sarsaparilla
Sassafras
Shavegrass
Soapwort
Spikenard
Spruce
Stillingia
Storax
Sumac (berries and
  leaves)
Tag alder
Thyme oil
Tormentil
Tragacanth
Turkey corn
Turpentine
Twin leaf
Uva ursi
White pine bark
White pond lily
White poplar
Wild sarsaparilla
Yellow dock
Yellow parilla

HERB SOURCES

Herbal remedies are not prescription items. However, you may wish to check with your doctor about any medical contraindications to employing them.

Thousands of herb distributors around the world provide the public with herbal products. Distributors include rare-plant nurseries, pharmacies, health food stores, tea producers, and live-cactus dealers. For herbs of the Orient, the Chinese community in a metropolitan area may be more useful inasmuch as you can deal directly with an herbalist and explain your requirements. Some herb companies deal in mail orders as well as over-the-counter sales.

To locate herb distributors in your area, check your local Yellow Pages. Local herb retailers may also be able to provide you with information on mail-order sources of herbs.

Chapter 5

NUTRITIONAL APHRODISIACS

Sex, sex, sex—I love it. The more I get, the more I want. I'm twenty years old and full of testosterone or something else. And now I've met Rosemary. The only trouble is that Rosemary isn't horny like me. I've got to find a way to make Rosemary want sex more. She's willing to try. I have her taking vitamins and bee pollen, and eating a natural-food diet, but something extra is needed for us to get it on near to my capacity. Unfortunately, there's no Spanish fly or powdered rhinoceros horn to be found anywhere.

My search is for the foolproof aphrodisiac to drive the girls—especially Rosemary—up a wall or into bed. There must be some hot stuff around—at least, I hear there is. What should I use? Is it available? Healthy to take? I don't want to do the girls any harm.

Bucky R.
Anchorage, Alaska

I get off on my boyfriend's body odor. From taking deep whiffs of the natural smells emitting from his crotch, armpits, and mouth, I become excited almost to the point of orgasm. These odors make me so wild that I lick and kiss his face, hairy chest, and genitals. My man thinks I'm a little nuts, but he doesn't mind because he's the beneficiary of my sexual antics.

Now, this is unusual for me, since I've been around with lots of men. I'm thirty-four and divorced. I know what to do in bed. No other man's body odor has ever affected me this way, and I'm wondering if this guy's smell is something special. Could it be bottled and sold as perfume? Is there any research or scientific history concerning odor as a source of sexual attraction? I know that animals are always sniffing and licking each other's private parts, but humans? I didn't know that!

Vicky S.
Concord, New Hampshire

People have been seeking the ultimate aphrodisiac for as long as they have been searching for the formula to change lead into gold. Until now, unfortunately, sex researchers have been laboring with little success, perhaps because they have been hunting for the uncompounded aphrodisiac in the wrong place—in the chemistry laboratory—when all the time people have been walking around with it as part of their own bodies.

An aphrodisiac is a substance or preparation that tends to increase or arouse sexual desire and heighten sexual excitement. For thousands of years, people in every part of the world have tried different items, internal and external, to enhance sexual response. The reputations that various plant and animal substances enjoy for having aphrodisiacal effects can be traced back to ancient beliefs. The physiological basis for some aphrodisiacal claims is that when the substance is eaten, drunk, or rubbed on the body, it acts on nerve centers in the brain to decrease inhibitions.

Substances considered aphrodisiacal have varied from human breast milk to the powder derived from ground-up dried beetles (cantharides) to cherry pits, which contain amygdalin. These many eatables—numbering about two thousand—have been applied as potency aids, sexual stimulators, or the means for "getting in the mood."

Women are using aphrodisiacs now, as well. Some females in foreign cultures in past years took aphrodisiacs to avoid the stigma of barrenness. The earliest record of an aphrodisiac being taken to bring on pregnancy is in Genesis 30:14–17:

> And Reuben went in the days of wheat harvest, and found mandrakes in the field, and brought them unto his mother Leah. Then Rachel said to Leah, Give me, I pray thee, of thy son's mandrakes.
>
> And she said unto her, Is it a small matter that thou hast taken my husband? and wouldest thou take away my son's mandrakes also? and Rachel said, Therefore he shall lie with thee tonight for thy son's mandrakes.
>
> And Jacob came out of the field in the evening, and Leah went out to meet him, and said, Thou must come in unto me; for surely I have hired thee with my son's mandrakes. And he lay with her that night.
>
> And God hearkened unto Leah, and she conceived, and bore Jacob the fifth son.

In the Hebrew language, *mandrake* has been translated, in the Song of Solomon, as *dudaim*, a fruit with a sweet and agreeable odor providing the pleasure of love—an aphrodisiac. Its root sometimes resembles a penis and testicles.

Modern Western societies—in contrast to Eastern civilizations, which have been using natural substances as aphrodisiacs for centuries—have been making aphrodisiacs in laboratories. These artificial substances have included drugs such as estrogens, progestogens, and androgens.

The modern synthetic aphrodisiacs have replaced the elixirs, herbs, and amulets of the ancients. Now the synthetics are considered the "fountain of youth" of sexual potency—so potent that women crave a man's favors, and other men tremble in his presence. After all, on television, in novels, and on the wide cinema screen, is it not the most virile (or feminine) and seductive among us who are the most successful businesspeople and athletes, the wildest adventurers, the best gamblers? Confidence and sexuality have always gone hand in hand, at least in the scripts of broadcasters, writers, and moviemakers.

Of course, there really is no single love potion for raising the libido. And if there was, you certainly would not find it in a chemical laboratory, unless it was something dangerous and addictive, such as methaqualones (Quaaludes and soporifics), which cause central nervous system disruption, withdrawal tremors, and, with prolonged use, exactly the opposite of what you are looking for—impotence. (In Chapter 13, I will discuss some of the more common recreational drugs, such as alcohol, marijuana, and caffeine.) Instead, there are foods and food supplements you can find in health food stores, herbal shops, pharmacies, and many supermarkets that may increase your sexual stamina and help bring you or your partner to greater passion more often.

However, before I describe what to ingest to elevate vitality, I would like to first acknowledge the validity of Vicky S.'s letter, at the beginning of this chapter. Vicky has been responding to something that is emanating from the genitals, axillary areas (armpits), and oral cavity of her lover and affecting her sense of smell. Vicki's boyfriend is a walking aphrodisiac for Vicki because the "something special" that he is giving off is a distinctive scent that is sexually attractive.

PHEROMONES

Scientists, especially those working for commercial perfumers, are on the scent of something big—or small—microscopic chemical messengers called pheromones that affect sexual desire, sexual readiness, hormone levels, fertility, maturity, aggression, submission, and the deepest emotions. Pheromones are arousal stimulators given off by people noted as "sexy." They affect the behavior of the opposite sex through the brain and nervous system, entering the receiver's thought processes through the nose.

It has long been suspected by some scientists that humans, in common with most other animals, secrete and react to pheromones. These catalysts of sexual attraction are components of perspiration. Thus, the sweat theory of sexual attraction strikes at the foundation of one of the big commercial industries of the United States—deodorant and antiperspirant manufacturing. Underarm products are based on the odoriferous qualities of limes, musk, and certain other scents. All this time, the manufacturers should merely have bottled the sweat of someone like Tom Cruise or Sharon Stone.

About 10 percent of all men have a particular pheromone in their perspiration that gives them a heightened sexual attractiveness to women. Androsterone is this mysterious, sexy "messenger" chemical. Androsterone, found in human skin and hair, broadcasts a powerful subconscious sexual call to women. Women do not know why they are attracted to a particular man; they just find the man sexy and want to know him better. The same type of pheromone is present in women who project a "come hither" call to men. In women, the pheromone is copulins, and it is present mainly in the vaginal fluids.

Women are approximately one thousand times more sensitive to smells than are men. They react most to musklike odors, which form the base of many expensive perfumes. When a woman has her ovaries removed, she loses this sexual-odor sensitivity, but she can have this sensitivity restored if she is given the ovarian hormone estrogen. Interestingly, police departments are aware that female officers are much more sensitive to the presence of a burglar on a premises than are male officers. Olfactory sensitivity may be one explanation for this so-called intuition.

It is common knowledge that the way people smell often determines how others feel about them, but no scientific basis has been established for the mystery of "turn-on" and "turn-off" odors. The science of smell research is known by two names—*osphresiology* and *osmology*. If you are sexually excited by an odor, you are in a state of osphresiolagnia or osmolagnia.

Some people are smell sensitive; others are smell deficient (the technical term is *anosmic*). Blind pianist George Shearing was so sensitive to odors that he could tell how attractive a woman was as soon as she entered the room. John Amoore, Ph.D., testing women and men in England for smell deficiency, found that 10 percent of the subjects were anosmic to the odor of sperm. The researcher himself admitted to being anosmic to certain smells.

French scientist J. Le Magnen, Ph.D., reported that women are quite sensitive to the smell of a substance called exaltolide, the musky fragrance found in a number of perfumes. This type of musky odor is perceived most clearly by sexually mature females at about the time of ovulation. Males may become more sensitive to the odor after receiving an injection of estrogen. The chemicals making up exaltolide, as well as parts of other perfume ingredients such as moskone, civetone, and castoreum, are similar to those produced by the human body. They are sexual attractors.

Many men and women are able to identify while blindfolded which shirt or dress belongs to their sexual partner. The nose knows. Copulins, given off in vaginal juices, as just mentioned, are pheromones that men find attractive. Dr. Alex Comfort postulated that they are secreted particularly by blondes and redheads. Copulins are a mixture of vaginal acids secreted in greatest quantity by women at the time of ovulation.[1]

Dr. Comfort, author of *The Joy of Sex* and *The Facts of Love*, also said that the scents of clean human skin and hair are natural human sexual attractors, with functions analogous, if not identical, to the sexual attractors of other organisms. Dr. Comfort has described scent glands that are usually assumed to be vestigial in humans but are probably present in the anal/genital region, around the breasts, and under the arms.[2]

The question arises: Are deodorants and douches, used maniacally by Americans, making people less sexy? Social scientists suggest that our effort to eliminate odors is from a preference for olfactory blandness because of the decrease in personal space brought about by overcrowding in urban areas. Also, because of food sterilization, smoke detectors, and other items and processes that have reduced our need to use our noses, few of us find it necessary to perceive odors for survival in these modern times. Smell is no longer a way of communicating, as it was for primitive man. This loss has given people a greater capacity to withstand crowding. It is too bad that the resultant loss has also meant a deficiency in our sexual awareness.

In the late 1970s, an aerosol spray containing the male pheromone androsterone was developed and sold broadly in Great Britain and other European countries. Originally marketed as Aeolus 7, the spray was exported to the United States under the name Bodywise. Bodywise was supposed to attract and arouse a woman subconsciously, making her perceive the male wearer as sexy. Numerous experiments in England and in the United States confirmed the product's sexual attraction and excitation effects. For example, men who had secretly applied the product were rated much higher by women in several "masculine" traits. Moreover, in other experiments, Bodywise was atomized in phone booths and on waiting room chairs at Birmingham University, Birmingham, England. Records compiled by hidden observers indicated that women were attracted to and stayed longer in the treated phone booths and chairs.

Bodywise and other products containing pheromones can be used for correcting sexual dysfunction. Masters and Johnson say that the sense of smell is tremendously underused in the treatment of people with sexual problems. These researchers have for many years been employing scented lotions in their clinic to help lovers enjoy the "touching therapy" offered there. They also conducted a ten-year study on scent and sexuality, and discovered once again what has long been suspected—the scent of a pheromone is a sexual "turn on."

The odorous steroid androsterone is normally secreted in trace amounts in human urine. The excretion rate in men is three to four times of that in women. Androsterone is present in human armpit sweat, as already explained, and is predominantly secreted by males. High androsterone secretors do have more drive than do low secretors.

Androsterone is produced in the adrenal glands of both men and women, and possibly in the testes. One finding about the substance concerns its presence in smegma, the material secreted by the sebaceous glands of the penis foreskin and of the vaginal labia minora. In smegma, androsterone has a signaling function for the opposite sex and promotes attraction.

What osphresiologists do not know is how the attraction effect works and what sort of individual is attracted. The one proven fact is that males who are high androsterone secretors are likely to attract females who are low androsterone secretors. While this is not a true aphrodisiacal effect, it has helped to combine certain women and men. And a pheromone is the exciting agent. It is obvious in this instance that if you want an aphrodisiac, you have to sniff it out. The sexual stimulator for the opposite sex most readily at hand may be going unrecognized under your very nose.

SUPEROXIDE DISMUTATES

Named after Aphrodite, the Greek goddess of love, beauty, and fruitfulness, aphrodisiacs have been sought by humans to drive the opposite sex wild with desire and to rekindle bodily appetite in those whose sex drive has been flagging. Nothing works quite that simply, according to my literature search, but nutritional research suggests that antioxidant nutrients such as superoxide dismutase can help prevent the sexual apparatus—male or female—from aging prematurely. Antioxidant nutrients hold off much of the damage caused by free radicals, which are created in the body as a result of extreme weather changes or exposure to the sun or pollutants.

Free radicals can be defined simply as foreign bodies that invade cell membranes and cut off the oxygen supply. They also stop the development of a cell's regenerative material, playing havoc with the genetic components so that the cell cannot duplicate itself exactly. Spermatozoan cells exposed to free radicals become abnormal, for example, resulting in at least temporary infertility. This kind of cell damage is known as cellular degeneration, and free radicals are among the most destructive causes.

A particularly powerful free radical is the minor product of the many biochemical reactions with oxygen. This destructive free radical is called the superoxide anion radical, and it is dangerous to the neurogenital attachments, among other entities, in the nervous system. Normally, the body keeps single superoxide anions under control by combining them with other superoxide radicals. The body encourages this kind of deactivation—called dismutation—through its use of a family of enzymes known as superoxide dismutates (SOD).

Superoxide dismutates are a class of proteins whose common feature is that they speed the dismutation of the superoxide radical. As food supplements, SOD are part of the armamentarium you can utilize to combat free radicals after overexposure to mutagens, carcinogens, or other pollutants. There are three distinct SOD, each having a different mineral component.

Copper-containing SOD is a large molecule with one atom of copper plus one atom of zinc. The zinc is involved only to give structure to the molecule.

Manganese-containing SOD is present in the body in appreciable amounts and appears to be the most widely distributed in nature. Iron-containing SOD has been found in bacteria. In 1973, an anti-inflammatory protein that had been isolated several years earlier by Dr. J. McCord of Duke University Medical Center was identified as being an SOD.[3]

An oral form of SOD derived from a natural source is now available to the public. The 1-milligram tablets each provide 2,000 units of activity. The principal SOD in this food supplement is copper-containing SOD, while a minor component is manganese-containing SOD, estimated to comprise about 5 to 8 percent. In the body, normal levels of SOD are 50 to 80 micrograms of SOD per 1 milliliter of blood, with the average SOD level being near 60 micrograms. Medical scientists theorize that levels in the blood of less than 50 percent of the norm are lethal, due to the increased toxicity of uncontrolled superoxide radicals.

There is a strong scientific basis for taking SOD supplements for sexual stamina and aphrodisiaclike action. Since exogenous (not made in the body) SOD is a large molecule and may not cross cell membranes, the protein is not likely to work inside the cells. But evidence shows that superoxide radicals are neutralized by SOD in the extracellular spaces, the spaces surrounding the cells. When cellular degeneration begins in the gonads, the release of large numbers of enzymes and flavoproteins takes place in these extracellular spaces. And that is where the supplemental SOD you pop does its main work, which is to offset inflammation.

At this time, the most accepted working hypothesis for the beneficial mechanism of SOD is based on the anti-inflammatory effect. SOD stabilizes the cell membranes or cell components involved in inflammatory events. By reducing cell-membrane damage, premature aging is held back; sexual activity follows a natural course.

"As a physician who specializes in nutritional medicine, I have been involved in the study of SOD for the past several years," said Dr. Milton Fried of Atlanta, Georgia, in *Let's Live.* "The therapeutic possibilities of SOD are mind-boggling, for we have in our grasp a system of enzymes which may allow us to slow down and possibly reverse aging."

Gerontologist and sexologist Dr. Alex Comfort has described the free radicals that SOD counteracts as being somewhat like convention delegates away from their wives. Each free radical is a highly reactive chemical agent running rampant through the body, combining with anything that is nearby and interfering with the functioning of the other molecules in the body. Cumulatively, these free-spirited free radicals can slow down or annihilate sexual response and performance.

SOD research is still in its infancy. While enzymes such as SOD have been used by people since prehistoric times, only recently has the scientific community realized just how and why they work. SOD was not even isolated until 1938, and the importance of the enzyme system has only been recognized since 1960. Traditionally trained nutritionists and dietitians still are not cognizant of SOD's importance in human physiology. However, wholistic nutritionists recommend a daily dosage of 2,000 SOD units, which they feel can do wonders for a person's sexuality, as well as for other bodily functions.

RIBONUCLEIC ACID AND DEOXYRIBONUCLEIC ACID

Ribonucleic acid (RNA) and deoxyribonucleic acid (DNA), taken together or separately as food supplements in pill form, are excellent preservers of the sexual self. And they are mild aphrodisiacs through a unique action.

RNA and DNA are nucleic acids that are similar in structure and synergistic in function. The nucleic acid RNA contains ribose, while DNA has deoxyribose, a five-carbon sugar. Rather than DNA's pyrimidine thymine, RNA has uracil. Pyrimidine and uracil are important heterocyclic organic compounds containing nitrogen atoms. RNA also contains the amino acids adenine and guanine, various bases of the purine groups, and cytosine, a purine-containing compound. As I just stated, almost identical components make up the structure of DNA. All of these constituents form nucleotides, which are the structural units of nucleic acid.

DNA and RNA comprise the master file of instructions for the creation of every type of protein in a body. These instruction carriers are transmitted in the genetic material received at conception. DNA never leaves the nucleus of cells, each one of which has access to the total inherited information but is specialized and calls on just the instructions needed for its own cellular functions. To inform a cell of the proper sequence of amino acids for a needed protein, a type of "photocopy" of the appropriate portion of DNA is made. This copy is messenger RNA (mRNA), which is able to leave the nucleus and seek out and attach itself to one of the ribosomes (protein-makers in cells). Ribosomes receive specifications for amino acids that need to be made and then linked into a protein strand.

Another form of RNA, called transfer RNA (tRNA), collects amino acids from cellular fluid and brings them to the mRNA. For each of the twenty-two amino acids, there is a specific tRNA. Many thousands of tRNA's with amino-acid loads cluster around the ribosomes, much the way vegetable-laden trucks idle around a farmer's market awaiting their turn to unload. When an amino acid is called for by a messenger RNA, a transfer RNA carrying the particular amino acid snaps into position for bonding by an enzyme to complete a protein strand. Then the tRNA and mRNA return for another load of amino acid. In less than a second, forty to one hundred amino acids can be tacked to a growing protein strand.

Proteins are broken down by enzymes (which are themselves proteins) into amino acids. The proteins come from food. The amino acids enter the body cells, where other enzymes put them into long chains using sequences specified by the DNA assisted by RNA. If something could be done to improve this entire metabolic action, all the body systems would benefit—particularly the genital system.

RNA and DNA taken as food supplements are capable of youthful restorations, such as fading age spots, smoothing the complexion, softening skin wrinkles, lessening facial lines, increasing energy levels, improving memory and coordination, and giving new zest to the sex drive. Yet RNA and DNA cannot be absorbed in any appreciable quantities when swallowed as pills. The two nucleic acids are not used by cells in this form, so their effectiveness hinges on the supplying of their "precursors." Such DNA-RNA precursors are common in all organisms, including human beings.

There are four nucleotide precursors into which the nucleic acids are broken down in the intestine. These four nucleotide precursors are absorbed directly into the cells. When a body's sexual apparatus begins to slow down and not do what it should, part of the reason is that the gonadal cells have lost their capacity to transcribe the information contained in their nuclei into protein (protein synthesis). One of the fundamental metabolic abilities whose loss leads to this loss of capacity is the ability to synthesize RNA and DNA precursors, which consist of carbohydrate, amino, purine, pyrimidine, and other molecules. The synthesis requires a great deal of energy from each cell, in addition to an elaborate amount of cellular machinery in the form of enzymes.

If the RNA and DNA precursors are supplied in extra amounts, the cells can more easily produce their own RNA and DNA. They will take carbohydrate precursors, amine precursors, and one- and two-carbon fragment precursors and synthesize them into the purine and pyrimidine molecules that go on to make the nucleotides that are ultimately generated and transformed into the RNA and DNA polymers of the nucleotides. To get extra precursors, you must supplement your diet with DNA and RNA compounds that can generate them. The body, which is the greatest synthesizer of them all, will then produce its own RNA and DNA on its own genetic template.

Anyone can tell if RNA and DNA supplementation is needed. Age spots on the hands or face are indications of the loss of certain cells in the skin. This means that the cells have an inability to regenerate themselves as they normally would. This degeneration comes about from the cells' feebleness in producing the RNA and DNA precursors. Lack of libido indicates the same thing.

A usual supplementation dose is 324.0 milligrams of ribonucleic acid and 32.4 milligrams of deoxyribonucleic acid (a ratio of 10 milligrams of RNA to 1 milligram of DNA) in a base of primary-grown yeast, which is an ancient mineral sea deposit perfectly chelated by nature. (Sometimes the RNA–DNA ratio is one to one, with 100 milligrams of each nucleic acid made into a single tablet.) You might also add freeze-dried *Lactobacillus acidophilus* and *Lactobacillus bifidus* (two yogurt-forming bacteria), lactose, associated B-complex vitamins, and trace minerals such as silica, chromium, selenium, calcium, magnesium, and other natural factors occurring in the yeast and mineral sea deposit for which no particular nutritional or dietary claims are made. However, know that they are probably doing you some good.

ALOE VERA

A relative of the lily and onion, aloe vera looks like a cactus plant and grows in warm, arid regions. It has long, slender leaves that are filled with a gelatinous liquid, the source of the benefits this plant supplies. The gel, made into a drink, is an excellent aphrodisiac for men in particular but also for women.

There are nearly 200 types of aloe plants. All of them have the same genus name of *Aloe*, but they spring from different species, such as *Aloe africana*, *Aloe perryi*, *Aloe ferox*, *Aloe spicata*, *Aloe succotrina*, and *Aloe vera*. The rich gel of each of these species is a storehouse of nutrition and water. In recent years, the aloe vera species has been the center of a multimillion-dollar industry as a health food, skin-care preparation, cosmetic, and now aphrodisiac.

Aloe vera is known for its ability to thrive in climates where there may be no soil moisture for long periods. The plant produces flowers and has a stem that is short and squat. Its fleshy leaves can grow to lengths of two feet and are arranged in a rosette. The plant's outer skin is smooth, fairly thick, and rubbery in texture. For thousands of years, in tropical climates, humans have applied the tart juice of the leaves to the body as a treatment for sunburn and other skin problems. In millions of Western homes, aloe has been cultivated for its use as a first aid in the treatment of cuts, burns, and abrasions.

Some people talk about aloe vera juice as if it were just one juice, confusing the characteristics of the two separate liquids in the aloe vera leaf. The yellow liquid lying just under the leaf rind has been incorporated into pharmaceuticals as a natural laxative for many years. The clear interior cellular gel, on the other hand, is not a pharmaceutical. Instead, it is a natural food product and can be consumed like any other fruit or vegetable drink. This clear gel from the central portion of the leaf has a clean, fresh taste, improved lately by the newer methods of processing, which remove certain nonbeneficial components. If you desire, mix the gel in equal parts with fruit or vegetable juices to vary the aloe vera taste. Additionally, some manufac-turers mix the gel with citrus flavoring and water at the factory. You can also drink aloe juice directly from the bottle; the daily dose is one-half cupful. In its pure form, aloe vera is an excellent aphrodisiacal drink.

Dr. Robert Picker of Berkeley, California, explained in an interview reported in the magazine *Public Scrutiny*:

> I've known about aloe vera for quite some time. . . . About five months ago, the general manager of a local company contacted me with a whole list of cases she had known about—people who had obtained fantastic results from this aloe vera juice. Out of curiosity, I started calling these people and documenting the stories I heard and, indeed, they were pretty remarkable stories. I talked to a few doctors around the country who had been using this. One of them in Arizona told me this was the closest thing to a panacea he'd ever found. I got curious enough to start using it in my practice. . . . I've used it now with over three hundred people. I started seeing results that corroborated the kind of stories that I'd been hearing.

In my own interview of another aloe vera distributor, I learned about women who have been marveling over the effects of aloe vera on their husbands. The distributor said that these women have reported how their husbands "chase their wives around the room" after drinking aloe. Many of the principal oils, vitamins, minerals, amino acids, and other ingredients of aloe vera juice have sexually stimulating qualities. These ingredients, many of which have already been described, include:

Inorganic ingredients. Calcium, chlorine, manganese, potassium, and sodium.

Monosaccharides and polysaccharides. Glucose, mannose, and uric acid.

Vitamins. Thiamine (vitamin B_1), riboflavin (vitamin B_2), niacinamide (vitamin B_3), pyridoxine (vitamin B_6), vitamin C, and choline.

Amino acids. Alanine, arginine, aspartic acid, glutamic acid, glycine, half-cystine, histidine, hydroxyproline, isoleucine, leucine, lysine, methionine, phenylalanine, proline, serine, threonine, tyrosine, and valine.

Other. Aloin, barbaloin, cinnamic acid, emodin, emoding lucosides of d arabinose, esther of cinnamic acid, ethereal oil, isobarbaloin, and resitannol.

In addition to its aphrodisiacal properties, aloe vera has certain health and medicinal characteristics that make it quite valuable. It is approved by the FDA for the treatment of burns and minor skin problems. Inasmuch as aloe vera is known to be safe for internal application, both physicians and laypersons take it as an adjunct to their regular health programs. Aloe vera, when used topically or internally:

- Is an unusually good natural skin cleanser and bowel cleanser.

- Penetrates tissue almost like dimethyl sulfoxide (DMSO). (For a discussion of DMSO, see page 190.)
- Anesthetizes the tissue in the area to which it is applied, relieving pain deep beneath the surface, including in joints and muscles.
- Is bactericidal when applied in high concentrations for several hours directly on infectious bacteria.
- Is viricidal when applied in high concentrations for long periods directly on viruses.
- Is fungicidal when applied in high concentrations for long periods directly on fungi.
- Reduces bleeding time.
- Is antipyretic, or reduces fever.
- Is anti-inflammatory, with an action similar to that of a steroid.
- Is antipruritic, or stops itching.
- Is nutritional, providing a wide range of vitamins, minerals, and simple carbohydrates.
- Dilates capillaries, increasing blood supply in the area to which it is applied.[4]
- Breaks down and digests dead tissue including pus through the action of proteolytic enzymes, hastening the degenerative phase of healing.[5]
- Enhances epithelization, or normal cell proliferation, hastening the regenerative phase of healing.
- Moisturizes tissue.
- Is safe for both internal and external use. It is comparable in safety, in fact, with any edible tropical fruit or vegetable and has been swallowed as a drink by hundreds of thousands of people of all ages from infants to the elderly in the United States and throughout the world since 400 B.C. In the laboratory, test animals have been fed aloe vera to the capacity of their stomachs and have had no ill effects.

Aloe vera comes in capsules or as a drink in liquid or gel form.

SPIRULINA

Spirulina is a blue-green alga that is eaten by many people to increase their energy, clarity of mind, or sexual vigor. Spirulina has a high chlorophyll content and is extremely rich in nutrients such as vitamins A, B3, B6, B12, and E. It is also high in the nutritional pigments phycocyanin, xanthophyll, and carotene. Japanese researchers have shown that in humans, spirulina activates the production of hormones, especially adrenaline and insulin, as well as increasing the efficiency of the nervous system and supplying glycogen reserves to the muscles.

Furthermore, there are several essential minerals present in spirulina, the most notable being iron and calcium gluconate. During processing, sodium ascorbate (vitamin C) is added to preserve spirulina's nutritional value. In his book *Spirulina: Nature's Diet Supplement Rediscovered*, Maurice Hanssen presents a nutritional analysis of the microalga. He points out that it is the richest source of natural protein yet found, containing 60 to 71 percent protein, of which 37 percent (a bit less than that of dried egg but more than that of powdered skim milk, brewer's yeast, or soy flour) is usable. Spirulina has all eight essential amino acids—without cholesterol—and stands on a par with honeybee pollen as one of the world's most perfect foods. (For a discussion of honeybee pollen, see Chapter 6.)

Spirulina is now recognized as the most promising of all microalgae as a food source for starving populations. It can be grown continuously and harvested inexpensively on a large scale. The United Nations has performed in-depth studies of the substance and has concluded that it is high in complete protein, vitamins, and minerals while, at the same time, being more easily digestible than any other food because of its lack of cellulose. The ingredients of spirulina, according to the United Nations Laboratories' chemical analyses, include:

Essential amino acids. Isoleucine, leucine, lysine, methionine, phenylalanine, threonine, tryptophan, and valine.

Nonessential amino acids. Alanine, arginine, aspartic acid, cystine, glutamic acid, glycine, histidine, proline, serine, and tyrosine.

Vitamins. Thiamine (vitamin B_1), riboflavin (vitamin B_2), nicotinic acid (a form of vitamin B_3), pyridoxine (vitamin B_6), cyanocobalamin (vitamin B_{12}), tocopherol (vitamin E), biotin, d-ca-pantothenate, folic acid, and inositol.

Minerals. Calcium, chloride, iron, magnesium, manganese, phosphorus, potassium, sodium, and zinc.

Included in spirulina's 8-percent fat content is gamma-linolenic acid, which previously had been found only in human milk and evening primrose oil (see page 109). Gamma-linolenic acid has been found valuable in treating an assortment of physical problems including impotency, frigidity, lack of libido, and premature ejaculation. It is a natural aphrodisiac.

Among its other uses, spirulina is also a diet aid. The protein substance in the microalga helps you to lose weight safely and steadily, and to maintain permanent loss without too much effort. It is not a drug and is therefore completely safe. When taken an hour before a meal, spirulina coats the lining of the stomach and provides a feeling of satisfying fullness. At mealtime, although you will want to eat, you will not eat as much.

Spirulina grows in alkaline lakes, in which the saline conditions limit the development of other organisms. It grows very rapidly on the surface of the lake until it is so dense that light, necessary for its growth, cannot penetrate it. The spirulina is then scooped off the lake and dried by a spraying process, without any discharge of industrial waste, just the recycling of lake water. The lakes from which spirulina is extracted are not polluted, rendering the substance contamination-free. The yield is potentially enormous, on an area basis some twenty times more than that of soybeans, over forty times more than that of corn, and five hundred times more than that of beef. Furthermore, no arable land is required for spirulina's growth. It fixes nitrogen from the atmosphere and requires no chemical fertilizer.

Spirulina is one of the oldest plants in the world, dating back 3 billion years. It was popular with the Aztecs, who mixed it with maize. However, when the Spanish conquistadors arrived in Mexico, they restricted its use. History indicates that the Spanish wanted to hold down the birth rate of the Aztecs, who in large numbers would have proven a danger to the conquistadors. Still, spirulina remains a staple of the Kanenbu people, who live in Africa near Lake Chad, one of the rare unpolluted spots left in the world. The Kanenbu eat spirulina as part of a dish called *dihe*, a mixture of millet, spirulina, vegetables, herbs, and spices. Dihe is delicious, nutritious, and aphrodisiacal. For a recipe, see page 105.

Spirulina is available at most health food stores. It comes in powder, tablet, or capsule form.

EICOSAPENTAENOIC ACID (EPA)
AND DOCOSAHEXAENOIC ACID (DHA)

In the 1970s, epidemiological studies of Eskimos and Japanese living by the sea were conducted. The studies showed that both of these populations had a relatively low incidence of coronary heart disease and were exceedingly active sexually. And, correspondingly, both populations had diets that included substantial amounts of fatty fish, fish oil, and other marine life.

The results of the studies stimulated researchers to wonder if there is a link between the frequency of sexual intercourse, the number of heart attacks, and the amount of fish oil ingested. If so, they wondered, what is the link?

All the animal, vegetable, and seed fats and oils that enter the human body are converted by the body's metabolism into more fundamental chemical materials. One category of these materials is fatty acids, which play an important metabolic role. Fatty acids supply nearly half of the calories burned by the body for energy and are utilized by almost all of the tissues. The gonads in particular make use of fatty acids, for hormone production and for the transfer of neurogenital impulse waves to the brain. Remarkably, there are relatively few fatty acids—only nineteen are commonly found in fats and oils. Most fatty acids are naturally produced by the body, but some must be obtained through the diet.

Dihe

One of the main ingredients of this popular Kanenbu dish is spirulina, a blue-green alga that increases energy, clarity of mind, and sexual vigor.

3 cups water
1 cup raw millet
1/2 cup vegetable stock or water
1 tablespoon spirulina powder
1/4 cup chopped onion
1 clove garlic, finely chopped
1 tablespoon oil
1/2 cup chopped red and green sweet pepper
1/4 cup chopped pimiento

1. *In a medium-size saucepan, combine the 3 cups water and the raw millet. Bring to a boil, then cover the saucepan, reduce the heat, and simmer the millet until all the liquid has evaporated, about 30 minutes. Drain the millet if necessary.*

2. *Meanwhile, in a blender, combine the vegetable stock or water with the spirulina powder.*

3. *In a large saucepan, sauté the onion and garlic in the oil. Add the sweet pepper and pimiento, and continue to sauté. Add the diluted spirulina and stir until the mixture reaches a uniform sauce consistency.*

4. *To serve, ladle a portion of the millet into a bowl and cover with sauce. If desired, season with salt and pepper to taste (limit the salt).*

Makes 4 servings.

Fatty acids, which were discussed in part in Chapter 2, can be described as the chemical building blocks from which fats and oils (or lipids) are made. They are composed of chains of molecules. The backbone of this chain is carbon atoms, which can be pictured as linking up in a line. Each fatty acid has a particular number of carbon atoms in its chain. The number of carbon atoms can range from two to as many as twenty-six. The most common chain has eighteen carbon atoms.

Once the body converts fat into fatty acids, it continues the metabolic process, synthesizing the acids into what are termed prostaglandins. Prostaglandins are hormonelike substances present in a wide variety of tissues and body fluids, including the uterus, testicles, semen, brain, lungs, and kidneys. Prostaglandins have many actions, one of which causes contractions of the uterus; for this reason, prostaglandins have been used therapeutically to aid labor and induce abortion. Prostaglandins were discovered in the 1970s.

Another acknowledged role of prostaglandins is helping with blood clotting. Blood clotting is controlled by tiny disc-shaped particles that are carried in the bloodstream. These particles, called platelets, group together, or aggregate, around injured blood vessels. Prostaglandins and prostaglandin derivatives affect blood clotting by either promoting or inhibiting this aggregation of platelets. Whether a prostaglandin is pro-aggregative or anti-aggregative is believed to be determined by the fatty acid from which the prostaglandin is synthesized. Normally, prostaglandins from saturated fats promote aggregation, and those from unsaturated or polyunsaturated fats inhibit it.

The danger of platelet aggregation is that sometimes platelets continue to congregate in the same sites in arteries and eventually help to create a clot that obstructs or completely blocks blood flow. When this occurs in an artery leading to the heart, a heart attack (myocardial infarction) can result. When an artery that supplies blood to the brain is blocked, a stroke can result. Even a clot that forms in an arm or leg can be extremely serious because blood flow to the limb can be blocked or the clot can break off from its original site and be carried through the bloodstream until it lodges in another part of the body. Clotting in any of the blood vessels supplying the gonads or other sexual organs can cause sexual dysfunction resulting in impotence, lack of libido, poor orgasmic response, or a similar problem.

Blood-platelet aggregation can also promote the buildup in the blood vessels of the fatty substance known as cholesterol. Cholesterol exists in all animal tissues and is found in high levels in saturated fats. Most cholesterol comes from the diet, although the human body itself also produces some cholesterol. Scientists are now able to detect five different kinds of cholesterol in the blood. Research findings show that one type of cholesterol—low-density lipoprotein (LDL) cholesterol—is bad and has a greater likelihood of building up along artery walls. Another form of cholesterol—high-density lipoprotein (HDL) cholesterol—is good and may play a role in removing unwanted types of cholesterol from the body.

If cholesterol accumulates along artery walls, it promotes atherosclerosis, commonly known as hardening of the arteries. Atherosclerosis causes arteries to narrow, which restricts or even blocks blood flow. And, like blood clots, atherosclerosis can lead to stroke, heart attack, poor sexual performance, and apathetic sexual response.

A final factor to consider in the relationship between diet, sexuality, and metabolism are triglycerides. Glyceride particles are formed during the digestion of dietary fat. High levels of triglycerides in the blood (serum triglycerides) have been shown to be associated with increased risk of degenerative disease involving the heart, blood vessels, gonads, general endocrine system, nervous system, or almost any other system of the body.

Exactly what was shown by the studies of the sexually active Eskimos and Japanese living near the sea? The diets of both these populations were very high in fatty fish, fish oil, and other marine life. The people were found to have low levels of bad, or LDL, cholesterol and a relatively reduced tendency for their blood to clot. And, as would be expected from the serum levels, both populations had a very low incidence of coronary heart disease. Both were an exceedingly healthy people naturally performing the sexual act in the way their strong sexual instincts directed.

Further study showed that the Eskimos and Japanese living by the sea had high levels of two particular fatty acids, namely eicosapentaenoic acid (EPA) and docosahexaenoic acid (DHA). EPA and DHA originate far down the food chain, in minute free-floating plants and animals that serve as the direct or indirect food sources for all sea creatures. These nutrient acids are found only in fish, fish oils, and the fat of marine mammals that live on fish. Of course, fish is the mainstay of the diet of both of the populations studied. EPA and DHA are not found in vegetable oils, land animals, or dairy products.

In examining the effects of EPA and DHA on the human body, the researchers reflected on the historical changes in the eating habits of Western society. The investigation showed that over the past one hundred years, the amount of fatty fish consumed and the amount of EPA and DHA taken in have dropped significantly. The researchers attributed this change largely to the public's preference for nonoily fish, which became more readily available with the advent of modern transportation, and to the increase in the price of oily fish relative to other forms of protein. The American diet as well as the diets of other nations changed to include higher amounts of animal meat, vegetable oils, and other saturated fats. The Western diet became almost devoid of EPA and DHA. And, at the same time, sexual dysfunction and cardiovascular disease escalated.

Only a few isolated populations—such as the Eskimos and Japanese living by the sea—continue to consume a diet rich in fatty fish. What further information could researchers gain from these populations about the relevance of diet to frequency of lovemaking and protection from heart problems?

In order to better assess the significance of a diet rich in fatty fish, a comparative study was made of fishing communities and farming communities in Japan. The study showed that the fishing communities had a higher daily intake of fish than did the farming communities and that the fishermen had correspondingly higher levels of EPA and DHA in their blood. The fishermen also had a reduced tendency toward blood-platelet aggregation. Based on the results of this and other studies, the researchers theorized that a diet including large amounts of fatty fish may increase the levels of EPA and DHA in the blood, which might, in turn, help deter cardiovascular problems and enhance sexual ability.

A new question then arose: Was there a need to supplement the diets of Western populations with foods rich in EPA and DHA, and if so, what effect would this have? In accordance with accepted scientific practice, these questions were examined through experiments with animals. Various researchers around the world conducted experiments to explore the significance and safety of an EPA-and-DHA-rich diet. The results of the studies showed conclusively that animals fed EPA- and DHA-rich foods and oils had lower levels of LDL cholesterol, reduced blood-clotting tendencies, better protection from cardiovascular disease, and improved production of progeny in comparison to control groups. Importantly, these experiments with laboratory animals clearly demonstrated the safety of a diet rich in EPA and DHA.

K.J. Kingsbury and associates fed volunteers 50 grams of cod-liver oil per day for up to twenty-three days. They reported in *The Lancet* that they found a decrease in serum cholesterol of approximately 27 percent. This reduction was not sustained after the oil supplement was discontinued.[6]

In *The Journal of the American Medical Association,* a study conducted at the University of Oregon Health Sciences Center, Portland, Oregon, was reported. During a ten-day diet of salmon, which contains both EPA and DHA, plasma cholesterol levels dropped by 17 percent in presumably healthy volunteers and by 20 percent or more in patients who had elevated cholesterol levels. The triglyceride levels fell by as much as 67 percent in those whose levels had been elevated originally.[7]

What recommendations can be drawn from the results of these studies? Most authorities agree that the consumption of saturated fats should be controlled, and while the role of cholesterol is still being debated, the American Heart Association, the U.S. Department of Agriculture, and the U.S. Department of Health and Human Services all recommend that the consumption of foods high in cholesterol should be limited.

Evidence shows that EPA and DHA are not naturally produced in the human body but instead must come from dietary sources. It is possible to do as one researcher did and adopt the eating habits of Eskimos, but it is unlikely that many people will choose to do so. In fact, there is probably a limit to the number of times each week that anyone would want to eat fatty fish. In addition, many people also strongly dislike the taste of oils such as cod-liver oil and are unwilling to use them.

A specially formulated dietary supplement of EPA and DHA is available in capsule form. The capsules also have free fatty acids, vitamin A, and vitamin E. The capsules contain a natural concentrate of selected marine oils. The concentrate is based on triglycerides, which have been shown to promote the positive effects of EPA and DHA in the body. The capsules themselves are made of natural gelatin, glycerin, and water, with no sugars, starches, colors, flavorings, or preservatives added. For more information about these capsules, or to purchase a supply, contact your local health food store.

EVENING PRIMROSE OIL

There is a superb aphrodisiacal nutrient that is neither a vitamin nor a hormone. Rather, this nutrient is the herb that is the source of two of the unsaturated fatty acids essential in nutrition. Vitamins are organic chemicals that are present in foods in very small amounts. They are, of course, necessary for good health. If a vitamin is missing from the diet, a specific disease will likely occur because certain vitamins—such as ascorbic acid—cannot be made by the body. Hormones are similar to vitamins; the difference is that hormones are made by the endocrine glands. If the normal body chemistry does not produce certain hormones adequately, then related symptoms or diseases may occur.

The source of the specific fatty acids that produce heightened sexual response is the natural oil of evening primrose. Evening primrose oil is known as the only source—other than mother's milk—of both linoleic acid and gamma-linolenic acid (GLA). These two acids help the body to manufacture the beneficial compounds known as prostaglandins, which regulate a wide range of body functions including blood pressure, cholesterol levels, and sexual hormone response.

At a semiannual meeting of the American Academy of Medical Preventics, David Horrobin, Ph.D., of Montreal, Canada, gave a lecture on evening primrose oil. Dr. Horrobin, an acknowledged expert on the subject, said that the level of prostaglandins is crucial to the body. A fall in the level will lead to a potentially catastrophic series of events including increased blood clotting, elevated cholesterol levels in the blood, diabeticlike changes in insulin release, weakening of the immune system, susceptibility to depression, greater risk of inflammation, disruption in the transmittal of nerve impulses, deregulation of calcium ions in the blood, and disruption of all types of cellular responses to stimuli including sexual stimuli.

Indeed, insufficient prostaglandins in the body due to an inadequate intake of GLA will produce any number of sexual symptoms. In a woman, menstrual cramps may become more severe. During intercourse or masturbation, a man may have insufficient ejaculate. Both men and women may become infertile. The diets eaten in modern Western societies can bring on these symptoms because they are low in linoleic acid and gamma-linolenic acid.

A woman who is suffering from premenstrual tension or cystic mastitis (hollow tumors in the breasts) can get relief by using evening primrose oil in combination with other nutrients. It is well-known, for instance, that vitamin B6 helps reduce fluid accumulation just prior to menstruation. Vitamin E also aids at that time. Together, vitamin B6, vitamin E, and evening primrose oil do an excellent job of preventing premenstrual tension.

Vitamin B6 helps the effort by converting linoleic acid into prostaglandins. Vitamin E keeps away disadvantageous compounds called leukotrienes and stimulates the production of prostaglandins. Evening primrose oil allows GLA to bypass inefficient linoleic acid conversion and work directly on the body to enhance prostaglandin production. Dr. Horrobin explained that the secret is for the woman not to wait until she begins to experience PMS; rather, about a week before her period is due, the woman should begin taking 1,000 milligrams of evening primrose oil three times a day. She should also take 50 milligrams of Vitamin B6 daily and 200 to 600 IU of vitamin E daily, split into two or three doses.

Additionally, women who are troubled by prolonged or heavy menstrual bleeding should remain on the combination of nutrients throughout the month, not just at the monthly period. After a few cycles, the monthly hemorrhaging should be normalized.

Benign breast disease, or cystic mastitis, which affects about 20 percent of menstruating women, may come from an overproduction of the hormone prolactin and a shortage of prostaglandins. Hard, lumpy cystic tumors are usually felt in the upper, outer sections of the breasts. These tumors become larger during menstruation and then diminish in size when menstruation is over. Benign cystic growths are not the forerunners of cancer, but they do hurt occasionally and certainly are frightening.

Evening primrose oil in the same dosage taken for PMS can help prevent cyst development and may cause existing lumps to resolve themselves. The softening and eventual disappearance of the cysts usually takes place within two to four months. And while a woman is taking the nutrient, she will also experience an elevation in sexual desire because evening primrose oil is a natural, nutritional aphrodisiac.

EXTERNALLY APPLIED APHRODISIACS

There are two ways in which to use food supplements for sustaining an erection. One is to eat the food, and the other is to apply it externally.

To prevent slackness of the penis, a man should indulge in a short period of preparation before a prolonged sexual session. About one hour prior to the sexual encounter, the man should wash his penis with warm water and milk, dry it, and rub in some musk oil or ambergris. Musk oil and ambergris are two highly prized products of the perfume industry. They are available at most perfume counters. Musk oil is derived from the musk ox and has traces of sheep testosterone in it. Ambergris is a grayish waxy substance excreted in the intestines of sperm whales. Usually found floating on the surface of the ocean in regions frequented by whales, it comes in masses of 60 to 225 pounds. Ambergris tends to concentrate perfume odors.

Ambergris and musk oil can cause a contractile reaction in the muscles of the penis, so that erectile tissues can remain stiff. While not strictly food for the digestive system, they definitely are food for the male sex organ. They are good for erecting the female sex organ, too, since the clitoris is stimulated by their direct application.

Another way to stimulate a full erection is to wash the penis before intercourse with an infusion of celery seeds. Follow this with a penis massage of oil of purslane. Oil of lily of the valley is said by herbologists to have the same effect. These three plant products—lily-of-the-valley oil, purslane oil, and celery seed—can be ordered from an herbologist. Before employing them, however, you should get advice from a competent doctor or herbologist.

Chapter 6

HONEYBEE POLLEN FOR SEXUAL VIGOR

I am good looking, twenty-nine years old, five feet ten inches tall, and 175 pounds in weight, and I have a problem that may make you laugh. I have never had sex with any woman in my life. I'm not afraid to get involved. It's just that I seem to have no strength even to try an approach. Any time I'm in the right place at the right time to make out with a desirable female, I lose my energy. Total tiredness comes over me. My eyelids actually shut, and I could fall into a deep sleep standing right there in the singles bar with couples drinking, talking, dancing, smoking, and making out all around me.

My pickup may have let me know that she's willing to go to bed, and I may feel extremely horny, but I always have barely enough energy left to just get in my car and go home.

This is a serious problem, for without energy, I will never be able to enjoy a fulfilling sexual relationship. I've gone to a shrink, and he studied my background but couldn't seem to find any psychological reason for my chronic fatigue. I'm beginning to suspect my fatigue is physical—maybe nutritional. Is there something I could eat during the day or at dinner that might help me hold on to my energy? I want so much to try having sex with a woman without losing the strength it takes.

Joseph C.
Chicago, Illinois

I am a forty-four-year-old married woman who has never experienced an orgasm during sexual intercourse. I'm not frigid. I've managed to climax by myself through masturbation with my vibrator.

At first I thought my husband was at fault because of an inability to make love to a woman properly. My husband and I have been married almost twenty years. But now I'm having an affair with a man who is thirteen years my junior, and I can't feel an orgasm with his penis inside me either.

However, this younger man has awakened sexual desires in me that I didn't know existed. When I am near him, I long to be touched, kissed, and hugged. Our sex life is fantastic, except that I never have a penis-stimulated orgasm. And my lover ejaculates only after he has worked hard trying to bring me to a climax.

It's not that I just lie there and let my lover do the work. I get on top and take control. But the main part of my problem is that I run out of steam. My breathing quickens, my heart beats furiously, my pelvis pumps forcefully, my excitement mounts, and then suddenly my stamina gives out. It just abandons me. I lose my energy, gasp for air, become weak, and collapse, frustrated and longing for a resurgence of strength to rub my "love button" just a little bit more. In the meantime, my man lets his orgasm come.

If only I could find some way to get more energy. What am I going to do? I believe that if my stamina stayed with me longer, I would reach an orgasm. Can you suggest a solution—a food, an exercise, or a technique to give me the vitality I'm lacking? I want to feel that glorious penis-induced climax that I hear other women describe.

Phyllis C.
Cleveland, Ohio

Many men and women who have a diminished or unsatisfactory sex life are being swindled by their lack of energy. Without enough energy, it is not possible to fully enjoy a sexual relationship—no matter how much it is desired.

In the movie *Everything You Always Wanted to Know About Sex*, Woody Allen's character was living with a woman. Both the Allen character and his girlfriend were having psychological problems. In one scene, Allen visited a psychiatrist and complained that his sex life was dismally poor. He described his unhappiness over engaging in sexual relations less than three times a week. In another scene, Allen's girlfriend was talking to the same psychiatrist. She complained that Woody was a sex maniac—he wanted her to have sex more than twice a week.

Sometimes people who are short on energy see others who attain sexual satisfaction on a regular basis as being "oversexed." Yet sexuality usually is not the problem—low energy levels are. Energy, or vigor, is staying power; it is the feeling of readiness to accomplish an act of joy, do a piece of work, meet a challenge, or chalk up some other achievement. Feelings of vigor often have a nutritional basis. Certain foods have the ability to produce energy in the people who eat them.

SEARCHING OUT FOODS FOR SEXUAL VIGOR

Unfortunately, when people attempt to find foods that heighten sexual response, they are frequently blocked in their search by the technological realities of industrialized Western civilization. Technology has interfered with the food supply. Robert Rodale, former publisher of *Prevention* and *Organic Gardening and Farming* magazines, said:

> For all our endless variety of available food, it is close to impos-
> sible to be well-nourished on what you can buy at our deceptively

plentiful supermarkets. Nature is perfectly willing to provide us with a richness of nutrition. . . . But alas, nature is no longer in command. . . . As a result the food does not reach us as proper food anymore.[1]

The processed food that is eaten today is inadequate for maintaining proper sexual health. Nutrients are lost through unnatural farming and food processing methods, and poisonous chemicals are introduced into foods by agriculture and industry. Nutritionist Carlton Fredericks, Ph.D., has been warning of the effects of technology on food production for more than fifty years. Dr. Fredericks believes that many of our foods spring from soil that has been overcultivated or underfertilized, yielding vegetables or fruits that are below standard in vitamin and mineral content.

The New York Times, on December 6, 1972, quoted Dr. George M. Briggs, nutrition expert formerly with the University of California, Berkeley, who testified before the U.S. Senate Committee on Nutrition and Human Needs. Dr. Briggs said:

Americans have turned into a nation of nutritional illiterates who know so little about what to eat that the annual cost of malnutrition among rich and poor alike may be $30 billion. . . . Mother is no longer the major source of knowledge for food selection. The sources are now the label, the ad, the menu, the grocery store or the school. People are eating less than in 1900, but exercise has decreased so much faster that the resulting excess of food is there for all to see . . . around people's middles. The development of fabricated foods containing nothing but calories is irresponsible.

In his book *Please, Doctor, Do Something!* Dr. Joe D. Nichols of Atlanta, Texas, founder of National Food Associates, said:

From those wonderful people who gave us DDT and white enriched bread and chemical additives and white sugar and sodium cyclamates, we learn that America is a healthy nation and that our food supply is safe, abundant, and nourishing. . . . We are faced with the inescapable conclusion that America is *not* a healthy nation. . . . This is the reason Americans have become frantic in their search for health.

Additionally, people are poorly nourished because they eat so many meals in restaurants. The National Restaurant Association reported that in 1987, food-away-from-home expenditures accounted for 60 percent of the total food dollar; this figure is anticipated to increase to 74 percent by 1996.[2] Few urban families still routinely gather around the dining room table; this once-sacred family-life institution has been gradually eroding. Hamburgers, hot dogs, fish and chips, fried chicken, pizza, pancakes, seafood, tacos, and roast beef are the more common limited-menu foods served up in fast-food restaurants today. Sales at such fast-food chains as McDonald's and Roy Rogers have been increasing by about 15 percent every year.

What has been the result of this sort of nutrition adulteration? The late Dr. Henry G. Bieler, an orthomolecular physician who corrected sexual dysfunction using nutrition, said that few people in the United States today are sexually healthy. He wrote:

> We have flouted, mutilated, and broken all the simple laws of Nature. Man, out of his frustration and his conditioning and his desire for ease has created unnatural food substitutes which offer little or no nutritional value. And in his ignorance, he has stuffed himself with these foods, disturbing his digestive system, punishing his liver and kidneys, forcing other parts of the body, such as his endocrine glands, sex glands, and finally his heart to eliminate the accumulated toxins vicariously, eventually causing ill health as we know it and sometimes premature death.[3]

During fifty-five years of medical practice, this veteran physician treated many patients for sexual problems resulting from poor eating. Dr. Bieler believed that since sex is expressed in terms of energy (the orgasm, in fact, being a discharge of excess energy), no one can have a complete orgasm if he or she is ill and malfunctioning due to toxic substances being present in the body.

Dr. Bieler had many female patients who complained about sexual problems. The most common problems were frigidity and a feeling of being used as a sex machine, lack of tactile feeling in the nipples of the breasts (usually one of the most sensitive areas in a woman), difficulty in achieving orgasm, lack of feeling in the vagina, and, in many cases, a burning, acid sensation from a man's seminal discharge.

The sexual complaints of Dr. Bieler's male patients were varied. The men complained of impotence, premature ejaculation, and acid burns on the penis after entering a woman. The acid burns, Dr. Bieler said, were caused by toxic secretions eliminated through women's vaginas. "Most men do not establish erective response to effective sexual stimulation for a matter of minutes . . . the erection may not be as full or as demanding as that to which the older man was previously accustomed."

The solution to most sexual problems is improved sexual nutrition, declared Dr. Bieler and his disciples, who practice wholistically. Too bad foods that build sexual vigor are rare in our daily diet. Honeybee pollen is definitely among the energy foods, but how many people do you know who regularly eat honeybee pollen?

HEIGHTEN YOUR SEX LIFE WITH HONEYBEE POLLEN

Physicians who are members of the Academy of Orthomolecular Psychiatry say that most of the foods in the daily Western diet are merely artifacts recombined by processors into products designed to please consumers' palates. These "foods" contain little actual nutrition. In consequence, it is difficult to find a really complete food for building up sexual vigor.

The human digestive tract will need several thousand years to evolve and learn how best to utilize the new "plastic" foods. The artificial and processed foods of modern society provide insufficient energy for full sexual vigor. The producers of packaged supermarket foods tend to ignore the fundamental orchestra principle of harmony in the human digestive and absorption processes. Refined foods offer metabolic discord. They lack the accessory factors found in whole, natural foods. A missing nutrient makes the body like a fiddle with a broken string.

Honeybee pollen not only produces no discord in the body, but it also acts as a neutralizer of any artificial substances that may be present in other foods consumed. It is one of the foods that offer greater amounts of vigor and can be considered primary sources of sexual vigor.

Honeybee pollen provides vigor through the release of high-energy chemical bonds and the generation of adenosine triphosphate (ATP). ATP, a compound that contains adenine, ribose, and three phosphate molecular groups, occurs in human body cells. The chemical bonds of the phosphate groups comprise the stored energy needed by the cell for nervous response, metabolic maintenance, and muscle contraction. The stored energy is released when ATP is created from adenosine diphosphate (ADP) or adenosine monophosphate (AMP) using energy derived from the breakdown of carbohydrates or other food substances.

To visualize how phosphate-group chemical bonds provide immense quantities of quick energy when the demand arises suddenly, picture the chemical bonds of bee pollen as twisted rubber cables tied to a helium-filled balloon. See the balloon as latent sexual desire always ready to pop up to the surface of your psyche.

Into your surroundings comes a highly sensual person who excites your libido. To satisfy the urgency you feel, your body first searches for the required sexual vigor. Because you have eaten wisely, your body finds this energy quickly by splitting those hypothetical stretched rubber cables that are holding the energy from the bee pollen you consumed. Your balloon of desire and sexual vigor is released with an upward surge. The energy released by snapping those stretched cables is tremendous. The snap represents the staying power waiting to be used in the high-energy bonds of the phosphate groups—energy derived from eating bee pollen.

Honeybee pollen is a food that affords excellent energy potential. It

contains natural hormonal substances that stimulate and nourish the reproductive systems of both men and women, with a direct impact on sexual
ability. As mentioned, it provides stamina for a muscular staying power of
pelvic movement, so that orgasm can be attained. It is a natural, organic,
and sensational food substance.

Honeybee pollen could be a major food source for the world. It is one of
the most nutritionally complete foods in existence, causing no ill side effects
for most people. Honeybee pollen possesses 185 known nutritional ingredients, including 22 amino acids (and more of each of the 8 essential ones
by weight than do the traditional high-protein foods), 27 mineral salts, and
the full range of known vitamins, plus hormones, enzymes, carbohydrates,
and fats. But some of the greatest values of this product of the beehive may
stem from elements that are still unknown to science. Benefits are also
derived from the synergistic action of all the elements.

Since honeybee pollen is loaded with this variety of nutrients, it gives the
voluntary muscles a vast collection of food components to draw upon for
energy. Sexual vigor requires energy expenditure from different sources in
the production of hormones, neurotransmitters, enzymes, and cofactors.
The amount of energy needed for sexual intercourse depends on which
muscles are involved and to what extent (determined by sexual position),
body weight, and the duration of the sexual exercise. Muscular contraction
during foreplay, afterplay, and the actual act of coitus uses up a great many
calories. In addition, the heart must pump faster to send nutrients and
oxygen to the muscles, and the lungs must inflate faster to get rid of carbon
dioxide and bring in additional oxygen.

Heavier people obviously need more calories when performing sexual
intercourse than do lighter people because extra effort is needed to move
additional body weight. The longer the sexual activity continues, the more
calories are used. The measurement of energy needed for sexual relations,
then, is expressed in three units—*calories* per *weight* per *unit of time*. Sexologists have noted that a person's total energy needs for sexual vigor probably
decrease by 5 percent per decade after the age of twenty.

In his book *How Sex Can Keep You Slim*, Dr. Abraham I. Friedman laid out
a mathematical formula for predicting how many pounds of body weight
can be lost by having sexual intercourse. The formula is based on Dr.
Friedman's estimate that one act of coitus uses up 200 calories of energy:

> Dr. Alfred Kinsey has stated that the pulse of a sexually aroused
> person increases from a normal rate of about seventy per minute to
> as much as 150 per minute or more. This is equal to the pulse rate
> of an athlete during his maximum effort, or a man involved in
> heavy labor. In addition, there are multiple contractions of the
> muscles of the buttocks and pelvis, thighs, abdomen, thorax, arms,
> legs, and neck, sometimes of great intensity.

Dr. Friedman admitted that his 200-calorie figure is an approximation. "It may be a few calories more or less," he wrote. "Personal communication with the Masters and Johnson Foundation in St. Louis revealed that to date there has been no research done as to the exact number of calories consumed during sexual intercourse."[4] As of early 1993, that was still the case!

Tests by honeybee pollen harvesters have shown that the body expends relatively little energy in metabolizing pollen. When any food is taken into the body, many body cells that have been dormant become active. The muscles that move food through the intestinal tract speed up their rhythmic contractions; the cells that manufacture and secrete the digestive juices begin their tasks. All these cells, and others, need extra energy as they "wake up" to participate in the digestion, absorption, or metabolism of the food substance. In addition, the presence of the food stimulates the general metabolism. This stimulation is the specific dynamic effect (SDE), or specific dynamic activity (SDA), of food.

SDE, or SDA, is generally thought to represent about 6 to 10 percent of the total food energy taken in. Because the food energy ingested normally equals the energy expended, the SDE of any food eaten for sexual vigor is usually calculated as being 10 percent of the total calories used for basal metabolism and sexual muscular activity. The higher the SDE for a certain food is, the greater is the amount of energy required just to metabolize that food and integrate it throughout the body for use by the cells. Honeybee pollen has an exceedingly low SDE. Pollen puts little burden on the human body.

THERAPEUTIC PROPERTIES OF HONEYBEE POLLEN

When Professor Nicolai Vasilievich Tsitsin, a biologist and experimental botanist associated with the Longevity Institute of the USSR, did a study of centenarians in the Caucasus mountains of the Russian province of Georgia, he was looking for the common bond of the many Georgians who lived past 100 years, including some who had even reached 150 years old. Dr. Tsitsin discovered that the common bond was beekeeping, with products from the beehive being one of the elderly Georgians' principal foods. He found that the Georgian beekeepers sold the clear, so-called pure honey for income and kept the raw, unprocessed honey—the bee pollen—for themselves.

Knowingly or not, the elderly Georgians had been incorporating into their diet nature's richest and most nutritionally packed food, a food routinely consumed as nourishment by Russia's competitive international athletes.

After the 1972 Olympics in Munich, it was revealed that Finland's Lasse Viren, winner of the 5,000-meter and 10,000-meter track events, had been eating honeybee pollen regularly for years. Between training and competition, he swallowed four to ten capsules containing pollen every day. Now all the members of the Finnish Olympic team take honeybee pollen on a regular basis. They sprinkle it on their morning cereal, slip it into tall glasses of freshly squeezed fruit juice, pop it into their mouths as bee pollen granules, spread it as a honey paste on whole-grain bread, or take it in tablet form along with their daily quota of vitamins and minerals.

Many American athletes and Olympic stars use honeybee pollen. Muhammed Ali, former heavyweight boxing champion of the world, popped down pollen granules all the years he was actively defending his title. Steve Riddick, American Gold Medalist in the 1976 Olympics, drank bee pollen in milk shakes and vegetable juice.

European doctors began to experiment with pollen as a medicinal agent following the Second World War. They found that it is a strong biological stimulant with highly therapeutic properties. Pollen helps regenerate the human cell. Used in experiments with aging people, it seems to restore morale, encourage a sense of physical well-being, heighten sexual vigor, and generally return physical health, all of which were measurable by laboratory examination.

Dr. Naum Ioyrish, author of *Bees in the Service of Humanity*, credits bee pollen with aiding healing in chronic colitis, disturbances of the endocrine system, and certain nervous disorders. Bee pollen is low in sodium and calories, and being completely vegetable in origin, it has no cholesterol. It initially contains small quantities of natural sugars—mainly sucrose, fructose, and glucose—which are increased to 10 to 15 percent when honey is added by the bees to keep the grains from fluttering away during transport.

Pollen extracts were studied by scientists using first dysfunctional laboratory animals and then humans suffering from various diseases. According to the test results, pollen extracts:

- Promote rapid weight and energy increases in convalescents.
- Demonstrate a regulatory action on intestinal functions, including easing constipation and diarrhea.
- Have a calming, tranquilizing, and sedating action without any side effects.
- Cause rapid increase in hemoglobin, especially in cases of anemia.
- Help to flush out the impurities and toxins that constantly pile up in the capillaries from stress, medications, and the various pollutants of modern times.
- Facilitate more oxygen reaching body and brain cells by acting almost like an atherosclerotic flushing agent, or chelator.

In the studies, bee-pollen-treated individuals enjoyed increased stamina. Patients using the extracts on a regular basis witnessed enhanced vitality. And even though they were ill, the animal and human subjects in many instances showed an increase of libido and sexual activity.

Laboratory animals exposed to high doses of radiation were found to be protected when fed honeybee pollen. A substance in the pollen—rutin, one of the bioflavonoids (vitamin P)—is a glucoside that increases in the walls of the capillaries to protect a person from excessive radiation from X rays or atomic energy.

Another important medical role of honeybee pollen is regulation of the body's metabolism.

U.S. Department of Agriculture researchers came up with the startling conclusion that "ingestion of pollenized food delays the onset of mammary tumors." Thus, the substance was found to be useful as a cancer preventative and a restrainer of tumor development. The researchers, reporting in the *Journal of the National Cancer Institute*, said:

> These results indicate that under suitable conditions, the development of mammary tumors in mice can be influenced by ingestion of pollenized food. It is suggested that the use of extracted and standardized active principle from pollen might produce greater postponement. These experiments were based upon the postulation that pollen contains an anti-carcinogenic principle that can be added to the food.

Although many studies have been carried out worldwide, no additional research has been conducted in the United States on the anticancer properties of pollen, and the 1948 study is still considered valid.

Dr. William G. Peterson, a clinical allergist from Ada, Oklahoma, claimed that over 25,000 of his patients across the United States used honeybee pollen—along with customary medication—to relieve allergic symptoms. Many people are allergic to anemophile pollens, which are pollens that are carried by the wind or air, such as those of the conifers, willows, chestnuts, and other trees. Bee pollen helps immunize the body against anemophile-pollen allergies.

Dr. Peterson told a meeting of 150 beekeepers belonging to the Oklahoma Beekeepers Association that raw honey (which contains honeybee pollen) is an effective treatment for pollen allergies. He said:

> It must be raw honey, because raw honey contains all the pollen, dust, and molds that cause 90 percent of all allergies. What happens is that the patient builds up an immunity to the pollen, dust or mold that is causing his trouble in the first place. The raw honey must not be strained, not even through a cloth. I know the customer wants clear, strained, filtered honey and that's fine, but for health reasons, raw honey is what we need.

The raw honey, cloudy with bee pollen and taken in small amounts, helps build an immunity against anemophile pollens. The trick is to use coseasonal treatment in addition to preseasonal treatment. Preseasonal administration for hay fever is begun four weeks before the expected onset of symptoms.

Dr. Peterson recommended taking a 2-percent concentrated solution of bee pollen in a glucose-alcohol diluent beginning with one drop and increasing by one drop each day until twenty drops are reached. The twenty drops should be taken daily until the allergy season begins, at which point the dosage should be advanced rapidly—by five drops daily—until forty-five drops are reached. If the allergy symptoms disappear, record the dosage that worked best, but do not reduce the dosage until the pollen content of the air is past the peak.

The minimum and maximum dosages have been established at twenty and seventy drops daily, respectively. Dr. Peterson insisted that overdosage is infrequent and occurs only during the first few weeks of treatment in a few patients. Some patients are able to discontinue oral pollen treatment because they obtain complete relief from their sensitivities.

Translations of French scientific writings indicate that bee pollen, which is a popular sexual enhancer in France, also is used for curing lost appetite, weakness, weight loss, intestinal disorders, psychosis, neurasthenia, retarded growth, cerebral hemorrhage, memory loss, general debility, minimal brain dysfunction in children, and general malaise. It is also used in France for reducing convalescent time.

Dr. Bogdan Tekavcic, chief of the Ljubljana Centre for Gynaecology in what was Yugoslavia, conducted double-blind clinical experiments using a blend of specially selected honeybee pollens and royal jelly with one group of subjects and a placebo with another. A *double-blind study* compares the results achieved by two or more groups of patients who were deliberately subjected to different regimes. Neither the subjects nor the people assessing the results are aware of which therapy was used with which subject. A *placebo* is a preparation that contains nothing that can either help or harm the person who takes it. Sometimes just the act of taking something can relieve symptoms in a patient who believes he or she will be helped.

In the Tekavcic study, sixty women between the ages of eighteen and twenty-two who were suffering with menstrual problems were divided into two groups. The first group consisted of women who were underweight and had irregular and very painful periods. The second group of women had painful periods but no other menstrual difficulties. Half the women in each group took a placebo containing no active ingredients for two consecutive months. The remaining women in each group took the bee-pollen-and-royal-jelly compound for two months.

The results were striking. More than three-quarters of the underweight women gained weight (between two and six-and-a-half pounds), whereas only a quarter of the control group gained weight. In both groups taking the pollen compound, all the women except two found their menstrual difficulties had disappeared entirely or considered them much diminished. Those taking the placebo reported no improvement.

HOW TO TAKE HONEYBEE POLLEN

Honeybee pollen can be eaten as a food supplement, one or two tablespoons of granules daily. It can also be chewed or swallowed as a tablet, one tablet a day. Another method for taking this food for sexual vigor is to purchase empty gelatin capsules at a pharmacy, fill them with pollen granules, and swallow them as a supplement. Pollen granules can also be stirred into fruit juice, mixed with honey or peanut butter, added to yogurt or cottage cheese, blended into applesauce, dropped into milk shakes, sprinkled on cereals or salads, or ground and dusted on food like cinnamon. Do not heat pollen, however, since heat destroys many of the nutrients it contains.

Although honeybee pollen is a food and not a drug, it is possible to be sensitive to it, the same way that you might be sensitive to any food. To test for a sensitivity to pollen, place one granule under your tongue; leave the pollen granule there until it is absorbed completely into the mucous membrane. The components of the pollen will go directly into the bloodstream. This method is the usual way in which clinical ecologists test for hypersensitivity to food substances or other items in the personal environment. If you find that one pollen granule does not provoke a reaction—such as a headache, runny nose, teary eyes, depression, sweating, or something similar—test yourself using two granules. Then try three granules. Keep increasing the number of granules until you feel sure that you are not sensitive to honeybee pollen. Any reaction such as those just mentioned will merely be transitory. A reaction just means that pollen brings your body into adjustment much faster than your immunological system can comfortably tolerate. It signals either that you should not eat honeybee pollen or that the normalizing metabolic activity of the substance will eventually do you good. You must determine from experience with allergens and bodily reactions what the reaction means for you. Taking pollen may restore your body chemistry, if you can tolerate the sensitivity symptoms until they finally disappear and do not come back. Your decision about whether to use pollen must be made also by evaluating the benefit–risk ratio.

The best time to take honeybee pollen is after a meal, when other foodstuffs in your digestive system can buffer the pollen's metabolic activity. Many wholistic physicians recommend continuing to gradually increase the amount of pollen that you consume until:

• All your digestive and absorption processes are working correctly, causing the food you eat to be eliminated in eighteen to twenty-four hours, with no constipation.

Honeybee Pollen Recipes

A few recipes that feature honeybee pollen will raise your enthusiasm for this most perfect of foods. They will also afford you a delicious and handy way in which to get a daily intake of sexual nutrition.

Honeybee Pollen Nibble

1 tablespoon shelled almonds
1 tablespoon shelled sunflower seeds
1 tablespoon honeybee pollen
1 tablespoon raw wheat germ
1 tablespoon plain yogurt
1 teaspoon camomile flowers
Raw honey, to taste (optional)

1. *In a small bowl, combine the almonds, sunflower seeds, pollen, wheat germ, yogurt, and camomile flowers.*

2. *If desired, add raw honey to sweeten the mixture.*

Makes ³/₄ cup.

Honeybee Pollen Milk Shake

¹/₂ cup raw milk
2 tablespoons honeybee pollen
1 tablespoon carob powder
Raw honey, to taste
2 tablespoons shelled almonds, ground

1. *In a blender, combine the milk, pollen, carob, and honey; process for 10 seconds.*

2. *Add the ground almonds and process the mixture for at least 60 seconds more.*

Makes 1 cup.

Honeybee Pollen Candy

2 tablespoons carob powder
2 tablespoons water
2 tablespoons honeybee pollen
3 tablespoons raw honey
2 tablespoons crunchy peanut butter

---

1. *In a small bowl, dissolve the carob powder in the water.*

2. *In a medium bowl, combine the dissolved carob powder with the pollen; stir. Add the honey and mix. Add the peanut butter and mix thoroughly by hand.*

3. *Using a melon baller, scoop out a little mixture and roll it into a ball between two sheets of wax paper. Store the candy balls in the refrigerator.*

Makes 12 balls.

- You feel more energy and stamina surging through your body.
- All your allergic symptoms are gone.

After your body has become accustomed to this natural food and cleansing agent, bee pollen can be consumed whenever you feel the need for a pick-me-up. Pollen provides quick energy with perfect nutrition. It can be especially advantageous to pop down some honeybee pollen just before a sexual encounter.

ROYAL JELLY AND HONEY AS SEXUAL NUTRITION

Two other products from the beehive are useful sources of sexual nutrition.

Royal jelly is a salivary secretion of honeybees that has been recorded as being therapeutically beneficial in the treatment of sterility and sex-organ insufficiencies such as impotence and frigidity. A study of women going through menopause was conducted in France, where much research on royal jelly has been done. Astoundingly, the researchers reported that the women's youth was so restored that some were even able to conceive again.[5]

Royal jelly has been found by scientists to contain twenty amino acids and a rich supply of B-complex vitamins. However, about 3 percent of royal jelly defies analysis. In the laboratory, fruit flies, pigs, roosters, and chickens have grown bigger, lived longer, had greater fertility, and become more sexually active as a result of feeding programs that included royal jelly. Chickens fed royal jelly laid twice as many eggs as those eating the usual chicken feed.

Honey, the most popular product extracted from the beehive, is also considered to be a sexually nutritious food. Honey is utilized for general potency, being a wonderful natural food containing vitamins, minerals, carbohydrates, protein, enzymes, and other substances. Foods like honey tend to increase the body's production of sex hormones. Raw, unprocessed honey—the dark variety seldom found on supermarket shelves but available from mail-order houses or in health food stores—acts like a semi-aphrodisiac, a physical and mental tonic, a deterrent to approaching senility, and an excellent sweetening agent. It was part of many of the sex-enhancing mixtures advocated in ancient times by cultures throughout the world.

Former President Ronald Reagan, now in his eighties, has attributed his good health to the bee pollen and honey he has been eating for more than twenty years. Every day, he spreads four crackers with honey and bee pollen, and munches them with his four o'clock tea.

Honeybees are hard workers. To produce one pound of clover honey, bees must visit and pollinate about 10 million flowers. It would take one bee about ten years to do this. But worker bees live for only six weeks, worn out from their arduous life. While alive, however, bees consume pollen and honey to keep themselves going. I recommend that you make pollen and honey the basis of your own energetic sexuality.

For more information on honeybee pollen, honeybee propolis, royal jelly, and honey for nutritional vitality, health, beauty, and sexuality, see *Royden Brown's Bee Hive Product Bible*, by Royden Brown. This is one of the finest books written on the wondrous products from one of nature's most productive creatures, the bee.

Chapter 7

GLANDULAR EXTRACTS FOR VITALITY

Around my fifty-second birthday, I began losing interest in my hobbies, in exercising, and in having sexual relations with my wife. I couldn't concentrate on my work as a certified public accountant in a large firm, nor could I sleep soundly, sustain any sort of cheerful outlook, or eat with an appetite. I lost weight, drank too much, smoked even more, had occasional migraine headaches, and sometimes flirted with the attractive secretaries in my office. When one of the women in the secretarial pool unexpectedly returned my advances, I found myself impotent. It was then that I realized I had sexual troubles.

My internist diagnosed "possible male menopause" while at the same time admitting that the designation may actually be ridiculous because men don't have a menstrual cycle or lose their reproductive powers at mid-life. "Mid-life crisis" may be a better description, he said. Unfortunately, my doctor had no medical solution. "Just wait it out, Charlie, and it will pass in time," he said. But I'm fifty-four now. Almost two years have gone by without my wife and me having sexual intercourse. My accountancy practice is going to pot, my headaches are still awful, and I continue to suffer from insomnia. My symptoms lessened a little when I stopped drinking and smoking, but I need more help, especially since my sex interest is nil. I'm worried about the love in my relationship because I see the marriage deteriorating.

Believe me, male menopause is no myth, and I desperately need some kind of treatment. Do you have any suggestions for what I should do to help myself?

Charles R.
Madison, Wisconsin

Sixteen months ago, just before turning fifty, I recognized the first signs of menopause setting in. My menstrual periods became irregular, hot flashes hit me periodically, my loved ones began to complain that I was always crabby, and depression overcame me. I felt completely unsexy and let myself go by dressing unattractively and gaining weight. Vaginal dryness set in, but it doesn't disturb me as much as it would someone who is sexually active. I've never been married and rarely have been with a man.

The estrogen pills my gynecologist prescribed frighten me. The doctor explained that estrogen-replacement therapy would probably continue at the same dosage levels for the rest of my life. But I have learned from several other sources that taking artificial estrogen can cause side effects. These drugs have already been identified as the apparent cause of uterine cancer. I refuse to take estrogen.

On my own, I have decided to take vitamins and minerals, particularly vitamin B₆, vitamin E, manganese, and some other nutrients that I know from my reading relieve the symptoms of menopause. This drastic change in my life that began with menopause has begun to ease up now, but I still get hot flashes, flushes, and sweats. There must be something else that can relieve them besides synthetic hormones such as estrogen. What can I do to ease my change of life? Is there something available that's not dangerous and isn't generally used as an alternative by traditional gynecologists?

Alice W.
Portland, Oregon

For most women, menopause begins sometime in the late forties or early fifties. At this time, menstruation begins to occur less frequently, until eventually ovarian function stops and menstruation halts completely. This biological event marks the end of the childbearing period. The transition from monthly ovulation and menstruation to ovarian decline takes anywhere from half a year to three years or longer.

While a few women have no menopausal symptoms at all, many, if not most, experience hot flashes or patchy skin flushes, along with drenching perspiration in varying degrees of discomfort. Some women suffer from backache, nausea, loss of appetite, dizziness, or sudden rise in blood pressure. Others experience fatigue, nervous irritability, or a nervous irritation of the bladder that causes them to urinate frequently. The so-called female change of life also entails bodily shifts in general, such as sagging of the breasts, coarsening of the skin, weakening of the bones, and redistribution of body fat.

The symptoms of menopause are associated with a reduction in the production of estrogens, which actually are three different female hormones—estradiol, estrone, and estriol. In women, the estrogens are manufactured mainly in the ovaries, but small amounts also are manufactured in the adrenal glands. Men have an estrogen hormone, too, produced in the testicles.

Research at the National Institute of Aging in Bethesda, Maryland, showed that while the production of male sex hormones hits a peak when men are in their twenties, it remains relatively stable from age thirty onward. These findings conflicted with previous studies, but researchers at the government institute attributed the differences to the male groups examined. Most of the earlier investigations had been based on older men with illnesses that could have affected their testosterone levels, said Dr. S.

Mitchell Harman, the chief investigator of the newer study. In contrast, Dr. Harman's study looked at seventy-six healthy, active men who were neither alcoholic nor obese. They ranged in age from twenty-five to eighty-nine and were all upper-middle-class residents of Baltimore, Maryland.

Dr. Harman confirmed that the research showed that there is a decline in sexual activity among older men despite the maintenance of the sex-hormone levels. He said he suspected central-nervous-system changes to be responsible. But Seattle endocrine-system expert Dr. C. Alvin Paulsen disagreed; he said that changes in personal priorities and social expectations— and perhaps decreased opportunity—may play a big part in the waning of older men's sex lives. Dr. Paulsen declared that menopause is not a factor.

Follicle-stimulating hormone (FSH) is the pituitary hormone that controls sex-hormone secretion in both men and women. Probably the best laboratory indication of the change of life in a man is an increase in the level of FSH either in his blood or in urine collected from him over a twenty-four-hour period.

Many medical experts on male sexual problems believe that a man's psychological response to the process of aging or prospect of death can bring on the male climacteric, or menopause, faster or can cause a greater reaction. Experts investigating brain chemistry point to many degenerative diseases that were once labeled psychological but are now known to be caused by chemical alterations in the body. Scientists are aware that doubling or tripling the blood-testosterone level in a man will not increase his libido or potency. But the amount of free testosterone—testosterone not bound to protein and therefore "active"—in the blood does decline with age and may be linked to decreased potency.

While a man's "menopausal" state may last anywhere from several months to several years and then subside as unexpectedly as it began, a woman's may linger much longer if treatment is not instituted. However, it begins in the late forties to mid-fifties almost without fail. Of forty-seven-year-old women, 25 percent whose ovaries are intact will have entered menopause. Of fifty-year-old-women, half will have done so. Of fifty-two-year-olds, 75 percent will have. And of those aged fifty-five, 95 percent will have entered menopause.

To verify the beginning of menopause, a simple laboratory test has been developed. Called the estrogen urine test, it works for both women and men, and indicates whether menopause has begun even before any symptoms have gotten to the annoying stage. The test involves taking a sample of urine to a local medical laboratory and asking for a measurement of male or female estrogen production.

The urine taken to the laboratory should be a twenty-four-hour sample, or the entire output of urine from one whole day. A normal, nonpregnant premenopausal woman secretes a total of 4 to 60 micrograms of estrogen during the first two weeks of the menstrual cycle and up to 100 micrograms during the last two weeks. A normal pregnant woman secretes as much as 40,000 micrograms of estrogen in twenty-four hours. After menopause, a normal woman's daily estrogen secretion drops to just 1 to 20 micrograms. By definition, a woman who has undergone menopause cannot become pregnant.

Men normally secrete up to 20 micrograms of estrogen in a twenty-four-hour period. An amount considerably less indicates that the man has entered menopause.

THE CAUSE OF MENOPAUSAL SIGNS AND SYMPTOMS

The symptoms of menopause are real enough; they have a physiological basis. For example, nervous irritability with edginess, sensitivity, unstable moods, tension, and insomnia is caused by the irritable control mechanism being lodged in the same area of the brain as the emotional center; when one is affected, so is the other. Mood changes and nervousness are caused by blood-vessel instability resulting from biochemical fluctuations in the brain. Brain-irritability attacks usually strike at regular intervals and may last for hours.

Drinking coffee, tea, or other caffeine-containing beverages stimulates the brain, increasing wakefulness and excitability. In high enough dosages—five or more cups of coffee a day—caffeine can even cause generalized twitching and convulsions. One change that takes place during menopause is a progressive failure by the liver to clear drugs, including caffeine, from the system as quickly as it once did; a menopausal woman can become high-strung and nervous by drinking the same amount of caffeine-containing beverage that a premenopausal woman handles comfortably.

Nicotine is also a stimulant. Given intravenously, it can bring on convulsions. Adding nicotine stimulation to the hormone-caused mood swings of menopause can overcharge even the toughest nervous system. Remember, cigarette smoke not only impairs the lungs and cardiovascular system but also burdens the brain.

Hot flashes, flushes, and other sensations of extreme heat usually are confined to the upper part of the body and are often accompanied by profuse sweating, chills, sleep disruption—and a feeling of embarrassment when the symptoms occur. Hot flashes are caused by disturbances in the hormone-regulating mechanism in the brain. As the blood-hormone levels bounce up and down, so do the nerve impulses to the blood vessels to the skin. The blood vessels open wide for minutes at a time, raising the skin temperature abnormally high. To counteract this, the sweat glands send fluid to the overheated area to cool it down.

In a hot flash, a woman's skin temperature often increases eight degrees Fahrenheit and may go up as much as twenty degrees. Dr. Howard Judd, whose clinic at the University of California, Los Angeles Medical Center is one of the few specialty clinics in the United States that is exploring the mysteries of menopause, found that the hot-flash temperature increase lasts about four minutes on the average. Other flash effects can continue for more than thirty minutes.[1]

In the years following the onset of female menopause, the vagina becomes less elastic; its lining gets thinner and its secretions decrease. This vaginal atrophy may result in itching, burning, or pain during intercourse. These symptoms are particularly prominent in women who had relatively inactive sex lives prior to menopause. Vaginal inelasticity and hot flashes are the only true physical signs distinctly characteristic of menopause, say gynecological experts.[2]

Dr. Sidney Wolfe of the Ralph Nader–affiliated Public Citizen Health Research Group in Washington, D.C., while being among the severest critics of synthetic hormones, agrees that estrogen-replacement therapy is a correction for the physical signs of menopause. But the data from medical studies of estrogens suggest that a woman taking these hormones runs an increased risk of developing cancer. Even taking estrogens for two years will not leave lasting benefits. Estrogen therapy is not generally recommended by medical consumer advocates and medical experts like Dr. Wolfe.

A consensus-development conference on estrogens and menopause held in Bethesda, Maryland, under the sponsorship of the National Institutes of Health also discouraged Americans from utilizing estrogen-replacement therapy. The conference compromised on a five-point set of guidelines for postmenopausal women. According to the guidelines, a postmenopausal woman should:

1. Talk to her physician in detail about the pros and cons of estrogen therapy in her individual case.

2. Take estrogens only by prescription, following all instructions carefully and remaining under the doctor's care.

3. Be alert for signs of side effects caused by the estrogen therapy.

4. Stay informed about estrogens, seeking out the latest information.

5. Find out about alternatives to estrogen, including improved nutrition, regular exercise, improved lifestyle, other glandular extracts, food supplements, and other, less-hazardous medicines that alleviate individual symptoms, such as lubricants to ease vaginal dryness.

Just as estrogen reduction is the source of female discomfort during change of life, the decrease in the secretion of testosterone, the hormone of the male sex gland, is the cause of male menopausal symptoms. Testosterone production is at the maximum when a man is between twenty-five and thirty-five years of age. By age fifty, a man's testosterone production is

tapering off. And when a man is sixty, his hormone production is down to
the prepuberty level. The man's energy and drive are less, but he will still
be producing enough testosterone to keep his beard growing and his voice
deep. By the time a man reaches ninety, he is still producing sperm—but
usually not in sufficient quantity to inaugurate pregnancy.

RAW GLANDULAR EXTRACTS AS SAFE HORMONE SUBSTITUTES

The dream of prolonging femininity with estrogen pills has proven dangerous because of estrogen's various side effects, such as vaginal spotting or
profuse bleeding, nausea, abdominal bloating or cramping, breast tenderness, fluid retention, and the tendency to develop breast or uterine cancer.
And giving testosterone to a premenopausal or postmenopausal male does
not extend or restore his youth. The way to ongoing sexual viability for both
sexes is *protomorphology*, the scientific use of enzymes and their activities.

Protomorphogens are proteins that are present in every cell as specialized components. They are fractional blueprints that determine what their
cell is going to build before it does any building. They are the catalyzers of
protein synthesis, much like the germ cells (sperm and egg) and other
building blocks that make up a whole animal. Offspring carry the characteristics of the parents, which are delivered by means of these blueprint
substances. Protomorphogens originate in each of the cells of the body and
are carried by the bloodstream to the gonads for assembly.

Protomorphogens are nonvitamin food factors and essential components
of the body's enzyme-protein construction. They are present in every single
cell of every organ in the body of every animal, including humans. Each cell
of a particular organ carries the blueprint of the whole organ. The protomorphogens, in the form of enzymes or determinants, promote the formation of a layer of protein molecules on the outer cell wall. They build and
repair the cell when it comes under stress. During the continuous process
of growth and repair, the cell wall is rebuilt outside this protein layer. The
guidance for the cell construction comes from the aggregate of enzymes,
trace minerals, and other nutrients furnished by what is eaten.

Protomorphogen substances can be taken from the raw organ parts of
other animals. They do not have to be created within the body in which they
are used. One of the newest methods of sexual nutrition is eating simple
extracts of various raw sex tissues or organs from farm animals. Since the
sex-organ extracts do not contain hormones, they are in one sense simply
meat juices. They are glandular extracts of meats that are manufactured and
distributed by nutritional laboratories as plain tablets, enteric-coated tablets, capsules, droplets, or powders for self-help or for dispensing by pharmacies on prescriptions from wholistic physicians. The glandular factors
involved in dietary supplementation have always been present in foods, the
same way that vitamins, enzymes, and organically combined minerals have

been; now they also are being concentrated and formed into food supplements. Consuming the concentrates helps prolong human sex-gland performance. The sexual cells from a cow or pig can be reconstructed by a human's body to extend the life function of that human's sexual organs.

It has been demonstrated in the laboratory that one kind of cell can be reconstructed as another kind of cell. For instance, scientists have cultured testicle cells in a flask and placed connective tissue from a kidney in with them. Since connective tissue has a special affinity for protomorphogens, the kidney cells were soon adapted by the testicle cells. By changing the culture medium's concentration of blueprint material, the new tissue tends to follow the pattern set up by the blueprint material. In this case, the testicular tissue gained size and strength from the kidney connective tissue.

Similarly, when a dermatologist grafts a piece of skin from the outside of the body onto the mucous membrane of the mouth, the skin becomes mucous membrane within a few weeks. The epithelial cells of the skin take in the blueprints of the mucous membrane and gradually convert the skin cells to mucous-membrane cells.

Experiments involving laboratory animals of different species have echoed these results. Pieces of live calf-embryo skin were grafted onto the belly of a guinea pig. Within a few months, the calf skin began growing guinea-pig hair instead of calf hair. These experiments showed that protomorphogens find their way into the culture medium and direct the growth processes of any appropriate cells that may be present. The protomorphogens also initiate a resurgence of growth and strength in the host animal's newly grafted organ.

Everything just described is also characteristic of glandular extracts taken in pill form as hormone substitutes. By swallowing raw extracts of a specific organ, such as the testes or ovaries of a healthy farm animal, you can influence the local nutritional environment of the same organ in your body.

Any enforced activity of the gonads causes an increased secretion of protomorphogens into surrounding tissue fluids. The effect is purely a body-response mechanism, whether the activity causes the increase in protomorphogen or the protomorphogen is supplied by the raw tissue extracts. The gonads respond when extracts from the matching animal sex organ are taken internally. Protomorphogen factors have shown some remarkable results in cases in which an individual's sex endocrines had been injured or overloaded, were showing premature aging, or were suffering from menopausal slowdown.

If a system has no specific need for an oral protomorphogen extract, the body treats the extract as merely nutritious protein. Extracts apparently produce no side effects. Reports from experts indicate that oral glandulars are harmless, with one possible exception. A person who has had a venereal disease, ovarian or uterine tumor, male genital lesion, or other sex-related pathology and all at once takes too much protomorphogen extract of animal gonads might experience a systemic histamine reaction. Histamine, a compound derived from an amino acid and found in nearly all the tissues of the body, can cause dilation of blood vessels and contractions of smooth muscle, giving rise to what can be considered an allergic response. A sex-related pathology may leave a person with a high level of sex-organ antibodies. Because of this, additional protomorphogen would make the person feel as though he or she were coming down with a cold. Cold symptoms are simply an indication of a generalized histamine reaction. This is why antihistamines are used as cold remedies.

It takes a fairly heavy dose of protomorphogen concentrate to bring about such a histamine reaction, even in people who had a severe sex-organ disease in the past and are loaded with gonadal antibodies now. To prevent histamine reaction, use a relatively conservative dosage of raw glandular extract, advised Royal Lee, D.D.S., who in 1930 was one of the pioneers in researching the benefits of raw beef-tissue extracts.

HOW RAW GLANDULAR CONCENTRATES WORK IN THE BODY

Only one biochemical mode of action by raw glandular concentrates has been demonstrated to take place within the human body. The therapeutic benefits of taking glandular extracts are powerful—much stronger than the effects from merely eating organ meats. You could not expect a piece of liver consumed for dinner, for instance, to repair your own damaged liver. Unlike raw liver extract, liver organ meat does not work that way. On the other hand, raw glandular tissues, after being refined, act like the enzymes secreted into the surrounding tissues by the organ's cells themselves. Enzymatic action is the only form in which glandular tissue can be assimilated for utilization by a target organ.

By the time a raw glandular extract has gone through one of the various refinement processes, it has actually become a nucleic acid, which forms the basis of ribonucleic acid (RNA) and deoxyribonucleic acid (DNA). In fact, scientists studying the structures of RNA and a raw glandular concentrate under a microscope would probably be hard put to explain the difference between them.

The protomorphogen tissue taken in pills, droplets, or powders is not the same tissue that actually becomes a part of the consumer and enhances his or her gonads. Rather, that material is a trigger mechanism. The form of protomorphogen that is taken interacts with the specific cellular system for which it was targeted by the manufacturer. Glandular extracts are made into manufactured products to enhance the functioning of the various sex organs, heart, pancreas, liver, kidneys, and other internal organs. Each designated protomorphogen extract enables the body to build the cells necessary to strengthen the target organ. Raw glandular concentrates provide the template, or pattern, from which the body can build cells.

Raw glandular extracts by themselves are not enough to restore sexual health or prevent premature aging. Also necessary are a nutritious diet, regular exercise, avoidance of smoking (and of secondhand smoke), and auxiliary wholistic health practices. These are the building blocks that form the foundation for a full lifetime of sexual power. Glandular concentrates provide protomorphogens and nucleic acids, which combine with nutrients taken from the digestive system to build gonadal cells.

Oral raw glandular products when swallowed must cross the gastrointestinal (GI) barrier and be transported in the blood to a selective site of action, such as the prostate, ovaries, testicles, uterus, or mammary glands. While Dr. Arthur Guyton's *Textbook of Medical Physiology* suggested that no intact peptide materials in the healthy adult human cross the GI barrier, more advanced views differ. Physiologists now know that the intestinal epithelium, a layer of thin tissue covering the interior walls of the gut, serves a dual role. It is a route for the active absorption of nutrients, and it is a physical barrier, segregating the contents of the GI tract from the tissues of the body. The barrier is incomplete, however, since various large molecules and particles, coming mostly from food and intestinal flora, do pass through the intestinal wall. The epithelium acts in this manner as a selective strainer.

Research has indicated that large polypeptide molecules—such as "tissue activating polypeptide-like (protein) material," as research biochemist Jeffrey Bland, Ph.D., described raw glandular concentrates in *Granular Based Food Supplements Helping to Separate Fact From Fiction*—are taken in small concentrations across the gastrointestinal barrier.[3] Moreover, the enzymes in organ extracts are not destroyed by stomach acid, since they are raw. Hydrochloric-acid secretion is minimal in the stomach. No acid action occurs for at least thirty minutes when food is eaten. As the extract capsule or tablet drops down the esophagus into the top portion of the stomach (the cardiac section), no hydrochloric acid is secreted. After a half hour, the bottom portion of the stomach opens and allows the glandular concentrate to pass through to the intestines. Because no stomach-acid action has taken place, there has been no breakdown of the pill in the stomach; the breakdown will occur only in the intestines.

An ever-evolving body of information supports the concept that small amounts of orally ingested enzyme preparations from raw glandular concentrates administered in pill form are absorbed intact and produce potentially tissue-specific physiologic effects. The effects result from protomorphogen stimulation. "Like affects like"—a homeopathic concept—explains why they are attracted to a sick organ. The sexual apparatus of a person whose sexual physiology is malfunctioning and who is fed raw normal sex glands from a healthy farm animal will eventually be restored to normal because a like cell from the animal helps to heal a like cell in the human.

Prestigious medical journals such as the British *Lancet* and *The New England Journal of Medicine* suggest that the protein part of raw glandular extracts is what does the healing. For instance, two separate articles by Dr. G. Goldstein and Dr. A. Rubinstein, both published in *The New England Journal of Medicine*, proved that oral tissue extracts are normalizing factors for malfunctioning organs in humans. Both researchers reported better immune-system function in people who were taking raw glandular thymus.[4] Indeed, research on the decline of immune defenses with age has focused new attention on the pinkish gray two-lobed organ called the thymus gland, located high in the chest. The thymus is an essential component of the immune system, but it reaches its greatest size at sexual maturity, around the age of fourteen, and then begins to lose bulk and diminish in function long before the body's overall immunological processes become noticeably weakened.

Now, the immune defenses of an adult's thymus can be extended by providing quantities of concentrated farm-animal thymus-gland extract. Dr. Raymond Hiramoto of the University of Alabama School of Medicine, with the support of the National Institute on Aging, gave thymic hormones to laboratory animals to see what effect the supplements would have.[5] Dr. Hiramoto's work was but one example among the dozens of experiments conducted throughout the world on glandular extracts and their protomorphogen effects on the endocrine glands, including the gonads.

TYPES OF GLANDULAR EXTRACTS

Endocrine specialists estimate that there are over 15,000 variations of the hormonal substances that trigger all the body's responses. The sex hormones, of course, spark the sexual feelings of desire and performance. Sight, touch, sound (in the form of seductive words), or even smell may signal the pineal gland (the regulator of emotion) to go into action. The pineal gland is a pea-sized mass of tissue attached by a stalk to the back wall of the third ventricle of the brain, deep between the cerebral hemispheres at the back of the skull. The hippocampus is a swelling containing complex folds of cortical tissue in the floor of the lateral ventricle of the brain.

A message travels from these parts of the brain to the base of the spine, where a cluster of nerves warns that something or someone sexually arousing is in the immediate vicinity. An escalating nervous and hormonal cycle then begins.

At sexual awakening, physical changes take place—extra energy is released, the pulse speeds up, the blood supply to the gonads is increased, the penis becomes erect or the vagina becomes lubricated, breathing becomes deeper, the nipples (of both men and women) become rigid, among other events signaling arousal. All these changes are a result of the pineal gland's stimulating the pituitary gland into flooding the body with follicle-stimulating hormone (FSH) and luteinizing hormone (LH). LH provides estrogen and progesterone synthesis for women and androgen synthesis for men by acting on the interstitial cells of the testes. LH is therefore also called interstitial-cell-stimulating hormone, or ICSH.

Unfortunately, even when outside stimulation is powerful, stress, fatigue, illness, aging, nutritional deficiency, or prolonged sexual inactivity that has weakened or depleted the hormone content of the sex glands may depress these signs of arousal. Because the glands that produce the sexual hormones are delicate, they are highly susceptible to deterioration if not given proper care continuously throughout life. Proper care may include supplementation with raw glandular extracts.

Manufacturers of oral raw glandular concentrates offer products to supply protomorphogens for many major glands and organs including the hypothalamus, pineal, pituitary, thyroid, parathyroid, thymus, pancreas, adrenals, liver, ovaries, testicles, spleen, uterus, placenta, prostate, mammary glands, duodenum, eye, lymph, heart, and parotid. Some of the products contain a mixture of a gland extract and important gland-stimulating vitamins or minerals. In the following list, I will focus only on those glandular extracts relating directly to the gonads; I will also mention vitamins and minerals that work in harmony with the extracts.

Self-help biological therapy using oral sex-gland extracts is for correcting the underlying cause of sexual dysfunction. It also helps to strengthen resistance to disease and to create the most favorable conditions in which the body can heal itself. The manufacturers of raw glandular concentrates recommend the following substances for alleviating problems related to the sexual endocrine system:

- *Raw mammary substance* can be used for disorders of the female breasts, such as lymph-node enlargement or congestion, nipple pain, general breast pain (especially during menses), lactation insufficiency (and for good general support for lactating mothers), and some cases of lumps or swelling. Raw mammary substance is not supposed to make the breasts larger or smaller, although manufacturers have received unsolicited reports from small-breasted women who have had to buy larger bras after engaging in a therapeutic program using raw mammary substance. It is recommended that high doses of folic acid and wheat-germ-oil capsules (for vitamin E) and a good general diet and exercise program be part of the therapy. The ordinary dosage of raw mammary extract, says the processor, is three to six tablets taken daily in divided doses.

- *Raw testicle substance* provides male-sex-gland support. It is indicated for use mainly by men over forty who are experiencing the tired businessperson syndrome (described in Chapter 2) or male menopause, which may manifest itself as nervous exhaustion or loss of strength. Impotency can originate with any of several glandular imbalances or nutrient deficiencies, or it can come from malabsorption or digestive inefficiency, which can result in protein malnutrition. In such a case, hydrochloric acid or enzyme products should be investigated for temporary use. Hydro-chloric-acid supplementation may be especially helpful for older men. Combined with wheat-germ-oil capsules, raw testicle substance can also help overcome sterility or inflammation of the testes. Some cases of libido loss will respond very dramatically, particularly if other substances such as dimethylglycine or bee pollen are taken at the same time. The manu-facturer suggests taking three to six pills of raw testicle extract a day.

- *Raw ovarian substance* provides female-sex-gland support. The indications for its use include failure to menstruate; painful or difficult menstruation; menopausal symptoms, such as depression, hot flashes, sweats, flushes, and irritability; and tired businessperson and tired homemaker syn-dromes (see Chapter 2) in women over age forty. Some cases of arthritis following menopause can be aided by raw ovarian substance accompa-nied by raw adrenal substance and high vitamin-C doses. Delayed pu-berty or lack of normal development in young women may respond as well. The manufacturer recommends taking two to six tablets of raw ovarian extract daily.

- *Raw placenta substance* may be taken as a synergist—a nutrient that interacts with another nutrient to produce increased systemic activity that is greater than the sum of the effects of the two nutrients taken separately. Alone, raw placenta extract promotes breast development in young women, encourages growth in underdeveloped children and in-fants, and checks overabundant lactation. The Russians have been experi-menting with raw placenta substance as a rejuvenator, prescribing it to slow down the aging process; they have found it highly effective, accord-ing to personal reports made by Russian scientists to foreign gerontolo-gists. The average daily dose of raw placenta extract is three to six tablets or capsules.

- *Raw prostate substance* provides therapy for prostate disorders of all types. In acute prostate conditions, the following supplements taken with the raw prostate extract should be quite beneficial—vitamin B_6; vitamin C; vitamin D; vitamin E; raw thymus, raw spleen, and raw lymph extracts; zinc; or high levels of calcium, magnesium, manganese, and potassium. For chronic prostatitis characterized by dribbling after urination, painful urination with burning sensations, premature ejaculation, or possible impotency, the raw prostate substance with its accompanying supple-ments should be taken regularly in moderate dosages. Experts recom-mend taking two prostate-substance tablets at each meal until the symp-toms begin to lessen, then one tablet per meal for several months. Bee pollen, pumpkin seeds, and most seafoods comprise part of a therapeutic diet for sufferers of prostate problems. Otherwise, the manufacturer says the recommended daily dose of raw prostate substance is two to six tablets.

- *Raw thymus substance* reduces the tendency towards premature aging.

The thymus gland has been called the gland for "love, joy, youth, and enthusiasm." The recommended dosage of this animal extract is three to six tablets daily.

- *Raw uterine substance* gives nutritional support to the uterus. It works synergistically with raw ovarian substance in cases of uterine congestion, uterine cysts, excessive or scanty menses, or prolapsed uterus, or when there is a history of spontaneous abortion (miscarriage). It also works as a mental stabilizer during female menopause. Wholistic physicians using raw glandular extracts as part of their treatment of gynecological disorders report that it helps in menopausal states when the patient's uterus is losing its function too fast. They also prescribe raw adrenal substance, as it stimulates the uterus to function again. To relieve endocervicitis (an inflammation of the membrane lining the cervix) or endometriosis (the presence of cells ordinarily lining the uterus but now growing in unusual or abnormal places, such as in the bladder or intestinal wall), many experts recommend that you use a combination of raw uterine substance and high doses of an herbal detergent (a cleansing solution such as chicory root douche). Douching with chlorophyll or lactobacillus culture, which is present in yogurt, may also help. In inflamed or infected conditions of the uterus, physicians treating with protomorphogens tell patients to take vitamin A, vitamin D, and thymus, spleen, and lymph glandular extracts. Raw thyroid substance and wheat germ oil added to raw uterine substance work well together for relieving painful menstruation and scanty or absent menstruation. The manufacturer suggests three or four tablets of raw uterine extract each day as the dosage.

There are a number of manufacturers and distributors of oral raw glandular extracts. For more information on any brand or to purchase a raw glandular extract, check your local health food store.

Chapter 8

CELLULAR THERAPIES FOR YOUTHFULNESS

I am sixty-seven years old, five feet seven inches tall, and 142 pounds in weight. The doctors tell me I'm in good health for a fellow my age, but I have difficulty ejaculating during masturbation or intercourse. If I manage an orgasm, there isn't any notice-able amount of fluid that comes out. Maybe a drop or two, but that's all. No longer is there the pressure behind the ejaculate that I used to feel in my younger years. The effect is that the sensation of orgasm is extremely diminished, and sometimes there is no feeling at all. I have been to physicians for tests, but everything appears to be normal with my sexual apparatus. "You're just getting old," the doctors say. I even visited a hypnotist, but nothing positive came of it.

My difficulty started about twenty years ago, when my wife and I began drifting apart. During the long time we were in conflict, we didn't have any sexual relations. I got really good at ignoring my sexual impulses, doing nothing to relieve them. Now that my wife and I are no longer together, I'm sorry, because the wonderful sensation of orgasm with ejaculation has never returned.

I recently met a woman who means a lot to me. My new lady friend really excites me. I satisfy her with intercourse, but I myself can't reach orgasm. I would love to feel that great sensation again, but it's gone. In a year and a half, I've only made it once. Now each time my girlfriend and I try, I know it won't work, so that's also against me. The only satisfaction I get is to see my lady enjoy herself.

I think if I hadn't met this woman, I would have said, "To hell with sex." But now I want it more than ever.

I have heard about some foreign rejuvenation injections given by specialists for my kind of trouble. Can you tell me about these injections, what they do, how they help, their side effects, and where to find them? I am looking desperately for something that will get me back sexually to where I was twenty years ago.

Ollie L.
Kansas City, Missouri

I've been married to my third husband for just four months. In the past—with my first two husbands and with other men—my sexual responsiveness was always very good. I have three children. Now, at age forty-three, I'm experiencing difficulty enjoying sex with my husband, who is five years younger than me.

Jeffrey claims that my vagina is too stretched for him; his penis just flops around inside and hardly rubs the walls. He says that he doesn't feel anything. This may be true, because Jeffrey's penis seems slimmer than others I've known.

Is there something I can do to tighten my vaginal canal? I have douched with astringent to no avail. My husband has tried slipping on thick-skinned condoms to take up room inside me, but this only reduces the sensations for his penis. We are in a terrible situation that is ruining our marriage, since Jeffrey says that part of the reason for getting married is now gone for him. Can you suggest any foods or other treatments that might restore my tight vagina?

Mrs. Jeffrey S.
Pittsburgh, Pennsylvania

It is not unusual for a woman who has had many years of sexual inter-course and three vaginal births to experience a lax vagina. The vaginal walls can lose their muscle tone and flexibility from extensive use or from a decreased blood supply due to premature aging.

The main muscular support of the vagina is the *levator ani*, a broad muscle made up of several components. Attached to the pelvic floor, it stretches when a penis is inserted into the vagina or when an infant emerges from the uterus. If overused, overstretched, or torn during childbirth, the levator ani muscle gives less support to the back wall of the vagina, where it is separated from the rectum. The bladder loses support, too, because the bladder sits on the levator ani when the woman is in an erect position.

Over time, the bladder pushes down on the levator ani muscle and causes the vaginal chamber to grow wider and looser than it should be, allowing less sexual sensation for both man and woman.

Furthermore, a lax vagina gives rise to less control over bladder function. A woman may experience urine loss when she coughs, sneezes, or strains in some way. Her straining puts stress on the bladder itself; the muscle that is supposed to be supporting the bladder has no power to perform its function anymore. Symptoms such as urine leakage will show in women with lax vaginas in the forty-, fifty-, and sixty-year age groups. An episiotomy, an incision made from the vaginal outlet toward the anus at the time of childbirth, may prevent some of the symptoms by averting overstretching of the levator ani muscle.

Dr. Peter A. Goodhue, chief of obstetrics and gynecology at Stamford Hospital, Stamford, Connecticut, said:

> We have patients who mention that their husbands don't find them as tight as they used to be before they had babies, and sexual intercourse is not being enjoyed as much by the husband. Knowing about this, a husband will jokingly say at the time of delivery, "Put

an extra stitch in for me!" He is referring to the episiotomy to be performed. The "husband's stitch" is talked about in jest, but some husbands are partly serious. However, sexual counselors have told me that the "husband's stitch" has no validity. If there is a significant complaint about lack of sexual enjoyment, there may be some other underlying psychological problem.[1]

There are two primary methods for overcoming a lax vagina. One uses a special exercise. The other combines several offbeat, unorthodox treatments that are well-recognized and applied in Europe, Asia, and parts of South and Central America but are forbidden in the United States by the FDA.

The special exercise to tighten a lax vagina is the Kegel exercise. To perform a Kegel exercise, contract the muscles around the vaginal opening as if you were trying to stop or prevent urination. One good way in which to practice the Kegel maneuver is to sit in a chair with your feet flat on the floor and a pillow held tightly between your knees. Contract your vaginal muscles, hold them tight for a few seconds, then slowly release them until the pillow falls to the floor. Perform the exercise several times per day.

Sheila Kitzinger, childbirth educator and author of *The Experience of Childbirth* and *Giving Birth*, suggests carrying the Kegel exercise a little further. In her books, she writes about Kegel exercises to reduce pregnancy discomfort from pelvic congestion before childbirth. To tighten a loose birth canal after delivery, she advises her clients to alternate contraction and relaxation of the gluteal muscles in the buttocks. This is an excellent self-help procedure for a lax vagina. Kegel exercises will tone up and firm the entire vaginal area and will especially reduce the size of the vaginal vault. However, it does take a while for the exercise to produce any results.

Perhaps a faster and more effective way to tone the vaginal muscles in women is cellular therapy, embryotherapy, or a combination of the two. These methods also help to reestablish the capacity to ejaculate in men. Cell therapy and embryotherapy have been practiced by medical innovators around the world for generations, although cell therapy is prohibited in the continental United States by the FDA.

CELL THERAPY

In 1889, seventy-two-year-old Charles-Edouard Brown-Sequard, professor of physiology at the University of Paris, announced to the French Societé de Biologie that "I have rejuvenated myself by thirty years, and today was able to 'pay a visit' to my young wife." Dr. Brown-Sequard's method was to inject himself with bull-testicle extract mixed with saline. His experiment presaged hormonal therapy in endocrinology.

The next year, Dr. Eugen Steinach of Austria perfected an operation that was predicated on Dr. Brown-Sequard's experiments. Dr. Steinach attempted to prevent a lab animal's testicles from producing spermatozoa in order to activate the hormone-producing part of the testicles. He accomplished this by tying off the animal's vas deferens. He theorized that backing up spermatozoa in sperm ducts would stimulate greater hormonal secretion and thus rejuvenate a lagging libido, end impotency, and encourage the formation of more fluid for ejaculation from the prostate and seminal vesicles. While Dr. Steinach's theory proved invalid for sexual rejuvenation, his operation is commonly performed on men today and is well-known as a *vasectomy*.

In 1920, Dr. Serge Voronoff from Russia set up a clinic in Italy near the French border where he performed the so-called monkey-glands transplant. Over a thousand elderly men visited Dr. Voronoff to have slices of chimpanzee testicles transplanted into their own testicles. The technique worked temporarily—the men did experience a short resurgence of sexual desire and capacity. The men's ejaculate increased in amount, and the men experienced a renewed sensation of orgasm with masturbation. (It is not known if female surrogates or prostitutes were employed in the experiments.) Unfortunately, the men enjoyed no *permanent* rejuvenating effect because the human host organ always rejected the foreign animal tissue. The treatment was abandoned by medical sexologists after Dr. Voronoff died.

Testosterone injections to renew sexual potency in men with a diminished sex drive were first used around 1936. Testosterone and other hormones have a kind of feedback effect on the body. The anterior portion of the pituitary gland and the hypothalamus register a hormone shortage in the blood. The pituitary, which is the body's master gland, sends a message to the sluggish endocrine gland—in this case, the testicles. In response, the endocrine gland secretes the missing hormone—here, testosterone. When the male hormone is raised to the appropriate level in the blood, the testicles cease their secretion because the pituitary and the hypothalamus stop calling for it.

Injecting testosterone makes the pituitary's function unnecessary. No work is demanded from the testicles, since the blood level of the male hormone remains elevated. This is bound to result in a lazy pair of testicles—they lose their ability to function well when the injection is skipped or altogether eliminated. The major shortcoming of testosterone injections therefore is that the recipient's testicles become dependent on the artificial supply of the hormone. Also, testosterone injections may increase a man's chances to get cancer.

On page 132, I described what may happen when artificial estrogens are given to a woman. The difficulties a man may experience when receiving testosterone are similar.

Homeopathy was founded on the belief that "like cures like" (*similia similibus curantur*). In the fifteenth century, Pope Innocent VIII had blood from young boys injected into himself because he believed that the blood contained a youth factor. Immediately after receiving the injections, however, the Pope died because of an immunologic rejection due to an incompatible blood type. (The people around Pope Innocent VIII came to condemn what they eventually considered an unnatural act—proven unnatural by the punishment God leveled upon the Pope.) Yet, the idea of rejuvenation through blood transfusion is being carried out hundreds of times every day in twentieth-century hospitals, except that the blood is first tested and typed.

Scottish physician John Hunter conducted laboratory experiments, reported in *Stay Young* by Dr. Ivan M. Popov, in which roosters' testicles were implanted in the gizzards of capons in an attempt to restore the capons' urge for sex. For the first time, living cells transferred to a sex-devoid animal rejuvenated the asexual animal's sexual functioning. In the mid-1800s, Dr. Claude Bernard, a French physiologist, confirmed this living-cells concept of "internal secretion"—in other words, that endocrine glands give off hormones—in the classic scientific manner.

Swiss endocrinologist Dr. Paul Niehans is the designated pioneer in cell therapy. Dr. Niehans solved the problems of immunologic rejection and anaphylactic shock caused by the injection of tissues from one adult into another adult of either the same or a different species by substituting the organs of fetuses as his material for injection. British zoologist Peter Brian Medawar later showed why the Niehans experiments succeeded—immunological competence of tissue develops only after birth. Thus, Dr. Niehans' technique avoided (perhaps by chance) the generalized, massive rejection syndrome, which can be fatal, because his injected cells lacked the antibodies that provoke allergic reactions. Dr. Niehans' laboratory experiments and clinical practice applications proved successful throughout the 1930s and 1940s. People traveled from all over Europe and North America to receive cellular injections of embryonic tissues for activating sluggish or nonfunctioning body organs—particularly sexual organs.

While the American Medical Association (AMA) totally rejects cell therapy as a viable form of glandular rejuvenation, AMA members in 1957 congratulated Dr. Georges Mathé of the Curie Institute in Paris for saving the lives of five Yugoslavian nuclear technicians using bone-marrow cells from donors. The five patients had been flown to Paris after their bone-marrow cells had been destroyed by accidental lethal doses of radiation in a nuclear reactor. The mens' immunocompetence had been destroyed. Although the live foreign bone-marrow cells that Dr. Mathé injected were eventually rejected by the mens' bodies, the Yugoslavians' own marrow cells had been given enough time to regenerate. The men survived.

William Sydney Bullough, Ph.D., an English scientist, isolated so-called aging factors that he called chalones. Chalones are tissue-specific but not species-specific. That is, pig skin cells transplanted into a mouse, calf, or human will inhibit the cellular growth and aging of the skin of the mouse, calf, or human. But the same pig skin cells will not slow the aging of a pig's liver, pancreas, or lymphocytes.[2] Although Dr. Bullough was not a cell therapist, his findings about chalones are employed in the practice of cell therapy.

HOW CELL THERAPY AIDS SEXUAL DYSFUNCTION

A vagina that lacks sufficient muscle-wall tone, a penis that produces a reduced orgasm because of a failure to ejaculate, and other dysfunctioning sex organs can all be aided by cellular therapy. Today in West Germany, thousands of physicians are practicing antiaging medicine utilizing the concept that embryonic cells contain vital elements that reinforce the functioning of deficient organ cells in the living. Embryonic cells are being freeze-dried in Germany at Heidelberg University under the control of the Ministry of Health. The freeze-dried cells are then being shipped to about fifty countries where doctors use them as treatment for dysfunctioning organs. The sex organs respond especially well to the injections of freeze-dried (lyophilized) embryonic cells. Freeze-dried cells are much less expensive than fresh placenta cells and can be administered on an outpatient basis. In the United States, the FDA does not authorize the use of cell therapy. Yet, around the world, several million patients have taken the treatment, and approximately 2,000 clinical journal articles have been published on the subject. The articles report positive results in extensive medical studies.

In cell therapy, injections of placenta cells usually accompany injections of organic-specific cells for the gonads. A man with a sexual problem such as loss of libido, impotence, or detained or diminished ejaculation will be given injections of testicular cells taken from a lamb, young sheep, or other young domestic animal. Combined with high doses of vitamin E, cell treatment has been successful in reversing male infertility, especially low sperm counts. For sexually dysfunctional women, injections of ovary cells from young animals are given to overcome frigidity, infertility, or difficulty with menopause. Placenta cells are also used as an adjunctive injection.

According to a former medical director of a major cell-therapy center in the Bahamas, the technique of cell therapy, after fifty years of clinical use, has devolved into the intramuscular implantation or injection of a Ringer-solution suspension of fetal or young animal cells. The injected cells have general as well as organ-specific effects. The precise mode of action of cell therapy is not known. The lyophilized cells are very close in activity to fresh cells. Lyophilized cells are, of course, easier to handle, ship, and store than fresh placenta cells, and the dosages are easier to establish. In addition to the cells for the gonads, over sixty cell types are available for the heart, pancreas, liver, spleen, stomach, thyroid, parathyroid, bone, adrenals, kidneys, and all the other human organs and glands. Several cell types (usually no more than five) can be given simultaneously to achieve a "revitalizing" effect, as well as to reactivate a particular organ or function.

The organotropic effect of cell therapy cannot be reduced by scientists to a simple hormonal action. Cell therapists accept that there may be a short-term hormonal effect due to the presence of small amounts of hormones in the cells. But they attribute the prolonged effect of sexual cell therapy to the stimulating influence of the young cells on the specific organ or on the entire person. This prolonged effect is in a way the opposite of that of hormonal injections, which can lead to dysfunction of natural hormone secretion from glandular disuse, as pointed out earlier in this chapter. Cell therapy aims to *activate* the receiver's genitals and gonads.

Animal experiments using cells that were marked with a radioactive isotope showed increased isotope density at the level of the sex organ (testes or ovaries). There was also increased division of the organ's own cells—the cells thrived. That activating substances migrate to a new site of action was shown by tracing the radioisotope with a Geiger counter.

Before cellular injections are given, a patient must undergo a physical examination and laboratory tests, and the doctor must take a careful history. These preliminaries are necessary because nearly 15 percent of people who want cellular injections show contraindications to the treatment. People who are allergic, heavily addicted to drugs or alcohol, or suffering with an inflammatory or infectious disease cannot take cell-therapy injections.

Lyophilized components of testicle or ovary cells are injected in the buttocks in a dosage of 10 cubic centimeters (cc) per injection. Although the solution feels cold when it first goes in, the patient feels no appreciable discomfort from being injected. The cell components travel through the bloodstream to the gonads, where the rejuvenation takes place. During the first few days of the injection procedure, exposure to the sun is forbidden and bed rest is mandatory; the cells need to have a chance to be absorbed by the sex organs. The patient also is not allowed to take a bath, smoke cigarettes, drink alcohol, or take other drugs. However, vitamins and anti-histamines are prescribed to ward off any possible allergic reaction. Cell-therapy patients smell pungent because of the cell absorption and the other odors escaping from the body. The other odors are from toxic products that have been lying dormant in the body and are finally being released.

For people over the age of forty, the initial reaction to the injection will probably be a surge of power and vitality. A couple of days later, however, they may feel as if they have the flu. Another delayed reaction may be redness at the site of the injection; the redness may then spread around the entire buttock region. The hip may ache as if suffering from a charley horse.

The cellular effects of energy and vigor will come on slowly, as the patient discovers a new interest in and capacity for sexual activity. Recipients of cellular injections report that the revitalizing treatment lasts a couple of years. A booster dose will then be needed.

Some very prominent people have taken cell therapy. Press reports have named the Duke and Duchess of Windsor, Pope Pius XII, Charles de Gaulle, Konrad Adenauer, Thomas Mann, Somerset Maugham, and Howard Hughes. Merle Oberon had cell therapy to preserve her Eurasian beauty.

If it seems that the rich and famous are more attuned to cellular therapy, it may be because of the price of the treatment. A course of treatment over ten days runs into the thousands of dollars. Some people take the full allotment of cell types permitted, which is five injections per day. Somerset Maugham said that it was worth the investment; he took the injections after he acknowledged losing his ability to write—and then he began writing again.

EMBRYOTHERAPY

The poor man's cellular therapy is embryotherapy, which is true sexual nutrition. Television and movie actor Bob Cummings took embryotherapy when he was sixty-three years old. He and his wife, Gigi, who was then thirty-four, took the therapy together. Although Cummings was almost twice her age, Gigi acknowledged that her husband's sexual ability came alive after he took the treatment. According to Bob:

> Gigi says I've never been better. She says that I have more energy and that I am more romantic toward her.
>
> As for my appearance, I used to worry in the mornings as I looked at myself shaving. There were lines in my forehead and grooves around my mouth. Today those worrisome lines in my forehead are gone and the grooves around my mouth have softened. Gigi looks, feels and acts much better too. If she keeps this up she'll look the same at sixty-five as she does today—and today she looks like a girl! I feel as if new energy is flowing through me and that every day I am growing younger rather than older.[3]

Embryotherapy treatments consist simply of swallowing the contents of a partially incubated chicken egg (the embryo and yolk of an egg incubated for seven or eight days) on an empty stomach. Eating fertilized eggs for seven to ten days has been effective—and it is absolutely harmless, without untoward side effects or contraindications, unless a person has an allergy to eggs.

Embryotherapy for abnormal sexual function, like cell therapy for sexual dysfunction, stems from original research by Dr. Alexis Carrel, who showed that embryonic extracts used alone kept certain tissue cultures alive for many years. The first experiments with embryotherapy were conducted by Dr. Ivan M. Popov, who had given raw fertilized eggs to recently released prisoners of war. In his book *Stay Young*, Dr. Popov wrote:

Many of those soldiers suffered from secondary impotence and were unable for some time to have an erection, whether by self-stimulation or in the presence of a woman. The men, of course, tried to fraternize with local girls, and an orderly handling the records remarked that the men whom I had put on embryotherapy fraternized much more successfully than the others not eating raw fertilized eggs.

I questioned the men about this, and the responses, checked against the records, revealed that the embryotherapy did speed up the return of normal sexual function. Fraternization records were then kept and compared in several paired groups, and they indeed showed the balance of improvement weighed heavily in favor of embryotherapy.[4]

Eating raw chicken eggs can be very dangerous. Swallowing dead embryos can lead to food poisoning or infection. Egg embryos are among the best culture media for viruses. Salmonella bacteria have also become a major problem in recent years. Therefore, the embryos must be prepared carefully.

An egg embryo should be alive and healthy when it is ingested. It should be swallowed on an empty stomach, so that some of its active elements can reach the bloodstream through the lining of the digestive tract. Otherwise, the embryo is mixed with the digestive bolus and destroyed by enzymes in the stomach or intestine.

Some chicken farmers in the United States specialize in egg-embryo production. However, the shelf life of eggs suitable for embryotherapy is just a few hours. Dr. Popov, in his treatment regimen, utilized biostimulins, turning the egg upside down a couple of times a day to make the embryo struggle against gravity to turn its head around. The struggle caused biostimulins to be produced to help the embryo overcome its stress. Biostimulins make an egg stronger and more potent.

While embryotherapy is not disapproved by the FDA nor criticized by American organized medicine, it still has not found favor in this country. In Europe and Mexico, it is used broadly. The doctors and clinics that dispense cell therapy generally also provide embryotherapy.

Biostimulated incubated fertilized egg yolks taken as a cocktail or sucked raw from their shells make a useful live-food additive. They are excellent stimulants for healthy cell growth and gonadal activity, and they reinvigorate sluggish or aging sexual organs.

Chapter 9

DMG FOR THE SEXUAL ORGANS

My testicles seldom stop moving. They twitch! I can feel them jumping when I put my hand in my pants pocket. This wouldn't be so bad if my testicles weren't so timid, but anytime I'm having intimate relations the pair of them noticeably shrink up into my groin.

I'm single, thirty-three, successful as a publicity agent, and relatively attractive to my clients in show business and modeling. I've had relationships with many of them. The only problem is that my testicles fade into my belly during sex.

It's not that I'm overly conscious of them. Their disappearing act has been remarked on by half the women with whom I've gone to bed. Having no apparent testicles makes me appear like a freak. It doesn't detract from my ability as a lover, but the shriveling of my scrotum against the bottom of my body has me worried and wondering. And the girls say they've never heard of timid testicles before. Is there something I could do to be like all the other guys in the locker room?

Sebastian B.
Beverly Hills, California

After twenty-six years of marriage, I became a widow suddenly. I remained alone for ten years, then met a man like my former husband and married him seven months ago. I love my new husband, but our sex life has been unsatisfactory due to my dry vagina. I am fifty-four years old and find myself with inadequate vaginal secretions. Years ago, I would be naturally lubricated within fifteen to thirty seconds of initiation of sex play. Now I don't get wet at all. When he inserts his penis into my opening, I get sore inside, and he can hardly slip in and out.

Worse, a watery and smelly discharge has been causing my vagina to itch, burn, and be generally irritated. Although my husband denies it, I think it's something he brought to me because I never had any discharge before I started to have sexual relations with him. I'm wondering if I'm infected with germs. What nutritional aid is there for my problem? Taking care of the body is something I believe in.

Mona F.
Cedar Rapids, Iowa

Testicle twitching, while not usual, certainly is possible, as is eye twitching, grimacing, head shaking, throat clearing, swallowing, thigh jerking, shoulder shrugging, or a more complex series of tics always carried out in a precise order. Tics are purposeless repetitive movements of a muscle or group of muscles. They can occur at any age and in either sex. Normal causes of tics are fatigue, overexertion, and anxiety. Basically, tics of the testicles are involuntary nervous twitches. They are not dangerous, except for the psychological damage caused by the underlying neurosis. An individual suffering from tics usually displays other signs of being nervous or highly geared, such as behavior problems, personality maladjustment, or another psychological manifestation. Anxiety intensifies the tic.

An associated problem, which Sebastian B. described as "timid testicles," may be due to the testicles being undescended. This is a condition in which one or both of the testicles failed to come down into the scrotum at birth. Undescended testicles are often arrested somewhere between the abdomen and the scrotum. The reason for this remains unknown. Unfortunately, sperm cannot be produced at normal body temperature; they need the cooler environment of the scrotum. Thus, sterility will result if both testicles are undescended. Men with undescended testicles also are susceptible to a high incidence of tumors, and 90 percent of victims develop hernia. (For a technique to examine for undescended testicles, see page 15.)

When a man with undescended testicles is excited sexually, his scrotum and testicles will retract into his abdominal region. This retraction is dangerous if a harsh movement causes torsion, or twisting, of the spermatic cords, which hold the testicles. Each cord is made up of muscles, ducts, and blood vessels; twisting a cord will cut off the blood supply and result in gangrene of the involved testicle.

Vaginal dryness and inelasticity sometimes come with menopause. The lining of the vagina becomes thinner, and vaginal secretions and lubrications decrease to the point where vaginal "atrophy" sets in. Itching, burning, or pain during intercourse may be present, along with a watery, whitish, vile-smelling discharge. Alternately, vaginitis can develop when the normal chemical balance of the vagina has been disrupted, commonly from eating a poor diet or from being infected with a parasite, yeast, bacteria, or venereal disease. The vagina's chemical balance is maintained by certain beneficial bacteria that grow there normally and make the secretions acidic. The female hormone estrogen, secreted by the body, also helps to keep the cells of the vagina healthy. Vaginitis, with its subsequent discharge, may result from a lack of estrogen, as in menopause; from taking antibiotics or douching too much; or from a systemic disease such as diabetes.

The various conditions just discussed—dry vagina, vaginitis, twitching testicles, and undescended testicles—although dissimilar, may all be helped by a particular nutrient. Although it has been called vitamin B15, this nutrient is not a vitamin. It has a controversial history in clinical nutrition.

but the FDA seems to have matters well in hand. A trial in Chicago's Federal District Court about ten years ago clarified the status of N, N-Dimethylglycine (DMG), the active ingredient behind what has been designated as B_{15}.

DMG is useful as a sexuality enhancer. Its properties benefit the internal and external genitalia, as well as the entire urogenital system. The reason will become clear when the DMG metabolic effect is explained.

THE MAIN DMG ACTION IN THE BODY

The pure food supplement N, N-Dimethylglycine helps to reduce sexual inadequacy caused by subtle or unrecognized malnourishment. DMG's biochemical role in the body was discovered in 1941 by Philip Handler, Ph.D. With his coworkers, Dr. Handler published a paper in the United States in which he demonstrated, among other things, that DMG exists as a metabolic substance and that it provides essential building blocks to cells. Dr. Handler also showed that DMG goes into action halfway through the process in which foods are transformed into the basic elements utilized by the body for energy and growth. Similar to the action of a vitamin (but not itself a vitamin), DMG is a cofactor in metabolism, suggested Dr. Handler.

Two years after Handler's discovery, Niels Nielson, Ph.D., of Denmark, demonstrated that DMG is a nonfuel nutrient. Dr. Nielson explained that DMG does not add directly to the energy pool but instead provides a series of biologically active substances, including methyl groups, required by the body. A methyl group is a molecular fragment consisting of one carbon (C) and three hydrogen (H) atoms, bonded together in the following way:

Every DMG molecule gives up two methyl groups to the cell through a process called *oxidative demethylation*. Each DMG molecule is therefore an indirect transmethylic agent. In the transmethylation process, one-carbon units, such as the methyl group shown, are transferred from one molecule to another. By making this "methyl donation," DMG acts as a cofactor, aiding vitamins, fats, hormones, and proteins in completing their metabolic action or cycle. It is through this same transmethylation process that DMG aids the body in detoxification.

It appears that the effects of this "molecular motion" may lead to an increase in oxygen utilization by cellular tissue. The exact process by which DMG enhances oxygen utilization has not been worked out in detail by nutritional scientists. However, all body cells need oxygen to function, and by assisting in the oxygenation process, DMG can and does significantly affect health and health-related problems, especially those related to the sex organs.

With this as a background, it should now be easier to focus on what DMG is supposed to be. While DMG has other physiological properties, which will be described later in this chapter, its main function in the body is as an "intermediary metabolite" of the choline cycle. DMG occurs naturally in food and in the body, and it helps to increase the efficiency of certain biochemical functions at the cellular level. It improves the body's well-being. By increasing the efficiency of operations within the cell, DMG becomes important as a "metabolic enhancer."

The definition of DMG is continually being refined, as scientists are understanding DMG's role in the body better and better. At present, no category exists within official government standards for what DMG is supposed to be; therefore, nutritionists at the FDA have had difficulty classifying DMG as a food. DMG can be defined as a nonfuel nutrient. It is nonfuel because it contributes no significant calories to the system; it is a nutrient because it does provide building blocks for the synthesis of many biologically active molecules such as hormones, proteins, and even DNA itself.

Although research on the chemical pathways and nutritional value of DMG has taken years to complete, studies have revealed that DMG is so important that it has a place beside other known metabolic enhancers, such as choline, PABA, and omega-linolenic acid, an important fatty acid.

REDUCING FATIGUE FOR MORE SEXUAL FUN

Some nutritional researchers believe that DMG increases cellular efficiency. They say it can help combat health problems like chronic fatigue and hypoxia (a lack of oxygen in certain body tissues, such as those of the penis or vagina). Providing organs with enhanced oxygen nutrition permits the organs to function more efficiently. The organs regain muscle tone. If the penile or vaginal muscles lose their tone, a lack of elasticity from muscular weakness results; the organs lose the ability to expand or contract indefinitely. Taking the food substance DMG, however, helps the penis to stand erect when stimulated and the vagina to properly contract.

Dr. Robert C. Atkins, diet specialist and author of *Dr. Atkins' Superenergy Diet* and *Dr. Atkins' Nutrition Breakthrough*, reported several case histories of patients whose health improved after using DMG. He said, "DMG is noticeable for being one of several fatigue-fighting nutrients. For some people, it is the best." He described a thirty-year-old housewife from Nebraska who complained that she was retaining water, craving sweets, crying often, and unable to make decisions. "We put her on a regimen involving DMG and about a week later she called to say everything was fantastic."

Dr. Atkins added, "She went in for an operation and was up walking the first day. One month later, she wrote to say she never felt better in her life."[1]

Dr. Howard Lutz, former medical research scientist with the National Institutes of Health as well as former medical director of the Institute of Preventive Medicine, used DMG to treat sexual inadequacy of various types. He also usually recommended one or two 90-milligram tablets of DMG daily as an energy booster.

Sexual inadequacy often results from a lack of endurance, since the energy that the body needs for the sex act is above and beyond what it normally needs to carry on life-supporting functions. Maintenance of body systems in as close to optimum health as possible is the first priority for the body's energy. Only after performing maintenance will the body spare any excess calories to satisfy the sex drive. This is why sexual functions are frequently the first thing to go when the body becomes ill, fatigued, or similarly stressed.

"I am convinced that DMG is a miracle substance," declared Dr. Lutz. "It works wonders. Its effect is dramatic. Patients quickly have an improvement in energy levels and in stamina. They sleep and rest better." Dr. Lutz said that in one three-year period, he treated more than 3,000 people with DMG. Unlike some other nutrients, DMG offers incredible results in a short time; Dr. Lutz reported that his patients seemed to feel the substance's effects in thirty to sixty minutes.

"Depending on the individual's body metabolism, the effects of DMG last from six to eighteen hours," said Dr. Garry F. Gordon, former medical director of Mineralab, Inc., and former president and board chairman of the American Academy of Medical Preventics, a group of wholistic physicians who advocate the use of chelation therapy.

DMG fights the tendency to feel fatigue by cutting down on waste products such as lactic acid that normally build up in the blood when you exercise heavily. It is believed to do this by increasing the amount of oxygen that reaches the body cells and therefore improving energy production within the cells.

"Basically, it helps the body utilize energy reserves when normal energy sources are too low," said Jerzy W. Meduski, M.D., Ph.D., a nutritional biochemist in the Department of Neurology at the University of Southern California School of Medicine. Dr. Meduski has studied one-carbon transfer reactions in the body. In connection with his interest, he has investigated DMG as an important intermediary metabolite. DMG had been neglected due to a lack of appropriate methodology and differences in behavior from the nutrient choline, which was the popular oxygen enhancer for the cells, until Dr. Meduski began his investigations in 1976.

Early in his studies, Meduski worked out ways to identify DMG and to produce it in tablet form for easy handling. He also carried out DMG toxicity studies during his preliminary investigations. Included in the toxicity studies were LD-50 toxicity tests on rats. The LD-50 tests determined how fast it would take DMG, and in what dosage, to kill one-half of the test rats. The results showed that more than 5,000 milligrams of DMG powder could be ingested by each medium-size rat before any one of the test animals died. The LD-50 tests indicated that DMG is proportionately safer than aspirin. "DMG is less than half as toxic as table salt," reported Dr. Meduski.[2]

Meduski also conducted long-range chronicity studies on DMG. He examined the characteristics of animals consuming large quantities of DMG while participating in toxic experiments. He especially compared behavior in high- and low-oxygen atmospheres. DMG "peps people up when they need it, when the wear and tear of the day drags you down," said Meduski. "It's amazing. It gives an immense boost to your sexual energy level."

CELLULAR OXYGEN EFFECTS FROM DMG

Dr. Mitchell Pries, a cardiologist from Palm Springs, California, conducted a study using DMG on 103 elderly people. The study program included two regimens—DMG given alone to one group, and DMG given along with several minerals including selenium and silica to a second group. The group given the DMG and minerals did noticeably better than the group given DMG alone. But both groups reported a marked increase in sex drive. The men reported awakening with erections more frequently during the test period, and the women expressed a renewed desire for sex. Additionally, Dr. Pries found other marked improvements in patients of both groups, including lessening of the pain associated with angina pectoris, lowering of abnormally high blood pressure, reductions in blood cholesterol and triglyceride levels, noticeable improvement in the electrocardiogram (EKG) patterns of heart patients, and general improvement in the blood-flow characteristics of all subjects.

Pries also conducted a second study on 50 patients—30 supplemented with DMG and 20 supplemented with a placebo. Among the findings were visible and positive effects of DMG supplementation.

In one four-year period, Pries had 400 patients in his private practice who regularly took DMG and did not have even one incident of toxic response.

Earlier in this chapter, I noted that DMG works by donating methyl groups to potentially toxic substances, thereby rendering the toxic substances harmless. When DMG is ingested, less oxygen is consumed in detoxification metabolism, leaving more oxygen available for the cells. Additionally, the methyl group can transform serotonin, a hormone that constricts blood vessels, into a substance that does not constrict blood vessels. Methyl groups also convert the hormone norepinephrine into epinephrine (adrenaline), which is a major hormone required for sexual performance. Without epinephrine, the body would not experience a reaction to even the most exciting sexual stimulus.

Thus, acting as an indirect methyl donor, DMG improves circulation and enhances the supply of oxygen to the cells. A secondary benefit of methyl-group production is increased production of cellular lecithin, also required for sexuality (see page 47).

In 1940, S.V. Maksimov and colleagues at the Endocrinology Laboratory of Kar'kov Institute Endokrinol, Khim, Formon, in Kar'kov, Russia, noted that DMG normalizes the blood levels of several hormones by stimulating the adrenals and regulating adrenal corticoid activity. Thus, there is evidence that DMG stimulates at least two body organs, the hypophysis and the adrenals, both important sexual endocrine glands.

CONFUSION CONCERNING DMG

DMG has as complex and controversial a background as do the FDA, IRS, and CIA. In fact, the IRS (Internal Revenue Service), the CIA (Central Intelligence Agency, and the FDA—especially the FDA—have all shown an interest in DMG.

N, N-Dimethylglycine has erroneously been labeled "vitamin B_{15}." In fact, there is no vitamin B_{15}. DMG does not meet the requirements to be a vitamin. In order to hold the title of "vitamin," absence of the food from the diet must lead to a deficiency disease, the way a lack of niacin causes pellagra or a lack of ascorbic acid causes scurvy. This is not the case with DMG, nor with either of DMG's analogs, pangamic acid and calcium pangamate.

THE RULING ON DMG

DMG has its enemies; Victor Herbert, M.D., J.D., and Neville Colman, M.D., both of the Hematology and Nutrition Laboratory of the Bronx Veterans Administration Medical Center, New York, are chief among them. Dr. Colman told nutrition scientists that several of the components of DMG are mutagenic, as shown by the Ames test, a widely used *in vitro* (test tube) assay.

The FDA sued FoodScience Corporation of Essex Junction, Vermont, the primary manufacturer of DMG, to stop the production and sale of DMG. The outcome of the FDA's litigation against N, N-Dimethylglycine was that DMG is classed as a food additive when it is mixed with other ingredients, such as the binder dicalcium phosphate. In order to sell a DMG tableted-and-bound product, the manufacturer has to apply for a food-additive petition. The court found for the FDA, even though Judge Roszkowsky clearly stated that DMG is present as a natural substance in many foods. Judge Roszkowsky ruled that DMG's status as a food is not the immediate issue. Because he felt that DMG was a newly discovered nutrient without a long history, he bent the food-additive regulations in favor of the FDA. He said that DMG cannot be sold as a food if it is mixed with other ingredients; if mixed with other ingredients, it must be labeled as a food additive and therefore falls under FDA jurisdiction. The judge added, however, that no company would be prohibited from manufacturing and marketing a *pure* N, N-Dimethylglycine tablet for food use.

The only substantial concept that came out of the four-year battle by the FDA against DMG is that the product must be free of all the usual tablet-making excipients. When pure and unbound, the substance can be considered a food and not an additive. Four DMG product manufacturers—FoodScience, DaVinci, Pro-Science, and SportScience Laboratories—have responded by producing pure DMG products, which represent the only legal DMG products to date.

DMG, DIPA, AND VITAMIN B$_{15}$

The shock waves emanating from a 1978 *New York* magazine cover article set the stage for the widespread introduction of diisopropylammonium dichloracetate (DIPA) to the vitamin B$_{15}$ market. Producers of bootleg vitamin B$_{15}$ sprung up all over the country. Realizing that there was a vacuum in the market, they increased their production, the bulk of which was based on DIPA.

DIPA is chemically similar to DMG, but it has very different effects. The public rush in the late 1970s for any product even vaguely associated with vitamin B$_{15}$ was unfortunate. Many consumers who experimented with B$_{15}$ products at that time were dissatisfied. DIPA simply cannot produce the continued sexual benefits that DMG has shown in successful formulations over the years.

Thus, there is *good* B$_{15}$ and *bad* B$_{15}$. Market research has shown that DIPA has been imported heavily from Spain, Monaco, Italy, Germany, and the United Kingdom, among other countries. FDA rules do not apply to these products, which may be deleterious. The notion of vitamin B$_{15}$ must therefore be left behind when looking for the promised B$_{15}$ activity. The product you buy and take should have N, N-Dimethylglycine as part of its formula and clearly show the presence of DMG on the label. In addition to DIPA, inexpensive common amino acids such as lysine, glycine, methionine, and vitamins like PABA are also being substituted for DMG by many companies. Although they are excellent nutrients and considerably safer than DIPA, these foods have nothing to do with the metabolic activity and sexual enhancement of DMG. DMG is the sexual enhancer that you are after.

Chapter 10

CHELATION THERAPY FOR ORGASMIC PROBLEMS

I am recently retired from the U.S. Army after forty years of service, mostly overseas. At sixty-two, it's time for me to settle down with a fine woman. I've whored with different races and nationalities around the world, but now when I'm anxious to make one woman happy, I don't seem to be able to.

My trouble is an inability to sustain an erection. My penis appears burned out. When first becoming stimulated, I may get an erection, but it does not last. My penis stands up but then drops down, becoming too limp to use for sexual intercourse. This condition has evolved gradually, growing serious over the last ten years.

I had a complete physical examination for impotency by military doctors just before my Army retirement. The diagnosis was that the blood pressure in my penis is just too low. An additional bank of medical tests given to me by civilian doctors last week uncovered that my failure to hold an erection comes from a lack of blood remaining in the penis after arousal has begun. The penile arteries are clogged. The tissues surrounding the shaft do not fill with sufficient blood to hold the penis firm and hard. The docs said some stiffening could be provided by an implant, but I refused this sort of artificial erection.

It has been over a year since I've enjoyed sexual relations with the woman I've been dating. We've tried a couple of times but have found it disastrous for both of us. She wants to have sex with me, and I'm fearful that I'll lose her interest if I don't come across soon. She says it doesn't matter, but I know better.

Is there any medical or self help treatment that I could try to stiffen my flaccid penis? It's not that I'm entirely impotent, since initially the penis does get erect. What can I do to keep it hard?

Major Austin C.
U.S. Army (Retired)
Dallas, Texas

I'm a forty-eight-year-old woman with trouble that may affect my future happiness. Having never before been married, I now find myself deeply involved with a dashing widower my own age. He wants to marry me for a variety of reasons, not the least of which is sex. He's let me know in many ways that he desires an intimate relationship. In younger years, I did engage in sexual intercourse with various men, but my attitude has long since changed.

The fact is, I don't want to be intimate anymore—not ever. I just feel nothing at all about sex. Every time my fiancé and I are together, he wants to have intercourse; I continue to put him off with an implied promise that we will when we're married. I don't mind when my fiancé kisses, cuddles, or fondles me from the waist up; however, when he puts his hand under my dress, I'm compelled to break off our familiarity. It's as if some blockage cuts off my feelings for any touching below, despite my wish to be married to and supported by the man.

I probably need a sex therapist, but I can't afford the cost. Because of leg cramps and high blood pressure, I've had to visit my internist frequently, and I incidentally told him of my turn-off to sex. The doctor thinks it may be related to the cause of my other health problems—hardening of the arteries. Is there any way for me to change my negative feelings toward sex? Can I do something on my own, without a sex counselor? I do want a good marriage with the widower, but I'm afraid that my frigidity may get in our way.

Virginia C.
South Bend, Indiana

The mechanisms of orgasm, as described in earlier chapters, appear to be parallel in men and women, except for the male ejaculation and the female capacity for multiple orgasms. Masters and Johnson, among other sex researchers, have found that the contractions of the voluntary genital-pelvic muscles during orgasm are identical in the two sexes. Investigators at the University of Washington found that sex therapists and other professional sexual counselors could not tell whether descriptions of orgasm were written by men or women.

Sexologists have found that even concerning ejaculation, some women appear to be similar to men in that they release fluid at orgasm (see page 10). Female ejaculation comes from the vestigial female prostate, the Skene's glands, which are located in the vaginal wall. Female orgasm, therefore, is potentially the same as male orgasm in all respects.

Writing in *Psychology Today*, Julian M. Davidson, Ph.D., professor of physiology at Stanford University, said:

> The orgasmic experience itself is no doubt associated with activa-
> tion of nerves somewhere in the cortex [of the brain], but we have
> no strong clues as to precisely where. . . . Activation of neurons in
> the septum, a part of the limbic system at the top of the brainstem,
> is reportedly associated with orgasm. Two areas in the spinal cord
> in the middle and lower back apparently coordinate the mechanics
> of ejaculation, including the movement of semen into the urethra
> and the contractions that ejaculate it, as well as the comparable
> movements and contractions associated with female orgasm.

Dr. Davidson went on to explain that when sexual stimuli from the brain and genitals pass a critical threshold, neural signals are sent simultaneously in two directions from a control point in the central nervous system. Neural signals go upward to higher brain areas in the cortex to trigger the intense subjective experience of orgasm and the sense of sexual satiety. Neural signals also travel downward to produce orgasm's physiological reactions in the genital-pelvic region.

THE PREORGASMIC WOMAN

The definition of successful sexual functioning for a woman includes effective arousal with a desire for sex, vaginal penetration, and orgasmic release. All three factors need to be present. (Success can also be achieved if a woman experiences orgasm after penile penetration but without coital stimulation, the orgasm brought on by oral or manual stimulation.)

Arousal and orgasm cause the autonomic nervous system to discharge nerve impulses. Lubrication and arousal involve the parasympathetic nervous system. The muscular contractions that accompany orgasmic release are controlled primarily by the sympathetic nervous system. The smooth muscle of the uterus is controlled by the same sympathetic hypogastric nerve as is the muscle of the male reproductive tract that, when contracting, moves semen into the urethra before orgasm. Thus, the little-studied contractions of the uterus during orgasm may be the counterpart of seminal emission in men.

Virginia C., our female letter writer at the beginning of this chapter, has hypertension (high blood pressure) and no doubt is being treated with antihypertensive drugs. Antihypertensives relieve high blood pressure by acting directly on the nervous system, by relaxing the blood vessels, or by draining the body of excess fluid. Ismelin, generically known as guanethidine, is an antihypertensive that interferes with erection and ejaculation. In men, it often produces "dry orgasm," that is, orgasm without ejaculation of semen, as described by our letter writer in Chapter 8, Ollie L. Ollie did not mention having high blood pressure or taking antihypertensive drugs, but he did allude to a type of retrograde ejaculation in which his semen was drawn back into his bladder rather than expelled from his penis. Aldomet or Aldoril (methyldopa), Hydropres, Rauzide, Salutensin, and Ser-Ap-Es (reserpine) all can cause impotence and lower the sex drive. Since they do this in men, if male orgasm works similarly to female orgasm, Virginia C.'s preorgasmic response could be connected to her antihypertensive medication.

Instead of mental or emotional factors, a physical problem could be the reason a preorgasmic woman (formerly called frigid) is unable to experience total sexual pleasure and satisfaction. The woman could be inhibited in her response due to a failure to lubricate or dilate properly. This type of physical dysfunction may be the result of abnormally structured genitalia; low levels of female hormones; irregular blood-sugar levels; dysfunctioning thyroid;

stress; poor nutrition; localized disease such as endometriosis, cystitis, or vaginitis; systemic disease such as diabetes; peripheral or central nervous system disorders such as multiple sclerosis; muscular disorders such as muscular dystrophy; drugs such as oral contraceptives, tranquilizers, or blood-pressure medicines; ablative surgery such as hysterectomy or mastectomy; or physiologic changes such as atrophy of the vagina. Many of these difficulties are related in some degree to systemic hardening of the arteries. All of them except abnormal genitalia are the specific results of a degenerative disease process taking place in the woman's body.

When a preorgasmic patient is suffering from an organic disorder, no amount of sexual counseling will help very much. For example, the Masters and Johnson three-stage sensate-focus exercises consisting of nongenital pleasuring, genital pleasuring, and nondemanding coitus are generally beneficial if mental or emotional factors are the cause of the preorgasmic disturbance, but they seem to fail completely when the problem is due to physical factors. The exercises also may fail for a woman who manages to achieve orgasm with clitoral masturbation but cannot do so through coitus, especially if the woman has some physical disorder involving hardening of the arteries. Hardening of the arteries can even occur in young adults. The treatment for this type of woman has to be leveled at reversing the medical condition.

Experts say that at least 10 percent of women never experience orgasm, either from masturbation, clitoral stimulation, or coitus. Of the less than 90 percent who do enjoy orgasm, 75 percent experience it regularly, but only 50 percent are orgasmic during sexual intercourse. The reasons a large percentage of women are not orgasmic during coitus are not completely known.

Psychic factors were at one time blamed for "frigidity." These mental or emotional disorders included inadequate sexual excitement, marital discord, anger, fear, guilt, psychiatric disturbances (depression being the most frequent), and stressful life situations (such as divorce or death). The preorgasmic woman frequently suffers from feelings of inadequacy, inhibition connected with religious training, or fear of losing control, which together comprise about 80 percent of psychic complications. The remaining 20 percent are psychological factors involving performance anxiety, "spectatoring" (whereby a woman objectively observes her responses rather than enjoying them), excessive need to please the partner, rationalization about why orgasm should be enjoyed, and communication failure between partners.

Finally, ignorance on the part of either partner concerning female genital anatomy and function or techniques of effective arousal and stimulation sometimes hurt a woman's ability to have a positive sexual response. All these factors—mental, emotional, educational, and physical—are possible reasons why a woman is sexually dysfunctional.

THE IMPOTENT MAN

Many doctors have long believed that impotence is usually caused by emotional factors, so men experiencing this problem have usually found themselves in psychiatrists' offices or sex therapy classes. Results have been mixed. A man's ability to get an erection and sustain it, even after long psychotherapy, remains unreliable, leaving the man in a state of anxiety. Anxiety tends to reduce potency, adding even further to the victim's incidence of penile flaccidity.

The erection process is a physical phenomenon that begins with an increased flow of blood into the penis and ends with the blood slowly returning to the body's general circulation. Sometimes the blood starts to recede sluggishly while the erection is still in progress because of a contraction of blood vessel "valves" in the penis; this decreases the hardness of an erection. A number of medical scientists believe that the erection valves become rigid as part of the aging process and lose the ability to contract or relax. Hardening of the arteries, which often accompanies aging, may narrow the erection blood vessels, preventing enough blood from entering the penis and producing the degree of hardness a man experienced when young. Thus, the main physical causes of impotence in middle-aged men are clogging of blood circulation in the penis, dropping of penile blood pressure, lack of mobility of penile vein valves, and a combination of all three. Also, as mentioned in relationship to preorgasmic women, many prescription drugs affect sexual performance, causing impotence, delayed ejaculation, retrograde ejaculation, loss of libido, or even development of female sex characteristics in men.

According to Dr. Dorothy Perloff, staff cardiologist at the University of California, San Francisco School of Medicine, many of the factors affecting blood pressure also affect sexual enjoyment and performance. "When you alter the nervous system, you alter sexuality," said Dr. Perloff. "The whole process of having an erection, maintaining an erection and achieving orgasm depends on a wide variety of muscular and circulatory factors, all of which are tied into the nervous system. The whole process is a very complex one and it depends on a very delicate balance happening in the brain. If you upset that balance, it will affect you sexually."[1]

The problem of impotence has become quite common. An estimated 10 percent of men are incapable of getting a firm penis no matter how physically or psychologically stimulated they become. As many as 50 percent of men experience impotence some of the time. In fact, nearly all men struggle with impotence at least once in their lives.

The first time a man suffers from impotence, he may become anxious and begin to question his manhood. The second time, his anxiety builds and what happened previously takes on greater emotional significance. The third bout of impotence may actually be brought on by recalling the prior incidents. Repetition sets up a vicious cycle of psychogenic—caused by the mind—impotence, which adds to any actual physical problem.

Obviously, treatment of impotence must begin with finding the cause. To test whether the problem is psychological, a man should wrap a single band of moistened postage stamps around his penis before going to bed. If any of the stamps are ripped in the morning, an erection probably occurred while he slept. This indicates that his impotence is physical, not psychological.

If a man has sexual desires but fails to get or hold an erection when excited—with all partners and from masturbation—and does not have an erection during sleep or upon awakening, his problem probably has an organic or physical basis.

CHELATION THERAPY

One solution for impotent men and preorgasmic women could be chelation therapy. Chelation therapy is a safe and effective way to open clogged arteries and increase blood flow to areas of the body with impaired blood circulation.

Chelation therapy has not been accepted by most mainstream physicians as a technique to reverse hardening of the arteries. Many physicians do not know how the procedure works. Doctors who do know something about chelation therapy think that the procedure is too new or that it has been inadequately tested. Consequently, relatively few patients with sexual dysfunction caused by hardening of the arteries have been informed that a valid, specific, albeit controversial medical treatment is available to unblock their narrowed arteries.

Chelation therapy, contrary to what many physicians believe, is not new; it was introduced into the United States in 1948. Long before its migration to this country, it was employed as a chemical medical procedure in Europe. Chelation is well-recognized in most countries as an excellent treatment to reverse lead poisoning; it has been used in the United States for this specific purpose. Chelation therapy has been the primary means for removing toxic lead from the bodies of children and adults for over forty years.

Chelation is administered intravenously under a physician's supervision when it is necessary to restore adequate blood flow through a patient's clogged arteries. The therapy is able to relieve symptoms of arterial insufficiency anywhere in the body, including throughout the penile blood channels of impotent elderly men with hardening of the arteries.

In 1976, Dr. John H. Olwin, clinical professor of surgery at Rush Medical College in Chicago, appeared before the *ad hoc* committee of the Advisory Panel on Internal Medicine of the Scientific Board of the California Medical Association. The committee was investigating the safety, effectiveness, and medical legitimacy of chelation therapy for hardening of the arteries. Dr. Olwin presented the results of the more than 16,000 chelation treatments he had administered to patients for hardening of the arteries. He also described a number of psychological and internal medical benefits that he had observed, among them increases in libido and sexual potency. Dr. Olwin presented the following case history as an example:

> An eighty-year-old formerly brilliant lawyer in Chicago had had a chronic brain syndrome (senility) for many years. His neurologist asked about this chelation treatment; I explained the experience that we'd had, and the family wished to have the elderly man treated. The patient was treated in collaboration with the neurologist, and after about a year there was no improvement in the patient's chronic brain syndrome.
>
> However, the eighty-year-old man's wife called me one day and asked, "Is this supposed to increase sexual desire?" I said, "We've had that recorded." And she replied, "Well, James has not been interested in sex for fifteen years and last night he tried to make love to me!"

"Perhaps this effect was an indication that the man's sexual problem was not a functional affair but an organic change," Dr. Olwin concluded. "It seems reasonable that if blood supply is being improved, all organs of the body may benefit from this improvement."

At present, less than 1,000 physicians in the United States offer chelation treatment. Those who do usually use it to reverse or repair the effects of hardening of the arteries including heart disease, diabetes, senility, stroke, Parkinson's disease, and multiple sclerosis. Approximately 3,000,000 intravenous injections have been administered by chelating physicians to around 300,000 patients. The results have been most impressive and often lifesaving. How chelation works is no mystery. The facts have been published in medical journals—in some 1,700 articles.

The chief agent used to clear arteries is a synthetic amino acid called ethylene diamine tetraacetic acid (EDTA). Since the component of EDTA that is employed for unclogging the arteries is sodium salt, the substance is also called disodium edetate.

AN EXPLANATION OF EDTA CHELATION

EDTA, when administered to a patient, is known to "chelate," or bind with, certain metals in the body. This manmade amino acid is able to grasp ionic calcium from the bloodstream and from cells within the walls of blood vessels. The term *chelation* comes from the Greek *chele*, which refers to the claw of a crab, implying a firm, pinchlike binding with certain minerals. Chelation is defined as the incorporation of a metal or mineral ion into a chemical heterocyclic ring structure. EDTA encircles or sequesters metals or calcium and causes them to lose their physiologic and toxic properties. Thus, when chelation therapy is administered, the calcium or heavy metal within the body comes in contact with the chelating amino acid, becomes imprisoned by it, and then is excreted from the body in a bound and inert form. Atherosclerotic plaques (which are the substance blocking the arteries) collapse and break up like a bridge that has had all its rivets removed. The calcium was the binder, or glue, that held the plaques together and caused the arteries to harden.

The EDTA solution is given in a very slow intravenous drip that takes about three or four hours to administer. No pain is connected with the treatment. While receiving the infusion, a patient can perform many passive activities such as talking on the phone, writing, reading, or watching television.

EDTA first binds with the circulating unbound calcium in the blood to form a calcium-EDTA complex. This is a unique property of EDTA, and its importance in reversing hardening of the arteries cannot be overemphasized. Much of the complex is excreted through the kidney, bypassing the normal renal conservation of calcium. Dr. Garry F. Gordon of Tempe, Arizona, and Dr. Robert B. Vance of Las Vegas, Nevada, confirmed this kidney action in a medical-journal article. They wrote:

> Approximately 80 percent is cleared through the kidney in the first six hours, and 95 percent in the first 24 hours. Some of the EDTA-calcium complex may dissociate, and calcium is dropped when a metal such as lead or chromium, for which EDTA has a higher affinity, becomes available.[2]

Gordon and Vance went on to explain that the loss of calcium through the kidney produces a temporary lowering of serum phosphorous, as well as an increase in serum magnesium. All of these chemical alterations with serum heavy metals benefit the heart muscle's contraction. Another possible plus is holding electrons in balance. Altogether, a person experiences a number of improvements in heart-muscle contraction, function, and rate.

The body's homeostatic mechanisms try to return the serum calcium levels to normal. They do this partly by increasing the levels of parathyroid hormone, the hormone of the parathyroid gland. The calcium initially lost is replaced from the calcium states of the body, which fluctuate according to the parathyroid hormone concentration of the blood. Some of the replacement is provided by metastatic (pathologic) calcium that has been deposited in scattered remote tissues, particularly tissues lining blood-vessel walls.

The human body is capable of replacing calcium in the blood at a rate of 50 milligrams per minute. Therefore, up to seven times the accepted dose of EDTA could be given in as little as one-tenth the normal administration time—in fifteen minutes instead of in three hours or more, as it is administered now—without serious ill effect. Consequently, EDTA is obviously quite a safe therapeutic aid. (It is safer than aspirin.)

No unusual complications have been noted when EDTA has been given by intravenous injection under the supervision of a physician following the protocol advocated by the American College of Advancement in Medicine, the organization of medical professionals who use chelation therapy as one of their subspecialties. Physicians who would like to become trained and certified as a Diplomate in Chelation Therapy should contact the American College of Advancement in Medicine (23121 Verdugo Drive, Suite 204, Laguna Hills, California 92653; telephone 800–532–3688 or 714–583–7666).

The chemical principle of chelation in many processes has been known for more than a century. Aspirin, for example, is a form of chelate. The action of penicillin is also one of chelation. Another chelation process is the softening of water, and certain ion-exchange materials such as zeolite are chelates.

More common examples of chelators are household detergents. When used to wash clothes or dishes, a detergent forms soluble chelates with calcium and magnesium, which are readily rinsed out with water. Thus, no scum builds up as a ring around the sink or washing machine. EDTA pulls calcium out of blood the way detergents pull it out of hard wash water. No calcium scum is left to line the walls of arteries.

It seems odd that the FDA will label so many chelation agents as safe for human use, yet deny EDTA for cleansing arteries.

NATURAL CHELATION FOODS FOR OPTIMAL SEXUAL HEALTH

It is not feasible to give EDTA chelation therapy to yourself. EDTA must be administered by intravenous drip by a knowledgeable physician. If you cannot find a chelating physician in your local area, you can utilize oral chelators, which are relatively common foods. Since chelation is a physiological process that occurs in your body on an ongoing basis, eating foods that encourage this natural mechanism would certainly be beneficial. I also feel that dietary chelation therapy using oral chelators is life-preserving and sexually enhancing.

The chelating nutrients, several of which have already been discussed in earlier chapters, are vitamins B_3, B_6, C, and E; the minerals magnesium, manganese, and selenium; N, N-dimethylglycine (DMG); the enzyme bromelain; the mineral salts orotic acid and aspartic acid; and garlic, onions, and high-fiber foods.

Bromelain

Tropical fruits such as bananas, kiwis, pineapples, mangos, and papayas are high in chelating minerals and in the enzyme bromelain, which has a chelationlike effect. Bromelain acts like a "pipe cleaner" for the blood vessels throughout the entire cardiovascular system. It reduces the incidence of phlebitis, assists in thinning the blood, delays red corpuscle clumping, and lowers the risk of blood clots. You can buy bromelain enzyme tablets in your local health food store. Better yet, eat whole fruits for bromelain, since whole fruits also supply fiber, as well as valuable chelating minerals and vitamins.

Bananas and other tropical fruits are rich in nutrients such as vitamins A, B$_1$, B$_2$, B$_3$, B$_6$, and C, and the minerals calcium, cobalt, iodine, iron, manganese, and zinc. They supply an ample amount of fiber, which is a natural chelator due to its roughage effect.

Papayas contain twice the vitamin C of oranges and as much vitamin A as carrots, and they are easily digested by young and old alike. Since they are low in sodium and are cholesterol free, they are also an excellent choice for people on special diets. In addition, papayas contain vitamins B$_1$ and D.

One large kiwi contains only about 55 calories, yet it has more vitamin C than a medium orange—more than the U.S. Reference Daily Intake. The fuzzy brown exterior hides a dazzling emerald green interior that tastes like melon with a hint of citrus and strawberry. Kiwi is delicious combined with yogurt, but try it alone, too. You can eat everything—including the tiny black seeds—except for the skin. Peel and slice it or cut it in half and scoop out the meat melon-style with a spoon. For some wonderful recipes using kiwis as well as papayas, mangos, bananas, and other exotic fruits, see pages 169–171.

Selenium

Almost half of a man's total supply of body selenium is concentrated in his testicles and in portions of the seminal ducts adjacent to his prostate gland. He loses selenium is his semen. Selenium deficiency seems to be a factor in cancer of the prostate, since the mineral is necessary in sufficient concentration in the body for life and health. Hair analyses have shown that men with prostate cancer are invariably deficient in body selenium.

In 1957, Klaus Schwarz, M.D., Ph.D., a medical biochemist at the University of California, Los Angeles School of Medicine, established with the help of various associates that selenium is an essential trace mineral, the active principle of the so-called Factor 3, an agent found in yeast, liver, kidney, and other food sources. Unfortunately, 75 percent of the selenium content of wheat is removed when the grain is milled into white flour.

M.L. Scott, Ph.D., a researcher at the Graduate School of Nutrition, Cornell University, found that selenium works in conjunction with vitamin E, inasmuch as both are natural chelators.

Selenium has a detoxifying action against pollutants. The average American's diet contains about 35 to 60 micrograms of selenium, equivalent to 0.1

Recipes From Paradise

Following are some sexy tropical-fruit recipes. Mix one up, take a bite, close your eyes, and enjoy.

Polynesian Paradise Papaya Salad

$1^1\!/_2$ cups cleaned and cooked medium shrimp
1 tablespoon chopped celery
1 tablespoon sliced green onion
$^1\!/_2$ teaspoon lemon juice
$^1\!/_4$ teaspoon celery powder
1 ripe papaya
Lemon wedges, optional

1. *In a small bowl, gently mix the shrimp, celery, green onion, lemon juice, and celery powder.*

2. *Cut the papaya in half lengthwise and remove the seeds. Fill each papaya cavity with half of the shrimp mixture. If desired, garnish each filled papaya half with lemon wedges.*

Makes 2 servings.

Paradise Papaya Parfaits

6 cups (16 ounces) plain low-fat yogurt
$^3\!/_4$ cup coconut flakes
$^1\!/_3$ cup frozen orange juice concentrate, defrosted
1 ripe banana, mashed
2 ripe bananas, sliced
1 ripe papaya, peeled, seeded, and cubed
20-ounce can pineapple chunks, drained
$^1\!/_4$ cup almond slivers

1. *In a large bowl, mix together the yogurt, coconut flakes, orange juice concentrate, and mashed banana.*

2. *In eight parfait glasses, layer one-third of the banana slices, one-third of the papaya cubes, and one-third of the pineapple chunks. Spoon half of the yogurt mixture over the fruit. Repeat with another one-third of the fruit and the remaining yogurt mixture. End with the remaining fruit. Top with the almonds.*

Makes 8 servings.

Papaya-Kiwi Paradise Oven Pancakes

$1/4$ cup butter or margarine
5 eggs
$1^{1}/4$ cups milk
$1^{1}/4$ cups flour
2 ripe papayas, peeled, seeded, and sliced lengthwise
2 ripe kiwis, peeled and sliced
Juice from $1/2$ lemon
Sesame seeds, as garnish

1. *Preheat the oven to 425°F.*

2. *In two 9-inch pie pans, place $1/8$ cup butter each. Place the pie pans in the oven to melt the butter. Remove the pans when the butter has melted.*

3. *Meanwhile, in a blender, whir the eggs for one minute. Add the milk and flour, and blend until smooth.*

4. *Pour half of the batter into each pie pan. Return the pie pans to the oven and bake until the pancakes are fluffy and lightly browned, about 20–25 minutes.*

5. *While the pancakes are baking, in a large bowl, toss the papaya and kiwi slices with the lemon juice; set aside.*

6. *To serve, remove the pancakes from the pie pans and place on large serving plates. Spoon half of the fruit mixture over each pancake and top with a sprinkling of sesame seeds. Cut the pancakes into wedges.*

Makes 8 servings.

Added to the sexual appeal of the following two breakfast dishes are their versatility. They can be made for one person or adapted to serve six. And the parfait is as comfortable in a paper cup for a "grab-as-you-can" breakfast as it is on the dining room table amidst your favorite china and other fancy Sunday brunch dishes.

Kiwi Paradise Breakfast Parfait

$1/4$ cup wheat germ
1 teaspoon cinnamon
1 cup plain low-fat yogurt
$1/2$ cup crushed pineapple packed in juice
1 kiwi, peeled and diced

1. *In a small dish, combine the wheat germ and cinnamon.*

2. *In a small bowl, combine the yogurt and pineapple.*

3. *In a parfait glass, spoon about one-fourth of the yogurt mixture into the bottom. Sprinkle one-fourth of the wheat-germ mixture over the yogurt mixture and top with one-fourth of the kiwi chunks. Repeat layering until all the ingredients are used.*

Makes 1 serving.

Mango-Yogurt Paradise Drink

1 soft mango, peeled, seeded, and sliced
$\frac{1}{2}$ cup plain low-fat yogurt
$\frac{1}{4}$ cup fresh-squeezed orange juice
2 one-inch ice cubes
Fresh mint, as garnish

1. *In a blender, process all of the ingredients until smooth. (Add additional milk, if desired.)*
2. *Pour the drink into a tall glass and garnish with fresh mint, if desired.*

Makes 1 serving.

part per million in the diet. Below-average diets contain substantially less of the mineral, and certain low-selenium geographical areas around the world sometimes show an elevation of cancer rates. The optimum daily intake of selenium seems to be in the range of 50 to 200 micrograms.

The National Academy of Science reports that 50 micrograms of selenium is supplied by 2.75 ounces of lobster, 4 ounces of codfish, 4 ounces of beef liver, or 1.5 ounces of beef kidney. But as much as 66 percent of the selenium present in seafood or land animals may be tied to the creatures' detoxification mechanisms against such dangerous elements as mercury or cadmium. Therefore, a good portion of the selenium from a food source may not be biologically effective in the human body.

Foods High in Selenium

The following list names foods that are high in selenium. Also given for each food is the number of micrograms of selenium per 100 grams (3.5 ounces) of edible portion of food. For example, butter has 146 micrograms of selenium in every 100 grams of edible food.

146	Butter	103	Brazil nuts
141	Herring, smoked	89	Apple cider vinegar
123	Smelt	77	Scallops
111	Wheat germ	66	Barley

66	Whole wheat bread	19	Beer
65	Lobster	18	Beef liver
63	Wheat bran	18	Lamb chops
59	Shrimp	18	Egg yolks, raw
57	Red Swiss chard	12	Mushrooms
56	Oats	12	Chicken
55	Clams	10	Swiss cheese
51	King crab	5	Cottage cheese
49	Oysters	5	Wine
48	Cow's milk, whole	4	Radishes
43	Codfish	4	Grape juice
39	Brown rice	3	Pecans
34	Top round steak	2	Hazelnuts
30	Lamb	2	Almonds
27	Turnips	2	Green beans
26	Molasses	2	Kidney beans
25	Garlic	2	Onions
24	Barley	2	Carrots
19	Orange juice	2	Cabbage
19	Gelatin	1	Oranges

Manganese

The mineral manganese is one of the essential trace metals, a necessary dietary constituent obtained from nuts, seeds, and whole-grain cereals. It is not uncommon for the hair analysis of an impotent man to show insufficient manganese.

Manganese offers natural oral chelation therapy. It works better as a calcium blocking agent against spasm of the coronary arteries than even the calcium-channel-blocking agents approved by the FDA. Manganese deficiency has been shown to be a cause of hardening of the arteries, diabetes, poor lipid and glucose metabolism, and hypothyroidism.

The more primitive people in the Philippines and in Vilcabamba, Ecuador, have a much higher manganese content according to hair mineral analyses than do most of the people in the industrialized West. The primitives have a much more normal calcium–phosphorous ratio than do Western societies; therefore, the primitives do not have hyperparathyroidism, which sends calcium into the cells and prevents manganese protection. These factors hold off the incidence of hardening of the arteries among these "backwards" peoples.

Try to put more manganese in your diet. Taking a manganese food supplement of 5 to 25 milligrams will not cause a marked improvement in a hair mineral analysis, but it will prompt a slight change. A better practice is to consume more manganese-rich whole foods.

Foods High in Manganese

The following list names foods that are high in manganese. Also given for each food is the number of milligrams of manganese per 100 grams (3.5 ounces) of edible portion of food. For example, pecans have 3.50 milligrams of manganese in every 100 grams of edible food.

3.50	Pecans	0.13	Swiss cheese
2.80	Brazil nuts	0.13	Corn
2.50	Almonds	0.11	Cabbage
1.80	Barley	0.10	Peaches
1.30	Rye	0.09	Butter
1.30	Buckwheat	0.06	Tangerines
1.30	Split peas, dried	0.06	Split peas, dried
1.10	Whole wheat	0.05	Eggs
0.80	Walnuts	0.04	Coconut meat, fresh
0.80	Spinach, fresh	0.03	Apples
0.70	Peanuts	0.03	Oranges
0.60	Oats	0.03	Pears
0.50	Raisins	0.03	Lamb chops
0.50	Turnip greens	0.03	Pork chops
0.50	Rhubarb	0.03	Cantaloupes
0.40	Beet greens	0.03	Tomatoes
0.30	Oatmeal	0.02	Cow's milk, whole
0.20	Cornmeal	0.02	Chicken breast
0.20	Millet	0.02	Green beans
0.19	Gorgonzola cheese	0.02	Apricots
0.16	Carrots	0.01	Beef liver
0.15	Broccoli	0.01	Scallops
0.14	Brown rice	0.01	Halibut
0.14	Whole wheat bread	0.01	Cucumbers

Cloves, ginger, thyme, bay leaves, and tea are also high in manganese.

Salts of Orotic Acid and Aspartic Acid

Wholistic medical experts who treat sexual disorders with nutrition suggest using salts of orotic acid, which have an orotic chelation action, when calcium, zinc, potassium, or magnesium are taken in supplemental form. Orotic acid has been called vitamin B_{13} and may or may not be correctly labeled. Orotates, which are the mineral salts of this nutrient, are "mineral carrier molecules." They take minerals to selected parts of the body and home in on certain aspects of the cell. By definition, such mineral transporters are chelation agents, non-toxic and highly efficient helpers that deliver selected minerals to the parts of the body where they are most needed.

Orotic acid is an organic molecule found in milk whey. It is also synthesized in the body from an amino acid known as aspartic acid. Orotic acid has three main functions in the body:

1. It becomes part of the DNA and RNA, the two molecules that mastermind and initiate the body's entire growth and development.
2. It stimulates oxygen-dependent pentose pathway tissue such as bone, cartilage, blood vessels, heart, and liver.
3. It forms a strong bond with various minerals, such as calcium, magnesium, potassium, zinc, and iron, and takes them to parts of the body where they are put to use.

Orotates show their superiority over the other mineral salts by their stability and their ability to penetrate the various body cells. Their absorption rate is from 60 to 80 percent, compared with an absorption rate of 1 to 9 percent for the phosphates, carbonates, and oxides. The orotates have an absorption rate that is even better than that of the amino-acid chelates. No secondary carrier systems are necessary, and no other chelates are formed.

Aspartic acid forms an organic complex with both magnesium and potassium. Magnesium aspartate and potassium aspartate transport their minerals to the inner layer of the outer cell membrane. They have been shown to reverse hardening of the arteries and to reduce the syndrome of cirrhosis of the liver. After releasing the mineral, the aspartic-acid carrier molecule is either incorporated into new protein or broken down to supply extra energy for the cell.

Aspartic acid and orotic acid work well as chelating-type nutrients for both men and women in the self-treatment or prevention of blood-flow blockage to the genitals. Dr. Hans Nieper, chief of the Department of Medicine, Silbersee Hospital, Hanover, Germany, in an interview during the Atlantic Southeastern Conference of Nutrition and Holistic Health in April 1981, described how he treats impotent males and preorgasmic females. Dr. Nieper said that he uses 1.5 grams of magnesium orotate, 300 milligrams of potassium aspartate, and 400 milligrams of bromelain, which are all megadoses. Persons treating themselves should avoid these extremely high doses, however; megadoses should only be taken by patients under the supervision of a wholistic physician knowledgeable about the chelation action of orotates and aspartates.

Chapter 11

NUTRITIONAL HELP FOR HERPES

I contracted genital herpes about five years ago, when my wife brought it home after having an extramarital affair while vacationing without me. I've been divorced for three years now, and I've not had sexual intercourse during most of that time. My celibacy is due strictly to the herpes infection. At my relatively young age of thirty-one, the virus has permanently messed up my sex life.

Any time I consider having a sexual relationship with a woman I really care for, I agonize over telling my prospective partner about my venereal disease. I can't do it, so I break off the friendship. I feel impaired, damaged, dirty, and terribly ashamed. For a year, I told nobody about my condition, not even giving it as a reason for dumping my ex-wife. Then I had sex with one-night stands I picked up in bars. But after a while, my conscience began to bother me, so I just stopped going out.

Right now, I'm seeing a psychiatrist because I can't find a solution. I feel depressed. My doctor says that I'm in the midst of the "herpes syndrome"—shock and denial, followed by loneliness, anger, and fear.

Traditional doctors have nothing to offer in the way of a cure. I'm wondering if I can find relief through something besides regular medicine?

Vernon S.
Detroit, Michigan

I've been plagued by painful herpes blisters for fourteen months and eight days. I know the exact moment I got the infection and the creep who gave it to me. The lesions on the man's genitals weren't noticeable until I took his penis in my mouth and turned on the light to better see what I was doing. Now I get herpes flare-ups once a month on the lips of my vagina and of my mouth. I experience a sort of burning sensation in both places about two or three days before the blisters begin to form. Sex for me at those times is taboo because I'm infectious and don't want to pass on the herpes.

Recently I met a wonderful man about whom I care a great deal. He has asked me to marry him, and I would like to. I'm twenty-six years old and want to be a wife and mother. But I'm afraid. I've told this man exactly what the score is about my *having herpes. He agrees that having sex together maybe two weeks out of every month might be a hardship, but he's willing to accept it. I'm not! The herpes would pose a grave danger to any unborn child I might carry. It would force me to deliver by cesarean section to prevent the child from being infected while passing through my birth canal. It would keep me from giving birth naturally. Marriage and motherhood are not for me until either medical scientists find a viable treatment for herpes or nontraditional researchers find some kind of alternative help. Is there such a thing as nutritional help for herpes?*

Sonya D.
New Orleans, Louisiana

Experts at the National Centers for Disease Control estimate that approximately 100 million Americans have contracted labial herpes, which produces sores resembling cold sores on and around the lips of the mouth, or ·the sexually transmitted and epidemic genital herpes, which is also called herpes genitalis. The National Institute of Allergy and Infectious Disease focuses on herpes genitalis, reporting that an estimated 36 million to 54 million people are active carriers. And every year, another half-million people contract this most prevalent sexually transmitted disease (STD).

Genital herpes is but one of eight major venereal diseases; gonorrhea and syphilis are by far the best known. One out of every seven American teenagers has a venereal disease. Gonorrhea, syphilis, and three others— chancroid, lymphogranuloma venereum, and granuloma inguinale—must be reported in most states. But the three remaining, little-known venereal diseases, which often go unreported by public health agencies, are becoming major health problems. They are trichomoniasis, an infection of the vagina that causes inflammation with vaginal discharge and that can be transmitted to males, in whom it causes urethral damage; nongonococcal urethritis (NGU), which affects men the same way that gonorrhea does and causes permanent sterility in women; and herpes genitalis, the fastest spreading and most serious STD because it is associated with cancer at the mouth of the womb and is occasionally transferred to infants.

While all eight STD's are serious and deserve discussion, I will concentrate on genital herpes in this chapter for ten significant reasons:

1. The disease was virtually unknown in the 1960s, but the sexual freedom of the 1970s and 1980s released it.

2. It reached epidemic proportions in the late 1970s and early 1980s.

3. It has probably become the most common infection of young, sexually active adults in the United States and other developed countries.

4. It is having a major impact on the lives of men, women, and even children.

5. It continues to be unrecognized by many primary-care physicians.
6. It produces painful sores on and around the genitals.
7. It recurs.
8. It is highly contagious.
9. It has no known cure, and regular medical treatment gives little relief.
10. It responds to nutritional therapy and other nonstandard methods of care.

Studies at STD clinics document the sharp increase in the genital herpes case load over the last decade. Among patients attending such medical facilities, the relative incidence of this viral infection versus gonorrhea has increased from two in ten persons to two in five, and seven cases of herpes genitalis are now diagnosed for every one of syphilis. These studies also indicate that the largest increase is among educated, single whites in their mid-twenties to mid-thirties.

CHARACTERISTICS OF GENITAL HERPES

Herpes genitalis can be overwhelming both physically and emotionally. Persistent, sometimes frequent recurrence can be painful, and social and sexual relations may be seriously disrupted because of embarrassment, marital discord, or fear. Many patients experience periods of diminished sex drive or impotence; some become celibate to avoid spreading the disease. Relationships often dissolve, and depression is common. In one study, over 20 percent of patients contemplated suicide at one time or another.[1]

Herpes genitalis is caused by the herpes simplex virus (HSV), which is related to other herpes viruses, such as the varicella-zoster virus, which causes chickenpox in children and shingles in adults, and the Epstein-Barr virus, which causes mononucleosis and is one of half a dozen causes of chronic fatigue syndrome.

The infections generally associated with herpes simplex virus type 1 (HSV-1) are herpes labialis, commonly seen as fever blisters and cold sores around the mouth and nose, and herpes gingivostomatitis, which affects the gums and mucous lining inside the mouth. HSV-1 infections are usually contracted early in life; over half of all children below age five have such an infection. HSV-1 infections result in the production of antibodies that are found in at least 80 percent of adults.

Herpes simplex virus type 2 (HSV-2) is generally associated with skin outbreaks near or directly involving the genital organs.

But some viral isolates from infected genital areas turn out to be HSV-1, and some oral isolates are identified as HSV-2. These "crossover" infections are presumably the result of oral-genital contact or autoinoculation.

Autoinoculation is a secondary infection by a disease already present in the body.

In genital herpes, there is virtually no difference between the clinical picture resulting from infection by HSV-1 and that resulting from infection by HSV-2. However, there is evidence that genital herpes caused by HSV-1 recurs less frequently than does an infection caused by HSV-2.

Although normally localized, herpes infections may disseminate in infants, whose immune systems are not yet fully developed. This may also happen in the immunocompromised, such as cancer patients on chemotherapy or kidney- or bone-marrow-transplant recipients, whose immune systems have been suppressed to prevent rejection and graft-versus-host disease. Dissemination can result in ravaging invasion of organs, the bloodstream, or the brain, causing diseases such as hepatitis, pneumonitis, and encephalitis.

Persons who have never had an oral or genital HSV infection usually have an especially severe form of initial herpes genitalis. That an infection is a primary initial infection can be documented by a blood test showing the absence of HSV-specific antibodies.

After an incubation period of two to twenty days, a patient suffering a primary episode of genital herpes may experience pain, twitching, urethral discharge, swollen glands, neuralgia, pain on urination, fever, headache, or malaise. These symptoms gradually increase in intensity during the first few days of active infection, and a few infections are accompanied by herpetic meningitis.

There is also an association between the persistence of the symptoms and the duration of viral shedding. Viral shedding is when the herpes organism flakes off with the peeling skin of disintegrated blisters. Recent evidence indicates that viral shedding, during which the victim is highly contagious, sometimes persists after the disappearance of overt symptoms.

Approximately 75 percent of patients experience the formation of new vesicles after the initial lesion onset. The new vesicles last about a week.

In primary infections, the symptoms last an average of two weeks but may persist for three to six weeks. Viral shedding begins with the onset of lesion formation and continues for an average of eleven days.

Primary infections usually produce many lesions, which begin as maculas or papules and then progress to vesicles or pustules. The lesions eventually become ulcers, form a crust, scab over, and finally heal.

Lesions may appear on the genitals, buttocks, or thighs, and can also form inside such organs as the urethra, vagina, and cervix.

Nonprimary initial infections, which occur in patients who previously have been exposed to the herpes virus (usually in childhood), are somewhat less severe because the victim has antibodies to HSV. Generally, the symptoms also last a shorter period of time than those of primary initial infections, and the lesions tend to be fewer in number and to heal in two to three weeks.

People who contract a herpes infection almost always harbor the virus forever. Following infection, sufferers of both HSV-1 and HSV-2 may enter a period of latency or dormancy. The virus leaves the infected site in the skin or mucous membrane and travels along the nerve fiber to the dorsal root (spinal) ganglia. Once it has entered the ganglia, it becomes dormant, remaining that way until it is reactivated to begin replicating. The length of time the virus remains dormant varies. When reactivated, it migrates back toward the spot where it first entered the body, usually taking the same pathway, and recurrence of symptoms results.

Recurrence, then, is a reactivation of the virus that produced the original infection; it is this latency feature that permits the virus to resume its ability to cause disease symptoms despite the presence of extracellular antibodies. In addition, reactivated HSV can spread directly from cell to cell without circulating in extracellular spaces, thereby temporarily avoiding potentially neutralizing antibodies.

Recurrent HSV infections are usually not as severe as primary infections, nor do they generally last as long. The frequency of recurrences varies greatly, and a pattern of recurrences may develop and then change. In one common pattern, the first recurrence is seen three to four months after the primary episode, with other recurrences following every six to eight weeks.

About 60 percent of patients experience prodromal, or early warning, symptoms such as itching, burning, tingling, or numbness in the spot where the lesions will develop. This generally happens somewhere between two to forty-eight hours before the recurrence begins. Although many victims find that this signals a recurrence quite accurately, about 10 percent report that it is unreliable as a predictor.

The major symptoms in recurrence are pain, pruritus (itching), and neuralgia. There are usually somewhat fewer lesions (a mean of three to eight), and the lesions generally advance from vesicle or pustule to crusting within ten days. The lesions usually occur at or near the original site of outbreak.

Viral shedding in recurrent infections begins with lesion formation and usually lasts four to five days. However, live virus has been isolated from the skin during the earliest disease manifestations, before severe symptoms have developed.

Again, the duration of viral shedding has been related to symptom duration, but viral shedders are sometimes asymptomatic. This may explain why some victims acquired herpes genitalis infections from people who were apparently clinically free of the disease. It may also explain why the mothers of many infected newborns had no history of HSV infection.[2] There is also believed to be a large reservoir of people with asymptomatic disease.

There has been a lot of conjecture surrounding the identity of the "trigger mechanisms" of recurrences, but conclusive evidence is lacking. Nevertheless, many patients and physicians have noted correlations between outbreaks and stressors such as fever, respiratory infection, lack of sleep, poor nutrition, emotional upset, menstruation, sexual intercourse, hormonal imbalance, mechanical friction from wearing tight clothing, and excessive exposure to sun, cold, or wind.

The past decade's increase in the incidence of herpes genitalis appears to be due mainly to persons of higher socioeconomic status acquiring the disease. Until recently, HSV-2 antibodies (indicating prior infection) were found much more frequently in persons of lower socioeconomic status. Antibodies were seen in almost 30 percent of the adults of lower socioeconomic groups, as opposed to about 10 percent of the adults of higher groups. However, while the frequency of occurrence in the lower socioeconomic groups has been stable, it has increased for college students and professionals over the past ten years or so.[3]

It should also be noted that regardless of economic status as a factor, the level of sexual activity and number of sexual partners increase the risk of contracting any STD. By way of illustration, one study found HSV-2 antibodies in over 50 percent of prostitutes but in only 1 percent of nuns.

EFFECTS OF GENITAL HERPES

Many patients react to a diagnosis of genital herpes with strong emotional distress, particularly when they realize they have contracted an *incurable* condition. Anger, frustration, and hostility are common. Some patients feel that the most damaging consequences of genital herpes are emotional. One study showed that a third of the victims surveyed had experienced impotence or diminished sexual drive. Almost half said their work performance had suffered. A fifth said that herpes had contributed to the dissolution of their marriages, and a fifth said that at times they were preoccupied with suicidal thoughts.[4]

A feature of genital herpes that generates great anxiety is its contagiousness. Many patients have described themselves as feeling "like a leper." But a more positive attitude is encouraged by organizations such as the American Social Health Association, or ASHA (P.O. Box 13827, Research Triangle Park, North Carolina 27709; telephone 919–361–8400). Around 100,000 calls a year come in to the ASHA Hot Line, about 40 percent of which are from new genital herpes patients. The Hot Line number is 919–361–8488.

It is estimated that about 90 percent of herpes in newborn babies can be traced to a maternal source; neonatal herpes is usually contracted during passage through an infected birth canal. It is estimated that an infant delivered vaginally to a mother with an active genital HSV infection has a 40 to 60 percent chance of acquiring the infection.

The mortality rate among newborns with herpes infections has been estimated at 50 percent or greater, and at least half of the infant survivors suffer serious neurological damage. (In addition, women with herpes genitalis have an increased rate of miscarriage.)

Infants appear to be at greater risk if a primary maternal infection developed during the final two weeks of pregnancy. Although cesarean section is usually recommended to allow the baby to bypass the potentially infected birth canal, it has been found that women with herpes genitalis can deliver vaginally and with no increased risk to the neonate if cultures are taken weekly and the two latest after the thirty-sixth week of gestation are negative. Taking into account the risks associated with cesarean section, doctors now recommend that culturing be performed for all pregnant women with a history of herpes infections. The drawback is that weekly culturing is readily available only in large medical centers and research laboratories.

Evidence that the herpes simplex virus has carcinogenic potential has been noted for more than twenty-five years. Most studies of the relationship between HSV-2 and human cancers have centered on a possible connection between the virus and cervical cancer and, more recently, between the virus and cancer of the vulva. The belief that there is a statistical association between HSV-2 and cervical cancer is based on the higher-than-normal frequency of prior HSV-2 infection in women with cervical carcinoma at the infection site, as well as dysplasia and carcinoma at the infection site, than in women without cervical cancer. The belief that there is a relationship between HSV-2 and vulvar cancer is based on HSV-2 particles being found in carcinomatous cells. Investigators have also noted a rise in the incidence of HSV-2 infections paralleling a rise in vulvar carcinoma at the infection site, particularly in women under forty.

However, it is still not known whether HSV-2 comes first, weakening the body and allowing the cancerous process to begin, or if the virus is an opportunistic infection, simply invading cells that have already been weakened by cancer. Defining the roles of herpesviruses in the development of cancer is of great importance, since various herpesviruses share many structural and biologic properties; demonstrating the tendency of one to form tumors would increase suspicion of the others.

Dr. Fred Rapp, chairman of the Microbiology Department at Hershey Medical Center, Pennsylvania State University, has suggested one possible tumor-forming process. During infection, he postulates, thousands of viral particles are released; some do not have all the DNA necessary to be infectious. But a defective elementary virus particle can still attack a normal cell and cause chromosomal damage. When the cell attempts to repair the damage, part of the invading viral DNA is taken up by a host-cell chromosome, with which it then multiplies. Dr. Rapp hypothesizes that if resulting new cells have tumor-forming properties, cancer may result.[5]

Unlike bacteria, viruses are completely parasitic—they cannot metabolize or reproduce on their own. A virus is a string of chemicals that requires the environment of a living cell to survive and replicate. It is the smallest known infectious agent.

Replication of HSV begins two to twenty days after infection. The virion, the infectious viral particle, attaches itself to a receptor on a host cell. The virion is engulfed, and it sheds its envelope. The viral DNA is transported to the host cell's nucleus, where it is transcribed into messenger RNA (mRNA). Thus, the viral DNA and mRNA are synthesized and the viral parts are assembled, with the host cell regarding the viral DNA as its own and converting its own machinery to that for viral replication. Finally, enveloped by an outer structure, newly replicated viruses are released to spread the infection.

Before it dies, an invaded host cell can produce up to 200,000 viral progeny, many of which go on to widen the infection.

The body's immune system responds by producing HSV-specific antibodies, which appear to play an important role in mediating the course of the infection. Evidence of this process includes the fact that neutralizing antibodies can inactivate extracellular viruses. In addition, the lesions seen in recurrent herpes genitalis are generally more localized. Patients with HSV-1 antibodies usually have less severe nonprimary HSV-2 infections than do people without such antibodies. Moreover, as noted earlier, immunodeficient neonates and immunocompromised or immunosuppressed patients are particularly at risk for disseminated infection.

Most herpes infections can probably be diagnosed clinically with a high degree of accuracy; a diagnosis of herpes genitalis is usually based on historical data along with signs and symptoms. However, genital lesions are a common manifestation of other diseases, and a patient history will sometimes lead a physician to believe that better diagnostic methods are needed. Some physicians examine smears prepared from lesions.

A more sensitive diagnostic method involves the demonstration of antibody titer in blood sera during acute and convalescent periods. However, HSV-1 and HSV-2 share many antigenic properties, so cross-reactive antibodies frequently will develop. Furthermore, although a primary or initial infection may cause a large rise in HSV-specific antibodies, the level varies widely after the primary infection.

The main definitive diagnostic test for genital herpes involves isolation of the virus from genital lesions; unfortunately, this test is not widely available. Alternative methods such as immunofluorescence, Papanicolaou, and crystal violet smear techniques are not totally satisfactory; their usefulness in diagnosing herpes simplex infections varies widely, and none is consistent in the accuracy of its results.

TREATMENT OF GENITAL HERPES

Physicians usually advise herpes genitalis patients to keep lesions clean and dry, and to reduce stress and other factors that seem to trigger recurrences. There is no pharmaceutical cure. Intense private research is continuing in an effort to learn more about the herpesvirus and to gain a better under-standing of latency and recurrence. However, of the total $10.6 billion budget of the National Institutes of Health, a mere $48 million is spent on all venereal diseases, not counting acquired immune deficiency syndrome (AIDS), and only $3 million is spent on herpes research.

A medicine chestful of self-help remedies has been devised to offset the symptoms of herpes genitalis. Victims seek and often find pain relief with a variety of alternative methods—some of them not acknowledged as effec-tive by orthodox medical practitioners, and one of them, dimethyl sulfoxide, not approved for herpes treatment by the FDA. The nutritional treatments for genital herpes that I describe in the following pages have evolved from this self-help mindset. Unfortunately, the traditional medical profession to this point has done little to help herpes victims. "Other" treatment proce-dures do seem to work for longer or shorter periods, depending on the victim's biochemical individuality. They are certainly worth a try. A herpes sufferer needs to find help wherever it is available.

BEE PROPOLIS FOR GENITAL HERPES

Dr. Franz Klemens Feiks of the Klosterneuberg Hospital, Klosterneuberg, Austria, reported to a symposium on apitherapy (treatment using honeybee products) held in Portoroz, a city in former Yugoslavia, that painting on bee propolis with a brush was useful in clearing up local sores of herpes zoster (shingles). In shingles, the herpesvirus causes lesions to appear on the skin along the paths of the affected nerves. The lesions take the form of crops of small blisters, which set in usually on just one side of the chest, back, or face and are accompanied by intense pain. Dr. Feiks' treatment was used in twenty-one cases, and for all of the patients, the pain disappeared. In only three did the itching persist. In nineteen cases, the sores healed and did not recur; in only two cases did the lesions redevelop. Dr. Feiks concluded that the bee propolis had a direct influence on the inflamed nerve fibers and that the herpesvirus must have been killed by the substance. After using the same technique, victims of genital herpes reported that bee propolis brought them similar relief.

Dr N. Mihailescu, endocrinologist and former director of the Apitherapy Clinic at Tital University Polyclinic Hospital, Bucharest, Rumania, de scribed bee propolis as a waxy resinous substance collected by bees from the bark and buds of balsam poplar, balm of Gilead, and other conifer trees in the late summer and early fall. The bees pack the substance into basketlike pouches on their hind legs and carry it back to the hive, where it is mixed with wax flakes and used as a cement or disinfectant.

Bee propolis is available as a waxy chunk, just as it comes from the hive, or as granules, powder, tablets, capsules, an extract, or a liquid tincture, which contains alcohol. According to Dr. Mihailescu, the best bee propolis is fluid, clear rather than amber, and collected from the upper part of the hive. It is available from health food stores and beekeepers.

In a study conducted in Rumania by Dr. Mihailescu, bee propolis was tested on 300 patients afflicted with endemic cysts (benign skin tumors). The doctor reported successful healing in 80 percent of the cases with the diffuse form of the disease and in 50 percent of the cases with the nodular form; this was over a three-month period of treatment. Dr. Mihailescu also reported a healing rate of 70 percent in 150 cases of chronic inflammation of the prostate.

Bee propolis has been hailed as a major breakthrough in the quest for an all-natural medicine to help battle viruses, soothe and heal stomach ulcers, create an antibiotic disease-fighting reaction within the body, and even help control runaway cell breakdown, which is symptomatic of cancer. Although it was known to the ancients two thousand years ago, only recently has propolis been "rediscovered" by modern scientists in the healing professions.

The word "propolis" is derived from the Greek *pro*, meaning "before," and *polis*, meaning "city," since in its natural state, propolis is used by bees to reduce the entrance to their wax cities to keep out harmful intruders. The bees also use the substance to seal off and disinfect intruders who do get into the hive and are killed, and to sanitize the cells that will house eggs and babies. Additionally, propolis is used as a cement to seal up structural holes and cracks, and to affix the wax combs in place.

Hippocrates (400–377 B.C.), the Father of Medicine, prescribed propolis to heal sores and ulcers both external and internal. The ancient Egyptians saw bee propolis as a source of eternal health and long life. Legend says that Jupiter transformed the beautiful Melissa into a bee so that she could prepare propolis as a miracle substance for use in healing.

Pliny the Elder (A.D. 23–70), a Roman scholar, said that "current physicians use propolis as a medicine because it extracts stings and all substances embedded in the flesh, reduces swelling, softens indurations, and soothes pains of the sinews and heals sores when it appears hopeless for them to mend."

For relief from the blisters of genital herpes, make a bee-propolis tincture and apply it to the area. To prepare the tincture, mix proportionately (by weight) two parts rubbing alcohol and one part propolis. Use a small postage scale for accuracy in measuring. Refrigerate the mixture for four days before using it. Herpes sufferers have described the results from this remedy as excellent.

Paint the propolis tincture on all herpes nodules and blisters. It will tend to sting where it touches an open lesion, but itching will cease immediately for twelve to twenty-four hours. Apply the remedy twice daily—upon awakening in the morning and before retiring for the night. In a couple of days, the sores should be gone entirely, but reapply the mixture in the general area even after they have disappeared. A mild rash may develop as a side reaction to the mixture, but this is expected. The sores of herpes genitalis may stay away for six months or more from the use of propolis tincture.

Bee propolis has also proven effective for other purposes. Dr. Mihailescu reported that it has been successful in dentistry in treating paradentosis (inflammation of the tissues around the teeth). For sore lips and gums, put a few drops of bee propolis in a half glass of water; the water should turn milky. Drink a little of the propolis water in the morning, in the afternoon, and again in the evening. The drink will help remove the gum soreness and heal wounds, scratches, and ulcers. Propolis makes a fine toothpaste, as well, for treating gum disease and dental plaque.

Bee propolis is effective against sore throat, nasal congestion, skin blemishes, respiratory difficulties, burns, and infections. Rumanian doctors have noted its usefulness in a variety of dermatological problems besides herpes.

As mentioned previously, bee propolis works well against all kinds of skin lesions. Put five drops of propolis in four ounces of water, then soak a small pad of cotton or wool in the solution and smear the solution all over skin spots such as acne, pimples, bumps, and rashes. Repeat as often as possible, especially after washing. The solution is also effective if left on overnight.

Put a few drops of propolis solution on burns as a cooling healer or use it for any health problem requiring an antibiotic. Combine it with honey and paint it on with gauze or a cotton-tipped applicator. Cover the wound with gauze, which should be kept on overnight. Renew the solution and dressing daily until the blemish, bruise, or burn is gone. This is also an effective application technique for open sores of genital herpes to avoid the stinging produced by propolis tincture.

Dr. Edith Lauda, an Austrian dermatologist, told of using a propolis tincture or ointment to treat her patients troubled with acne or other skin disorders. Dr. Lauda was able to completely heal her problem patients with a few applications of bee propolis, even cases that had lasted longer than thirty years. One woman suffering with acne conglobata on her chin for thirty years had not responded to chemotherapy. After only two propolis treatments, her skin was free of inflammation. Another woman, age forty, had acne papulosa covering her entire face; she also had not responded to chemotherapy. But within two weeks of placing a combination of propolis tincture and ointment on her skin, the acne cleared up completely.

Propolis tincture can also be used as a gargle for throat disorders. Put four or five drops in half a glass of warm water or a few drops on a lump of sugar to be sucked to ease a throat infection. Put a few flakes of propolis on a piece of bread for a natural antibiotic to fight the microbes responsible for the throat soreness.

For nasal congestion or vasomotor rhinitis accompanied by difficult breathing and stuffy nose, take a few drops of propolis in a liquid at least three times daily. The solution will help clear up any nasal infection, decrease nasal secretions, and open up clogged passages to permit healthier breathing.

For scratchy throat, stubborn cough, or other respiratory distress, try this European remedy: Combine a few flakes of propolis with honey and drop the mixture into a cup of herbal tea. The tea will leave the throat feeling silky. Repeat this several times per day.

Indeed, bee propolis has proven to be effective as an antibiotic, antihistamine, antiviral, and antifungal. Favorable results were noted by Dr. Mihailescu in treating thyroid nodules.

The viral infection of influenza was treated by Dr. Izet Osmanagic of the University of Sarajevo. Dr. Osmanagic selected eighty-five students and teachers who had no influenza symptoms but who, because they were in daily contact with so many people, were at high risk of getting the condition. The researcher wanted to give these subjects immunity.

Dr. Osmanagic gave each of his subjects two bottles of bee propolis diluted with honey. He prescribed one teaspoonful each day for forty to fifty days. Out of the group taking the bee preparation, only 9 percent became infected with influenza; the rest enjoyed healthy immunity. Thus, bee propolis could act as a more natural antibiotic than the type prepared in a drug factory. It has proven better than any drug in the treatment of genital herpes.

L-LYSINE FOR GENITAL HERPES

Proteins are chemical compounds composed of carbon, hydrogen, oxygen, and nitrogen atoms arranged into amino acids, which are linked into chains. There are twenty-two common amino acids. When a protein molecule is subjected to heat, acid, or another condition that disturbs its stability, it changes shape, thus losing its function to some extent. This is what happens to an egg when it is cooked; alterations of the egg proteins during cooking account for the observable changes in the egg white and yolk.

Amino acids serve as the primary units of synthesis both of tissue proteins and of nonprotein nitrogenous compounds. Upon entering the body, many freeform amino acids undergo complex interconversions into substances necessary for maintaining the metabolic pathways of the body. For example, the arginine amino-acid pathway is important in the formation of urea and in the maintenance of the body's nitrogen balance and carbon dioxide balance. This characteristic of arginine, which is shared by the amino acid L-lysine, plays a role in relieving symptoms of genital and labial herpes.

Dr. Richard S. Griffith, professor of medicine at Indiana University School of Medicine, Indianapolis, reported in *Dermatalogica* that he and his coworker, Dr. Arthur L. Norins, treated some 200 herpes genitalis patients with L-lysine. The two doctors had found that L-lysine suppresses the growth of the genital herpes virus. Dr. Griffith said that in virtually all of

45 patients, the pain, along with the herpes symptoms, disappeared within twenty-four hours. Although lysine cannot heal a blister once it has erupted, it can stop the tender nodule that forms first from beginning a blister.

Drs. Griffith and Norins gave their patients 312 to 1,200 milligrams of L-lysine daily. In a controlled study carried out by the Department of Infectious Diseases in Copenhagen, Denmark, a significant number of patients were recurrence-free when treated with lysine in the same dosage range; the placebo used in the double-blind study proved ineffective in keeping away the herpes symptoms, but the lysine worked well.

L-lysine is an essential amino acid, that is, it is essential that it be supplied in the diet because the body cannot make it from fats or sugar and free nitrogen. L-lysine controls herpesvirus eruptions by changing the nutrition of the cells involved so that the virus is unable to produce the type of protein it needs to survive. Because this amino acid is not a cure but rather a natural, drugless suppressant, lesions could recur within a month or two; however, they do not recur while small maintenance doses of lysine are taken.

The use of L-lysine as an agent against herpes goes back to 1970, when Dr. Christopher Kagan, then with the University of California, Los Angeles Center for the Health Sciences, found that when a virus invades a cell, it shifts the cell's nutrient-intake requirements so that the need for lysine is reduced while the need for arginine is increased. An abundance of lysine in relation to arginine appears to create an environment that is hostile to the herpes simplex virus.

The human diet consists of foods that can be rated as high or low in lysine or arginine. When there is a high arginine–lysine ratio in a particular diet, such as in the chocolate-and-nuts diet eaten at holiday time, herpes lesions may occur in people susceptible to the virus. Arginine seems to bring on blisters of herpes genitalis. Listed below are foods high in L-lysine, which should be added to the diet as much as possible by herpes victims, and foods high in arginine, which should be avoided. However, foods high in L-lysine tend to neutralize the arginine content of even the foods high in arginine.

Foods High in L-Lysine

The following list names foods that are high in L-lysine.

Avocado	Peanuts
Beef	Pork
Brewer's yeast	Potatoes
Chick peas	Pumpernickel
Cottage cheese	Salami with no preservatives added
Flounder	Shrimp
Lentils	Soybeans
Lima beans	

Foods High in Arginine

The following list names foods that are high in arginine.

Beef (also high in L-lysine)	Lamb
Bran	Nuts
Buckwheat	Seeds
Cereals	Soybeans (also high in L-lysine)
Chick peas (also high in L-lysine)	Sunflower cake
Chocolate	Veal

VITAMIN C, HERBS, AND HOMEOPATHIC REMEDIES FOR GENITAL HERPES

Vitamin C taken in megadoses such as 10 grams daily has been reported as relieving herpes genitalis. Dr. Frederick Klenner of Readsville, North Carolina, has used tremendous amounts of the vitamin in treating the condition. However, such high doses of ascorbic acid should not be taken without a physician's supervision. Instead, take smaller doses and load up on citrus fruits and juices. Grapefruit has been praised by herpes sufferers as helpful against the blisters. (See page 57 for a list of foods that are high in vitamin C.)

Three herbs tend to counteract the symptoms of herpes genitalis:

- White willow (*Salix alba*). White willow relieves the pain of herpes blisters by reducing the body's production of prostaglandins. A wash can be made from white willow powder and used as a douche. White willow powder is available from herbalists. Make the douche using 15 to 30 grains (about one-half to one teaspoon) of powder. Or, drink an infusion made by steeping one ounce of the herb in one pint of boiling water for twenty minutes.
- Goldenseal (*Hydrastis canadensis*). Goldenseal alleviates the irritation and inflammation of herpes genitalis when it is taken internally or applied externally to treat lesions of the mucous membranes. Because it is a strong stimulant and contains alkaloids that the body eliminates without difficulty, goldenseal should not be used for more than seven days in a row, according to herbalists. To make an infusion of goldenseal root, steep one gram (about two teaspoons) of the herb in eight ounces of boiling water for fifteen minutes. Drink the infusion in tablespoon doses.
- Chickweed (*Stellaria media*). Chickweed can be applied in poultice form directly on genital herpes sores, but be sure to change the poultice every two to three hours. Cook one part fresh chickweed in two parts lard, strain the mixture, and soak up the solution in flannel for the application. Or, make an infusion of chickweed by steeping one gram (about two teaspoons) of fresh herb in eight ounces of boiling water for five minutes.

Herbalist John Christopher, N.D., developed a healing ointment for herpes made from chickweed, beeswax, and leaf lard. Cut up one pound of chickweed and place it in a stainless steel pot along with two ounces of beeswax and one and a half pounds of leaf lard. Cover the pot and place it in a 200°F oven for three hours, then remove the pot from the oven, strain the mixture through a fine wire sieve, and let it cool. The beeswax helps thicken the ointment. Keep the ointment refrigerated and apply it to any lesions as needed.[6]

Certain athlete's foot ointments, creams, and solutions dabbed on herpes lesions that are in full bloom and causing pain have been known to bring about good results. Those winning the most praise are the ones that contain a lot of zinc, such as Ting. Ting is an over-the-counter topical product sold as an antifungal remedy primarily for athlete's foot. It contains boric acid and two types of zinc. Taking up to 50 milligrams of zinc tablets daily in divided doses while also using a zinc-containing cream or ointment works synergistically, sometimes overnight, to clear lesions.

Osteopathic physicians and other doctors who practice homeopathic medicine have experienced success in treating herpes genitalis. Homeopathy is a medical system that uses microdoses, or highly diluted doses, of natural substances to stimulate a person's own natural healing process. According to homeopathic laws, a substance that causes the symptoms of an illness in a healthy person can be used to cure the same illness in an unhealthy person when it is used in a highly diluted form. A century ago, homeopathy was practiced in the United States by nearly 50 percent of all clinical physicians. With the advent of the modern "wonder drugs," it fell out of favor, but certain physicians still practice it with good results. (To locate a homeopathic physician, contact Homeopathic Educational Services, 2124 Kittredge Street, Berkeley, California 94701, telephone 510–649–0294; or the National Center for Homeopathy, 801 North Fairfax, Suite 306, Alexandria, Virginia 22314, telephone 703–548–7790.)

In the treatment of genital herpes, homeopaths use calendula tincture, which can be ordered from the Standard Homeopathic Company (154 West 131 Street, Los Angeles, California 90061; telephone 213–021–4204). Using a cotton swab, apply the tincture directly on the blisters. It may sting a little; when the calendula tincture dries, apply cornstarch to soothe the area. If the stinging continues, add a coating of Lanacaine ointment, which is an over-the-counter topical anesthetic. Paint the lesions with tincture during every trip to the bathroom. This is when the blisters are exposed and should serve as a reminder that the moment for treatment has arrived again.

After applying calendula tincture, take an acidophilus tablet with a glass of milk. Also take a small dose of vitamin B_{12}, plus a 50-milligram tablet of B-complex to balance the B_{12}.

DIMETHYL SULFOXIDE FOR GENITAL HERPES

Genital herpes also yields to the antiviral properties of dimethyl sulfoxide (DMSO), which has already been proven effective in eradicating HSV-1 infections around the mouth. Considered an experimental drug in the United States, DMSO is available on a prescription basis in many other countries.

DMSO is a solvent and a membrane penetrant that has the ability to pass through every tissue of the body except the enamel of teeth and fingernails. When it passes through a tissue, it can take other substances, including antiviral agents, along with it.

Dimethyl sulfoxide reduces pain by impeding its conduction in the smaller nerve fibers. It alleviates inflammation, inhibits the growth of viruses and other microorganisms, dissolves scar tissue, improves blood supply, and acts generally in ways that medical scientists do not yet understand.

Dr. William Campbell Douglass of Atlanta, Georgia, had some fine results when he studied DMSO's effectiveness against herpes zoster and other forms of herpes infection. His clinical applications illustrated that the sooner DMSO treatment is begun, the better the skin lesions will respond. Dr. Campbell also succeeded at relieving genital herpes patients of their troublesome symptoms for short periods.

To treat a herpes outbreak, paint DMSO directly on the skin lesions. Apply a 75-percent liquid strength directly on the sensitive area as often as it is tolerable, realizing that it will sting. If the blisters are too sensitive for this high-strength DMSO, dilute the solution with water; experiment with how much water to add. Sitting in front of a revolving fan may also help to cool the burning sensation. *Caution:* While it is less effective, a 50-percent or weaker DMSO solution should be used for treating herpes lesions on the face, neck, or scalp.

DMSO is becoming a specific remedy for the symptoms of herpes zoster (shingles), particularly for the neuralgia, which is the pain along the affected nerve. In patients with itching but no neuralgia, the itching may increase. In general, though, DMSO appears to shorten the course of herpes zoster with skin eruption and to prevent postherpetic neuralgia, that is, pain after the illness is gone. DMSO is already relied upon in informed medical circles for the treatment of herpes genitalis. It is used mainly by wholistic physicians.

A research group in Oxford, England, investigated the use of DMSO in combination with the antiviral drug idoxuridine for shingles. Although systemic idoxuridine had been tried against the viral nerve disease with equivocal results, the Oxford investigators reasoned that since the varicella-zoster virus is related to the herpes simplex virus, and since DMSO-idoxuridine is useful against herpes simplex lesions on the skin and mucous membranes, it was worth a try. The idea was to prevent virus replication, thus ameliorating the disease and, not incidentally, the pain.

The trick worked. Continuously applied 40-percent idoxuridine in purified DMSO cleared up herpes zoster lesions quickly. The continuous administration was achieved by placing a piece of lint over the vesicles. The lint had been soaked in the DMSO solution and was kept on the skin using a gauze bandage. The lint was resoaked daily.

"The patients were delighted, for the pain disappeared within a median of two days. Healing also appeared to be accelerated," the researchers reported in the *British Medical Journal.*[7] Some skin peeling was experienced, but only one subject in this uncontrolled trial developed a secondary bacterial infection.

The English investigators attempted a double-blind study pitting 40-percent idoxuridine in purified DMSO against both DMSO alone and a salt solution with garlic. (The garlic was supposed to simulate the characteristic odor of DMSO, which is strong, unique, and a problem in double-blind studies.) The DMSO-idoxuridine combination worked even better against the simpler virus infection, herpes simplex, than it had against herpes zoster. By itself, DMSO was only moderately successful against the cold sores or fever blisters of the simplex virus.

DMSO mixed with vitamin-C crystals appears to be quite an effective treatment for herpes labialis and other genital herpes. Some doctors have had success using this combination for herpes genitalis, herpes simplex, and herpes zoster, too. These doctors administered 60,000 milligrams of pure vitamin C by intravenous (IV) drip and painted the DMSO–vitamin C solution directly on the lesions. The lesions must be kept wet. After two and a half hours of IV drip, the redness was gone.

One fifty-eight-year-old woman got rid of the herpes simplex symptoms on her scalp permanently within three days. The lesions on the right side of her head had run from the back of her head over her scalp and down to her right eye. She could have developed an ophthalmic herpes—highly dangerous to eyesight—if the vitamin C and DMSO had not worked so fast.

For a more complete discussion of the efficacy and usage of DMSO, as well as additional case studies, see my book *DMSO: Nature's Healer.*

PREVENTION OF GENITAL HERPES

Despite the lack of a cure for genital herpes in the orthodox sense, prolonged relief of symptoms and signs does exist. The only way to check the spread of the disease, of course, is prevention. Since herpes is passed on only by skin contact while it is in an active stage, infection can easily be avoided through the use of common-sense precautions.

Once you have been infected with genital herpes, you must change your lifestyle to lessen the effects and recurrences. Emotions, stress, and other psychic factors may cause a physical reaction in your body. Therefore, you must try to eliminate negative thoughts such as guilt, anger, resentment, and anxiety. Substitute the positive feeling that you will be well and make it your strong personal commitment to work toward that goal.

Meanwhile, try the various remedies suggested in this chapter after checking with your physician. Maybe your doctor has something different to offer; new information is funneling into doctors' offices all the time through medical journals and scientific meetings.

Additionally, be scrupulously clean when it comes to your body. Use hygienic techniques for avoiding secondary infections and take actions that minimize the risks of inadvertent transfer of the virus. Try hard to eat the best possible diet and be serious about taking your dietary supplements. Stay on top of the newest findings in nutrition by reading and studying books and magazine articles. Get an adequate amount of sleep every night and avoid unnecessary environmental trauma. As a herpes patient, you have become a victim of altered body ecology; therefore, you must do everything possible to preserve the personal ecology you have left and the ecology of your surroundings.

HIV TRANSMISSION AND SAFE SEX

Now that the world has entered the second decade with acquired immune deficiency syndrome (AIDS) as an established clinical entity, I would be remiss if I failed to discuss the epidemiology and transmission of the human immunodeficiency virus (HIV). I would also like to provide a nutritional program to offset this virus. Much of the HIV epidemiological information offered here comes from *Acquired Immune Deficiency Syndrome: Biological, Medical, Social, and Legal Issues,* an excellent book by Gerald J. Stine of the University of North Florida in Jacksonville.

AIDS, caused by the HIV discovered by French scientist Dr. Luc Montagnier in 1983, is a syndrome, not a single disease. In 1985, HIV-2 was isolated in West Africa. Since then, an unbroken chain of HIV transmission has been established between the infected and the newly infected. The major route of HIV transmission involves body fluids that are exchanged during sexual activities, intravenous drug use, blood transfusions, use of blood products, or birth. Currently, there are nearly 250,000 verified AIDS cases in the United States.

The highest frequency of HIV transmission in the United States is among homosexual and bisexual males and among intravenous drug users. However, I will focus on the heterosexual transmission of HIV infections.

About 90 percent of the HIV infections that occur within the heterosexual population are transmitted sexually from men to women, from women to men, or from men to men and then to women. (HIV transmission among lesbians is very low even though, according to the Centers for Disease Control and Prevention, vaginal secretions and menstrual blood from infected lesbians are potential sources of HIV for noninfected lesbians.)

For promiscuous heterosexuals, the more sexual partners a person has, the greater is the probability of HIV infection. In heterosexual sex that produces skin, anal, or vaginal membrane abrasions prior to or during intercourse, there is an increased risk of HIV infection.

HIV transmission can be prevented by practicing "safe sex"; the responsibility rests with the involved individuals. "Safe sex" essentially means using condoms and not having intercourse with an HIV-infected person. Correct nutrition is also a component of "safe sex." Food is the source of life-sustaining nutrients and includes the all-important vitamins, minerals, proteins, fats, carbohydrates, enzymes, amino acids, herbs, essential fatty acids, and other natural substances that boost the immune system. The following list names foods and food supplements that keep the immune system functioning well:

Acidophilus	Coenzyme Q10	Mushrooms
Algae	Echinacea	Sea cucumbers
Astragalus	Garlic	Vitamin A
Beta-carotene	Ginseng	Vitamin B complex
Bioflavonoids	Lecithin	Vitamin C
Brewer's yeast	Licorice	Vitamin E
Carnivora	Multiple minerals	Wheat germ

Physical protection during sex is also vital. At least fifty brands of condoms (also called rubbers, bags, skins, raincoats, sheaths, French letters, and prophylactics) are manufactured in the United States to fit every need and fancy. Condoms may be lubricated; have reservoir tips; contain spermicide; be flavored, perfumed, brightly colored, stippled, or phosphorescent; be ribbed; or contain so many "safeguarding" chemicals that they cause an allergic skin reaction called contact dermatitis. However, a no-go with latex condoms are oil-based lubricants such as petroleum jelly, cooking oil or shortening, or baby oil because such oils make the latex porous and nullify the protection the condom provides against HIV. Sexual authorities recommend the use of condoms containing a spermicide.

The name "condom" came from Dr. Alois Condom, a physician to King Charles II of England. In the early 1700s, Dr. Condom designed a penile sheath for his majesty.

A female condom, or vaginal pouch worn internally by women, was approved by the FDA in 1993. Made of 15-centimeter polyurethane, it is a sheath with rings at each end designed to cover the base of the penis and a large portion of the female perineum to provide a barrier against microorganisms. The polyurethane is stronger than the latex used in the usual male condom.

For more information on AIDS, its history and treatment, and protection methods, check your local library or bookstore. Many excellent books are now available.

Chapter 12

SEX AND SENIOR CITIZENS

During all of my 88 years, I've considered sex to be a crucial part of my life. It gives me a general sense of well-being and a good feeling about myself. And it's no different for me now than when I was a girl, for having sexual relations helps me realize an exhilaration, an awareness of being desirable and beautiful. I still love to take a man's penis within me or to stroke it, kiss it, or suck it.

My need for sex is one of my strongest drives and very important to my self-image. My only problem is in finding a partner. Young men don't want an old lady. Old men seemingly don't have any sex drive left, at least not the ones I have met; most apparently have erection difficulties and shy away from facing them. My husband died five years ago at the age of ninety-one. Until then, we enjoyed sexual intercourse at least twice a week and often more.

The trouble with living long and remaining sexually active is that your sexual partners tend to die off. Now I've been left alone and looking for that rare man who feels as uninhibited in his old age as I do. Where am I to find someone who believes in himself and feels that he's getting better as he gets older?

Brenda P.
Toronto, Ontario

A few years ago, at the age of 79, I married for the second time. My wife, who is now 71, agrees with me that our later marriage has allowed us to relax sexually. We devote long periods to pleasuring each other, for time is something we have plenty of. Before marriage, since I was a very sexual person, I would spend practically my whole Social Security check on prostitutes. The situation is all different for me today.

Since my wife and I share the belief that sex keeps a person young and healthy, we sure are lucky to have found each other. For us, sex is emotional nutrition. It's our main preoccupation besides our individual hobbies; it's the icing on the cake of our marriage. The difficulty is that my wife has an even higher level of sexuality than I do. She wants to have intercourse every day, sometimes even more frequently. I can't quite keep up with her, so now she's talking about my sharing her with other men. This idea doesn't sit well with me. Do you think I'm being too narrow-minded?

Should I not object to my wife fulfilling her sexual needs beyond what I can manage? Is it all right for an elderly woman to sleep around?

Walter T.
Richmond, Virginia

The facts about sex in the mature years are that it is as good when you are older as when you were younger—and for many, it is better. A widely held myth is that people lose their sexuality in their later years, experiencing declining performance, poor responsiveness, and lack of libido. This will occur only if you let it. A sexual wasteland will not be waiting for you when you hit 70, 80, or beyond if you pursue a proper, natural lifestyle.

THE DIET OF THE ANDES CENTENARIANS

To come up with the lifestyle that is most conducive to sexual longevity, I decided ten years ago to visit the longest-lived people in the Western hemisphere, the Vilcabambans, who resided high in the Andes mountains of Ecuador. Many Vilcabambans were surviving alert and active, all their faculties intact, well beyond 100 years of age. In a population of less than 4,000 people, more than 20 were known to be centenarians. This compared to 117 centenarians in a total population of 250,000,000 in the United States. I knew that these Vilcabamban "Old Ones" (*Los Viejos*), who remained in continuous close contact with nature, would have much to offer investigators from a medical-sexual standpoint. My goal was to spend time talking with *Los Viejos* (through Spanish interpreters) and to bring back samples of their hair, water, and blood for analysis. Primarily, I was anxious to discover the mineral content of their bodies, a result of what they ate and drank and of the way they lived in general. My findings revealed the reasons for the elderly Vilcabambans' intact sexuality.

Among the oldest living people in the world were the Abkhazians, living in Soviet Georgia; the Hunzas (Hunzakuts), in the Karakoram mountain range in the Pakistani-controlled Kashmir; and the Vilcabambans, in the Andean mountain village of Vilcabamba in Ecuador. The Vilcabambans were allegedly living much longer and remaining more vigorously sexual in old age than anyone else in the world. I met with *Los Viejos*, took their photographs, ate a few meals with them, followed them somewhat in their daily work routines, and went to the Vilcabamba village offices to make photographic copies of their birth certificates, baptismal certificates, and other records.

The centenarians of southern Ecuador lived in an arc of villages, the most noted of which was Vilcabamba. Many people living in these remote villages were truly old. They had been falsely accused by one bone physiologist of faking their ages for some undetermined motive. During a short stay in February 1978, the bone doctor, whom residents described as having spent his entire visit drinking beer at a cantina in the middle of Vilcabamba, concluded that *Los Viejos* were not really living so long. Yet he never went into the jungle, climbed the mountains, or traveled the dirt roads to find and talk with the centenarians.

My own investigation took me into the high, rugged back country. I traveled alternately by four-wheel-drive vehicle, pack animal, and foot, hacking my way through thick jungle growth, wading through shallow streams, and climbing up almost vertical inclines, looking for those infrequent patches of level ground where cabins had been built. In these cabins or tending a nearby plot of farm land, I sometimes found one or two of the Old Ones.

The Old Ones lived in isolated areas along with a few chickens and maybe a pig. They farmed a rich black soil that received strong sunshine and fairly good rainfall. The average temperature during the day was sixty-eight degrees Fahrenheit; it dropped to about fifty-eight degrees when the sun went down. Although located only four degrees latitude south of the equator, Vilcabamba, at a four-thousand-foot altitude, never suffered from the relentless equatorial heat.

Los Viejos grew maize and other grains, such as barley, millet, rice, rye, and wheat, which along with legumes formed the basis of what they ate. They also had every kind of tropical fruit available for the picking and were surrounded by an abundant supply of vegetables, which needed just the slightest of cultivation. They used sugar cane domestically as *panella*, a brown block of solid syrup from which chunks were taken for sweetening, and also exported it.

A look at the Vilcabambans' diet revealed that they ate an average of 1,200 calories a day. They consumed only about half the protein that Americans did, and interestingly, most of the protein and fats were of vegetable origin. By American standards, the Vilcabamban diet was exceedingly low in saturated animal fats and cholesterol, inasmuch as the people ate hardly any meat, reserving it for a once-a-month feast day, when a hog or some guinea pigs raised for the purpose were slaughtered and eaten.

The Vilcabambans lived along the Chamba, a relatively warm river that was formed by the merging of two flowing streams, the Yambala and the Capamaco. The Old Ones drank the water from these streams and river, and used them to wash their clothes and at times their bodies. They also obtained drinking water from artesian wells dug into underground streams flowing through mineral deposits. (I will have much more to say about these mineral waters later in this chapter.) The artesian-well water was cold, clear, and pure. It came from icy melted snow from ravines in the Mandango and Warango mountains, rocky sentinels that overlooked Vilcabamba. There were many lakes in the hollows of these mountains, and the Vilcabambans used the lakes as reservoirs by piping water from them down the mountainside and into the villages and surrounding homes in the valley.

The Vilcabambans grew wheat and barley on the mountain slopes and used the grains as staples at almost every meal along with potatoes, yucca (a root), and corn. They grew grapes, from which they made wine. They distilled some of the corn they grew into a fiery liquor that resembled Japanese *saki*. I had the privilege of sharing another liquor—a fresh form of rum—drawn off when sugar-cane juice was boiled down. The burning taste on the tongue brought tears to the eyes.

The Vilcabambans grew all kinds of greens and other vegetables, including cabbage, cauliflower, celery, broccoli, tomatoes, squash, zucchini, carrots, peas, Brussels sprouts, and beans. They ate these vegetables regularly. The soil was exceedingly fertile—a sandy humus—especially in the region where the Chamba river met the Uchima river. It was thick, black dirt from thousands of years worth of silt that had been brought down from higher up in the mountains. On the roads were pockets of clay and volcanic ash; red dust flew everywhere when cars passed, particularly during the dry season. The fields were heavily layered with carbon, phosphorus, and lime, and contained deposits of calcium, kaolin, gypsum, and other minerals. The land was particularly suited to the growing of wild fruit trees and was a veritable paradise of oranges, mangos, plums, grapefruits, pomegranates, guavas, limes, bananas, sweet lemons, avocados, papayas, apples, crab apples, pineapples, berries, and many indigenous types of fruit that I did not recognize but found delicious. There were also wild watermelons, honeydews, cantaloupes, and other kinds of melons growing everywhere. It did not seem that anyone could go hungry in or around Vilcabamba.

The centenarians lived mainly in the mountains, about 2,000 feet higher than the villagers, who lived on the valley floor. Their diet was slightly different from that of the villagers in that they seldom if ever ate anything processed; the mountaineers ate fresh foods picked directly from the fields or trees. There were a rare few extremely old people who lived in the heart of Vilcabamba village and had access to white-sugar and white-flour products, but overweight among the elderly was almost nonexistent. When I was there, the ex-mayor's wife, who ran a grocery and sold cola drinks, pastries, canned foods, and other refined foods, was the only obese elderly person I saw. The children, in fact, although they were well-fed, looked thin to the point of emaciation—the girls more so than the boys.

The Vilcabambans made cottage cheese and a thin yogurt from goat's milk or, less often, from cow's milk. (There were more goats than cows in Vilcabamba.) Often, they stored milk for eight days in the paunch of a recently killed domestic animal, where rennet, an enzyme, seeped into the liquid from the walls of the animal's stomach. The rennet transformed the milk, which was then mixed with orange peel, pressed slightly, and presented at the table, occasionally with pieces of meat. Eggs were drunk raw from the shell or eaten just slightly cooked.

A typical Vilcabamban evening meal consisted of a flat cake of white curd cheese, boiled corn cobs, boiled yucca, loose grains of corn, small wild potatoes, soybeans, eggs, a piece of homemade brown bread, and water from a nearby stream or artesian well. Sometimes a yellow corn soup garnished with goats' or pigs' eyes was added as a special treat. Melons were eaten for dessert.

Los Viejos nibbled on fruit throughout the day. Ripe fruit was always available, for there were no seasons owing to Vilcabamba's proximity to the equator, where the sun shines every day. The countryside was a veritable paradise of fruits, flowers, butterflies, and tranquility.

AIR QUALITY IN VILCABAMBA

The vilco tree was special; with its greener than normal leaves, the vilco seemed to somehow change the atmosphere in the valley and make the air fresher. Breathing seemed to be easier in Vilcabamba, and the lungs seemed to expand to a greater capacity. This physiologically improved breathing may have had something to do with the negatively charged particles—air ions—stimulated by the vilco tree. This air effect was the exact opposite of the "witches' winds" in certain other parts of the world, such as the Santa Ana wind in California, the Bitter Winds in Arizona and Mexico, the Chinook wind in western Canada, the Sharav in the Middle East, the Foehn in Germany, and the Mistral in southern France. These winds, and others like them, produce negative symptoms in people and animals.

Vilcabamba may possibly have been named after the vilco tree. Derived from the language of the Quechua Indians, *vilca* means "sacred" and *bamba* means "valley"; *Vilcabamba* therefore means "sacred valley." The benefits of living in the sacred valley may have come in part from the mystical effects of the vilco tree.

The vilco tree had attractive fernlike leaves, decorative branches, and pretty red fruit. An extraction from its bark made a hallucinatory drug. More than that, standing in the shade of a vilco tree promoted a feeling of well-being that was very sexually stimulating. This contrasted sharply with what is felt by inhabitants of the areas where witches' winds blow. Dr. Bernard Wissmer, a physician in Geneva, Switzerland, cared for patients (mostly foreigners) who complained of many of the same or similar ills—colds, fatigue, stomach problems, depression, and diminished sex drive. Dr. Wissmer explained to Fred Soyka, coauthor with Alan Edmonds of *The Ion Effect*, that his patients not only suffered from physical problems during the witches' wind in Geneva but also often behaved in manners he considered to be out of character. "He said there seemed to be an unusually high incidence of broken marriages among those of the foreign community . . . and this seemed to be linked to a dropping off in the sex drive of one of the partners," wrote Soyka and Edmonds. "For obvious reasons, men most commonly appeared to be the victims of this particular problem. They would complain that their wives no longer stimulated them.

"Wissmer suggested this was because in the ego-sensitive area of sexual potency a man was more likely to blame his wife than himself for his lowered performance, and at the same time seek reassurance by playing around behind his wife's back," continued Soyka and Edmonds. "Ultimately, this usually led either to a rift in the marriage or to break-up and divorce. Women, too, would complain of feeling tense and anxious and unhappy, and believed that this ill feeling was the cause of their diminished interest in sex." Dr. Wissmer believed that one does not cause the other but rather that the anxiety and lack of a sex drive are part of the same condition.[1]

Impotence and lack of sex drive seemed never to happen among Vilcabamban couples, partly for two reasons—no witches' wind blew through the sacred valley, and the vilco tree gave off pure, negatively charged oxygen molecules from leaves that converted carbon dioxide. The negatively charged air ion particles emitted by the leaves of the vilco tree are missing in most industrialized Western societies. Instead, Westerners are overexposed to positive air ions, which cause a sense of illness.

AIR POLLUTION AND SEXUALITY

There was absolutely no air pollution in Vilcabamba. No industrial chimneys spewed forth ash, smoke, soot, toxic heavy-metal particles, carbon monoxide, or any other pollutant into the region's pristine air. Only about 200 people from among the entire population of 819 in the villages and approximately 3,000 in the surrounding mountains owned and drove an automobile or truck; most of the people traveled by burro, horse, or shank's mare. Consequently, lead poisoning, which has affected the potency of every third adult male in industrialized Western countries, did not exist in Vilcabamba. Vilcabamban men were extraordinarily potent.

In a study conducted over a ten-year period at the University of Miami, the sperm counts of healthy young male students were recorded. The researchers produced a shocking report about the future of male virility. As a result of the high levels of lead in their bodies, one third of the Miami University subjects, then between the ages of 16 and 24, were predicted to be unable to impregnate their future wives. Their sperm counts had dropped over eight years from 150,000,000 spermatozoa per cubic centimeter (cc) to less than 60,000,000 per cc. Overexposure to low-level lead in the air from factory chimneys and automobile exhausts had brought about infertility in these men. The University of Miami students were representative of most young American males. Their fertility fell because of heavy-metal toxicity, especially from lead.

Stimulated by the Reagan administration, which in turn was pressured by American industry (particularly by automobile manufacturers), the U.S. House of Representatives Energy Committee's Subcommittee on Health and the Environment drafted legislation that made substantial changes in the Clean Air Act of 1970. These politicians tampered with the Clean Air Act to allow a higher level of lead in the air and gut many substantive portions of the law. The changes allowed states to "opt out" of requirements that air pollution be allowed to grow by no more than specified increments in particular areas. Changes doubled the allowed amount of pollutants in urban air, and also allowed additional lead pollution in such areas as national parks, where air quality was most strictly protected. Since Ronald Reagan left office in 1988, the only change has been that tetraethyl lead usage has been reduced in gasoline. There are no "sacred valleys" in the United States.

In contrast, the sacred valley of Vilcabamba was said to be the true Paradise from which Adam and Eve were expelled. This "Eden" in the 1980s still retained a pure atmosphere, brilliant sunshine, and crystal-clear sky surrounded by snow-capped mountains that rose to 14,000 feet. People traveled to the sacred valley and stayed for short periods at El Retiro, the Vilcabamba hotel.

Americans, meanwhile, were reacting to the heavy-metal toxicity surrounding them by developing impotency, vaginal atrophy, premature ejaculation, frigidity, menstrual difficulties, disturbed thinking about sex, loss of libido, retrograde ejaculation, infertility, and premature sexual aging. Especially hard hit were industrial workers regularly exposed to heavy metals such as mercury, nickel, copper, cadmium, arsenic, aluminum, or lead. These metal workers numbered in the millions. (For in-depth information about toxic metals and how they affect sexuality and other aspects of health, see my book *The Toxic Metal Syndrome: How Heavy Metal Poisonings Affect Your Brain.*)

HOW THE CENTENARIANS EXERCISED

The Vilcabamban centenarians were remarkable healthwise in that they had none of the degenerative diseases such as cancer, heart disease, diabetes, senility, liver disease, cataracts, kidney disease, arthritis, or stroke. Their diet was largely responsible for this freedom from illness. The amount of exercise the Old Ones received in the performance of their labors also protected them against disease. The mountain people went to their fields six days a week and put in a full day's work farming. The fields most often were located on the next available patch of ground, which often was 1,500 to 3,000 feet higher or lower on the mountain slope than their cabins. To reach their farm lands, the centenarians had to climb mountain paths, which were frequently angled at seventy-five degrees. It could take these elderly people two hours to climb up the face of the mountain, after which they worked their land a full eight to ten hours and then climbed down.

The work most of the Vilcabambans did consisted of chopping wood, digging out tree stumps, carrying away medium-size stones, levering out large rocks, scything tall grass, planting crops, weeding, sawing logs, dehusking corn, and shoveling debris. They did all their tasks with hand tools. They did not use modern machinery and had only a few oxen or burros. Men and women worked side by side using a long-handled hoe called a *lampa*. They hacked away brush and undergrowth with a sharp-bladed machete.

On Sundays, when they did not work but instead usually attended church in the villages, the centenarians walked a distance of six or seven miles each way. The paths they followed took them up and down steep hills, since there were almost no level grades in the area. On their trips home, they carried burdens from the shopping they had done in the open farmers' markets, where people congregated for a few hours after church and made their weekly purchases.

Exercise was an integral part of life for the Vilcabambans. The centenarians were ambulatory. Movement out-of-doors was part of the Vilcabamban culture. These people walked everywhere and used pack animals just for carrying burdens such as firewood, sugar cane, and banana stalks. They exemplified the old saying that each of us has two "doctors"—the left leg and the right leg. Exercise was another major reason these Old Ones were active sexually for so long (as I will discuss in the next section). As a natural chelating agent and cleanser of the atherosclerotic plaques that clog the arteries of so-called civilized people, continuous vigorous movement allowed *Los Viejos* to avoid almost all of the degenerative diseases. The centenarians' minds stayed alert and vital, fit for their supple bodies. When I asked these people if anyone among them had ever experienced memory loss from senility, nobody knew what I meant. Senility did not exist in Vilcabamban society. Excellent blood circulation from constant walking and working was probably the reason. The Old Ones provided themselves with their own built-in form of chelation therapy.

In *Rejuvenation*, Johan Bjorksten, Ph.D., developer of the crosslinkage theory of aging, wrote:

> That certain exercise is beneficial for health is no longer doubted. This has mostly been ascribed to improvements in circulation and in muscle tonus.
>
> It is an established fact that the lactic acid or lactate content of blood is about doubled during the time of moderate muscular exertion, and declines to the normal level abruptly, in a few minutes after cessation of the muscular action. *Since lactic acid is a fair-to-good chelating agent, it may help remove from the system potentially crosslinking aluminum, cadmium, mercury, lead, arsenic and excess iron, among others, thereby increasing longevity if depletion of the needed chelatable metals manganese, cobalt, zinc, iron, and perhaps molybdenum is counteracted by supplement medication or a couple quarts daily of skim milk* (Bjorksten's emphasis).

The time x mass product of circulation elevated lactic acid is more dependent on the duration of muscular exertion than on its intensity. Therefore, it is predictable that the beneficial effects of exercise on longevity will be found to be highest in endurance type activities such as walking, jogging, rowing, skiing and swimming, where an elevated lactic acid content of blood is maintained regularly and for a considerable time.[2]

SEXUAL PRACTICES OF THE VILCABAMBANS

Sex was a primary preoccupation of the Vilcabambans. Men and women alike were notorious for their love affairs, and passion was an important part of living for these people. The Vilcabambans made love to each other irrespective of age. In addition, the women made as many advances as did the men. The centenarians seemed extremely open about their passion, inasmuch as some were very boastful when I asked them about the number of lovers they could take in one night at the age of 80 and onward. The men made love to their wives on a steady schedule—the same three nights each week. They maintained extramarital sexual relations during the other days. The women did the same. The Vilcabamban culture just assumed that men and women had sexual relationships—in or outside of the home or both—whether or not they were married, this despite the fact that the Vilcabambans were a very spiritually inclined Catholic people who followed church doctrine in every way. Religion, in fact, played the key role in disciplining them; there was almost no criminal behavior in Vilcabamban society. There were no policemen in the villages. The mayor was the sole authority, and he was elected for short multiple terms.

There was also no "dirty old man" attitude in the villages or surrounding countryside, despite the number of sexual escapades a centenarian had. It was not unusual for a man of 108 to enjoy a sexual relationship with a woman 60 years his junior, married or unmarried. Centenarian men still fathered children in their early hundreds; records show that healthy sperm was taken from one man when he was 119 years old. The women continued to menstruate until they were nearly 70. The old men were much revered by women of all ages.

Of the women centenarians, very few had ever been married. Interestingly, married Vilcabamban women died much younger than did single Vilcabamban women—at around age 80 instead of over 100—perhaps because the married women bore and reared so many children (a dozen was common) and were treated as sexual objects for use at the convenience of their husbands. In an extramarital pursuit, the stimulated man romantically wooed the woman. The jungle undergrowth offered plenty of places for two people to meet and copulate. The couple then went back to their respective households. (Nevertheless, extramarital sex was considered against the law in Ecuador.)

When getting married for the first time, a woman was required to be a virgin. If the new husband suspected that his bride was not, he could divorce her immediately and send her back to her family in disgrace. The woman then probably did not marry again for the rest of her life. Vilcabambans generally married when the man was about 22 and the woman was 18. The woman usually had four children before she turned 25.

Vilcabamban men felt great satisfaction when their wives were pregnant. A wife's pregnancy was a sign of a man's sexual prowess, something that was esteemed in Vilcabamban society. The men admitted that they were happiest when they saw their women "full" and knew it was of their doing. They spoke of their pregnant wives with pride. The type of contraception that was the most popular was the rhythm method, although some Vilcabambans who were knowledgeable violated the Catholic rulings against the use of artificial means of birth control. No one ever admitted to this sort of religious transgression, however.

The women also used prolonged breastfeeding as a natural method of birth control. A Vilcabamban breastfed her child for two to three years, or until she and her husband decided to have another baby. Then husband and wife both took the fertility "drug" gayuna, a locally grown herb that tended to increase a man's sex drive and to diminish a woman's. The women breastfed everywhere without inhibition. My wife and I stood at a church service one Sunday and counted every fifth woman as holding a suckling child to her breast—maybe to keep the child quiet. Additionally, the women wore a carved wooden model of an erect penis nestled between their breasts. The men carried such sexual symbols in their pockets. These were a very sexy people.

Childbirth was accomplished at home, not in a hospital. Children born outside of wedlock were not uncommon. One family, that of Miguel Carpio (who died in 1980 at the age of 133), was exceptionally numerous. Grace Halsell wrote in her book *Los Viejos* that Carpio had acknowledged having fathered within wedlock twelve sons, who gave him ninety-eight grandsons, seventy great-grandsons, and seventy-two great-great-grandsons. He took no notice of his couple of hundred female progeny. Carpio also admitted frankly that he had fathered many children outside of wedlock.[3]

THE SOURCE OF THE VILCABAMBANS' PROLONGED SEX LIFE

The specific purpose of my Ecuadorian trek was to learn the secret of the Vilcabambans' long life and prolonged sexuality. I think I achieved my goal. Taking water, food, and hair samples and then matching their mineral contents uncovered the source of the longevity.

The water was probably part of the secret of the Vilcabambans' long life and super sexual capacity. I had a quantity of water from Vilcabamba's artesian wells analyzed by a laboratory in California. The results are presented in Table 12.1.

Table 12.1. The mineral content of water from Vilcabamba, Ecuador.

Mineral	Concentration (Parts Per Million)	Normal Range
Calcium	21	0–200
Magnesium	5.7	0–150
Sodium	7.1	not established
Potassium	1.4	not established
Iron	0.53	0–0.3
Copper	0.003	0–1.0
Manganese	0.005	0–0.05
Zinc	0.010	0–5.0
Chromium	0.010	0–0.05
Selenium	0.050	0–0.01
Lead	0.010	0–0.05
Cadmium	0.005	0–0.01
Mercury	0.001	0–0.005
Arsenic	0.050	0–0.1
Aluminum	0.030	not established
Cobalt	0.010	not established
Lithium	0.006	not established
Molybdenum	0.020	not established
Nickel	0.020	not established
Phosphorus	0.200	not established
Vanadium	0.020	not established

I have already described the food sources and chelation effects of some of the minerals in the Vilcabambans' water supply including calcium, magnesium, zinc, selenium, and phosphorus. The remaining natural mineral chelators that kept the centenarians' blood vessels unclogged included chromium, cobalt, iron, lithium, molybdenum, potassium, sodium, and vanadium. These minerals and their food sources are described in the following pages.

To get these chelating minerals the way the Vilcabambans did, you would need to drink Vilcabamban water, which is bottled in Vilcabamba but not imported into the United States. This water from the sacred valley of Vilcabamba is sold by the quart in Ecuadorian supermarkets, beverage shops, pharmacies, health food stores, and specialty grocery stores. It is bottled by Aqua d'Oro B.V. (de Loiressestraat 73, 1071 N. V. Amsterdam, Holland).

You may never be able to drink Vilcabamban water, but you can still enjoy the Vilcabambans' minerals of long life and sexual endurance by eating foods that are high in them. Or, you can supplement your diet with these minerals in the form of tablets, capsules, powders, drops, or injections.

One pair of mineral products available in the United States was inspired directly by the Vilcabambans. Called Fountain 2001, the products are marketed by Youngevity, Inc. of Dallas, Texas, and furnish beta-carotene, vitamin C, and vitamin E to rid the body of damaging free radicals. In a two-step program, Fountain 2001 begins the oral chelation process with Alpha Formula, which cleanses the system and prepares it for improved absorption. It continues the process with Beta Formula, which is intended to retard aging and enhance sexuality. (For more information on Fountain 2001 or to order the products, telephone Youngevity at 800–469–6864.)

Chromium

The trace mineral chromium is essential for good health. A daily dosage of 200 milligrams is most beneficial. Chromium prevents the formation of atherosclerotic plaques when it is eaten in sufficient quantity. An insufficiency of chromium in the diet results in an elevation of serum-cholesterol and serum-sugar levels and in hardening of the arteries. This is particularly true when refined white sugar is eaten. White sugar has chromium refined out of it, while raw sugar cane is loaded with the mineral. Raw cane sugar is a fine food; it has nutritional value, in contrast to the zero nutrition of white sugar.

Inasmuch as a sizable percentage of the people eating the ordinary Western diet are deficient in chromium, hardening of the arteries and death from the degenerative diseases that result such as heart disease and stroke are rampant. According to estimates based on organ weights, Africans have twice the chromium in their bodies that Westerners do, Near Easterners have almost four and a half times the amount, and Orientals have five times as much. The Eastern peoples do not have the high incidence of degenerative diseases characteristic of Westerners.[4]

Because chromium in pill form is poorly absorbed by the human gut unless it is chelated with an amino acid to fool the intestine into thinking it is an organic substance, it is better to get chromium from whole foods. The following list shows which foods supply a relatively high concentration of chromium. (*Note:* The values shown in the list are for the total chromium content of the foods, not for the amount that may be biologically active as Glucose Tolerance Factor. The foods marked with an asterisk [*] are high in Glucose Tolerance Factor.)

Foods High in Chromium

The following list names foods that are high in chromium. Also given for each food is the number of micrograms of chromium per 100 grams (3.5 ounces) of edible portion of food. For example, brewer's yeast has 112 micrograms of chromium in every 100 grams of edible food.

112	Brewer's yeast*	11	Scallops
57	Beef, round	11	Swiss cheese
55	Calf liver*	10	Bananas
42	Whole wheat bread*	10	Spinach
38	Wheat bran	10	Pork chops
30	Rye bread	9	Carrots
30	Chili peppers, fresh	8	Navy beans, dried
26	Oysters	7	Shrimp
24	Potatoes	7	Lettuce
23	Wheat germ	5	Oranges
19	Sweet peppers, green	5	Lobster tails
16	Eggs	5	Blueberries
15	Chicken	4	Green beans
14	Apples	4	Cabbage
13	Butter	4	Mushrooms
13	Parsnips	3	Beer
12	Cornmeal	3	Strawberries
12	Lamb chops	1	Cow's milk, whole

Cobalt

The trace element cobalt, which is part of the vitamin B_{12} molecule, is essential for life. The necessary average daily intake is 8 micrograms. Cobalt activates the enzyme systems in blood-vessel walls that respond to stressors. After it is consumed, it is stored in the red blood cells and blood plasma, liver, kidneys, pancreas, and spleen. The best food sources for cobalt are meats, especially liver and kidney; seafood, such as oysters and clams; dairy products; and sea vegetation, such as kelp. The foods rich in cobalt that are listed in the following table are also rich in cobalamin (vitamin B_{12}), to which cobalt is tied.

Foods High in Cobalt

The following list names foods that are high in cobalt. Also given for each food is the number of micrograms of cobalt per 100 grams (3.5 ounces) of edible portion of food. For example, lamb liver has 104.0 micrograms of cobalt in every 100 grams of edible food.

104.0	Lamb liver	25.0	Chicken liver
98.0	Clams	18.0	Oysters
80.0	Beef liver	17.0	Sardines
63.0	Lamb kidney	11.0	Beef heart
60.0	Calf liver	6.0	Egg yolks
31.0	Beef kidney	5.2	Lamb heart

5.0	Trout	1.6	Gruyère cheese
4.0	Brain, all kinds	1.4	Bleu cheese
4.0	Salmon, meat only	1.3	Haddock, meat only
3.0	Tuna, meat only	1.2	Flounder, meat only
2.1	Lamb	1.2	Scallops
2.1	Sweetbreads (thymus)	1.0	Cheddar cheese
2.0	Eggs	1.0	Cottage cheese
2.0	Whey, dried	1.0	Mozzarella cheese
1.8	Beef, lean	1.0	Halibut
1.8	Edam cheese	1.0	Perch, meat only
1.8	Swiss cheese	1.0	Swordfish, meat only
1.6	Brie cheese		

Iron

Despite iron's being a heavy metal, it is not toxic like lead, cadmium, mercury, aluminum, nickel, copper, or arsenic, unless it is ingested in extraordinary amounts. Taken in excess, iron causes problems in the liver and pancreas. When ingested in proper amounts, iron chelates with protein and copper to form hemoglobin, the transporter of oxygen in red blood cells. Thus, iron performs a basic life function by building blood, by producing myoglobin in muscle tissue, and by participating in enzyme metabolism and protein metabolism.

A daily iron intake of 18 milligrams is recommended for women and 10 milligrams is recommended for men. Women require extra iron during menstruation and other blood losses, during pregnancy, and while breastfeeding.

Foods High in Iron

The following list names foods that are high in iron. Also given for each food is the number of milligrams of iron per 100 grams (3.5 ounces) of edible portion of food. For example, kelp has 100.0 milligrams of iron in every 100 grams of edible food.

100.0	Kelp	6.1	Clams
17.3	Brewer's yeast	4.7	Almonds
16.1	Blackstrap molasses	3.9	Prunes, dried
14.9	Wheat bran	3.8	Cashews
11.2	Pumpkin seeds	3.7	Beef, lean
11.2	Squash seeds	3.5	Raisins
9.4	Wheat germ	3.4	Jerusalem artichokes
8.8	Beef liver	3.4	Brazil nuts
7.1	Sunflower seeds	3.3	Beet greens
6.8	Millet	3.2	Swiss chard
6.2	Parsley	3.1	Dandelion greens

3.1	English walnuts	0.8	Pumpkins
3.0	Dates	0.8	Mushrooms
2.9	Pork	0.7	Bananas
2.7	Dried beans, cooked	0.7	Beets
2.4	Sesame seeds, hulled	0.7	Carrots
2.4	Pecans	0.7	Eggplants
2.3	Eggs	0.7	Sweet potatoes
2.1	Lentils	0.6	Avocados
2.1	Peanuts	0.6	Figs, dried
1.9	Lamb	0.6	Potatoes
1.9	Tofu	0.6	Corn
1.8	Green peas, fresh	0.5	Pineapples
1.6	Brown rice, uncooked	0.5	Nectarines
1.5	Chicken	0.5	Watermelons
1.3	Mung bean sprouts	0.5	Winter squashes
1.2	Salmon	0.5	Brown rice, cooked
1.1	Broccoli	0.5	Tomatoes
1.1	Currants	0.4	Oranges
1.1	Whole wheat bread	0.4	Cherries
1.1	Cauliflower	0.4	Summer squashes
1.0	Cheddar cheese	0.3	Papayas
1.0	Strawberries	0.3	Celery
1.0	Asparagus	0.3	Cottage cheese
0.9	Blackberries	0.3	Apples
0.8	Red cabbage		

Lithium

In megadoses of 1,000 milligrams (1 gram) daily, lithium is used in psychiatry to treat manic-depressive psychosis. In areas where lithium levels in drinking water are in the range of 0.004 to 0.04 parts per million, overall criminal behavior among the population seems to be much diminished. An average person's daily diet contains about 2 milligrams of lithium. Since lithium occurs naturally in minuscule amounts in many foods—including most vegetables, all dairy products, and all meats—no listing of specific lithium-containing foods is necessary. Supplementation with lithium pills is not recommended unless done under the supervision of a psychiatrist familiar with orthomolecular nutrition.

Molybdenum

Without molybdenum, human life would not exist. Molybdenum is an essential trace mineral. It helps determine carbohydrate metabolism, dental decay, and the presence or absence of esophageal cancer in older people. The recommended daily intake is 300 micrograms daily.

Foods High in Molybdenum

The following list names foods that are high in molybdenum. Also given for each food is the number of micrograms of molybdenum per 100 grams (3.5 ounces) of edible portion of food. For example, lentils have 155 micrograms of molybdenum in every 100 grams of edible food.

155	Lentils	31	Cottage cheese
135	Beef liver	30	Beef
130	Split peas, dried	30	Potatoes
120	Cauliflower	25	Onions
110	Green peas, fresh	25	Peanuts
109	Brewer's yeast	25	Coconut meat
100	Wheat germ	25	Pork
100	Spinach	24	Lamb
77	Beef kidney	21	Green beans
75	Brown rice	19	Crab
70	Garlic	19	Molasses
60	Oats	16	Cantaloupes
53	Eggs	14	Apricots
50	Rye bread	10	Raisins
45	Corn	10	Butter
42	Barley	7	Strawberries
40	Fish	5	Carrots
36	Whole wheat	5	Cabbage
32	Whole wheat bread	3	Cow's milk, whole
32	Chicken	1	Goat's milk

Potassium

The same diuretics that help women combat premenstrual tension by increasing fluid discharge also cause potassium loss. Therefore, a woman taking a diuretic may need to supplement her diet with potassium pills. With a deficiency of potassium, both males and females suffer from poor neurogenital response. Potassium is necessary for the stimulation of nerve impulses from the sexual centers of the brain to the muscles required in vaginal-wall or scrotal-sac contractions. It is also needed for normal body growth, correct body-fluid alkalinity, healthy skin, good cell metabolism, and proper enzyme reactions, as well as for synthesis of muscle protein from amino acids in the blood, stimulation of the kidneys to eliminate poisonous body wastes, and conversion of glucose to glycogen for energy. It also works synergistically with other minerals to accomplish necessary bodily functions. For example, it joins with calcium to regulate neuromuscular activity, with phosphorus to send oxygen to the brain, and with sodium to normalize the heartbeat and nourish the muscles.

Potassium is found naturally in many different foods. Therefore, a person eating an average diet generally has no problem meeting the minimum requirement, which is about 2,500 milligrams (2.5 grams) per day.

Foods High in Potassium

The following list names foods that are high in potassium. Also given for each food is the number of milligrams of potassium per 100 grams (3.5 ounces) of edible portion of food. For example, dulse has 8,060 milligrams of potassium in every 100 grams of edible food.

8,060	Dulse	295	Cauliflower
5,273	Kelp	282	Watercress
920	Sunflower seeds	278	Asparagus
827	Wheat germ	268	Red cabbage
773	Almonds	264	Lettuce
763	Raisins	251	Cantaloupes
727	Parsley	249	Lentils, cooked
715	Brazil nuts	244	Tomatoes
674	Peanuts	243	Sweet potatoes
648	Dates	234	Papayas
640	Figs, dried	214	Eggplants
604	Avocados	213	Sweet peppers, green
603	Pecans	208	Beets
600	Yams	202	Peaches
550	Swiss chard	202	Summer squashes
540	Soybeans, cooked	200	Oranges
529	Garlic	199	Raspberries
470	Spinach	191	Cherries
450	English walnuts	164	Strawberries
430	Millet	162	Grapefruit juice
416	Dried beans, cooked	158	Grapes
414	Mushrooms	157	Onions
407	Potatoes, with skin	146	Pineapples
382	Broccoli	144	Cow's milk, whole
370	Bananas	141	Lemon juice
370	Red meats	130	Pears
369	Winter squashes	129	Eggs
366	Chicken	110	Apples
341	Carrots	100	Watermelons
341	Celery	70	Brown rice, cooked

Sodium

While sodium is an essential element in nutrition, the standard intake in modern Western diets far exceeds the need. For example, the average American every day ingests 3 to 7 grams of sodium that occurs naturally in food and another 6 to 18 grams in sodium chloride (table salt) that has been added to processed food. This is too much. The National Research Council recommends a daily sodium chloride intake of 1 gram for every 1 kilogram of water consumed. Ingesting too much sodium additionally causes potassium to be lost in the urine, bringing about the double health problems of too much sodium in the intercellular fluid and too little potassium in the cells. Ingesting 14 to 28 grams of sodium chloride daily in the form of table salt is considered toxic.

About 50 percent of the body's sodium is found in the fluids surrounding the cells. Furthermore, sodium is required for the fluids of ejaculation and vaginal lubrication.

Since most people get enough salt in their daily diets, salt supplementation is not recommended. Therefore, foods that are high in sodium (see the list below) generally not only do not need to be sought out but probably should be avoided—unless, of course, they offer other important nutritional benefits.

Foods High in Sodium

The following list names foods that are high in sodium. Also given for each food is the number of milligrams of sodium per 100 grams (3.5 ounces), unless otherwise noted, of edible portion of food. For example, kelp has 3,007 milligrams of sodium in every 100 grams of edible food.

3,007	Kelp	110	Cod
2,400	Olives, green	71	Spinach
2,132	Table salt (1 teaspoon)	70	Lamb
1,428	Pickles, dill	65	Pork
1,139	Soy sauce (1 tablespoon)	64	Chicken
828	Olives, ripe	60	Beef
747	Sauerkraut	60	Beets
700	Cheddar cheese	60	Sesame seeds
265	Scallops	52	Watercress
229	Cottage cheese	50	Cow's milk, whole
210	Lobster	49	Turnips
147	Swiss chard	47	Carrots
130	Beet greens	47	Yogurt
130	Buttermilk	45	Parsley
126	Celery	43	Jerusalem artichokes
122	Eggs	34	Figs, dried

30	Lentils, dried	10	Onions
30	Sunflower seeds	10	Sweet potatoes
27	Raisins	9	Brown rice
26	Red cabbage	9	Lettuce
19	Garlic	6	Cucumbers
19	White-colored beans	5	Peanuts
15	Broccoli	4	Avocados
15	Mushrooms	3	Tomatoes
13	Cauliflower	2	Eggplants

The following list names foods that contain large amounts of sodium chloride, which is added during processing. These foods generally should be avoided.

Barbecue sauce	Nuts, salted
Bouillon cubes	Peanut butter, commercial
Catsup	Salad dressings, commercial
Cheese, processed	Snack foods (potato chips, corn
Crackers, salted	chips, pretzels, etc.)
Fish, canned	Soups, canned or packaged
Luncheon meats	Spice mixes, packaged
Meat, cured, smoked, or canned	Vegetables, canned or frozen
Meat tenderizer	

Vanadium

The trace element vanadium is part of the natural mechanism in the body that regulates how much cholesterol is formed. When the right amount of vanadium is present in the brain, cholesterol formation is inhibited and hardening of the arteries is prevented. Vanadium also helps the central nervous system to function properly. For the entire body to work well biologically, about 2.1 milligrams of vanadium should be consumed daily.

Foods High in Vanadium

The following list names foods that are high in vanadium. Also given for each food is the number of micrograms of vanadium per 100 grams (3.5 ounces) of edible portion of food. For example, buckwheat has 100 micrograms of vanadium in every 100 grams of edible food.

100	Buckwheat	42	Eggs
80	Parsley	41	Sunflower seed oil
70	Soybeans	35	Oats
64	Safflower oil	30	Olive oil

15	Sunflower seeds	5	Onions
15	Corn	5	Whole wheat
14	Green beans	4	Lobster
11	Peanut oil	4	Beets
10	Carrots	3	Apples
10	Cabbage	2	Plums
10	Garlic	2	Lettuce
6	Tomatoes	2	Millet
5	Radishes		

Panella (Vilcabamban Cane Sugar)

One of the main staples in the Vilcabambans' diet was sugar cane, which was both eaten raw for its fiber and sweetness, and cooked down into a thick brown syrup and hardened into blocks. All of the minerals ordinarily present in cane sugar were ingested by the Vilcabambans daily inasmuch as the brown sugar block, called *panella*, was the only sweetening agent the people used.

Stalks of sugar cane were fed into a press that was powered by oxen turning wheels. The juice squeezed out of the stalks ran through a trough into a boiling cauldron. The juice was skimmed of impurities three times as it was alternately heated and cooled. The thickening syrup was poured by sugar workers into three-inch-thick square or rectangular molds and allowed to cool. When done, the blocks of sweetener were removed from the molds and sold to the public as a table sweetener or candy. The common practice was to use the side of a knife to shave off slivers of the hard chunk sugar for sweetening a cup of herb tea.

Panella was exceedingly rich in sexually enhancing minerals. Table 12.2 shows the mineral content of this natural food used at practically every meal by the centenarians in Vilcabamba. (Note that the minerals in panella were the same as those in the drinking water in Vilcabamba.)

HAIR MINERAL ANALYSIS FOR DETERMINING HEALTH STATUS

Dr. John A. Myers of Baltimore, Maryland, suspected that the longevity of the Vilcabambans was directly related to the minerals in their drinking water and diet. In the *Journal of Applied Nutrition*, Dr. Myers wrote that the mineral elements supplied by the Vilcabambans' agricultural lifestyle contributed to the Old Ones' long life and elevated capacity for sexual activity. "Each of [the Vilcabambans'] communities is situated in a valley supplied with water which washes silt from a mountain behind them," he said. "These people drink the silted water; they fertilize crops with it; they eat the flesh and milk of animals raised on it and have a constant supply of trace

Table 12.2. The mineral content of panella from Vilcabamba, Ecuador.

Mineral	Concentration (Parts Per Million)
Calcium	994
Magnesium	815
Sodium	233
Potassium	343
Iron	15
Copper	0.73
Manganese	3.4
Zinc	5.9
Chromium	0.20
Selenium	1.0
Lead	2.0
Cadmium	0.10
Mercury	0.030
Arsenic	0.000
Aluminum	21
Cobalt	0.20
Lithium	0.76
Molybdenum	0.20
Nickel	0.40
Phosphorus	533
Vanadium	0.20

elements throughout their lives that is as good or better than any other place on earth."[5]

Dr. Myers concluded that "these people maintain their health and longevity from activation of enzymes of their cells by these mineral elements supplied to them in a fortuitously balanced concentration."

I was able to have the concentration and balance of the old-timers' body minerals checked and compared to those of other Vilcabambans in various age groups by having trace-mineral hair analyses performed.

Minerals are present in every tissue of the body, including hair tissues. Metabolized minerals lodge in the hair tissues in proportional quantities, just as they do in other body tissues. However, they are more easily measured in the hair tissues than in the other tissues. Hair analysis has been found to be an accurate way to measure mineral absorption to the cells. Using the results of a laboratory analysis of strands of hair, experts are able to plan a program to balance the minerals in a person's body through proper nutrition and food supplementation. Hair trace-mineral analysis also facilitates the monitoring of toxicities and planning of appropriate detoxification measures.

By having newly grown hair tested by a lab for the presence of essential and toxic trace minerals, you can learn about the state of your health. The trace-mineral hair-analysis report lets you know exactly which mineral supplements you need. It also alerts you to the levels of toxic minerals in your body. This is all indicated in the trace-mineral hair-analysis computer printout that comes back to you from the laboratory.

The only things you need to do to get your hair analyzed are to cut about two to three tablespoons (about half a gram) worth of new-growth hair from the back of your head or nape of your neck; this should be the first inch or two of growth closest to the scalp. Place the hair in either a plastic bag or small envelope and mail it with the appropriate order form to the laboratory you have selected. Laboratories that perform hair mineral analyses include:

- Albion Clinical Laboratories, P.O. Box 750, Clearfield, Utah 84105.
- Analytico Laboratories, 100 East Cheyenne Road, Colorado Springs, Colorado 80906.
- Parmae Laboratories, Inc., 7101 Carpenter Freeway, Dallas, Texas 75080.
- Natural Health Institute, 7624 South Broadway, St. Louis, Missouri 63111.

The cost of a trace-mineral hair analysis varies according to how many minerals you have your hair analyzed for (from twelve, which is the number of basic minerals essential to life, to over forty). When you receive the report, you will know the status of each of the analyzed minerals in your body as it was four to six weeks earlier and as it possibly is currently. Follow the directions in your report about adding or subtracting minerals to achieve the proper balance in your body.

Mineral levels in blood are also measurable but subject to great fluctuations that reflect acute exposure. For this reason, hair mineral analysis is preferable because of the more stable readings it gives. Some toxic minerals are removed from the bloodstream fairly rapidly but are still present in the body in storage. They may be causing toxicity, even though the blood shows them to be within the normal range. Furthermore, some minerals can be deficient in body cells but shown as falling within normal levels according to blood analysis. Good examples are magnesium and potassium. The blood must maintain a certain equilibrium between these two minerals, and it will maintain this equilibrium even at the expense of the cells to which these minerals are so important. It is possible for the cells to be deficient in potassium and magnesium, although the blood shows normal levels. Hair analysis will reveal problems that might be missed in blood analysis.

HAIR MINERAL ANALYSES OF THE VILCABAMBANS

The oldest living Vilcabamban from whom I took a hair sample for mineral analysis was José Maria Roa, a 131-year-old Mestizo (a person of mixed Indian and Spanish blood, as were most of the Vilcabamban population). Roa was married to Maria Castilla Roa, 66, who was his third wife. Maria had given birth to a son twenty-four years earlier, which means that José Maria Roa had viable sperm and produced progeny at the age of 107.

In all, I had hair mineral analyses performed on forty adults and on ten children under the age of 10. Comparing the children's analyses to those of the adults provided a clue as to whether the long life and sexual longevity of the Vilcabambans were inherited or due to lifestyle. In summary, lifestyle was the answer. There was no common genetic mineral trait between the adults and the children, but there was a definite similarity among the centenarian mountain people. All the elderly mountain people had about the same concentrations of exactly the same minerals in their hair samples. But the children, coming from the village center and exposed to imported processed foods, had hair analyses that were closer to the standard analyses of Westerners.

In all, I took hair for analysis from seven Vilcabambans who were 100 years old or older, five who were 90 or older, ten who were 80 or older, eight who were 70 or older, three who were 60 or older, three who were 50 or older, and four who were 40 or older.

The reports relating to the hair mineral analyses indicated the reasons that these elderly Ecuadorians remained sexually active for so long. The reports proved that minerals in the water and food, including the panella, were the sources of the success. The water and unprocessed food provided the ingredients for a type of chelation process that took place within these people's bodies—particularly in the blood vessels. Additionally, the exercise the Vilcabambans enjoyed daily, the pure air with its negative ions, and the nonstressful existence within the community were major factors. Degenerative diseases such as cancer, heart disease, arthritis, kidney disease, Alzheimer's disease, cataracts, liver disease, glaucoma, diabetes, senility, and stroke did not exist in the elderly people's bodies. The centenarians and younger Vilcabambans were able to engage in activities that come quite naturally to a healthy and primitive people, especially sexual fulfillment in all its aspects.

An interesting scientific observation was that while the killer diseases were absent from the Vilcabamba population, they were still prevalent in the rest of Ecuador in the same rates as in the United States. When I examined public health records from Ecuadorian cities such as Quito, Loja, and Guayaquil, the facts became apparent.

The water and food the Vilcabambans consumed also protected them against heavy-metal toxicity such as lead poisoning. Even though part of the population had high body contamination of aluminum and iron, as shown by the hair analyses, these people were healthier than were most Americans. It is possible that many of these people were living on mountains of bauxite containing goodly deposits of aluminum ore. Additionally, the heavy red dust on the roads was composed of iron oxide. An excess of either of these metals in the body ordinarily is extremely toxic. Excess iron kills, and too much aluminum brings on memory loss, confusion, Alzheimer's disease, and other symptoms of senility. These long-lived people, however, did not suffer from heavy-metal toxicity. The chelating mechanisms brought about by the optimal exercise, drinking water, and fresh food seemed to protect them.

The main chelators present in the water and panella were selenium, magnesium, manganese, zinc, chromium, calcium, sodium, potassium, molybdenum, vanadium, and lithium. The sodium–potassium ratio in the old-timers was ideal. Their calcium–magnesium–phosphorus ratio was ideal. The high natural chelation property of manganese, combined with the antioxidative effect of selenium in their bodies, was ideal. These, with the exceedingly low heavy-metal contents of cadmium, mercury, lead, arsenic, aluminum, and nickel showing in the hair of the Old Ones, made Vilcabamban water and panella practically therapeutic for consumption.

In a verbal report on the Ecuadorian water, Dr. Garry F. Gordon, laboratory director of MineraLab, Inc., which performed all the analyses, said:

> The manganese levels alone in the Vilcabambans' bodies are the same as if the people were having chelation therapy. The manganese in their drinking water, taken into the cells lining their arterial walls, helps to keep calcium (which brings on heart and artery spasm) out of the cells. The high magnesium level also displaces the cells' calcium. Heart disease and hardening of the arteries are largely prevented just by the favorable mineral contents (including magnesium, chromium, zinc, selenium, potassium, calcium, and manganese) in the body tissues. These probably came from the Vilcabamban drinking water.
>
> Furthermore, from our hair analyses, we see that the Vilcabambans' lack of lead toxicity is incredible. The latest report from the *Danish Medical Journal* indicates that children are poisoned in Denmark by 13.9 ppm [parts per million] lead content; one third of American children are suffering from over 30 ppm lead poisoning. Vilcabamban children have essentially zero lead poisoning; Vilcabamban adults have no more than 4 ppm lead. This is absolutely amazing and may be due to the drinking water's chelation effect.

The drinking water, excellent unpolluted lifestyle, lack of stress, and fresh food may have made manganese biologically available to the Vilcabambans. This has not been so for Americans, who are likely to consume too much phosphorus, which tends to make blood vessels degenerate, in carbonated soft drinks, condensed milk, and beef. The Vilcabambans' phosphorus–calcium ratio was ideal, which may have permitted them to pick up bioavailable manganese more effectively than do people in industrialized Western civilizations.

In the United States, physicians do not find more than one in ten people with the proper calcium–magnesium ratio. Most Americans are not in calcium homeostasis, and calcium tends to leave the bones in order to line the walls of arteries. Calcium is the glue that holds together atherosclerotic plaque. Hair-calcium ranges are between 60 and 180 in unhealthy Americans. Normal is between 20 and 60. Some Americans have calcium analyses showing 800 or 900; these people are extremely unhealthy. The joints and arteries of these unhealthy Americans are likely to be calcifying virtually by the hour with calcinosclerosis disease. (See page 356 of *Calcifilaxis* by Hans Selye, M.D., D.Sc.) Yet disease caused by excess deposition of calcium did not happen to the people living in Vilcabamba. One of the reasons was that a natural calcium antagonist—manganese—appears to have been bioavailable in the environment, most likely in the drinking water and food. It is not bioavailable in the American environment. The result is that Americans are victims of over 6 million spontaneous bone fractures each year.

Only one out of seventy-five Americans shows a normal manganese level in hair mineral analysis, but more than nine out of ten Vilcabambans had normal manganese hair mineral analyses. The unadulterated drinking water and panella tended to extend Vilcabambans' sex lives because of the ideal mineral contents.

Scientists and members of the healing arts are increasingly aware of the importance of minerals in maintaining health and long life. Perhaps this is because the foods eaten by industrialized Western societies are stripped of so many of their valuable nutrients in the process of being dried, stored, refined, frozen, or canned—or because they are often grown in depleted or chemically treated soils. When insufficient amounts of vital elements are present in food, health, sexuality, and longevity are bound to be affected. The population will not enjoy sex and sexuality into old age.

You can add minerals to your diet, but which ones you should add can be determined only through accurate laboratory testing. To learn what the submolecular ratios of minerals are within bodies, doctors of all the healing arts are turning to hair mineral analysis. The method is inexpensive and rapid by atomic absorption spectroscopy, which provides microscopically accurate measurements of the trace elements in a body. Once the mineral ratios are known, the status of a person's health, sexuality, and longevity can be pinpointed and possibly predicted. The trace-mineral hair analyses that I had done of the Vilcabambans high in the Ecuadorian Andes proved this to be true.

Chapter 13

LIFESTYLE AND SEXUAL HEALTH

I'm only twenty-one years old, but my whole world is coming down around my ears. I am living with a guy. Both of us are between jobs, surviving on unemployment checks. We are subsisting on coffee, doughnuts, cola drinks, salty snacks, and occasional fast foods. We can hardly scrounge enough for marijuana.

I have an upset stomach all the time, am ridden with anxiety, show rashes on my skin, have a vaginal discharge, feel jumpy constantly, and blow my stack at any provocation. The worst part is that even though I have all this time on my hands, I don't want to have sex. I mean, the one release I have from all the pressures in my life doesn't come to pass. I have no orgasm. The few times my boyfriend and I have tried making love, we both found it ungratifying. Now he's moving out.

I don't think I can tolerate being alone. Recently, a couple of friends left me some whiskey to help me get over those bad times. I get high while I wait for something good to happen. During my dreaming, I have thoughts that maybe my problems are more physical than anything else. My body's not acting well. Could it be that the stuff you've written about sexual nutrition can apply to other life problems? I don't know!

Cornelia P.
Honolulu, Hawaii

I've always considered myself to be a healthy, normal male. I'm twenty-four with a strong sex drive. Lately, however, I've been alarmed by a series of incidents. For example, I may be with a sexy woman who is wearing an intoxicating new perfume. We've been kissing and touching, and both of us are excited and ready to go further. But then I catch a really heady whiff of her perfume, and suddenly, I lose all interest in making love. A feeling of nausea comes over me, and I just want to get away from the girl.

Or, at a bar or party, I'll be enjoying a few beers, smoking pot, and talking to women. I'll make my play for the woman I desire, and she'll accept. Before you know it, we're getting down to sex. Then suddenly, it becomes extremely difficult for me to maintain an erection. The woman is primed and waiting, but my organ is soft and won't go in. This has happened half a dozen times in the last several months.

Now, I know that I'm not old enough for permanent impotency, and I don't have any severe psychological problems. What's wrong with me?

Frank W.
Washington, D.C.

A certain concept circulating in the worlds of medicine and sexology is that a loss of interest in sex, possibly accompanied by depression or lethargy, may be due to allergies. There are many new allergic substances in our altered ecology.

The human digestive and breathing systems are tubes that are open to the environment. They draw sustenance from the environment, and they return wastes to it. These digestive and breathing systems are vulnerable to the unfamiliar allergens created by modern technology, for none of us has armor against surroundings that irritate us physically. The result is that most people suffer mental, sexual, emotional, or physical problems. In fact, more than 80 percent of people who are ill actually are victims of nonpersonal environmental excitants in air, water, food, drugs, or other substances that have been thrust upon modern civilization mostly by the technology of industrialization.

YOU MAY BE ALLERGIC TO SEX

The raped and polluted environment is striking back at people by bringing on an enormous amount of illness in the form of sexual dysfunctions, physical ailments, behavioral and perceptual disorders, psychoses, and neuroses, which the orthodox medical community—not recognizing as ecological—has labeled "psychosomatic."

Sexual disabilities such as impotency and frigidity, which had been generally assumed to be psychic problems, have now been proven to be cerebral allergies. The brain can be sensitive to an allergen the same way any other organ in the body can be.

The irritants that cause allergic reactions are in homes, workplaces, recreational areas, and other locations of easy access. All of these places comprise individual sophisticated chemical environments. According to studies conducted by internists, allergists, pediatricians, urologists, gynecologists, and other physician specialists who belong to the American Academy of Environmental Medicine (formerly the Society for Clinical Ecology), one in ten people shows sexual abnormality because of an allergy to substances such as:

- Automobile exhaust
- Chemical food additives
- Chlorinated water
- Cigarette smoke
- Cleaning products
- Coal-tar products
- Cosmetics
- Detergent

- Disinfectant
- Dust mites
- Fabric
- Floor wax
- Furniture polish
- Hair spray
- Heating-system fumes
- Hydrocarbons
- Inhalants
- Ink
- Insect repellant
- Mold
- Nail polish
- Nail polish remover
- Paint
- Perfume
- Pesticides
- Petrochemicals
- Pharmaceuticals
- Plastic
- Processed foods
- Rubber
- Rubber cement

After an allergic substance (an allergen or excitant) enters the circulatory system, it is carried to every potential shock tissue. In a sensitized person, the number of possible combinations of allergic symptoms is therefore very great. The allergic person not uncommonly experiences a rather peculiar series of symptoms (a syndrome) because various bizarre reactions originate in several unrelated anatomic areas. An allergen lodging in the urogenital system of a male may bring on impotence. An allergen stuck in the digestive system of a man or woman may cause stomach problems. An allergen lodging in the brain can bring about dizziness, nausea, or vomiting. If an allergen strikes a few places in the body, two or more syndromes may set in.

If you are a victim of undetected allergies and seek relief from an establishment physician who is uninformed about the newer methods of *clinical ecology* (the medical science of diagnosing and treating allergic illnesses created by changes in our ecology), chances are that the only diagnosis you will be given is that you are suffering from a "psychosomatic" illness. Doctors who are not educated in the techniques of clinical ecology cannot imagine that allergic ailments can manifest themselves in a variety of symptoms and signs that may seem unrelated. The concept that an allergic lifestyle could louse up a person's sex life is relatively new and has been the source of revolutionary thinking among sexologists in recent years.

Favorite foods that are eaten every day are particularly overlooked as possible allergens. After all, you eat them regularly. And practically every day you feel no inclination to enjoy sexual intercourse; you feel lazy and lethargic about making love—symptomatic especially of a woman who has a brain sensitivity to a supposedly wholesome food such as milk, potatoes, or salad greens. Common foods that bring on the loss of libido include:

- Baker's yeast
- Beef and other red meats
- Brewer's yeast
- Chicken

- Chocolate
- Citrus fruits
- Coffee
- Corn
- Eggs
- Food coloring
- Lettuce
- Malt (in beer)
- Milk

- Pineapples
- Potatoes
- Rye
- Sprouts
- Sweet peppers
- Tomatoes
- Tuna
- Wheat

Sexual weakness coming from hypersensitivity to foods or the products of modern chemical technology is a much-neglected area of medicine. Ecologic illness is not understood, least of all by the very people who are addicted to the allergens that are producing their loss of sexual power.

It is true! Many foods and chemicals have an addictive quality for the people who are sensitive to them. This is supported by the fact that allergic substances induce symptoms that are quickly alleviated when more of the allergen is taken. Cigarettes are an example. A person becomes jittery if he is in the habit of smoking regularly but cannot light up for a while. He goes into a state of withdrawal from the addictive allergen. Although he recognizes his addiction as something that is sure to cause future poor health, he cannot give up his habit no matter how much logic he uses because the excitant in the tobacco or in one of the substances used to process the tobacco will not let him. The smoker is simultaneously allergic to and addicted to the excitant.

The addictive quality of allergens has been verified by Dr. Theron G. Randolph of Chicago, coauthor of *An Alternative Approach to Allergies*. Dr. Randolph induced withdrawal symptoms in subjects, then quickly alleviated the withdrawal symptoms by giving the subjects the substances to which they were allergic. As already mentioned, victims of environmental sickness (allergy) can show many different recurring symptoms in various parts of their bodies. They may display headache, itching, cramps, hives, rhinitis, muscle aches, joint pains, depression, fatigue, and lost libido, all at the same time. Cerebral functions can be upset if the allergic substance acts on the brain. Strange emotional, behavioral, or perceptual changes, which can be termed ecologic mental illness, or cerebral allergy, may result. The number of body regions affected seemingly can be unlimited.

When an allergy involves nerves somewhere in the cerebral cortex, where the female orgasmic experience takes place, a woman may become preorgasmic and gain a reputation as being frigid. A man with an allergy that affects the activation of neurons in his septum, the part of the limbic system at the top of the brain stem that is reportedly associated with male orgasm, may not be able to ejaculate or may become entirely impotent. Cerebral allergy tends to block the impulse necessary for the emission of semen into the urethra or to interfere with the nerve circuits that tell the small arteries surrounding the muscular coating of the penis to surge with blood.

When you seem to be allergic to sex, you are not necessarily sensitive to the act of intercourse or love play itself but rather are reacting to an irritant in your immediate environment that is affecting your sexual desire or ability to perform. An unnatural or abusive lifestyle can bring on a negative brain response in the form of cerebral allergy. It may be the perfume of a bedmate, such as our letter writer, Frank W., described. Indeed, it could be any food or anything created by the industrial revolution. To overcome allergic manifestations, you must first figure out what the allergen is and then eliminate it from your lifestyle.

HOW TO PROVOKE SYMPTOMS
AND PROVE THEY ARE ALLERGIES

There are a few measures that you can take if you suspect that your symptoms of sexual disability are coming from a susceptibility to unrecognized changes in the ecology. You can try by yourself, using trial and error, to correct pollution in or remove allergens from your daily environment, or you can seek professional medical help. For the latter, ask friends, relatives, or your general practitioner to recommend a clinical ecologist, or check the Yellow Pages. Many good books have been published on clinical ecology in recent years; look for appendices that list names and addresses of local practitioners. You can also contact the American Academy of Environmental Medicine (P.O. Box 16106, Denver, Colorado 80216; telephone 303–622–9755). This organization of clinical ecologists will mail information to you regarding members practicing in your local area. In contrast to orthodox physicians, who offer symptomatic drug therapy, clinical ecologists emphasize prevention and management of ecologic illness through avoidance of allergens by environmental control or neutralization, when possible.

Dr. Marshall Mandell of Norwalk, Connecticut, author of *Dr. Mandell's 5-Day Allergy Relief System*, explained how the body can go haywire. He said:

> Anything you eat, drink, or breathe enters the bloodstream from the digestive tract or the lungs and then exposes every single cell in the body to numerous potential offenders from the environment. Every tissue of every organ is reached by the circulation. There is a very broad spectrum of environmental substances, such as foods, chemical agents, air pollutants, and airborne allergens that can make people sick, both physically and mentally. Medical practitioners do not know the cause of many ecological diseases so they often make diagnoses that describe only the illness, or misdiagnose

complex illnesses, calling symptoms "psychosomatic" conditions due to some assumed stress that the neurotic and hypochondriac patient cannot cope with. They simply do not have the knowledge of clinical ecology that is required in order to practice good medicine.

The orthodox physician lacking a bioecologic orientation might declare that your [sex] problem represents the effects of emotional stress and/or the many responsibilities he believes that you are unable to cope with. Or, he will decide the so-called psychosomatic illness he has incorrectly diagnosed stems from the trauma of being alive in the modern world, and your inability, as a second class individual, to adequately adjust to your situation. He places a psychosomatic label on your unrecognized bodywide allergies, a label that certainly doesn't belong. The [orthodox] doctor does this out of ignorance—from not knowing you have a *bona fide* bioecologic disease of the nervous system—a brain allergy along with an assortment of physical symptoms. This is an extremely important and very common type of illness that most physicians are not yet familiar with.

The brain, with its exceedingly rich blood supply, can malfunction in many ways. Any of the numerous brain activities may be altered, inhibited, stimulated, or distorted by the substances that enter this organ and affect brain cell function. Environmental impact can be extreme on an individual, since his or her brain is heavily exposed to outside influences because it is the most nourished organ in the body. It's like a highly organized, delicately balanced computer system. It has twelve billion neurons (nerve cells) and each of these nerve cells has hundreds of dendrites, little connecting fibers, so the number of available circuits in the nervous system is absolutely enormous. Many environmental factors can cause different types of brain malfunctioning that will affect your normal human behavior. Your intellect may be altered, forgetfulness and confusion may set in, nervousness, headache and fatigue may develop, changes in perception can occur and visual and auditory stimuli might become distorted. An individual may experience sexual malfunction as a mild to moderate dysfunction and psychotic reactions are the most extreme form. Different aspects of schizophrenia can manifest themselves because of brain allergy and unmet nutritional needs. And lesser indications that your brain is allergic are often indicated by unaccountable restlessness, irritability, mood swings, responses to situations blown out of proportion, inappropriate rage with the slightest provocation, depression, anxiety, and sexual incapacity.

People who feel tense, nervous, or withdraw into themselves do this from a malfunctioning of the brain. The usual cause, albeit an unrecognized one, is an environmental substance, such as a commonly eaten food or an inhaled or ingested chemical agent that may be part of everyday activities.[1]

From what clinical ecologists have stated on lecture platforms, in publications, and in personal interviews, it seems obvious that no body organ or system is invulnerable to ecological changes—the brain least of all, and the gonads along with it. The brain's reaction determines usual and customary behavior in society and responsive behavior in sexual relationships. Following a bizarre pattern in society will invite a label of neurotic, eccentric, or just plain crazy. Treating sexual advances with apathy will encourage being branded as frigid. All the while, behavior is controlled by a physical effect on the brain and gonads.

To provoke your symptoms and prove that they come from allergies, the fasting technique used by Dr. Michael Schachter (see page 32) is effective. The interval between the eating of an offending food and the appearance of physical, mental, or sexual symptoms can vary from person to person. Symptoms may come on in seconds or take several days. Total fasting—the elimination of all food for four, six, or eight days—is the best technique for finding the foods to which you are allergic. However, such an undertaking should be done under the supervision of an informed physician. After fasting for the selected number of days, you return to your diet one by one the foods you normally eat, while you are observed closely for any allergic symptoms.

The fasting technique is somewhat complex. In addition, you must take precautions. If you decide to fast on your own, be sure to first read the books I have cited that were written by Dr. Randolph, Dr. Mandell, and Dr. Schachter. Finally, you must make sure that your gastrointestinal tract is clear during the fast; drink two quarts of spring water every day. And be prepared to experience certain symptoms each day.

In another provocative test, foods that are possible allergens are prepared as extracts in minute proportions. Chemical provocateurs from the immediate environment are prepared in a similar way. The procedure for preparing food extracts and chemical provoking agents is explained in several allergy books.

Place a drop of food extract or chemical provocateur under your tongue and wait for a response. Any organ or system in your body that has been showing either normal or abnormal performance can be affected. If you have been experiencing sexual difficulties, you will probably find that they recur immediately upon taking the allergen into your system; sublingual testing is equivalent in effectiveness to intravenous injections. Thus, your disabling symptoms will become apparent as a result of the provocative test. You will now know which elements in your environment are reacting factors and can eliminate them from your life as much as possible.

Some food sensitization that you discover via provocative testing may be transitory in the sense that if you refrain from eating certain foods for several days or weeks, you may be able to reintroduce them into your diet on an occasional basis. Eating the foods repeatedly, unfortunately, may reestablish your sensitivity. By trial and error, however, you can devise a schedule that will allow you to enjoy favorite foods fairly regularly but without ill effects. This system is the basis for the Rotary Diversified Diet, developed by Dr. H.J. Rinkel.

Using Dr. Rinkel's Rotary Diversified Diet, you can construct menus and a safe diet for overcoming sexual allergies. To design such a diet for yourself, list available foods; locate the foods alphabetically on an index; classify the foods as animal, vegetable, or mineral; number them in the sequence that you try them in your diet (spreading them apart to prevent repeated consumption of the same family of foods); and alter the way you prepare them.

You may fit the chemical profile of the type of person who is hypersensitive and displays allergic symptoms. For example, if you generally detect fumes before others who are similarly exposed do, you may manifest the allergic profile. Various other symptoms are also generally tied to allergies. Among them are:

- Persistent fatigue that is not helped by rest.
- Overweight, underweight, or a history of fluctuation in weight.
- Occasional puffiness of the face, hands, abdomen, or ankles.
- Heart palpitations, particularly after provocative testing.
- Sweating that is excessive and unrelated to exercise.
- Perspiration that has an unpleasant odor that no amount of bathing dispels.
- Chronic symptoms such as irritability, headache, runny nose, joint pains, backache, anxiety, depression, breathing difficulties, skin rashes, prickly sensations, fainting, speeding pulse, asthma, and anger, as well as an inability to sustain an erection even in the presence of erotic stimuli or remaining preorgasmic despite direct vibratory, manual, or oral stimulation of the clitoris.

Some substances produce worse allergic reactions than do others. The balance of this chapter will focus on the ones more commonly known to elicit cerebral allergies and produce sexual dysfunction.

MANMADE HAZARDS IN THE FOOD SUPPLY

The American food system has come a long way. Humans started as hunters of meat and gatherers of nuts and fruits. They divided into different cultures, some of which developed agriculture. Subsistence farming gave way to commercial farming, freeing people for other activities and city living. Peddlers bowed to grocery stores, and grocery stores became supermarkets. These changes gave rise to food processors. And now humans, especially Americans, eat more processed foods than unprocessed foods. Sometimes we are not even aware that a food has been treated with chemicals; the food looks natural. For example, a Florida orange that is newly harvested is washed with detergent to remove pesticides, mold, and dirt. It is then sprayed with fungicide to retard rotting. Further, because customers expect oranges to be orange in color, the naturally green fruit is often dyed orange using ethylene gas and red coloring. To prevent excessive loss of moisture, a petroleum-based shellac is painted on the fruit.

Many chemicals are added to foods to enhance or improve their taste, texture, appearance, or shelf life. Often chemicals are substituted for more expensive food ingredients. Food additives seem to be ubiquitous in the food supply. Fresh eggs are sometimes coated with mineral oil to prevent moisture evaporation or loss of carbon dioxide. Tomatoes, cucumbers, and many other fruits and vegetables are waxed for the more attractive shiny appearance. Apples destined for temporary storage usually are treated with a decay inhibitor and an antioxidant. Baby foods are thickened with starch. White flour, after relieved of its nutrients during processing, is bleached, aged, and then re-enriched with nutrients. Altogether, American consumers ingest about 2,800 different additives in the foods they eat. Some of the various additives and their uses are:

- *Artificial flavor enhancers,* such as monosodium glutamate (MSG), "bring out" or "improve" the natural flavors of foods.
- *Artificial flavors* imitate real flavors like strawberry, coconut, or chocolate.
- *Antioxidants* control food discoloration caused by oxidation. Substances such as butylated hydroxytoluene (BHT) and butylated hydroxyanisole (BHA), which are petroleum products, prevent rancidity.
- *Antimicrobial preservatives* inhibit the growth of mold, bacteria, and yeast. Sorbic acid and sodium benzoate are examples of these types of preservatives. Sorbic acid is derived from the berry of the mountain ash, which is a tree, and sodium benzoate is a salt of benzoic acid.
- *Emulsifiers* such as monoglycerides and diglycerides keep water and oil mixed.
- *Stabilizers and thickeners* make a product look rich and thick. Examples of stabilizers are methylcellulose and carrageenan.
- *Food colors* restore natural colors to processed foods or give a pleasant color to manufactured products. An example is the caramel coloring that is added to some white breads to make them look like whole wheat bread.

Intentional additives are used in foods for one or more of the following four purposes:

1. To maintain or improve nutritional value.
2. To maintain freshness.
3. To help in the processing or preparation.
4. To improve appeal.

Food additives are more strictly regulated in the United States now than at any other time in history. Harvey Wiley, Ph.D., chief chemist at the U.S. Department of Agriculture from 1883 to 1912, is credited with the passage of the 1906 Food and Drug Act and the Meat Inspection Act, both of which led to the passage of the Food, Drug and Cosmetic Act of 1938. These acts gave the government the authority to remove adulterated or obviously poisonous foods from the market. But it was not until the Food Additives Amendment was enacted in 1958 and the Color Additive Amendment in 1960 that the United States had laws specifically regulating food additives. The amendments to these laws shifted the burden of proof concerning the safety of a food additive from the government to the manufacturer. Rather than the additive's being considered innocent until proven guilty, the additive was now considered unsafe until proven safe.

A provision to the 1958 law included the so-called Delaney Clause, which stated:

> No additive shall be deemed to be safe if it is found to induce cancer when ingested by man or animal, or if it is found after tests which are appropriate for the evaluation of safety of food additives to induce cancer in man or animal.

Also under the Food Additives Amendment of 1958, two major categories of additives were exempted from the testing and approval process. They were the "prior sanctioned substances," those additives approved before 1958, and the 700 substances "generally recognized as safe" (GRAS) by qualified experts.

Food additives are a highly controversial subject. The Manufacturing Chemists' Association defends all FDA-approved additives. But consumer advocates say, "Buyer beware."

A food additive is any substance that is added to a food and consumed with that food. This includes unintentional additives such as bacteria, rodent hairs, and pesticides, and the intentional substances that I have been discussing. The main concern is whether the chemicals intentionally placed in foods during processing are safe. If a scientific answer had to be given in one word, it would be *no!* My research indicates that synthetic additives in particular are partially responsible for sexual disorders being experienced by many men and women living in the industrialized Western nations. But the scientists who are working with additives do not believe that anyone is being hurt. The scientists, most of whom are dependent for their incomes on food processors, say that the public's alarm is exaggerated and that people fail to understand the difference between toxicity and hazard.

Toxicity is the capacity of a chemical substance to harm living organisms and is a general property of all matter. Hazard is the capacity of a chemical substance to produce injury under given conditions of use. All food substances are potentially toxic, but they are hazardous only if consumed in sufficiently large quantities.

Additive proponents say that if there is a hazard associated with additives, it is very small compared to the many other food-associated hazards, such as food-borne infection, inadequate nutrition, environmental contamination, naturally occurring toxicants in foods, and pesticide residues. The laws on the safety of additives are based on "margins of safety." Most chemicals that are allowed in foods are added in amounts up to only one-hundredth the level that produced a toxic effect in animals. And additive proponents declare that additive toxicities are not cumulative. "If you dosed yourself with a hundred different compounds," said Eleanor Noss Whitney and Eva May Nunnelley Hamilton in *Understanding Nutrition*, "each at a hundredth of what would cause toxicity, you would still have one-hundredth the chance of experiencing a toxic reaction. Often there are antagonists as well."[2] According to nutritionist J.M. Coone, "The toxicity of one element is offset by the presence of an adequate amount of another."[3] These types of statements are nonsense, however, and exactly the type of false information that is producing the high incidence of illness, disability, and degeneration that is affecting the endocrine and genital systems of people in industrialized societies.

The National Academy of Science's Food Protection Committee has stated its case this way: "No method is at hand—and none is in sight—for establishing, with absolute certainty, the safety of a food chemical under all conditions of use. Experience has shown, however, that properly conducted and interpreted animal experiments can provide that degree of assurance of safety reasonably expected in the evaluation of chemicals for use in human food."[4] Most consumer groups, which include people who have become victims of degenerative diseases, believe that the National Academy of Science's statement is just so much double talk.

Many of the controversies about additive safety involve the public's concern over the fact that the food testings are performed by the food manufacturing companies themselves. In contrast to the statements made in favor of the use of food additives, Jane Brody has written, "There are still other unknowns about the safety of food additives. In most cases each additive is tested by itself. Little is known about possible interactions with other substances that might be used in the same product or in products that are eaten together."[5]

Moreover, many more questions relating to chemical additives exist. Does an additive change chemically when it comes into contact with a food? Does it change when the food is packaged or when it is transported or stored? Do changes in temperature or humidity cause alterations in the additive? What happens to the additive during cooking? What can happen if humans ingest the additive in small quantities, repeatedly, over their lifetimes? How does the additive interact with other additives? Does it change when it comes into contact with vitamins, minerals, trace elements, or other substances? What effects does it have on fetuses? Does it affect pregnant or lactating women, or newly born or young children, or malnourished or chronically ill people, or the elderly, or people under great stress or with severe allergies, respiratory ailments, diabetes, or other health problems?

The anti-additive movement is troubled. The people in the movement are crying "fire" in the 1990s in much the same way that Rachel Carson did in 1962 in *Silent Spring*. Carson's warning about the overuse of insecticides and the potential destruction they would inflict on nature and mankind proved woefully true.

It is unrealistic to expect our highly technological society to return to using only unprocessed, additive-free foods. Most people would not want the inconvenience of having to food-shop frequently, along with having a limited food selection and higher prices. Many seasonal foods would be wasted through spoilage. We are stuck with our chemical additive–laden foods and the megacorporations that process them and make them available at local supermarkets. But we can help ourselves by eating more wisely. We can apply the principle of poison dilution by consuming a wide variety of foods. This helps to weaken the concentration of individual additives. If you are concerned about nitrates in preserved meats, avoid or limit your intake of bacon, cold cuts, hot dogs, and smoked fish. Worried about monosodium glutamate (MSG)? Do not cook with it, and when you go to a Chinese restaurant, avoid ordering soup and request that MSG not be used in the rest of your food.

Most of the items that have food coloring are junk foods. We can all profit by drastically reducing our intake of these items. Junk foods are usually high in sweeteners. Regardless of body weight, no one needs all the sugar that Americans are consuming. Saccharin is suspected of being a "minor" carcinogen, so avoid this, too. I question the value of saccharin and other artificial sweeteners in treating obesity and diabetes. Most of the overweight people I know (and I have been teaching weight-control classes for over twenty-five years) have been using artificial sweeteners for ages without losing weight. I believe that diabetics must reduce their taste for sweets by gradually lowering the amount of sweet flavoring they use until they phase out sweetness completely.

Use fresh or minimally processed foods. Make real, whole foods—not their artificial equivalents—a part of your lifestyle. Do not be fooled by the word "natural." Utilize only fresh or frozen fruit juices. Avoid powdered mixes and fruit drinks; they are make-believe foods. The fewer canned or packed foods you eat, the better off you will be.

Manmade hazards in foods can harm you in part by being disadvantageous to your sexuality, yet you must learn to live with them. Avoid food additives whenever possible. Be aware of the risk–benefit ratio connected with whatever you put in your mouth. Make educated food choices. Do not waste your taste. Read labels and be informed.

BOOZING IT UP BRINGS YOU DOWN

Dr. Eugene Schoenfeld of San Francisco, author of the syndicated *Dr. Hippocrates* column running in many newspapers in the United States, said: "Alcohol is an example of a drug so widely used most people don't think of it as a drug. In moderation, the drug has beneficial tranquilizing effects. With larger doses, there is depression and slowing of reflexes. The 'stimulation' due to alcohol is actually caused by release of inhibitions."

Prolonged drinking causes the liver to produce excessive amounts of an enzyme that destroys testosterone, the male libido hormone. In fact, university research has shown that most men cannot achieve an erection even after just three 1-ounce swallows of liquor. Also, since alcohol decreases testosterone production, heavy regular drinking can produce permanent impotence and a tendency toward feminization in men.

Drinking hard liquor or prodigious quantities of beer or wine also causes depletion of folic acid, a B vitamin that is known to be low in at least one out of three people. Some medical studies have shown a lack of folic acid in 80 percent of women. Symptoms of folic-acid deficiency include irritability, forgetfulness, weakness, fatigue, diarrhea, headache, palpitations, shortness of breath, moodiness, and, most of all, decreased sex drive. This complex of symptoms is similar to the allergy syndrome. Heavy drinkers are especially in need of folic-acid supplementation. (For more on folic acid, see page 66.)

Another nutrient that is exhausted in the body by imbibing alcohol is zinc, a mineral that is needed for sexual response and performance (see page 51). Shakespeare said, "Drink provokes the desire, but it takes away the performance." By depleting yourself of zinc, you will hardly be able to perform.

A study conducted by psychologist Dr. George Greaves showed that although there appears to be a strong relationship between alcoholic-beverage drinking and the willingness to engage in sexual activity, this is due mostly to the liberal attitudes of those who use alcohol and commonly interact sexually.

Two other psychologists, Dr. C.W. Sheppard and Dr. G.R. Gay, proved through research that alcohol reduces sexuality by decreasing the desire for sexual intimacy and by promoting impotency. Yet certain personal and social characteristics of a man may be so strong that he can raise an erection even though he is dead drunk. Biochemical individuality, therefore, must be factored into the equation. Sex researchers Sheppard and Gay concluded, "Considering the dubious benefits of excessive amounts, it makes little sense to use this artificial stimulant. The individual who is unable to respond to ordinary psychosexual stimulation should probably seek professional help. For the most part, sexual disappointment rather than enhancement is to be expected from drinking."

A pathologist at Mount Sinai School of Medicine in New York City, after studying the effects of alcohol on males who used the drug for a lift before sexual encounters, said: "Anybody who drinks can get a lift of the spirit but only a temporary lift of the penis. Erection, in fact, is just a semi-rigid occurrence. The pure effect of alcohol in any form you take it—whiskey, wine, or beer—will leave the penis flaccid. And the total amount of alcohol is the really important thing. The more drunk, the less rigid."

Reports in the scientific literature on the effects of alcohol on women have been contradictory and unclear. Dr. Frank Lemere and Dr. J.W. Smith found evidence of sexual disorders in women drinkers. And there have been recurring reports in the medical literature that alcoholic women are chronically preorgasmic. In contrast, other evidence indicates that alcohol may enhance feelings of sexuality for some female imbibers.

Several sexually dysfunctional women were given alcoholic beverages by psychologists Dr. G.T. Wilson and Dr. D.M. Lawson. The women said, in contrast to prior reports, that the drinks made them feel sexually excited. One woman described the sexy feeling as "clitoral tingling or itching with a warm sensation that spreads through the groin area." The women's vaginal pressure pulse, when tested with a vaginal photopleythysmograph (a blood volume–measuring instrument), increased because the extra alcohol seemed to cause the vaginal areas to become flooded with blood.

Writing in the *Journal of Abnormal Psychology*, Drs. Wilson and Lawson said, "Based on our study of the relationship between increasing levels of alcohol consumption and sexual arousal, we suggest that the perceived association between increasing levels of alcohol intoxication and sexual arousal may be instrumental in the development and/or maintenance of moderate or excessive drinking patterns." In other words, some women may become problem drinkers in part because of an effort to increase their sense of sexuality and femininity, and an attempt to induce "warm, loving, and sexy feelings." The liquor industry is known to be targeting women with its advertising.

One good thing that drinking liquor is known to do for women is to relieve premenstrual tension; therefore, some women are encouraged to self-medicate in this way. The beverage, which is recognized as an effective diuretic, alleviates discomforts such as headache, irritability, and the feeling of being bloated. It tends to relieve the pain and cramps experienced during the premenstruum and menstruation because it depresses uterine contractions during the expulsion of the endometrium.

In a study conducted by two physicians, Drs. Jones and Jones, the same dose of alcohol produced extremely variable blood-alcohol levels in men and women. The study revealed that:

- The women subjects consistently obtained higher peak blood alcohol than did the men subjects.
- The women absorbed the alcohol faster and sooner than did the men.
- The women held the alcohol in their blood longer than did the men.

Stated another way, the women became drunker, got drunk quicker, and stayed drunk longer than did the men.

One more item concerning drinking by women: Scientists at the University of North Carolina at Chapel Hill have found evidence that only one or two episodes of heavy drinking by a woman early in pregnancy can seriously damage an unborn child. The evidence, which comes from animal studies, indicates that the condition, known as Fetal Alcohol Syndrome (FAS), can be caused as early as the third week after conception, well before most women suspect they are pregnant. At that stage of development, an embryo is about the size of a pinhead and consists of only a few thousand cells. FAS has been estimated to affect between 1 in 300 and 1 in 750 births in the United States.

GETTING HIGH SHOULD BE LOW ON THE LIST

Marijuana at one time was the number-four crop ($1 billion per year) in California and the number-one cash crop ($500 million per year) in Hawaii. At one point it was grown in all fifty states. *The Marijuana Growers' Guide* sold more than 1 million copies when it was published. Marijuana was, and still is, one of the most abused drugs ever. While marijuana has not been proven to cause death, it has been shown to bring about brain damage, sterility, impotence, and insanity, and it is a known precursor to drug addiction. Socially and medically, marijuana is deadly.

Marijuana comes from the Indian hemp plant *Cannabis sativa*, a hardy weed that grows all over the world. It can be grown in backyard gardens. Often uncultivated, it can be extremely difficult to eradicate. Street buyers know marijuana as a prepared mixture of chopped dried leaves, stems, flowers, and seeds. It ranges in color from gray to green to brown to red to blond, and it resembles in texture small granules of oregano or large leaves of tea. When smoked, marijuana smells sweet, like burning rope or dried grasses.

The active ingredient of marijuana—found in the gooey, yellow, fragrant resin of the upper leaves and flowers—is delta-9-tetrahydrocannabinol, more familiarly known as THC. This is the substance that produces the characteristic chemical and psychological effects. Different for different people, marijuana is employed as a light hallucinogen, a relaxant, a tranquilizer, an appetite stimulant, a sexual stimulant, or an intoxicant. The effects depend on the amount smoked and on the potency, as well as on the expectations and perceptions of the user. Therein lies marijuana's only value and effectiveness as a sexual stimulant.

The act of thinking about how sensations will be heightened tends to cause a person to feel sensations as heightened, especially when under the influence of marijuana. Although marijuana is not a clinically proven aphrodisiac, it tends to produce a happy, relaxed mood, setting a comfortable stage for sexual enjoyment. Inhibitions may be washed away by a dreamy wave of joyous freedom. Sensations swirl; every action seems smoother and feels glorious.

Under the influence, marijuana smokers munch on anything that resembles food. Most are obsessed with eating. Everything looks juicy and tastes good. The throat, mouth, and lips feel dry and parched during marijuana use.

Another common obsession of many people when "stoned" is music to accompany sex. The music industry has long been aware of the connection between pot, sex, and the magic carpet of music. Cash registers have rung up astronomical sales thanks to smokers purchasing records and tapes for the purpose of heightening their sensibilities. In dance clubs, flashing lights, mirrors, and glittery clothing add extra stimulation.

When marijuana is smoked, its effects usually are felt within a few minutes and last for a relatively short period of time. When the drug is ingested, usually as a more purified resin, it may take thirty to sixty minutes before any effects are felt, but the influence may persist for three to five hours. Among the effects, the pulse rate increases, the blood pressure rises slightly, and the eyes become bloodshot. Blood sugar becomes elevated, and an excessive amount of urine is passed. Nausea, vomiting, and occasional diarrhea have also been noted. The appetite increases markedly, especially for sweets, and hunger intensifies.

Two University of California lawyers, Lloyd Haines and Warren Green, conducted a study on the sexual ramifications of marijuana use. Their findings were later confirmed in a paper published by Dr. Martin H. Keeler in the *American Journal of Psychiatry*. Haines and Green wrote:

> This is not to say that when one smokes marijuana he or she immediately engages in sexual activity. The responses show that most subjects have regular sexual partners whether it be a spouse or lover. The incidences occur when they are together and have the

opportunity. Only one unattached subject in the test group (out of a sample of 131 users) claimed to go out and "hustle" or try to "pick up" a partner. All the other unattached subjects found that their ability to "hustle" was impaired after smoking marijuana. They had little ambition to get up, get dressed and attempt to meet people.[6]

A more detailed study of the sexual ramifications of smoking pot was conducted by Erich Goode, Ph.D., assistant professor of sociology at the State University of New York at Stony Brook. In Goode's sample, perhaps due to what the doctor described as "cultural associations, expectations, and a feeling of increased sensual awareness," 50 percent of the women and 39 percent of the men stated that marijuana increased their sexual desire. On the issue of sexual enjoyment, however, the effect of the drug seemed to be somewhat greater on the men. In all, 74 percent of the men and 63 percent of the women said that they enjoyed sex more while under the influence.

Haines and Green had also reached this conclusion in their study, reporting that about four-fifths of their subjects who engaged in coitus while under the influence of the drug felt that sex was "more enjoyable" than it was when they were not under the influence.

All these effects, however, may be due just to susceptibility to suggestion or to the knowledge that something has been taken to enhance the sexual experience. Or, the effects might be facilitated by the quiet, relaxed settings in which two people, alone together, smoke marijuana. Very likely, though, the effects are a result of both the feeling of increased sensory awareness and of the time distortion that makes orgasm seem to last much longer for many people.

Attempts to define the psychotomimetic effects of pot in terms of the properties and behavior of the brain and its neurons have presented a number of challenges to neurophysiologists. Marijuana has an effect on the medial and intralaminar nonspecific nuclei of the hypothalamus, the large ovoid mass of gray matter of the brain that houses the sexual center. It is perhaps not surprising that a drug that causes a reaction in this area will produce dramatic effects.

Low-frequency stimulation of medial hypothalamic nuclei causes a characteristic type of activity in the cerebral cortex. This activity has been called the recruiting response and is a synchronizing activity in the brain cortex. Suffice it to say that anything interfering with synchronizing thought waves is going to distort reality for and prompt unusual behavior in the victim. Hypothalamic neuronal activity is affected by activation of neuronal organizations, which in turn are responsive to outside irritants such as cannabis. In brief, using marijuana may temporarily heighten your senses sexually, but it will do so at a price to your body and mind in the future.

BOTH SUGAR AND SALT SOUR YOUR SEX LIFE

You can put sweetness back into sex by removing one of the biggest causes of energy depletion. Refined carbohydrates, exemplified most commonly by white sugar and white flour, actually lower the level of blood sugar and throw the body and mind into detrimental metabolism, known as *catabolism.*

Each year, the average American consumes 125 pounds of refined sugar, compared to 11 pounds used per person during the last century. The British and French are estimated to use even more sugar. This excess intake of a totally worthless carbohydrate certainly sours the sex life.

An example of sugar's detrimental sexual effects is that hypoglycemic men (men who have low blood-sugar levels) cannot awaken in the morning with an erection, which is common among normal men. Hypoglycemic women tend to substitute high carbohydrates for sex. Hypoglycemics, as described on page 25, tend to be uninterested in sexual activity. Hypoglycemia is one of the precursors of diabetes, and mature-onset diabetes is aggravated by excessive sugar consumption.

The ingestion of sugar products has been directly linked with the development of toxemia in cells and tissues. Infectious bacteria give off putrefactive acids. Hypoadrenalism (a deficiency of adrenaline) sets in when the body squanders its stress-fighting hormones; people with this condition have no energy left for the act of love.

A number of mineral and food supplements have been found useful in offsetting the destruction of body cells induced by the excessive consumption of refined sugar. For example, some natural nutrients that help regulate blood sugar are chromium, manganese, and licorice root.

White sugar—refined white crystalline sugar and confectioners' white powdered sugar—is virtually useless to the human body. It contains no protein, thiamine, riboflavin, or niacin; and no calcium, phosphorus, or other important minerals except a trace of iron, sodium, and potassium. White sugar fares miserably when compared to even molasses, honey, or brown unrefined sugar for these important elements. All it does is add flavor to food. By itself, sugar has no qualities—nutritional or otherwise—that are indispensable in the human diet.

Research has shown that with the increase in sugar use, there have been related jumps in the incidence of sexual dysfunction among older married people and of diabetes, arthritis, dental cavities, premature aging, fatigue, general aches and pains, cancer, and heart disease among all age groups. This research was cited in *The Folklore and Facts of Natural Nutrition* by Fay Lavan and Jean Dalrymple.

In a listing of the sugar contents of popular processed foods, the sugar contents are shown to be amazingly high. Table 13.1 presents a sampling, provided by Kurt Donsbach, Ph.D., former president of the International

Table 13.1. "Hidden Sugar" in Popular Processed Foods.

Food Item	Portion Size	Sugar Content (in approx. teaspoons of granulated sugar)
Beverages		
Cola drink	6 ounces	3½
Cordial	¾ ounce	1½
Ginger ale	6 ounces	5
Orangeade	8 ounces	5
Root beer	10 ounces	4½
7-Up	6 ounces	3¾
Sweet cider	8 ounces	6
Whiskey sour	3 ounces	1½
Cakes and Pastries		
Angel food cake	4 ounces	7
Applesauce cake	4 ounces	5½
Banana cake	2 ounces	2
Cheesecake	4 ounces	2
Chocolate cake (plain)	4 ounces	6
Chocolate cake (iced)	4 ounces	10
Chocolate eclair	1 average	7
Coffee cake	4 ounces	4½
Cream puff	1 average	2
Cupcake (iced)	1 average	6
Doughnut (plain)	1 average	3
Doughnut (glazed)	1 average	6
Fruit cake	4 ounces	5
Jellyroll	2 ounces	2½
Orange cake	4 ounces	4
Pound cake	4 ounces	5
Sponge cake	1 ounce	2
Candies		
Butterscotch chew	1 average	1
Chewing gum	1 average stick	½
Chocolate mint	1 average	2
Fudge	1 ounce	4½
Gum drop	1 average	2
Life Savers candy	1 average	⅔
Milk chocolate bar (plain)	1 average	2½
Peanut brittle	1 ounce	3½

Food Item	Portion Size	Sugar Content (in approx. teaspoons of granulated sugar)
Canned Fruits and Juices		
Apricots	4 halves with 1 tablespoon syrup	3½
Fruit juice (sweetened)	4 ounces	2
Fruit salad	½ cup	3½
Fruit syrup	2 tablespoons	2½
Peaches	2 halves with 1 tablespoon syrup	3½
Stewed fruit	½ cup	2
Cookies		
Brownie (plain)	¾ ounce	3
Chocolate cookie	1 average	1½
Fig Newtons cookie	1 average	5
Ginger snap	1 average	3
Macaroon	1 average	6
Nut cookie	1 average	1½
Oatmeal cookie	1 average	2
Sugar cookie	1 average	1½
Dairy Products		
Ice cream	1 pint	10½
Ice cream bar	1 average	1–7
Ice cream cone	1 average	3½
Ice cream soda	1 average	5
Ice cream sundae	1 average	7
Malted milk shake	10 ounces	5
Desserts		
Apple cobbler	½ cup	3
Blueberry cobbler	½ cup	3
Custard	½ cup	2
French pastry	4 ounces	5
Jell-O	½ cup	4½
Jams and Jellies		
Apple butter	1 tablespoon	1
Jelly	1 tablespoon	4–6
Orange marmalade	1 tablespoon	4–6
Peach butter	1 tablespoon	1
Strawberry jam	1 tablespoon	1

Institute of National Health Sciences, Inc. Table 13.2 shows the sugar contents of twenty-four leading cereals.

The high-sugar diet of the average modern Westerner is quite the reverse of what the human species evolved on, and now it is wending its way to the East. For example, American fast food and cola drinks are taking the joy out of sex in Japan. Medical researchers at six Japanese universities have complained about the sugar addiction to which the Japanese are succumbing and about the elevated incidence of heart attacks from the overconsumption of fatty hamburgers. (To learn more about sugar, its effects, and what you can do to break a sugar addiction, see *Lick the Sugar Habit* by Nancy Appleton, Ph.D.)

Another pervasive threat to sexual health is sodium chloride, which has been around at least five thousand years but is today consumed in more

Table 13.2. The Sugar Content of Leading Cereals.

Cereal	Percentage of Sugar
Kellogg's Apple Jacks	52.04
Post Fruity Pebbles	48.51
Ralstin Purina Cookie Crisp	45.45
Quaker King Vitamin	42.40
Post Super Sugar Crisp	42.16
Quaker Cap'n Crisp	39.09
Kellogg's Frosted Flakes	39.07
General Mills Trix	37.27
General Mills Golden Grahams	29.90
Kellogg's Cracklin Bran	27.50
Kellogg's Country Morning	21.85
Nabisco 100% Bran	19.77
Kellogg's Frosted Mini Wheats	19.77
C.W. Post	18.20
Quaker 100% Natural	17.09
Krotschmer Sun Country Granola With Almonds	16.82
Ralstin Purina Bran Chex	14.25
Post Raisin Bran	12.97
Kellogg's 40% Bran Flakes	12.88
Kellogg's Raisin Bran	12.20
Kellogg's Rice Krispies	8.62
Wheaties	8.60
Kellogg's Corn Flakes	5.03
Cheerios	3.07

extravagant amounts than ever. The results? Among them are extreme symptoms of premenstrual tension (see page 72). Some women experience bloating, headache, irritability, tearfulness, and even uncontrollable rage just before menstruation. These discomforts are due largely to retention of salt and water, and they are best relieved by following a low-salt diet for ten days before menstruation is expected.

The elaborate mechanism that regulates the body's internal supply of water and its balance of sodium and potassium dates from the time when sodium was relatively scarce in the human diet and potassium, a common mineral in fruits and vegetables, was plentiful. Thus, the kidneys and the chemicals that govern their activity function to conserve sodium and get rid of excess potassium. But today, sodium is consumed in considerable excess, while potassium is woefully lacking in the diet.

The sensory pleasure associated with the taste of salt in certain foods is a powerful force in typical Western diets. Researchers have noted in the journal published by the American Dietetic Association that in light of the public's addiction to salt, it is critical that more is learned about why the taste is so attractive.

The average consumption of salt per person in the United States is approximately 6 to 18 grams per day, averaging 11.4 pounds a year—about 7 to 21 times the presumed requirement. Although many foods come to the table in processed form and therefore are high in salt, "much of the salt individuals and manufacturers place in foods is there because people 'like' the taste of salty food better than the taste of the same food without salt," researchers noted in the journal of the American Dietetic Association. It takes over a month of salt restriction to break a salt habit.

As astounding as it may be, a single serving of instant chocolate pudding may have twice as much sodium as does a small bag of potato chips, and a scoop of cottage cheese (a food ordinarily thought of as "healthy") may contain 3 times the salt of a handful of salted peanuts. Because of the sodium in baking powder and baking soda, baked goods and cereals often are the top sources of sodium in the diets of Westernized people. Canned peas are 250 times as salty as fresh peas. Vitamin C may even be a culprit when it is added to foods in the form of sodium ascorbate. Much of the salt that modern Westerners eat is hidden in foods not thought of as salty.

The way that excessive salt intake affects sexuality is tied to the body's regulation of blood pressure. The complex system of blood-pressure control works by means of nerve signals, hormones, and chemicals to widen or narrow the arterioles, which are small, muscular blood vessels that carry oxygen and nutrients from the arteries to the tissues. If the genital organs need a lot of nourishment at a particular time, such as during coitus, the arterioles in the genitals expand to allow increased blood flow. Arterioles in other parts of the body will constrict to maintain normal blood pressure. However, if the regulatory system of a person who eats too much salt goes awry, arterioles all over the body constrict at the same time and stay constricted. The pressure in the larger arterioles will go up and stay up, the same way that the pressure will rise in a water hose when the nozzle is turned off. The result is abnormally elevated blood pressure all the time. With constant high blood pressure, dilation of the genital arterioles will not be possible and the necessary infusion of blood will not come about. The penis will become only semirigid; or vaginal contraction, elasticity, and lubrication will be inadequate, and clitoral sensitization will not happen.

As discussed in Chapter 10, antihypertensive drugs can cause side effects that are so unpleasant that patients frequently stop using the medications. Also, patients must take the medications for the rest of their lives, while questions about possible long-term ill effects from their chronic use still remain unanswered. Therefore, the best way to handle high blood pressure is to never get it. And one of the best ways to avoid getting high blood pressure is to stay away from salty foods.

CAFFEINE AND THE GONADS

While caffeine has been linked to many health problems—heart disease, hypertension, bladder cancer, peptic ulcer, and "coffee nerves," to name a few—it is often overlooked as a drug that also adversely affects the gonads. The caffeine in coffee, tea, cola, chocolate, and some over-the-counter medications is a hidden addiction.

Finding evidence of caffeine's addictive properties is not difficult. Just ask any coffee drinker what happens when he or she abstains for a day; headache, fatigue, stomach pains, and other withdrawal symptoms will be described. The white crystalline alkaloid—caffeine—stimulates the brain and artificially lessens fatigue. Every time a person drinks a cup of coffee or eight ounces of cola, the following physiological changes take place in the body:

- The stomach temperature rises ten to fifteen degrees Fahrenheit.
- The stomach's secretion of hydrochloric acid is increased 400 percent.
- The salivary glands double their output.
- The heart speeds up its beating.
- The lungs work harder.
- The blood vessels around the brain become constricted, and the ones around the heart become dilated.
- The metabolic rate is increased.
- The kidneys manufacture and discharge up to 100 percent more urine.[7]

Regular coffee produces dose-related changes in most standard electro-encephalogram-electrooculogram sleep parameters of normal adult males monitored in a sleep laboratory. The changes are always in a direction that indicates sleep disturbance. The equivalents to four cups of regular coffee did not affect sleep patterns.

As with alcohol, a pregnant woman who drinks coffee will hurt her fetus. Michael Jacobson, Ph.D., director of the Center for Science in the Public Interest and Nutrition Action of Washington, D.C., urged the FDA in the early 1980s to launch a campaign to warn pregnant women of caffeine's possible hazards. He said that tests on animals and humans had linked caffeine with such birth defects as cleft palate, heart defects, and missing fingers and toes. Tests had also indicated that the drug may bring on reproductive problems.

Two of the studies described by Jacobson when he made his appeal to the FDA showed that five cups of coffee a day could have "significant effects" on a fetus, and according to statistics, 400,000 pregnant women drank that much coffee on a routine basis in the 1980s. However, Jacobson could not say how many problem pregnancies and abnormal births were the fault of coffee drinking.

The caffeine content of coffee ranges from 3 milligrams per five-ounce cup of decaffeinated coffee to up to 110 milligrams per five-ounce cup of brewed coffee. Tea contains between 30 and 50 milligrams of caffeine per five-ounce cup. About 88 percent of the caffeine consumed by the public comes from coffee and tea, but caffeine from chocolate or soft drinks is also a real danger. Table 13.3 shows the caffeine levels in today's most common sources of the drug.

Medical nutritionists want caffeine removed from the list of food chemicals that are "generally recognized as safe" (GRAS). Among the main reasons is that coffee has been acknowledged by health authorities to produce benign breast lumps. In *The Journal of the American Medical Association*, Dr. John Peter Minton, a surgeon with Ohio State University College of Medicine, published his findings that two-thirds of benign breast lumps disappeared in women who completely eliminated all forms of methylxanthines—caffeine, theophylline, and theobromine—from their diets. The title of the article was "Benign Breast Lumps May Regress With Change in Diet."

According to the article, Dr. Minton advised forty-seven women with breast lumps who had come to his clinic for breast biopsy to eliminate all coffee, tea, chocolate, and cola from their daily diets. Twenty of the women did so. The breast disease disappeared completely in two to six months in thirteen (65 percent) of the twenty women, as indicated by physical examination, mammography, and echogram. Three of the remaining seven women who followed the diet found their symptoms gone within one and a half years after starting the diet and stopping cigarette smoking. Of the twenty-seven women who did not follow Dr. Minton's advice and continued ingesting coffee, tea, chocolate, and cola, only one witnessed the disappearance of her breast disease.

Most of the women in Dr. Minton's study who saw their breast nodules disappear on the restricted diet found that the lumps returned when they

Table 13.3. Caffeine Levels in Common Sources

Source	Milligrams of Caffeine
Coffee, brewed, 5 ounces	85–110
Coffee, instant, 5 ounces	66
Coffee, decaffeinated, 5 ounces	3
Tea, black, 5 ounces	50
Tea, instant, 5 ounces	30
Jolt, 12 ounces	71
Mellow Yello, 12 ounces	51
Cola, 12 ounces	50
Kick, 12 ounces	31
Cocoa, 8 ounces	6–42
Chocolate bar, 1 average	20
Excedrin or Anacin, 1 tablet	60

resumed drinking or eating the forbidden substances. This is because biochemical individuality determines sensitivity to methylxanthine chemicals. Dr. Minton found that cyclic nucleotides, which stimulate cell division and growth, are appreciably elevated in biopsy tissue from women with fibrocystic disease (cystic mastitis) and fibroadenoma (noncancerous tumor). He theorized that methylxanthine, which inhibits phosphodiesterase, the chemical that breaks down cyclic nucleotides, is the reason. Methylxanthine prevents the phosphodiesterase chemical from breaking up the cyclic nucleotides, which then stimulate the development of cysts. Every woman with breast lumps should be warned that coffee, tea, cola, chocolate, and over-the-counter medications containing caffeine such as Excedrin, Anacin, and Midol might be implicated in her condition.[8]

AIDS AND YOUR HEALTH

The pendulum of sexual freedom has swung more wildly during this century, especially during the last few decades, than at any other time in recorded history. We moved from sexual repression in the forties and fifties to total sexual freedom in the sixties and seventies. Now, the pendulum has come not to rest but has settled into a calmer, steadier motion.

In this time marked by the epidemic of AIDS, it is important for all of us to become much more aware of the consequences of our sexual behavior. There are risks associated with everything, including sex. There are also protective measures that can be taken. One is to always know your health status. If you are enjoying an active sex life, have yourself tested periodically for AIDS. The test is simple, safe, inexpensive, and available upon request at most medical laboratories and doctors offices. Also encourage your partner to be tested. The relief brought by a negative test result will more than make up for the few dollars and minutes spent in taking the test.

However, it is important to remember that the test for AIDS is not 100-percent accurate; many negative tests come back positive, and some positive tests, sadly, come back negative. Practicing safe sex therefore becomes all the more important.

Be selective in your sexual partners. Be aware that intravenous drug users and homosexual and bisexual men are at high risk for the AIDS virus. In addition, current statistics show a rapid increase in the heterosexual population as well. Further, while your prospective partner may be "safe," what about his or her former or other lovers?

Use physical protection. Always use a condom, and know how to use it properly. For instance, a condom should not be used with petroleum jelly, which makes it porous and ineffective. A wide variety of condoms is available in pharmacies and many other stores. Female condoms are also available now. Ask your doctor for details.

Finally, take care of your general health. A healthy body is better able to fight off any virus that it may encounter. For a list of foods that boost the immune system, as well as for more information about HIV and safe sex, see page 192.

When approached wisely, sex is healthy, for all the reasons discussed in the earlier chapters of this book. Sex in itself is not "dangerous." The abuse of sex, as is true of almost everything is life, is what creates the danger. If you use your intelligence and wisdom, you, too, can—and will—enjoy a healthy sex life!

CONCLUSION

Sexologists are claiming now that there is no biological reason why sexual satisfaction should not get better as the years go by. In fact, they say that the peak period of sexual enjoyment is during the middle or later years. Why, then, do so many bedmates experience sexual slowdowns? Most people blame themselves—or their partners. And they may not be entirely wrong, for too many people are unaware of the vital role that good nutrition plays in sexuality. An inadequate sex life may result from poor nutrition, which many people just do not realize. That problem, however, can easily be remedied through the use of the nutritional ingredients described in this book. Sexual frustration from nutritional deficiency does not have to happen.

I have described in this book the nutritional substances that bring the sexual senses into healthy harmony. For achieving the pinnacle of pleasure in all things sexual, you must be attuned to the biochemical and nutritional fluctuations of your body. Your responses come from the total sexual experience—what has gone before as it relates to how you are feeling now. Are your body, mind, emotions, and spirit sufficiently healthy to carry you from the first stages of interest and arousal to desire, rapture, and final fulfillment? If you routinely consume sexual nutrients, the answer will be *yes!* Your body will be capable of taking you to the heights of sexual ecstasy.

I also touched on that special kind of chemistry that ignites when two people become intimately involved. Body temperature rises, skin flushes slightly, pulse accelerates, and bodily secretions such as saliva, perspiration, and vaginal juice increase. For the moment to be really right—when passion finds its most fulfilling outlet—many physical changes must occur and intermingle with the psychology of sexuality—the phenomenon known as libido. All the information on sexual nutrition that I presented in this book is dedicated to helping the physiological facets of sexual arousal, desire, response, and performance.

Despite having deep, loving feelings and desire, couples sometimes experience disappointment in their relationships. One or both partners may be missing a link in the sexual-fulfillment cycle. This link may be a sex hormone that is supposed to trigger sexual activity. Without adequate nutritional support, this sensitivity-sparking system may become drained and unable to carry out its role as igniter of sexual ardor. Without proper nourishment, one or more endocrine glands may become susceptible to deterioration through wear and tear. General healthcare and nutrition rules apply to the gonads in the same way they apply to the heart, liver, pancreas, and other internal organs.

Everyone has the right to have good sex. If you do not suffer from any major physical or psychological impairment, natural foods and dietary supplements should be able to help your body manufacture whatever is needed in sufficient quantities to strengthen and enhance your sexuality. The magic ingredient in any love potion, when analyzed in the light of today's knowledge, invariably is good nutrition. Sexual nutrition is nature's most potent aphrodisiac.

NOTES

Chapter 1
The Totally Balanced Lover

1. William H. Masters and Virginia E. Johnson, *Human Sexual Response* (Boston: Little, Brown, and Co., 1966), pp. 206–207.
2. Ibid., p. 183.
3. John Perry and Beverly Whipple, "Can Women Ejaculate? Yes!" *Forum: The International Journal of Human Relations*, April 1981, pp. 54–58.

Chapter 2
The Diet for Healthy Lovemaking

1. Gerald G. Griffin, *The Silent Misery: Why Marriages Fail* (Springfield, IL: Charles C. Thomas, 1974), pp. 29–30.
2. *Diet Related to Killer Diseases, V: Nutrition and Mental Health.* Hearings before the Select Committee on Nutrition and Human Needs for the U.S. Senate, Ninety-Fifth Congress, first session. "Mental Health and Mental Development," June 22, 1977 (Washington, DC: U.S. Government Printing Office, 1977).

3. Somasundaram Addanki, "Doctor Reveals How Being Overweight Causes Sexual Problems," *Body Forum Magazine*, 1981.
4. David Shenkin, Michael Schachter, and Richard Hutton, *Food, Mind and Mood* (New York: Warner, 1980), p. 78.
5. M.C. Crim and H.N. Munro, "Protein," in *Nutrition Reviews' Present Knowledge in Nutrition*, 4th ed. (Washington, DC: Nutrition Foundation, 1976), pp. 43–54.

Chapter 3
Nutrients for the Libido

1. Arnold Lorand, *Health and Longevity Through Rational Diet* (Philadelphia: F.A. Davis Co., 1916), pp. 384–391.
2. J. Rivers and M. Devine, "Plasma Ascorbic Acid and Concentrations and Oral Contraceptives," *American Journal of Clinical Nutrition* 25:684–689, 1972.
3. William J. Robinson, *Treatment of Sexual Impotence in Men and Women*, 16th ed. (New York: Eugenics Publishing Co., 1931), p. 173.

4. Michael Lesser, *Nutrition and Vitamin Therapy* (New York: Bantam Books, 1980), p. 94.
5. I. Fraser MacKenzie, *Social Health and Morals* (London: Gollancz, 1947), p. 20.

Chapter 4
Sexual Health With Herbs

1. Penny Wise Budoff, *No More Menstrual Cramps and Other Good News* (New York: G.P. Putnam's Sons, 1980), pp. 24–35.
2. John R. Christopher, "Cramp Bark Tea Is the Most Effective Natural Remedy for Alleviating Menstrual Cramps...," *The Healthview Newsletter* 18 (1978):2.
3. Thomas Murr, *Herbal Combinations From Authoritative Sources* (Provo, UT: Nulife Publishing, 1978), p. 2.

Chapter 5
Nutritional Aphrodisiacs

1. Tom Clark, "Whose Pheromone Are You?" *World Medicine*, July 26, 1978, pp. 21–23.
2. Janet L. Hopson, "The Sexone Signal," *Family Health*, April 1980, pp. 38–53.
3. A. Michaelson, J. McCord, and I. Fridovick, *Superoxide and Superoxide Dismutase* (New York: Academic Press, 1977), p. 129.
4. C.E. Collins and C. Collins, "Roentgen Dermatitis Treated With Fresh Whole Leaf of Aloe Vera," *American Journal of Roentgenology and Radium Therapy* 33 (March 1935):396–397.
5. M.E. Zawahry, M.R. Hegazy, and

M. Helal, "Use of Aloe in Treating Leg Ulcers and Dermatoses," *International Journal of Dermatology* 12 (January–February 1973):68–73.
6. K.J. Kingsbury, P.M. Morgan, C. Aylott, and R. Emmerson, "Effects of Ethyl Arachidonate, Cod Liver Oil and Corn Oil on the Plasma Cholesterol Level," *Lancet* i (1961):739.
7. Phil Gunby, "It's Not Fishy: Fruit of the Sea May Foil Cardiovascular Disease," *The Journal of the American Medical Association* 247 (February 12, 1982):729–731.

Chapter 6
Honeybee Pollen for Sexual Vigor

1. *Organic Directory* (Emmaus, PA: Rodale Press, 1979).
2. *National Restaurant Association's Washington Report*, 1993.
3. Henry G. Bieler, *Dr. Bieler's Natural Way to Sexual Health* (Los Angeles: Charles Publishing Co., 1972), pp. 4–6.
4. Abraham I. Friedman, *How Sex Can Keep You Slim* (New York: Bantam Books, 1973), p. 28.
5. Linda Lyngheim and Jack Scagnetti, *Bee Pollen* (North Hollywood, CA: Wilshire Book Co., 1979), p. 67.

Chapter 7
Glandular Extracts for Vitality

1. Alan Parachini, "Researchers Finally Study Menopause Problems and Treatments," *The Advocate*, March 3, 1981, p. 9.
2. Caroline Derbyshire, *The New*

Woman's Guide to Health and Medicine (New York: Appleton-Century-Crofts, 1980), p. 272.

3. J. Bland, *Granular Based Food Supplements Helping to Separate Fact From Fiction* (Niles, IL: Nutri-Dyn Products, 1980); R.L. Owen, "Transport of Horseradish Peroxidase Across the G-I Barrier," *Gastroenterology* 72 (1977):440.

4. G. Goldstein, M.P. Scheid, and J. Wauwe, "A Synthetic Pentapeptide With Biological Activity Characteristic of Thymic Hormone," *Science* 204 (1979):1309; A. Rubinstein, R. Hirschhorn, and M. Sicklick, "In Vivo and In Vitro Effects of Thymosis and Adenosine Deaminase on ADP Deficient Lymphocytes," *The New England Journal of Medicine* 300 (1979):387.

5. Harold M. Schmeck, Jr., "Mysterious Thymus Gland May Hold the Key to Aging," *The New York Times*, January 26, 1982, p. C1.

Chapter 8
Cellular Therapies for Youthfulness

1. Morton Walker, Bernice Yoffee, and Parke H. Gray, *The Complete Book of Birth* (New York: Simon and Schuster, 1979), p. 251.

2. W.S. Bullough, *The Evolution of Differentiation* (London: Academic Press, 1967).

3. "Bob Cummings, 63: 'I Feel 10 Years Younger—Even My Memory Has Improved,'" *National Enquirer*, February 17, 1974.

4. Ivan Popov, *Stay Young* (New York: Grosset and Dunlap, 1975), pp. 235–236.

Chapter 9
DMG for the Sexual Organs

1. Leslie Kane, "Court Battle Looms Over Wonder Drug B-15 As Federal Officers Confiscate Shipments," *The Star*, April 11, 1978.

2. Richard A. Passwater, "The Truth About DMG," *Bestways*, February 1982, pp. 72–77.

Chapter 10
Chelation Therapy for Orgasmic Problems

1. Thom Willenbecher, "Impotence by Prescription," *Forum: The International Journal of Human Relations*, August 1981, pp. 18–22.

2. Garry F. Gordon and Robert B. Vance, "EDTA Chelation Therapy for Arteriosclerosis: History and Mechanisms of Action," *Osteopathic Annals* 4 (February 1976):38–62.

Chapter 11
Nutritional Help for Herpes

1. H. Blough and E.D. Luby, "Psychological Aspects of HSV Infections," American Social Health Association Conference, Philadelphia, September 18–19, 1981.

2. J.H. Grossman, W.C. Walker, and J.C. Sever, "Management of Genital Herpes Simplex Virus Infection During Pregnancy," *Obstetrics and Gynecology* 58 (1981):1–4.

3. A.J. Nahmias, "Diagnosis: Clinical and Laboratory," American Social Health Association Conference, Philadelphia, September 18–19, 1981.

4. H. Blough and E.D. Luby, op. cit.
5. F. Rapp, "Herpes Simplex Virus and Cancer," American Social Health Association Conference, Philadelphia, September 18–19, 1981.
6. John R. Christopher, *School of Natural Healing* (Provo, UT: Biworld Publishers, 1976), p. 323.
7. "Antiviral Drug, DMSO Teamed Against Shingles," *Drug Topics*, February 15, 1971.

Chapter 12
Sex and Senior Citizens

1. Fred Soyka with Alan Edmonds, *The Ion Effect* (New York: Bantam Books, 1978), pp. 9, 10.
2. Johan Bjorksten, "The Crosslinkage Theory of Aging as a Predictive Indicator," *Rejuvenation* 8 (September 1980):62.
3. Grace Halsell, *Los Viejos* (Emmaus, PA: Rodale Press, 1976), p. 31.
4. Henry A. Schroeder, *The Trace Elements and Man* (Old Greenwich, CT: Devin-Adair, 1973), pp. 72–73.
5. John A. Myers, "Biological Transmutation of Cobalt and Magnesium in the Support of Good Teeth and Health," *Journal of Applied Nutrition* 27 (Spring 1975): 28–50.

Chapter 13
Lifestyle and Sexual Health

1. Marshall Mandell and Lynne Waller Scanlon, *Dr. Mandell's 5-Day Allergy Relief System* (New York: Pocket Books, 1980).
2. Eleanor Noss Whitney and Eva May Nunnelley Hamilton, *Understanding Nutrition* (St. Paul, MN: West Publishing Co., 1981), p. 483.
3. J.M. Coon, "Natural Food Toxicants: A Perspective," *Nutrition Review's Present Knowledge in Nutrition*, 4th ed. (Washington, DC: Nutrition Foundation, 1976), pp. 528–526.
4. Food Protection Committee, *The Use of Chemicals in Food Production, Processing, Storage and Distribution* (Washington, DC: National Academy of Sciences, 1973).
5. Jane Brody, *Jane Brody's Nutrition Book* (New York: W.W. Norton, 1981), pp. 475–476.
6. Lloyd Haines and Warren Green, "Marijuana Use Patterns," thesis, University of California, 1969, p. 20.
7. Kurt W. Donsbach, *The National Addiction, Coffee* (Huntington Beach, CA: International Institute of Natural Health Sciences, 1977).
8. Michael Lerner, "Coffee Causes Benign Breast Lumps," *Common Knowledge* 13 (Fall 1979).

Index